ALL

DOCTOR WHO – THE NEW ADVENTURES

Also available

THE NEW

DOCTOR WHO

ADVENTURES

ALL-CONSUMING FIRE

Andy Lane

First published in Great Britain in 1994 by
Doctor Who Books
an imprint of Virgin Publishing Ltd
332 Ladbroke Grove
London W10 5AH

ISBN 0 426 20415 8

Cover illustration by Jeff Cummins

Internal illustrations by Mike Nicholson

Typeset by Intype, London
Printed and bound in Great Britain by
Cox & Wyman Ltd, Reading, Berks

To: Chris Amies, Tina Anghelatos, Ian Atkins, Molly Brown, Mr Fandango, Craig Hinton, Liz Holliday, Ben Jeapes, Rebecca Levene, Andrew Martin, Jim Mortimore, Amanda Murray, Mike Nicholson, David Owen, Justin Richards, Gus Smith, Helen Stirling, Charles Stross and James Wallis. If you don't like it, you know who to blame.

'May I marry Holmes?'
> *Cable of enquiry from dramatist/actor William Gillette to Arthur Conan Doyle during writing of Gillette's* Sherlock Holmes *play.*

'You may marry or murder or do what you like with him.'
> *Doyle's reply*

Prologue

March 1843 – Jabalhabad, India

'Boy! I say, boy! Two more *burra pegs, chelo!*'

The man in the British Army uniform waved an imperious hand as the turbaned servant glided silently from the veranda.

The old man in the cane chair beside him cackled gently. 'Most kind of you, hmm?' he said, and glanced over to where his granddaughter was attempting to capture the distant mountains in water-colour. The setting sun was behind the bungalow, casting a deep shadow over the patchy *doob* grass but catching the snowy peaks in a net of scarlet and purple.

She glanced up and caught his gaze.

'Grandfather?'

'Nothing, child.'

The soldier batted at a cloud of insects with his pith helmet. The motion caused a fresh rash of sweat to break out across his forehead. He mopped half-heartedly at it.

'Deuced if I know how you cope in this heat,' he muttered.

'Oh, I've been in hotter places than this, my boy,' said the old man.

'There's nowhere on Earth hotter than India during the dry season. If there was, I'd have been posted to it.'

'Perhaps you're right,' the old man agreed. He looked over towards a group of three people – a man and two women – who were sitting and taking tea upon the lawn in the shade of a large parasol. There was something familiar about the man, but he couldn't quite place him.

The servant appeared from the shadows of the bungalow with two double whiskies on a tray. The ice had already melted. A mosquito was struggling weakly in the old man's glass.

'Now, where was I?' the soldier asked, frowning slightly.

'You were telling me about a rather strange temple up in the hills.'

'So I was,' the soldier replied, faintly surprised. 'A rum tale, and no mistake. Let's see what you make of it, what?'

The old man said nothing, but glanced again at the trio happily chatting near his granddaughter. The women were young, but the man . . .

He managed to catch the man's eye. A look passed between them, and the old man shivered.

'Are you all right?' the soldier asked.

'Hmm? I think somebody just walked over my graves.'

'If you're feeling a bit under the weather, you'd better see the medic. Corporal Forbes is rife around here.'

'Corporal Forbes?' the old man asked.

'*Cholera Morbus*. Cholera, you know.'

'I wouldn't worry about that,' the old man said. 'Please, go on.'

'Right-ho. As I said earlier, the palace was a sight to be seen . . .'

'So this is where it all started?' Bernice said politely.

'Indeed,' the Doctor replied, and took a sip of tea. 'And we've seen where it ends. If I hadn't listened to Siger's tale on that veranda . . .'

'Yeah, we know,' Ace said dismissively. She fiddled with her frilly dress. Bernice could tell that she felt uncomfortable in something that wasn't bullet-proof and laser-resistant. 'Ultimate evil, and all that guff. It's a bit hard to swallow, Professor. If you hadn't stopped it, somebody else would have done. I've seen the future, remember? The future of all this. I was born in it.'

'Time's a funny thing,' the Doctor mused, gazing with a strange expression at the girl who was painting the water-colour landscape. 'Didn't the business with the Monk and his pet chronovore illustrate precisely that

2

point? The lives of every planet, every person and every proton are like trickles of water running down a window. Their courses may look fixed, but if you disturb them early on then they can trickle into another path entirely.'

Ace summed up her viewpoint in one succinct word.

Before the Doctor's temper boiled over, Bernice said, 'So, do I take it that the old man sitting over there is you?'

'In a sense.'

'In what sort of sense, precisely?'

'In a rather imprecise sense.'

'He doesn't look very much like you.'

'I was five hundred years younger then,' the Doctor said gloomily. 'You may not believe it, but age has mellowed me.'

Ace snorted.

'You should write your autobiography,' she said. '*Confessions of a Roving Time Lord*. You'd sell a billion.'

'Ah,' said the Doctor, 'that reminds me . . .'

He reached inside his jacket and pulled out a small, leather-bound book.

'A present for you both,' he said.

Bernice took the book from his outstretched hand.

'*All-Consuming Fire*,' she read, grinning. '*Being a Reprint From the Reminiscences of Doctor John Watson As Edited by Arthur Conan Doyle.*'

She rifled through the pages.

'This is weird, seeing them called Holmes and Watson.'

'That's how history remembers them. That's how Arthur protected their identities.'

'Arthur?' Ace looked interested. 'Mate of yours, this Doyle character?'

The Doctor looked away.

'Oh, our paths crossed, longer ago that I care to remember. Arthur Conan Doyle and Rudyard Kipling. Do you like Kipling?'

'I don't know,' Ace replied with a cheeky grin, 'I've never kippled.'

3

Bernice, who had been flicking through the book looking for her first appearance, laughed suddenly.

'What is it?' the Doctor asked.

'You, after that creature fell on you,' she giggled. 'I still remember the look on your face.'

The Doctor frowned, and gazed at the faded pink stains on his linen jacket.

'I'll never get these blood-stains out,' he murmured.

Bernice hardly heard him. She had flipped back to the start of the book and was already reading the first few words.

Chapter 1

In which Holmes and Watson return from holiday and an illustrious client commissions their services

A reprint from the reminiscences of John H. Watson M.D.

As I flick through the thirty-five volumes of my diary I find records of the many bizarre cases that my friend Sherlock Holmes and I were engaged in over the years. In the volume for eighteen eighty four, to take an example, I see the repulsive story of the red leech and the tale of the terrible death of Crosby the banker. Again, in the tome devoted to eighteen eighty six my eye is caught by the singular affair of the aluminium crutch and its connection with an attempt upon the life of our dear sovereign: a story for which the world is singularly unprepared. It is, however, the year eighteen eighty seven which occupies no less that three volumes of my diary. Following the tragic curtailment of my marriage to Constance Adams of California I was again living under the same roof as Holmes. I still maintained a small practice in Paddington, but my work was undemanding – so much so that I had turned my hand to writing an account of my meeting with Holmes for private publication – and I always managed to make myself available on those occasion when Holmes requested my presence (I cannot, in all honesty, say help) on a case.

All through the spring and summer of that year the brass knocker on the door of 221b Baker Street seemed never to be still, and our carpet was almost worn away by the constant stream of visitors. Twice Mrs Hudson threatened to withdraw from her role as provider of light refreshments to Holmes's clients. The unceasing round of snatched sleep and snatched meals caused Holmes's naturally gaunt features to become so emaciated that I became worried for his health. Eventually I managed to persuade him that he deserved a holiday. Typically of Holmes, he chose to spend it in Vienna researching his theory that many of Mozart's symphonies were plagiarized from obscure works by Orlando Lassus. To mollify me, for he had no interest in bodily comfort himself, he arranged for us to travel in some considerable style. The cost, he claimed, was of no concern, for he had recently been generously remunerated by Lord Rotherfield for proving to the satisfaction of the various Court circulars and scandal sheets that Lady Rotherfield was not a female impersonator. Whilst he delved into archives and, much to the dismay of the maids, buried his hotel suite in mounds of dusty paper, I admired the architecture, the ladies and the horseflesh at the famous Riding Academy. Finally, completely restored to health and happiness, we returned to England on the Orient Express. I should have known that our luck could not last for ever. The shadow of the Library of Saint John the Beheaded lay over us, even as we pulled out of Vienna.

Holmes and I were in the habit of taking dinner with Colonel Warburton and his charming wife Gloria. Returning from an extended holiday, they were heading for Marseilles to pick up the ship to India, where the Colonel was the Resident in the native state of Jabalhabad. Warburton had been with my old regiment, the Fifth Northumberland Fusiliers. Our paths had never crossed before, as he had arrived after my transfer to the Berkshires during the Second Afghan War. My subsequent wounding and invalidity precluded any chance meeting. He was a beefy, florid man with a greying moustache and piercing blue eyes. His wife was a dainty creature, as fragile as a porcelain miniature, but they were obviously devoted to one another despite their differences.

We first became aware of something amiss in the dining carriage. Holmes was in an unusually expansive mood that night, entertaining us with anecdotes of his long and varied life as we dined on an excellent fillet of beef washed down with a surprisingly mediocre Medoc. Having heard Holmes's stories before, I spent some time admiring the carriage we sat in. The ornate ceiling, mahogany panelling and embossed leather seats put me in mind of the finest London clubs, although the paintings (by Schwind and Delacroix, Holmes had assured me) were not to my taste. Give me Landseer's *Monarch of the Glen* any day.

Eventually my gaze shifted to the window, and to the snow-bound Austrian landscape which flashed past too quickly to identify any features. There was a full moon in the sky, and occasionally clouds scudded across its face like dirty rags carried by the wind. Moonlight glinted on the metal of a set of rail tracks which ran parallel to ours. I was about to turn my attention back to the table when a movement caught my eye. I craned my neck, and saw that a second train was racing along behind us, moving at such a pace that it would overtake us within moments. I watched, fascinated, as it pulled alongside. Against the fiery glow from the engine I could see the silhouette of the stoker shovelling like a clockwork figure in the cabin. As the train overtook us I was amazed to discover that it consisted of only one carriage. If anything it was even more ornate than ours from the outside; a gleaming white shape with scarlet velvet drapes drawn across the windows and a golden crest on its flank. Who owned it? What was it doing there? I turned to ask Holmes, but he was engaged in deep conversation and I could not find it in my heart to interrupt. By the time I turned my face back to the window the mystery train had almost passed us.

Holmes was now waxing lyrical about violins, explaining to the Colonel and his wife the difference between an Amati and a Stradivarius. I thanked God that Holmes's own violin lay back in Baker Street. When the mood took him Holmes could play like an angel, but more often than not his raucous meanderings put the cats to shame. Whilst

7

we waited for our third course I glanced over Holmes's shoulder. Apart from the four of us around the dinner table there were two other travellers travelling first class, but only the Reverend Hawkins was present in the dining car. Baden-Powell, a self-proclaimed expert on butterflies whose tan and manner indicated military service, was absent. I looked again at the Reverend Hawkins. Something about him bothered me, but I could not say what.

'You see, but you do not understand,' said Holmes, interrupting my train of thought.

'I beg your pardon?'

'Our clerical fellow traveller is an agent for the British Government.'

'Good Lord, Holmes. Are you sure?'

Colonel and Mrs Warburton were listening intently. I suddenly became aware that the train was slowing but I found myself, as always, fascinated by Holmes's display of his talents.

'The *Compagnie Internationale des Wagons-Lits* have provided spies of all nations with a golden ribbon across Europe. It would be unusual were they not to take advantage of it. When I see an English clergyman travelling first class my suspicions are raised; when I notice that the knees of his trousers do not shine, my suspicions positively levitate.'

'Knees?' asked Warburton.

'Shine?' murmured his wife.

'You do not see the connection?' Holmes asked. 'Forgive me, I thought it was obvious. The Reverend Hawkins may pray, but not I suspect for his immortal soul, and certainly not in the conventional position. You may also note the callous on the index finger of his right hand, indicating a familiarity with firearms of which the Archbishop of Canterbury would strongly disapprove.'

The train was just crawling along now, but Holmes continued.

'The man is obviously an undercover agent of some sort. The assertion that he works for our dear Queen rather than one of her foreign relatives is, I will admit, a shot in the dark. However, given his calm manner I would suggest that he is returning from an assignment rather than travelling to one.'

'But how did you know . . .?'

'That you were watching him? If I catch you staring fixedly over my shoulder it doesn't take much to know that you aren't keeping an eye on an empty table. You were watching one of our fellow travellers.'

The train had been brought to a stop now. Glancing out of the window I saw what I had expected; the white train with the gold crest was stationary on the other track.

'But,' I protested, gathering my wits, 'Hawkins entered after us, and your back has been to him all the time. How did you know it wasn't Mr Baden-Powell who had entered?'

'Simplicity itself. When the *serveur* brought in the soup, he was carrying five dishes. Someone had obviously entered behind me. It must have been either Baden-Powell or Hawkins, since they are the only other first class travellers.' He leaned back and steepled his fingers upon the tablecloth. The candle on the table cast a hawk-like shadow behind him. 'When we received the soup, we began immediately. There was a gap of almost forty-five seconds before I heard the clink of a spoon on a dish behind us. Conclusion: the Reverend Hawkins had been saying grace.' Holmes smiled. 'Either that or Mr Baden-Powell had been straining the soup for botanical specimens. I chose the most probable alternative.'

'Bravo!' said the Colonel. His wife applauded daintily.

'As usual, Holmes,' I said, a touch acerbically, 'you make it appear so simple.'

Before Holmes could reply the imposing figure of the *chef de train* appeared at our table. Bending low, he murmured something into my friend's ear. Holmes stood, and turned to the Colonel and his wife.

'I'm afraid that I will have to leave you for a moment,' he announced, and turning to me he said, 'Watson, perhaps you would like to accompany me.'

Together we made our way from the dining carriage to

9

the smoking salon. Baden-Powell was slumped in a heavy leather *fauteuil* with a sketchbook in his hands. As the *chef de train* led us past I noticed that the naturalist was painstakingly filling in patterns on a butterfly's wing.

Beyond the smoking salon, stairs had been lowered to the snowy ground. The white train lay twenty feet away. Footsteps led from that train to ours and back again. There was a chill in the air, but no worse than the bite of an April morning in London.

The *chef de train* halted and turned to us.

'Gentlemen,' he began, his breath steaming in front of his face. 'In the history of the *Compagnie Internationale des Wagons-Lits* this has happened not once before. Not once. We have been . . .' he searched for the right words, '. . . *flagged down*!'

'By whom?' Holmes inquired softly.

'By one whom I may not disobey,' the *chef* said, crossing himself briefly. 'Your presence is requested. We will wait for ten minutes. The schedule will allow no more.' With that he turned on his heel and strode back inside the salon.

'You saw it pass us by earlier?' Holmes asked, indicating the distant carriage. I nodded. 'That crest is familiar,' he continued. 'I have seen it before, on a letter or a document of some kind.' He shook his head. 'There is, of course, only one way to find out. Are you game?'

'I would consider it a privilege,' I replied.

We set out together across the snow-laden ground towards the white train.

The snow crunched underfoot. I could feel the cold begin to bite at the tips of my fingers. Behind us I could hear an increasing number of voices from the second-class compartments demanding to know of the *chef de train* what was causing the delay. I could not make out his answer.

Within moments we were approaching the train.

'Are you armed?' Holmes asked.

'No,' I replied. 'I had not anticipated the need. Are you?'

10

'My hair-trigger pistol is back in my valise.'

As we reached the steps leading up to the lone carriage a door opened above us. Back-lit by the light spilling from the carriage, a spindly, cloaked figure cast its shadow over us. I could make out nothing apart from the unnatural smoothness of its head. It gestured us inside, then retreated.

Holmes and I looked at each other, then Holmes climbed the steps. Casting a longing glance back at the Orient Express, I did likewise.

The bright light blinded me momentarily as we entered the carriage. Shielding my eyes, I managed to make out three figures before us. One was seated in an ornately carved chair in the centre of the otherwise empty space. The others stood behind. As my eyes grew accustomed to the glare I began to make out more. The carriage was lined in white silk, with the scarlet velvet curtains across the windows standing out like splashes of blood. Three massive gas-lit chandeliers hung from the ceiling, swaying slightly. The carpet was deep and red.

The figures standing behind the chair were tall and thin. Both wore long black robes with scarlet scarves draped across their shoulders, scarlet sashes around their waists and scarlet skullcaps half-covering what sparse hair they had. Each had a face that seemed to be made up of vertical lines. Neither showed any expression.

The man in the chair, swamped by his white robes, was the least impressive thing in the carriage. Thin and grey-haired, he might have been a banker or a grocer. His tiny white skullcap looked as if it could fall from his head at any moment.

Holmes walked to the centre of the carriage and stood before the man in the chair. I expected one of them to say something, and so I was completely unprepared when Holmes knelt upon one knee. The man extended his hand, upon which I saw a massive gold ring. Holmes's face tightened for a moment, then he knelt and kissed the ring.

I was hit by a sudden crashing realization, and so when Holmes turned his head and said, 'Watson, may I intro-

11

duce His Holiness, Pope Leo XIII,' I was at least half prepared. I bowed from where I stood. One of the men who flanked the Pope frowned and opened his mouth as if to rebuke me, but the Pope raised his hand. The other man spoke in excellent English.

'His Holiness understands that Doctor Watson shares the majority of his countrymen's antagonism towards the Holy See. There is no transgression.'

Holmes stood and took two steps backwards to join me.

'We are grateful, your Holiness,' he murmured. There was a undertone of sarcasm in his words.

The man spoke again.

'I am Cardinal Ruffo-Scilla, and this,' he gestured to his mirror image on the other side of the chair, 'is Cardinal Tosca. His Holiness wishes to express his regret for disrupting your journey.'

'His Holiness has no need to apologize for anything,' Holmes said. 'I have served the Holy Father from a distance before, although I had never expected to meet him in person.'

'His Holiness was most pleased with your discreet recovery of the Vatican cameos,' Ruffo-Scilla continued smoothly. 'Your actions prevented a scandal, and justified his Holiness's faith in you.'

'I did wonder how I had come to the Vatican's attention,' Holmes said carefully. 'After all, given Mr Gladstone's belated acknowledgement of the annexation of all papal lands by King Victor Emmanuel II, and the subsequent withdrawal of the Apostolic Delegation from British territory, I had assumed that his Holiness would use the extensive resources of the Vatican rather than resort to a British detective who regards himself as an atheist and whose fame,' and he spread his hands modestly, 'barely extends beyond the borders of a country currently regarded as *non grata*.'

His Holiness Pope Leo XIII smiled gently.

'His Holiness has followed your career with interest,' Cardinal Ruffo-Scilla said. 'There are certain things that a free agent can do that members of the Sacred College cannot. His Holiness believes, however, that such business should be "kept within the family", whenever possible and, despite your own regrettable lapse in faith, your family have served the Holy See faithfully before.'

Holmes nodded and turned to me.

'I remember Sherringford writing to tell me,' he murmured, 'that one of our distant ancestors had been Commander in Chief of the Naval Forces of his Holiness the Pope. I had never credited the story until now.'

I was amazed, not so much at what had been said, but at Holmes's uncharacteristic revelations concerning his family. After all, it had been five years before he revealed to me that he possessed a brother. I made a note to ask who Sherringford was when we got back to London.

His Holiness raised a hand, still smiling enigmatically.

'Time is short,' Cardinal Ruffo-Scilla said. 'Your train will be leaving shortly. His Holiness wishes to retain your professional services. You may demand any recompense that you wish.'

'My fees are on a fixed scale,' Holmes said severely, 'except in those cases where I remit them altogether. The problem is everything. Pray explain what you wish of me.'

His Holiness twisted his ring around his finger and looked thoughtful.

'Have you heard of the Library of Saint John the Beheaded?' Ruffo-Scilla asked. I saw Holmes's fingers twitch. Had we been back in Baker Street I knew he would have been demanding: 'Watson, pass my index for the letter L down from the shelf. Oh, and whilst you are at it, you may as well recover J and B as well.' Now, however, I could hear the chagrin in his voice as he admitted, 'The name is familiar, but I am afraid I cannot place it.'

'I would not expect you to,' the Cardinal said calmly. 'The Library does not advertise its presence. It is a repository for books which have been, or are, or may be, banned – either by us or by some other ... authority. Books so extreme and unusual that we cannot even acknowledge

13

that we are interested in them, for fear of exciting general opinion. Books that, some say, should never have been written. However' – he spread his hands wide in an unofficial benediction – 'we are reasonable men. We allow selected scholars and researchers to examine these books in the hope that they may shed a little light into the darker corners of God's creation for us. Because England is the centre of the rational world, and has always seemed to us to be more stable than many other countries, the Library is based in London. The present ... discommodation ... between our countries has, paradoxically, made things easier. The greater the perceived gap between the Library and the Church, the better.'

'Suppression of knowledge by the Church,' Holmes said bitterly. 'Why am I unsurprised?'

I cleared my throat. His Holiness looked up at me and smiled.

'I find myself confused,' I said. 'What sort of books are we talking about?'

'One of the three unexpurgated versions of the *Malleus Maleficarum* is in the Library,' the Cardinal replied from the Supreme Pontiff's side, 'the other two being held in the Vatican Library. The only complete transcript of Galileo Galilei's trial resides there, along with shelves of books on the Chinese *Si Fan* society and its leader, Doctor Fu Manchu – a man whom we in the Vatican believe to be as huge a menace to civilization as you believe anarchism to be. Five lost plays by Aristophanes. The only known copy of the Basra Fragment of the lost Dictionary of the Khazars, along with the proof of Fermat's Last Theorem. And,' he smiled, 'a copy of notes made by Doctor Watson and picturesquely entitled *The Affair of the Politician, The Lighthouse and the Trained Cormorant*, the publication of which was, I believe, suppressed at the highest levels.'

I took a step forward, ready to remonstrate with the Cardinal. Holmes raised a hand to stop me but His Holiness the Pope coughed, attracting my attention. The small man in the loose-fitting white robe who was believed by many to be God's mouthpiece on Earth looked full into

14

my eyes for the first time, and I was so struck by the calm and wise intelligence that shone like a beacon in his gaze that I stood with my mouth hanging open until Holmes interjected, 'This is all very interesting, but I'm afraid we have a train to catch. Perhaps you could get to the point.'

'The Library was been robbed,' Ruffo-Scilla said quietly. 'In the thousand years that the Library has existed, such a thing has never happened. Wars, fires, disasters ... these things have been as the beating of a moth's wing to the Library. And yet now, after all those long years, books are missing.'

Cardinal Ruffo-Scilla seemed genuinely upset, although I could not see why. Admittedly, the theft of historical relics was unfortunate, but the Cardinal was making it seem like a world catastrophe. I had seen enough looting in Afghanistan and in India to show me that nothing lasts forever.

Holmes cut to the nub of the issue.

'Do you have any idea who the thief might be?' he said.

'None.'

'When was the theft discovered?'

'Two days ago, when a member of the Library asked to see one of the books.'

'The news came through rapidly.'

'We have our methods.'

'I shall have to visit the scene of the crime, of course, although the evidence will almost certainly have been cleaned away by now.'

The Cardinal smiled. 'Cleaners are not allowed in the Library,' he said. 'Some of the documents are so old that a careless touch would crumble them to dust.'

'The police have not been informed?'

His Holiness frowned. For the first time Cardinal Tosca spoke from the other side of the Papal Throne. His voice was sibilant, his accent pronounced.

'The authorities must not be made aware of the Library,' he hissed. 'The whole point about conspiracies is that they have been suppressed by those in power.'

Outside a train whistle hooted mournfully.

'I believe that is our train,' Holmes said. 'I shall take your case, but I will require the location of this mysterious Library, and a letter of introduction to its custodian.'

Ruffo-Scilla reached into his robes and pulled out a sheaf of documents, which he passed to Holmes.

'His Holiness would like to extend his gratitude,' the Cardinal said. Holmes, uncomfortable with the display of subservience but too experienced in the ways of the world to object, knelt to kiss the ring on the Pope's outstretched hand again, and this time I did the same. Leo XIII leaned forward and made the sign of the cross above Holmes's forehead, and then above mine.

'*In nomine Patris, et Filii, et Spiritus Sancti,*' the Pope murmured, '*Amen.* God be with you, gentlemen.'

We left the carriage together.

'A rum business, what?' I said as we walked back across our footprints. The night had turned colder in the few minutes we had been inside.

'Returning overdue books to the library,' Holmes snapped. 'It's a bit beneath my dignity. And I have no great love for the Catholic Church. Our family was brought up in the faith, but my brothers and I were too aware of the inconsistencies and irrationalities inherent in the Bible to make good communicants.'

Brothers? I thought, but just then the Orient Express began to pull slowly away from us, and we had to sprint the last few yards or face a long walk home.

16

Chapter 2

In which Holmes and Watson visit the Library and Mr Jitter threatens to take a hand

'Cab!'

Holmes's strident cry rang out across the late afternoon hurly-burly outside Victoria Station. I added a single blast from my cab-whistle for good measure. A growler that had seen better days detached itself from the throng of vehicles and clattered towards us.

It was good to be back in London. The metropolis was labouring under a warm and muggy spell and despite the high, if not putrid, aroma of horse dung and refuse that greeted us as we left the station, I felt my spirits soar.

As Holmes and I sank gratefully back into the upholstered seats and the cabbie hoisted our considerable baggage on to the four-wheeler's roof, Holmes turned to me and said, 'You have been strangely quiet since our meeting with his Holiness last night.'

Indeed, we both had. After we had clambered back on to the Orient Express, Holmes had refused to be drawn on the matter. We had retired to our cabins with no more than a few words passing between us. We awoke in Paris, and spent most of the day so occupied in getting ourselves to the present point with the minimum inconvenience and our luggage intact that no opportunities for serious conversation had presented themselves. Even on the journey from Dover to London, Holmes had buried himself into the pages of the Daily Chronicle, eschewing the headlines for the agony columns.

In passing, I should say that, despite his frequent claims

to care 'not a whit' which party was in power, I could not help but notice that on the day that the *Daily Telegraph* switched its editorial allegiance from the Liberal camp to the Unionist persuasion, Holmes had given up reading it in favour of the newly published *Chronicle*.

'You,' I ventured, 'have been remarkably reticent on the subject as well.'

We jolted into motion. The ornate facade of the Grosvenor Hotel passed us by, followed moments later by the Metropolitan line Underground station ticket office.

'That is no more than anyone who knew my foibles would expect,' Holmes responded.

I glanced across at Holmes, suspecting some jibe. His eyes were closed and his mouth curved into a slight smile.

'However,' he added, 'since you are known as a clubbable sort of fellow, your silence is more surprising than mine.'

The growler's speed increased as it moved from the muddy area outside the station to the asphalted wooden blocks of Victoria Street. Within a few minutes we were rounding Parliament Square and trotting up Whitehall.

Holmes glanced at his watch.

'Mycroft will be clearing his desk at this very moment,' he said, 'in preparation for his usual walk to the Diogenes Club. As I may have remarked before, the daily rotation of my brother between his lodgings in Pall Mall, his office here in Westminster and his club is as unvarying as the motion of the stars.'

'If you must know,' I said, 'I have misgivings concerning this case.'

'I confess,' he replied, 'that the more I think about it, the less I like it. I suspect there are deep undercurrents here of which we have not been made aware.' He brightened up. 'Still, it is a capital mistake to theorize in the absence of the facts, and the case does hold certain interesting features.'

We took Trafalgar Square at a fast clip, and were heading up the newly built Charing Cross Road when Holmes said, 'How do you fancy a little run out tomorrow, old chap?'

His casual tone did not fool me.

'To the Library of Saint John the Beheaded?'

'I'll make a detective out of you yet,' he chuckled.

As we turned into Oxford Street we found ourselves behind a slow-moving bus – one of the dark green Atlas type – whose horses could not be raised from an idle canter. The press of traffic made it impossible for our own driver to overtake.

'These streets are becoming more crowded by the day,' Holmes remarked. 'There is only so much traffic the capital can take without grinding to a complete halt.'

It was twenty minutes later that we arrived at our lodgings in Baker Street. Mrs Hudson, our landlady, had been alerted by telegram to our impending arrival. Despite a sprained ankle which had occurred during our absence, and which my locum had treated, she had a large dinner awaiting us. At last I was home and comfortable again.

I descended the next morning to find Holmes slumped in his armchair in the same position he had been in when I retired. He was still wearing his mouse-coloured dressing-gown.

'Have you slept, Holmes?'

'Sleep is for tortoises.' A huge pile of newspapers was spread around him and he was clipping out articles and pasting them into his files. 'I have a deal of catching up to do. Mrs Hudson had been saving these for me every day. This,' he said, waving a copy of the *Globe*, 'is the nervous system of the city, Watson! The agony columns, the small advertisements, the snippets of news concerning lost parakeets and accidents involving brewers' drays . . . I can predict half the crimes in London for the next six months by keeping abreast of these sorts of minutiae and trivia!'

Whilst I breakfasted on scrambled eggs, bacon and kedgeree, all washed down with cups of strong, sweet tea, Holmes busied himself amongst his cuttings. I took the opportunity to look around the room – made fresh to me by a few days' absence. It struck me suddenly how *bohemian* our abode must have looked to the casual visitor – of which we had more than our fair share, given Holmes's vocation. The general arrangement of chairs and tables was, it must be said, unremarkable. The three windows looked down onto Baker Street, and provided ample light. The furniture was comfortable. A spirit case and gasogene in one corner were a welcome sign of refreshment, and a curtained recess in another provided privacy, should it be needed. No, it was the details that gave us away. The initials 'VR', which Holmes had patriotically inscribed in the wall adjoining his bedroom using a small-calibre revolver were, perhaps, the most obvious feature. Next to them his unanswered correspondence, affixed to the mantlepiece with a jack-knife, was a minor detail and the Persian slipper full of tobacco a mere frippery.

How did I put up with the man? More importantly, how did Mrs Hudson put up with him?

The answer to that was simple. Mrs Hudson's affection for Holmes was that same feeling that one would show for a precocious but wayward child. She had taken him under her wing, and Holmes, the great observer, never realized the extent to which she mothered him. The fact that the rent which – and I frankly admit this – he paid for both of us could have already bought the house many times over did not influence her in the slightest, I feel sure.

I glanced over at the side of the room which, by mutual agreement, was 'mine'. A few scattered volumes of short stories, a copy of Gray's *Anatomy*, a framed portrait of General Gordon and an unframed one of Henry Ward Beecher ... these were my possessions. Not for the first time, I compared my life to that of my friend, and I found myself wanting.

'I have been researching the Library of St John the Beheaded whilst you lay asleep,' Holmes announced, apropos of nothing. 'I have been able to find no reference to it anywhere, save some guarded comments in an obscure theological journal published almost a century ago. It appears to derive from the Venetian Church of S.

20

Giovanni Decollato, or S. Zan Degolà as the locals call it. According to the documentation we were provided with by his Holiness – ' he tapped a sheaf of vellum beside him which, I noticed, was already stained with marmalade ' – it is located in Holborn, in the notorious area known as the St Giles Rookery. A nasty neighbourhood it is too; a veritable rabbit-warren of alleys, cellars, tunnels, slums and stairwells. The police dare not go near it, save in teams.' He frowned slightly. 'I tracked down Lady Fantersham there, you may recall, when she was kidnapping girls for the white slave trade.'

'An unexpected location for a library. I would have expected something isolated and heavily guarded. A manor house, perhaps, in some remote corner of England.'

'I suspect that the location is not accidental. Given the value that we know must attach itself to such a collection, what better place to hide it than amongst thieves and rogues?'

'Ah,' I cried. '*The Purloined Letter* by Edgar Allen Poe! The best place to hide an incriminating letter is in a letter rack!'

'Poe is an American drunk and his fictional detective Dupin a fortunate blunderer,' Holmes snapped, and threw off his dressing gown to reveal impeccable morning attire.

'Surely,' I said, 'if we are descending into the lair of the criminal classes, a disguise of some sort . . .'

'No need.' He reached for his top hat. 'The one reference I have been able to find to the Library of St John the Beheaded implied that some form of immunity from harm was extended to its patrons.'

'Holmes, that was a hundred years ago!'

'Then we had better hope it is still accurate.'

Within a few minutes we were in a hansom heading for Holborn. Within sight of Newgate Prison, empty now but still a name to strike terror into the heart, we turned off into a series of narrow alleys, whose steep sides restricted the sky to a narrow, overcast strip and provided plentiful shadows for lurking muggers.

'Can't go no farther, Guv,' said the cabbie after a while.

I was not sure whether he was referring to the narrowness of the alleys or the danger of lingering. Holmes paid him off whilst I gazed around, convinced we were being watched.

'The St Giles Rookery,' Holmes murmured as the two wheeler clattered away to wider and safer thoroughfares. 'A portmanteau term born of St Giles's Church and the rook, a burglar's jemmy. Keep your eyes peeled and your hand on your revolver.'

'How did you . . .'

'Your topcoat hangs heavy on the right-hand side. No doubt the crows will have noticed.'

'Crows?'

'The look-outs, Watson. Five of them. You had not noticed?' He gave an exclamation and moved off. I followed, wishing I were somewhere else.

The alleys seemed to crowd in on us as we walked. The cobbles were more like sharp stones embedded in mud. Glassless windows and doorless doorways led to sparsely furnished rooms and stairwells with broken treads. Undernourished dogs paced us from a distance. Sneering men in grimy, collarless shirts watched us from doorways. Hollow-eyed women glanced quickly up at us from sinks and tables, only to look away if we met their gaze. Children ran in gangs, playing with shards of wood and frayed string, staring at us with hard, old eyes. The stench was appalling – worse than the fetid odour of gangrene and trenchfoot which was my overriding memory of Afghanistan.

'The dregs of London make their abode here, Watson,' Holmes warned, *sotto voce*. 'I would be surprised if there's a man or woman with an honest occupation within a mile of this spot.' His voice was bitter. 'The criminal underclasses do not call themselves the Family for nothing. They live ten to a room and teach their children to become dips and mutchers in their wake, and who can blame them? Those politicians who decry anarchy and socialism as dangerous foreign nonsense should look to their own back yards first. There is no law here; it is nature, red in tooth and claw.'

'Dips and mutchers?' I asked.

'Pickpockets and thieves who rob drunks,' he said. 'Really, Watson, your education is remarkably lacking in some areas.'

A pair of grimy ragamuffins ran past us. I was about to reach out and ruffle the hair on one of them – a small, blonde girl – when Holmes stopped me.

'Tosh-fakers,' he explained.

'I'm sorry?' I pulled my hand back.

'Urchins whose dubious profession it is to search the sewer mouths of the Thames, casting amongst the excrement for valuable trifles which have been lost down privies and drains.'

'How can a child endure this way of life?' I exclaimed.

'They survive,' he said.

Holmes seemed to have memorized the route, for he led me unhesitatingly through turn after turn. Within moments we were moving through what seemed to be a crowd of scarecrows who eyed us with envy and hatred, but we carried a bubble of privacy with us that pushed the crowd away before us and closed it again in our wake. As Holmes had said, we were protected. I could not have retraced even a fraction of our path, for every street and every face bore the same marks of hardship and violence.

'Does anything strike you as strange?' Holmes muttered after a while.

'Nothing in particular,' I replied.

'Hmmm. I would be prepared to swear that this rookery is less crowded than the last time I passed this way. Many of the male inhabitants appear to be absent.'

'*Less* crowded?' I couldn't see how any more people could be crammed into the area.

'Relatively speaking,' he added, and walked on.

I noticed after a while that, as well as the dogs, a gaggle of stooped and grey-haired women were following us.

'We appear to be the object of some attention,' I murmured to my friend.

23

'Not us,' he said, 'the dogs.'

Indeed, now he mentioned it, I noticed that the women were carefully watching what the dogs did. When one of the hounds took it into his head to ... delicacy forbids me to be specific ... perform a natural function, then one of the grey-haired hags would immediately rush forward and scoop the resulting ordure into a canvas sack.

'Collected for the tanneries south of the Thames,' Holmes said in answer to the question which I could not bring myself to utter. 'Too old to steal, they eke out a living this way.'

'Holmes, all this ... this *degradation* ... and within five minutes walk of Simpson's Tavern and Divan in the Strand.'

'Yes,' he said. 'Obscene, is it not?' He looked around. 'We have arrived.'

The doorway was no different to others we had passed; empty, with the timbers of the doorframe rotted and mossy. Inside there was darkness.

Holmes led the way.

I had expected shadows, rats and creaking floorboards. What I found was a black curtain that parted to reveal a carpeted corridor lined with damask. Oil lamps provided a warm yellow light. The ceiling was adorned with alabaster carvings. The contrast with the poverty outside was almost unbelievable. I could well have believed myself to be in a house in Cheyne Walk, having dreamed the journey here.

An emaciated attendant dressed in black silk robes came forward to greet us.

'Gentlemen,' he said in a voice so low it verged on the indistinguishable. 'Do you have an appointment?'

Holmes handed his card to the man, who looked at it in disdain.

'If you have no appointment, then I regret ...' He trailed off politely.

'Perhaps a letter of introduction?' Holmes suggested.

The man inclined his head.

'That would, of course, depend on ...'

Holmes handed over the vellum sheet sealed with the papal crest.

The man frowned.

'Yes, sir,' he finally intoned. 'I believe that will be sufficient.'

Holmes looked over at me and raised an eyebrow.

'Perhaps you would care to sign the visitors book,' the man continued, moving away. 'We do not allow documents to be removed from the premises, but you are at liberty to examine any that you wish whilst you are here. What is your area of interest?'

'Stolen books,' Holmes said succinctly.

'We have a small section on bibliographic theft, sir, including a treatise which casts an intriguing new light upon the fire which consumed the library at Alexandria in the sixth century.'

We both stared at him.

'My little joke,' he said quietly. 'Please follow me.'

We followed him to a little nook, where we both signed an ancient tome as thick as a large loaf and were issued with small slips of card with our names on them. He then led the way along the corridor and up two flights of stairs which groaned under the weight of the books piled upon them. His robes made no sound as he walked, and in the silence I was aware of the swish that our morning clothes made. Three rooms led off each landing, so thickly lined with laden shelves that the walls themselves were not visible. I glanced in one of them and saw a small man sitting at a desk and reading a book. His face was morose, an impression aided by his heavy eyebrows, and he looked as if he had selected his clothes in the dark from a wardrobe of remnants from the Eastcheap markets. His lightweight linen jacket was inappropriate for the time of year, the time of day and the occasion; his white trousers were baggy; his embroidered silk waistcoat belonged to another *ensemble* entirely. A paisley cravat was loosely knotted at his throat, and a battered fedora was crammed upon his head.

'Excuse me,' I said, and made as if to leave.

'Were you looking for anything in particular?' he asked.

'I'm not sure'.

He smiled cheerfully.

'I hope you find it,' he said. 'I myself am in search of universal peace, an end to strife and unlimited custard for all, but I have a feeling I'm looking in the wrong place.'

'Might I ask what you are reading?'

He held the book up so that I could see the title: *Adventures Amongst the Abominable Snowmen* by Redvers Fenn-Cooper. As a child I had doted on the adventures of the famous explorer. I remember the sense of loss I had experienced when reading about his disappearance, a decade or more ago.

'Are you interested in his work?' I asked.

'I'm searching for the man,' he replied.

'He vanished, did he not? Are you intending to set out on an expedition to look for him?'

'Oh I know where he is. I meant it metaphorically.'

'I see.' I began to withdraw. 'I hope that you find him.'

'Most kind,' his voice rang out as I ran to catch up with Holmes and our guide.

We turned left and walked for a few yards, passing another two such rooms, descended another flight of stairs and turned back on ourselves. We followed this curiously winding path in silence for some ten minutes or more, passing innumerable rooms, each containing innumerable books, folders and pamphlets. By the end of it, I estimated that we were in a cellar area a hundred yards or so deeper into the building and had passed more books than were in the possession of the British Library. In all that time, I had seen nobody but the small man with the lunatic grin.

As we turned a sharp corner and descended a ramp to a lower level, I heard a noise behind me. Turning, I caught sight of a robed and hooded figure, reminiscent of a monk, hobbling across the corridor behind me. It stopped at an ornately carved door and produced a small key. Before opening the door, the figure paused and glanced at me. I could not distinguish any features within the shadow of the hood. Conscious that I was staring, I turned and walked on.

After a few more minutes walk, our guide gestured for us to enter a room of bare, undecorated walls. A second man, also swathed in black robes, also thin, rose to greet us from behind a bare desk.

'Gentlemen,' he whispered. 'Are you looking for anything in particular?'

I looked around for our guide, but he had vanished.

'I have been retained,' said Holmes, moving forward, 'by Pope Leo XIII to investigate the theft of certain documents from this library. My time is short, and I would request your co-operation.'

'Of course,' the man whispered. 'My name is Ambrose, Jehosephat Ambrose. I am the Head Librarian of the Library of Saint John the Beheaded. Whatever questions you have, please ask them.'

'Which documents are missing?' my friend snapped.

'Three books from our alternative zoology and phantasmagorical anthropology section. Here are the titles.' He held out a sheet of paper.

'You were expecting us?'

'I was expecting someone.'

'What, pray tell,' I interjected, 'is "alternative zoology"?'

'The study of fabulous beasts,' Ambrose answered. 'Dragons and deamons, griffins and chimerae. You may have heard rumours concerning a sea creature which inhabits Loch Ness, near Inverness in Scotland. We have a number of manuscripts describing its habits and its physiognomy. You may also remember the discovery of the fossilized bones of what might be termed "primeval monsters" at Charing Cross some ten years ago, now. Again, we have quite a selection of books on that subject, going right back to the Bible.'

'The Bible?' I said, scandalized.

' "There were giants in the Earth in those days",' Ambrose quoted.

27

'And these books were kept where?' Holmes said tersely, trying to get the conversation back on the right track.

'In a room, not far from here.'

'And your security procedures?'

'Nobody is allowed to remove books from the library.'

'So I am informed. I am not concerned with what people are *allowed* to do, but with what they are *forbidden* to do.'

Ambrose had the grace to look discomfited.

'You will have noticed,' he began, 'that we have an *arrangement* with the local criminal fraternity. More precisely, two of the local gang leaders, or "scurfs" as the argot has it, guarantee the safety and integrity of the Library in return for financial recompense.'

'And how exactly do they operate?'

'Very simply. There is only one way out of the Library – the doorway through which you entered. At no other point do its bounds come near the outside world; apart from that door we are completely sealed in. Every visitor and every member of staff who leaves is searched by the skilled pickpockets, or "fine wirers", of each gang. If anybody is caught attempting to remove a book – and they will be caught – their hands are cut off. It's a very simple deterrent.'

'Bribery?' Holmes suggested.

Ambrose shook his head. 'It was obvious to the original creators of the Library that any one set of guards could be suborned by bribery or threats. Since time immemorial we have used two tribes, or gangs, who are in competition. Each watches the other, you see? Each would like nothing more than to catch the other one out, and so we avoid placing too much reliance on any one person or group of people.'

'An equitable arrangement,' Holmes said brusquely. 'Do these gang leaders have names?'

'They are known by the colourful sobriquets of Mr Jitter and Mack "The Knife" Yeovil.'

'I know of them. Men without any notion of decency or morals: thieves and killers whose catalogues of crimes are exceeded only by their hatred of each other. I have often suspected them of being linked to the Moriarty gang.'

Ambrose smiled.

'That rivalry assures our security,' he said. 'Each man would take great pleasure in catching the other one out, or discovering a theft that the other had overlooked.'

'What about ventilation?' I asked. 'Could somebody gain access through ventilation ducts?'

'There is no ventilation.'

'But the air ... it's fresh.'

Ambrose smiled. 'The Library has been designed to provide a natural channel for the transit of air from the doorway, around the many corridors and rooms, and out of the same doorway whilst still maintaining a constant temperature and humidity. Effectively, and without wanting to appear melodramatic, the Library breathes, just as you or I.'

'Very interesting, I am sure,' said Holmes, who could be very blinkered when he chose to be. 'But how soon would the theft have been discovered?'

'We had just completed a full inventory of the Library's stock a month back when an old and respected visitor asked to see the very books that were stolen. Thus we were able to narrow the time of the theft down considerably.'

'Most fortuitous,' Holmes said dryly. 'I will need the names and addresses of all visitors to the Library, starting a month before the theft.'

'Already prepared.' He held out another sheet of paper. Holmes took it and scanned the list. His eyes widened in surprise at one of the names. He cast a covert glance at me, and read on.

'This W. C. Minor ...' he said a few moments later. 'The name is familiar to me.'

'Ah,' Ambrose said, and trailed off. 'You have hit upon one of our more unusual members. Dr Minor is the only man who is allowed to read our books outside the library.'

'I believed you to say that nobody was allowed to remove books.'

'He does not remove them. We send them to him.'

'And why is that?' Holmes snapped.

'He is aiding in the compilation of a dictionary to rival that of Dr Johnson, one that will contain every word in the English language. Our archives of arcane documents are invaluable to his researches.'

'And why can he not consult them here?'

Ambrose blinked.

'Because he is confined within the hospital for the criminally insane at Broadmoor.'

'Of course!' Holmes cried. 'I thought I knew the name. He shot an innocent man under the delusion that he was being pursued by Irishmen. I was briefly involved in the case. I presume that you have recovered all of the books that you sent him?'

'Of course.'

'Then, assuming that he is still in captivity, we can provisionally rule him out as a suspect. This last one on the list interests me, however,' he said thoughtfully. 'You have him listed only as "The Doctor", and you give no address.'

'That is how he styles himself,' Ambrose said, and smiled reminiscently. 'The Doctor has been a visitor here since before my father's time. I believe his ticket was first issued ... oh, let me see ... five hundred years ago.'

'Not to him personally, I hope,' Holmes said.

'I would not have thought so,' Ambrose said, offended. 'Many families treat their visitors' tickets as family heirlooms, passing them down from generation to generation. Strangely enough, it was he who asked to see the missing books, and sparked off this business.'

I could see my friend's eyebrows lift slightly at this.

'I would like to see the room from which the thefts occurred,' he said. Ambrose nodded, levered himself from behind his desk and gestured for us to follow him out of the room. He led us another merry dance; switching back and forth along corridors, climbing stairs and descending

30

ramps until I felt quite dizzy and had no idea where we were or even upon which floor. Eventually we stopped by a room, no different from the myriad others we had passed.

'Alternative zoology and phantasmagorical anthropology,' he announced.

I stood on the threshold as Holmes leapt into action. I had seen my friend's methods put into effect before, and so I was not surprised when he dropped to the floor and began to crawl around the room like some huge, dun-coloured beetle.

'You must be terribly well read,' I said to Ambrose in an attempt to make small talk. He looked strangely at me.

'We do not read any of the documents here,' he said.

'What, not at all?'

'No, sir. We have all taken a vow for the sake of our own safety.'

'Why on Earth would you want to do that?'

'Too much knowledge can drive a man mad,' he said strangely, and would not be drawn further.

Using a small pair of scissors, Holmes took clippings from the ornate carpet and placed them into a series of envelopes. Eventually he tired of the floor, and turned his attention to the book-lined walls. He began by moving rapidly along them with his hands clasped behind his back, sniffing at the spines. He then took out his magnifying glass and spent ten minutes examining the spine of one book in particular in almost infinite detail. It was when he reached out a bony finger to remove the book from the shelf that Ambrose's expression changed from polite disdain to shock.

'Sir!' he exclaimed, and leapt forward. Using a pair of vellum-swathed tongs which he removed from a pocket in his robes, he carefully prised the book from its perch. Holding it in one hand, he removed a pair of dove-grey gloves from a hidden pocket of his robes and presented them to Holmes.

'How remiss of me,' Ambrose said.

Holmes flicked through the volume in a cursory manner and replaced it on the shelf.

'Ludwig Prinn's *De Vermiis Mysteriis*, German black letter edition, sixteenth century. A remarkably good copy.' He turned towards the door. 'I have seen enough,' he announced. 'I would inspect the rest of the Library.'

It took Holmes three hours to cover the entire extent of the Library of St John the Beheaded, during which time Mr Ambrose and I finished most of a bottle of sweet sherry, and I flicked through various volumes of morally suspect theology. Eventually he returned, downcast.

'He was right,' Holmes muttered. 'No concealed exits, no trapdoors, no skylights. I did, however, come across one locked room, which our host informed me was for members to entertain visitors in, should they so wish.'

'At the head of a ramp?'

'Indeed. You noticed it?'

'I saw a figure entering the room, covered from head to foot in robes of the type that monks wear. He walked strangely, as if he was deformed in some way.'

'Hmm. Well, I suppose that the Library does cater to Catholic tastes.' He smiled briefly. 'It may interest you to learn that I confirmed our host's statement to the effect that there is only one way in or out. I would suggest that we now avail ourselves of it.'

Ambrose escorted us to the egress.

'Good luck, gentlemen,' he said. We turned, blinking in the sudden sunlight, to thank him, but he had vanished into the gloom.

''Scuse us, gents,' said a voice from the alley. Standing in front of us was an oafish figure wearing stained trousers, a shirt with neither cuffs nor collar and a trilby whose band had almost become detached from its crown. 'Rules is rules,' he said and stepped forward, revealing a smaller, rat-faced man behind him. I prepared to remonstrate with him, whilst reaching in what I hoped was a surreptitious manner for the gun in my pocket, but Holmes put his hand on my arm.

'The search,' he reminded me.

The oaf stepped forward and ran his hands down the outside and inside of my topcoat, barely brushing my waistcoat.

'Five guineas in loose change and a Webley revolver,' he grinned, stepping away. I could smell the rank odour of his breath: stale ale, rancid meat and dental decay. He moved to Holmes and repeated the procedure whilst Rat-face – presumably a member of the rival gang – frisked me as well.

'What's this?' The ruffian searching Holmes smiled a vicious, tight little smile. His hand came away holding a book. Rat-face looked downcast, and my heart sank. It was the book that Holmes had been looking at in the Library. How could he have been so stupid?

'Well, it's been a time since a cove like you tried to smug the Library there, and you a peach, or so's they say.' A knife as big as my forearm appeared in his hand as if by magic. 'You take me for a queer diver, did you? In for a chivvin' then, aint'cha?'

I made a grab for my gun, but my arms were suddenly pinioned by Rat-face, who was surprisingly strong for a man of his size. The knife man raised his blade to the level of Holmes's eyes. My friend was calm, but I could see him looking from side to side, searching for some means of escape.

'Hold 'is 'ands up where's 'e can see 'em for the last time,' said the knife man.

'Let him be,' commanded a deep, authoritative voice. The knife man stepped back, contrite, his blade vanishing into thin air. The hands holding Holmes and I also disappeared.

A owner of the voice stepped into sight from beyond the edge of my vision. He was small, with oiled hair and a long frock coat that had seen better days, but which was still better than any other clothing I had seen in the area. His face was deeply pocked and his nose was almost eaten away by syphilis.

'Testing my security, were you?' he said. His eyes didn't seem to connect with ours; his gaze drifted across us like

33

smoke. 'Can't say I blame you. You'll be the jack from up West, then? Mr Sherlock Holmes?'

Holmes nodded.

'Well, Mr Holmes, you tell them that wants to know that Mr Jitter's turf is as tight as a drum, and always has been. You hear that? Always has been.' He looked away, down the street. 'I've already taken steps to check out my men here, me and Mack Yeovil between us. I'll be watching out for you, and you watch out for me, hear? I want to know who's been doing me over. Consider yourself hired.'

'Mr Yeovil's not gonna like this,' Rat-face whined.

'I'll sort out Yeovil's hash,' Jitter snarled. 'Mack and I are together on this. We've both been made monkeys of, an' we want to know who to see about it.'

Holmes glanced at me, then stepped forward to face Jitter.

'I will find the thief,' he said. 'Depend upon it.'

He extended his hand towards Jitter. The man looked down at it, and then, as quick as a striking snake, he grabbed the hand and raised it up in front of Holmes's face.

'You can keep this,' he snarled. 'Consider it to be payment in advance.'

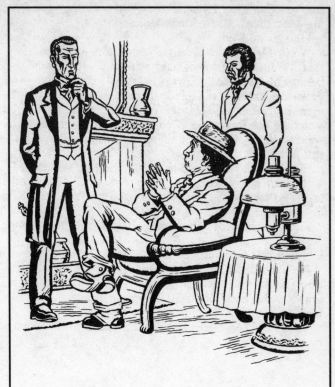

As I watched the clash of wills between the two
men . . .

Chapter 3

In which the Doctor is evasive and Watson cannot stand the heat

We decided to eat luncheon at Kean's Chop House, only a short walk away from the Rookery. Every step I took away from those rat-infested tenements made the sky seem bluer and my heart lighter. And yet, as we passed the elaborate frontages of the buildings which lined Holborn, I knew that a part of my mind would always remember the decay that lay behind the ornate facade: the skull beneath the skin.

I tried to discuss our adventure with Holmes as we walked, but he did not want to be drawn.

'Holmes,' I asked eventually, 'what on Earth did you think you were playing at, stealing that book from the Library?'

Holmes made no reply. A waiter brought menus to our table, but I was intent upon getting a straight answer from Holmes.

'Although the cellar here is generally acceptable, I believe that a frothing pint of porter would grace a good English chop better than any wine. What do you say?'

His face was hidden behind the menu. I was convinced that he was deliberately avoiding the issue.

'I have seen you do some pretty hare-brained things in your time, Holmes, but that really does take the biscuit!'

'Wilma Norman-Neruda is playing at the St James's Hall this evening, Watson. Chopin, followed by dinner at Simpsons: what better way to spend an evening?'

'*Holmes*! For God's sake, man, have the decency to answer a straight question when it is put to you!'

Holmes lowered the menu and met my eyes. His face was pale.

'Forgive me, Watson. I had not meant that little contretemps to go as far as it did. I needed to test the Library's security. The story about its efficacy was just that – a story – until I could test its veracity. I have always found it to be a capital mistake to theorize until one has access to the facts.' He looked away, to the window onto the street. 'There was no danger. I had five different means of escape from his gang of ruffians worked out.'

I would have been more reassured had the menu not been trembling slightly in his hands.

The conversation moved to different topics – old cases, the recent death of the well known *grande horizontale* Cora Pearl in Paris, Holmes's research into the effect of employment on the shape of the ear, and whether or not I should abandon my medical practice. We left the restaurant happier than we had arrived.

Urchins were turning somersaults amongst the wheels of carts, buses and cabs as we made our way home. The golden light of late afternoon made the stonework of Oxford Street glow. The squalor of St Giles was fading away like a bad dream.

As we scaled the steps to our rooms, our page-boy rushed up to the foot of the stairs bearing a silver platter.

'You got a visitor, Mr 'Olmes,' he announced, all puffed up in his new blue uniform. 'E's up in your rooms, and 'e's a strange one!'

'Thank you, Billy,' Holmes said kindly as he took the card from the tray. He tossed a coin to the child, who had to drop the tray to catch it. The clatter as it bounced on the floor bought Mrs Hudson limping out from her lair. Holmes and I beat a hasty retreat upstairs.

'Interesting.' Holmes passed the card across to me as we reached the landing. 'See what you make of it, Watson.'

Printed in a gothic script, it read: *The Doctor*; underneath, in the corner, was the word: *Travelling*. Rather flippant, I thought. I flexed it between my fingers. Good quality, judging by the rigidity of the stock.

'Not a gypsy,' I ventured, 'despite the obvious connection with the word "traveller". A man of some means.' I sniffed. 'Recently printed, I'll warrant. The smell of fresh ink is quite pronounced.'

'Bravo, Watson.'

'Have I missed anything of importance?'

He smiled, rather cruelly, I thought.

'Practically everything, dear chap. Despite the fact that the ink is still fresh there are no traces of it on the back of the card, as there would be had it been stacked with the rest of a recently printed batch. This would suggest that it was printed singly: presumably for us. The logical conclusion would be that this person is attempting to disguise his true identity, although – ' and Holmes frowned ' – the choice of *nom-de-plume* and the lack of address seem to suggest that he wishes us to come to that conclusion.' He frowned, then shook his head and continued. 'The slight but noticeable rounding of the card further indicates that it has been kept in a pocket, rather than a wallet. I would suggest a waistcoat pocket: trousers would have left it too rounded and a coat not rounded enough. And, most important of all, remember that "The Doctor" was one of the names on the lift of visitors to the Library of St John the Beheaded that we were given this morning.'

'The list that you did not wish me to see.'

Holmes looked away, discomfited, and said nothing. He took the card from my hand and walked into our sitting room.

The Doctor was standing in the window alcove. In his hands he held one of Holmes's files: the volume marked "T". I recognized him at once as the man I had conversed with in the Library, the one who had babbled of custard and metaphors.

'I will trouble you to put down that file,' Holmes snapped. Within two strides he was towering over the Doctor and removing the offending object from his hands. 'It ill behoves a visitor to rifle through private papers unasked.'

'It wasn't Spink, you know.'

'What?'

'I couldn't help reading the details of one of your cases. The terrible murder of the Atkinson brothers in Trincomalee. Spink was innocent.'

I noticed that the word "terrible" rolled off his tongue with relish. There was the hint of an accent in his voice that I could not place.

'The man robbed the world of justice by taking his own life.' Holmes strode across the room and replaced the volume. 'The case was simple; the solution obvious.'

'Ah,' said the Doctor, 'but did you take into account the significant delay in the onset of rigor mortis in tropical climates? It's all in that file.'

Holmes's face suffused with fury. I thought he was going to throw our visitor bodily through the window, so great was his rage, until a strange thing happened. A look passed across Holmes's face: a look of sudden realization and, even worse, shock.

'I . . .' he started to say, and trailed off into silence. His gaze travelled across the little man, and I had learned enough about reading expressions to tell that he was attempting to descry some detail about our visitor: his work, his character, his manner.

'I see from your appearance that you . . .' Holmes trailed off into silence; puzzled. 'Your cuffs suggest . . .' Again, he halted. He frowned. I could see that he was at a loss. 'That soil on your gaiter, I do not recognize it,' he said finally.

The Doctor grabbed at his foot and pulled it up to eye level.

'Ah,' he said, 'a slurry of clay and dust from Menaxus. Now *there's* a place to go for a show.'

'Menaxus? I am not familiar with the name: it must be a small village. Greek, I would venture.'

The Doctor tilted his head back and smiled a toothy grin.

'Menaxus is close to the Rippearean cluster.'

'And the spatulate appearance of your right forefinger. It is similar to that seen in typists, but I would have expected an indentation across your right thumb from the space bar.'

The Doctor peered at the offending digit as if he had just found it on his dinner plate.

'Ah, he said, relieved, and jabbed at the air with the finger. 'Too much prodding of large, metal creatures.'

Holmes and I looked across at each other. The man was obviously deranged.

'I see that you dabble in chemistry,' the Doctor said, walking across to the deal-topped table where Holmes kept his retorts and flasks.

'I am presently researching into coal-tar derivatives,' Holmes replied, drawing himself up stiffly. 'Now, may I ask what your business is with us?'

'Take precautions if you ever manage to distil coronic acid,' the Doctor muttered, picked up three flasks filled with liquid and juggling with them. 'It's a nasty substance. Very nasty indeed.'

'I would be obliged if you would . . .'

'Yes, I know. You would be obliged if I put down these flasks. Oh, very well.'

He placed them back on the table and turned to Holmes.

'I have no business with you,' he said, finally answering Holmes's question. 'But you have business with me.'

The Doctor threw himself into Holmes's armchair and grinned up at us. Holmes opened his mouth to make a cutting reply, but a knock at the door interrupted him. We turned as Mrs Hudson limped into the room with a tray bearing cups, saucers, plates, cakes and a teapot.

'I took the liberty of ordering tea,' the Doctor said, grinning up ingenuously at Mrs Hudson. 'Your landlady is a treasure.'

Mrs Hudson pampered the Doctor as if he were the vicar come to call: pouring his tea, sweetening it and cutting him a slice of Madeira cake. Holmes and I looked on, aghast. Her usual attitude to our visitors ranged from disinterest to barely veiled contempt. Despite my recent lunch the sight of the Doctor gobbling down the cake made my stomach rumble. I sat in my usual chair, cut myself a slice and poured a cup of tea. Holmes remained, raging impotently, on his feet.

'Now,' the Doctor babbled on after three slices and two cups had gone the way of all things. 'Where were we? Ah yes, the robbery at the Library of St John the Beheaded. I presume you will have questioned Mr Ambrose, and received from him a list of recent visitors to the Library. My name will be on that list. I suspect that I want to know who took those books just as much as you do, and that's why I am here, to pool resources, share information, spread panic and sow the seeds of defeat in the fields of our enemies. Now I realize that I am just as much a suspect as anybody else on that list – ' he suddenly frowned and looked away ' – a position I find myself adopting with monotonous regularity – ' he smiled sunnily and looked back at us again ' – but I don't see why that can't be just as much the basis for a long and fruitful relationship as mutual trust. Now, any questions?'

Holmes held up the Doctor's card.

'You give no address.'

'Ah.' The Doctor stood. 'I travel.'

'No fixed abode,' said Holmes, towering over the dim-inutive figure.

'Oh, I have a fixed abode.' The Doctor plucked the card from Holmes's hand and slipped it into his waistcoat. 'But *it* travels. "Not bound to swear allegiance to any master, wherever the wind takes me I travel as a visitor".'

'I do not appreciate flippancy,' Holmes snapped.

'I always try to mix a little foolishness with my serious plans,' the Doctor replied, gazing up into Holmes's face. 'It's lovely to be silly at the right moment. But, if it makes you feel any better, I am currently lodging in Hampstead.'

'With whom?'

'Professor Litefoot. You may know of him.'

At this juncture I interjected, 'Not Professor George Litefoot, the eminent pathologist?'

'The very same!'

Holmes was not to be put off so easily.

'And what exactly are you a Doctor of?' he growled.

'Metaphysico-theologico-cosmologo-nigology!' announced the Doctor triumphantly.

Holmes pursed his lips and strode to the window.

'Facile quotations from Voltaire will not help your case,' he barked. 'If you remain unwilling to provide a straight answer then I can only surmise that you are unwilling to co-operate with our investigations.'

'Oh very well.' The little man pouted, and stared down at his gaiters. 'If it helps, I took a medical degree in Edinburgh in eighteen seventy.'

'What a coincidence!' I exclaimed. 'I studied for my Bachelor's degree and my baccalaureate at the University of Edinburgh from that very year onwards! I must say,' and I studied his features more closely, 'that I do not remember you.'

The Doctor shifted uneasily in Holmes's armchair.

'I can't say I'm surprised. I looked different then.'

I stroked my moustache and looked ruefully down at my figure: stockier now than it had been seventeen years ago.

'So did I,' I admitted.

'This is getting us nowhere,' Holmes pronounced, staring out of the window. 'Be so good as to tell me what your researches were at the Library, Doctor.'

'India.'

'More specifically.'

'Hindu mythology.'

'More specifically still.'

'Legends concerning the rakshassi.'

'Rakshassi?' I asked.

'Demons from the pantheon of the Indian subcontinent,' Holmes replied tersely.

'Usually associated with the worship of Kali,' the

43

Doctor added. 'Kali being the Indian goddess of death and destruction.'

'I thought you had been in India, Watson,' Holmes asked.

'I passed through ten years ago on my way to Afghanistan,' I replied, 'but I confess I took little interest in the heathen ceremonies of the natives.'

The Doctor glanced over at me, and there was something dark and unpleasant in his eyes.

'God's in his heaven and all's right in the world,' he sneered.

I drew myself up to respond to the gibe, but Holmes interrupted, saying, 'And the books that were stolen: they were all associated with this subject?'

'As you well know.'

As I watched the clash of wills between the two men I could not help but recall the words that I had written about Holmes some six years before, soon after the occasion of our first meeting. I had been drawing up a list of his interests in an attempt to more closely understand his character. I had jotted down, in no particular order, that he was well up on poisons generally, that he could tell at a glance different soils from each other, that his knowledge of anatomy was accurate but limited, that his knowledge of sensational crime and criminal law was immense and that he was an expert boxer, singlestick player and swordsman, but that he knew nothing of astronomy, philosophy or literature. At this point I had thrown the list away, crying: 'If I can only find what the fellow is driving at by reconciling all these accomplishments . . .!' I could see something of the same thought process concerning the Doctor going through Holmes's mind.

'Perhaps we might be better employed,' the Doctor said finally, breaking both Holmes's and my train of thought, 'in examining the list of other visitors to the Library. Accepting that I am naturally a suspect, we should question the others as soon as possible. May I see the list?'

Holmes turned away to gaze out of the window onto the Baker Street bustle below.

'I retain an accurate memory of the names,' he said, 'and there is, therefore, no necessity to examine the list. Your own name appears, of course, Doctor, as does that of a Mrs Kate Prendersly of Whitefields Lodge in Deptford, an inmate of Broadmoor named Minor, a certain Baron Maupertuis, his manservant, Surd . . .'

'How do you know he is the Baron's manservant, Holmes?' I interjected.

'The address is the same, Watson,' Holmes said, pityingly. 'And since he is only referred to by a surname, without any qualifier, the conclusion is obvious.'

'Any other names?' the Doctor asked.

'A Professor Challenger, whose address is given as "care of the Royal Society".'

'And?' The Doctor's expression was carefully neutral.

Holmes's voice was level as he replied: 'No other names appear on the list.'

'Are you sure, Mr Holmes?'

'Do you accuse me of dishonesty, sir?'

'How should I presume?' the Doctor murmured.

'Perhaps,' I ventured, sensing the sudden hostility between Holmes and the Doctor, but not understanding its cause, 'we should visit these people. Talk to them. Ascertain their reasons for visiting the Library. Perhaps some pertinent fact might emerge of which we are at present unaware.'

'A capital idea,' the Doctor said, leaping to his feet and rubbing his hands together gleefully. 'I'll start with Professor Challenger, Doctor Watson can tackle Miss Prendersly and you, Mr Holmes . . .' He was still smiling, but his eyes glinted coldly. '. . . You can choose your own suspects.'

'Since you yourself are still a suspect,' Holmes retorted, 'might I suggest that you accompany Watson to Deptford.'

'Very well.' The Doctor made for the door, picking a multicoloured umbrella from the umbrella stand as he did so. 'I'll hail a cab.'

He vanished from our rooms and scampered down the stairs.

'A rum character,' I observed.

'There is more to that man than meets the eye,' Holmes said. 'He may seem to be at times almost ridiculous, almost the fool, but he has a shrewd brain. Watch him, Watson. Don't let him out of your sight. I want to know everything he says and everything he does.'

'But why on Earth do you want to associate him with this investigation?'

'I suspect that he will be associated with it whether we want him to be or not. At least this way we get to keep a close eye on him.'

I moved to take my walking stick from the coat rack, and exclaimed, 'Not raining outside, is it Holmes?'

'Not for days,' he replied. 'Why?'

'There's some water in the bottom of the coat rack.'

He bent to examine it, and came up rubbing his fingers together.

'Not water, Watson, but oil.'

'Oil?' I reiterated stupidly.

'Indeed. Most singular.' He wiped his hands on his jacket. 'You had better not keep the Doctor waiting.'

'And what of you, Holmes? What are your plans?'

'I shall endeavour to meet up with Mr Jitter's opposite number,' he said, 'Mack Yeovil and I have crossed swords before, and so I think some form of disguise is called for.'

I discovered the Doctor sitting at the bottom of our stairs and conversing with our page-boy in a casual manner that I felt was unsuited to dealings with a servant. I curtly bade him accompany me, and whistled down a hansom almost immediately. As the cab trotted off he planted his umbrella on the floor, rested his forearms upon its handle and frowned. A melancholic expression shadowed his features, and I found myself wondering who he was and where he came from.

'Gallifrey,' he muttered.

'I'm sorry?'

46

'You were wondering where I came from.'

'That's astounding. How did you know?'

'Elementary.'

'Gallifrey . . . that sounds Irish.'

He looked sideways at me and said nothing.

The cab clattered through London, with us sitting inside in silence. I watched with confused feelings the loungers, shop girls, street-sweepers and dollymoppers who thronged the streets. It was so easy to see them as a backdrop: a featureless, characterless crowd of extras, called on stage as we came near and sent back to their dressing rooms as we passed. Most of Holmes's cases were conducted amongst people of our own class or above; it was rare, especially since Holmes's reputation had spread and my medical practice in Paddington had become established, that we mixed with people below our station. And yet the events of that morning were still clear enough in my mind that I knew these people must have lives, homes, families, desires and hates that I never usually gave any consideration to. The aegis of the British Empire stretched across many foreign lands, but it occurred to me for the first time that the division between rich and poor in London matched anything to be found in Bangalore or Calcutta.

' "The poor always ye have with you",' the Doctor quoted in a doom-laden voice, and then sighed. 'Wherever I go, certain universal truths always hold. There is always evil, and there are always those with and those without.'

We were passing across the balustraded expanse of London Bridge now. The Doctor's words set me thinking about the course my life had taken. When I made the decision to be a surgeon I had wanted to relieve human suffering: a noble enough aim, I suppose, if a trifle naive. I joined the army for the same reason, but the Afghan War cured me of my youthful innocence. I quickly realized that human suffering was largely due to humans, and the meagre amount of relief I could give was like trying to bale out the ocean with a teaspoon. During the eight hours or so that the battle of Maiwand lasted almost two hundred of us had been wounded, and almost a thousand killed. I had contracted enteric fever, was invalided out, and drifted to London: depressed over the scale of misery, horror and ignorance I had encountered and powerless to do anything about it. I had fallen in with Holmes, but what had I achieved since our chance meeting and my decision to chronicle some of his adventures? We had returned various stolen sets of jewels to their rightful owners and averted a handful of scandals in high society. What was the point? How did this square with my youthful aims?

My mood when we drew up at our destination was not light.

Whitefields Lodge was a large, square house set in its own grounds and girt around with a low stone wall. It made quite a contrast to the regular run of houses in the locality; squat, dark terraces, snaking downhill to the Thames and relieved only by the tawdry glare of public houses on every corner. Raucous dockers' songs drifted through the late afternoon.

As we paid off the driver and crossed the road, I became aware that somebody was watching us. My instincts – developed on the Afghan front and finely honed through years of working with Holmes – were jangling. I glanced around, trying not to attract attention.

'The shadow on the wall, to the left of the dilapidated house,' the Doctor hissed.

'You sensed it too?'

'Of course.'

All I could see in the lee of the wall was a jumble of upright sticks, bamboo I believed, and a sack of some kind; the detritus of some child's game, perhaps. The sticks had been arranged as a support, holding the sack some five or six feet above the ground. The sack swayed gently in the breeze. It looked as if it might be half full of water. If there was a human form hiding somewhere in the shadows behind that bizarre sculpture I could not say. I turned to move on, but at the sight of the Doctor's

48

blazing eyes I stumbled and stopped. His gaze was fixed on that same patch of shadows. I turned to look.

The sticks and the sack were gone.

'Good Lord!' I exclaimed.

'No,' the Doctor whispered. 'Not a very good one at all.'

He shivered, and drew his coat tighter about his body.

'On with the motley,' he murmured, smiling hesitantly at me, then strode up to the front door as if he owned the place and rapped upon the door with the head of his umbrella. A maid left us in a room full of books whilst she took our cards in to her mistress. We sat, side by side, on an antimacassared sofa until Mrs Kate Prendersly swept into the room.

'Gentlemen,' she said softly, 'what can I do for you?'

We stood. I cannot speak for the Doctor, but for myself I was overawed. In an experience of women that encompasses many nations and three separate continents, I cannot recall seeing so striking a woman. Her hair was auburn and piled high in tresses. Her eyes were a smoky purple, matching the warm tones of her voice. She was dressed in a long blue skirt, with a peacock jacket over a frilly white blouse. I felt envious of Mr Prendersly, wherever he was.

'We . . . ah, that is . . . I . . .'

'May I say,' the Doctor interrupted, raising his hat, 'what a great pleasure it is to meet you. This house is lovely, and so close to the river as well. I love rivers, don't you? I do believe there's a pie-and-eel shop nearby – Fred's, or is it Frank's? – no matter, in which I spent many a happy day in my youth, or perhaps somebody else's youth. Do you read a lot? I only ask because you have a great deal of books scattered around. Law books, aren't they? Are you studying?'

'Yes,' she said, and I could tell that she was struggling to suppress some deep emotion. 'For my husband's sake.'

'And your husband is dead?'

'Yes, how did you know?'

'The footprints outside. We have been the first men to walk from the gate to the door in some time.'

I reached across to pat her hand. She was really a most attractive woman.

'Patrick was killed in . . .' she sobbed, and took a tiny lace handkerchief from her sleeve '. . . the most *terrible* manner. He had been in London on business . . . he was the captain of a lighter, you see, and he had to go to Admiralty House . . . something to do with his licence . . . and he was making his way back through Trafalgar Square, and . . .'

She broke down in tears, dabbing at her eyes with the lace. I could fill in the rest of the story myself. The Trafalgar Square riots were still a fresh scar in the mind of every decent Englishman. The summer had been completely rainless. Sewage, instead of being washed away, had been left to rot in the streets. The heat had aggravated the unsanitary conditions. Squalor bred disaffection, disaffection turned to unrest, and unrest led to riots. Trafalgar Square had seen the worse: a mob of drunken and enraged loungers who destroyed property in a wild orgy of wanton behaviour. General Sir Charles Warren, Commissioner for Police in the Metropolitan Area, had taken it into his incompetent head to order a sabre-charge by the Life Guards. The riot became a rout, but at the cost of men's lives. It had been a black day for British justice.

'My dear woman,' I murmured, placing a reassuring hand on her shoulder.

'He was just passing through . . .' she wailed. 'He wasn't even *involved*! But he was wearing his uniform, and they mistook him for a policeman . . .'

'You said that you were studying for his sake? Is this studying connected to the Library of St John the Beheaded, in Holborn?'

She looked up at the Doctor, so surprised that she forgot she was crying.

'Yes, but how . . .?'

'There has been some trouble,' I said. 'Nothing that

should bother you, but we need to talk to all the people who have visited the Library recently.'

'I was there last week.' She looked more closely at the Doctor. 'In fact, I do believe that you were as well.'

She glanced over at me. A thrill ran through my nerves, a feeling similar to the descriptions written by those who have received shocks from electrical equipment.

'I am sure I would have remembered your face, Dr Watson, had you been there,' she said, and lowered her gaze.

'If you don't mind me asking,' I said, 'for what reason were you at the Library?'

'My husband was in fear of his life, even before he left for London that day,' she said simply. 'He ... ah!' She raised a hand to her heaving bosom. 'Excuse me, gentlemen, a touch of heartburn, I fear.'

'I am a doctor,' I said quickly. 'Perhaps . . .?'

'I am sure it will pass,' she said, and smiled slightly. 'But thank you for your kind offer. My husband, as I said, was in fear for his life. He talked of some plan that he had stumbled on, something hideous and important, but no matter how I pleaded, he would not tell me. 'Best not to know,' he said. She sighed. 'I believe that he was killed because of his knowledge. I believe that he was lured to Trafalgar Square and, under cover of the riot, he was murdered.'

Her plain statement caused shivers to run up and down my spine.

'And the Library?' the Doctor prompted.

'I said that Alexander would not talk of his discovery. That is not quite true. He would have nightmares, and during them he would murmur words which were strange to me. When I was sorting through his possessions following . . . following the riots, I discovered a membership card for the Library of St John the Beheaded. Such a macabre name. I had never heard of it, but scribbled on the back were some of the words I had heard him cry out. I presumed that he had been attempting to research them, and so I habituated it too.'

'And did you find anything?' I asked.

'No,' she said, and frowned, clutching again at her chest. Her face was redder than it had been when we entered. I ran through lists of symptoms in my mind, but I could make no specific determination without examining her more closely.

'Those words, do you remember them?' the Doctor asked.

'I'm not sure that I can,' she said. 'The librarian kept the card. They were more like groans than words.'

The Doctor was insistent. 'Perhaps you could try to recall them for me.'

She screwed her face up, and started to speak. Subsequent events have seared those words on my memory, and I reproduce them here as first I heard them.

'*I-ay, I-ay,*' she croaked in a hideous parody of speech. '*Naghaa, naghai-ghai! Shoggog fathaghn!*'

A cold chill seemed to seep through my bones.

'Thank you,' said the Doctor. His face was sombre.

'The Library was a strange place,' she said, seemingly having to force the words out. 'And the approach to it was simply horrendous. Fortunately, having been around sailors for most of my life, and after what happened to poor Patrick, I always take precautions when I go out. I also found a number of guns amongst his possessions, and they make a most effective deterrent.'

A thin sheen of perspiration had appeared upon her brow. I was about to tactfully suggest that she should take to her bed whilst I attended her when the Doctor spoke.

'Have you ever seen anything out of the ordinary happen at the Library?'

'Oddly enough, I once saw a man eating books,' she said, with an effort. 'I was sitting at a table, checking the index of a large and rather fragile volume for any mention of the words in Patrick's nightmares, when a noise attracted my attention. I looked across to where a half-closed door hid a small side room. The gas-lamp in the room cast the shadow of a man over to the wall by the door, where I could see it. He was grotesquely large

52

and rough of feature, if his silhouette was anything to go by. As I watched, he raised a book in his hand, looked at it for a long moment, and then seemed to eat it whole! When he lowered his hand, the book was gone. And it was not a small book.'

I had forgotten that my hand still rested upon hers, until a faint tremor alerted me to the fact that she was shaking.

'Mrs Prendersly,' I said, 'I really think . . .'

Before I could finish my sentence, Mrs Prendersly half-rose and opened her mouth. A tremendous gout of yellow flame leapt from it, singeing the Doctor's hair. He leaped backwards. Mrs Prendersly's eyes widened in agony and shock. Flames were licking around her mouth and bursting from the crown of her head. I could not move. The Doctor whipped off his coat and attempted to smother the fire, but the heat drove him away. I spotted a gasogene on the sideboard and ran to grab it, but when I turned back her body was a blazing mass of orange and red. I directed the jet of water upon the conflagration, but it was no use. I could still make out her face, that beautiful face, blistering and running like wax. Her arms were flapping about, dragging flames with them like a bat's wings. A heavy orange smoke filled the room and a roaring sound filled my ears. Somewhere in the background I could hear the maid screaming. Mrs Prendersly's face was just a Hallowe'en mask now, a hollowed-out pumpkin filled with fire. She crumpled to the carpet, her legs and arms like burned branches. Her chest exploded outwards in a ball of flame, leaving charred ribs sticking from a pile of ashes. The ruin of her head flared for a few moments longer, and then the fire vanished as suddenly as it had appeared. My hands, my face, my clothes: all were greasy and black. The Doctor's face was shocked and there were blisters on his hands. I could see a rough circle of soot on the ceiling, directly over the charred mass that used to be Mrs Kate Prendersly.

And projecting from the remains, at the ends of those blackened, stick-like limbs, her hands and feet were

53

almost untouched by the fire. Light gleamed from the gold of her wedding ring.

I turned away, and I am not ashamed to say that it was the stench of cooked flesh that caused me to be violently ill.

Interlude

AF235/2/3/12
  V-ON, BRD-ABLE, WPU = 231.2
  VERBAL INPUT, SAVE AND COMPRESS
  MILITARY LOG FILE EPSILON
  CODE GREEN FIVE
  ENABLE
Rocky slope of a mountain, looking down. Plain spread out for some miles. No cover to speak of.

Some kind of experiment's going on. It must be important, 'cos every time they do it, they post sentries. Lot of singing, then a big sheet of some dark material appears. Could be some kind of transmat portal. Could be a lot of things.

Bit of a flap a few days back. One of the large three-legged rat-things that infest the foothills wandered into the area. The sentries tried to get it, but ended up panicking it. I saw it run for the dark sheet. It vanished, like I thought it might. That's why I shooed it in that direction.

The sentries aren't native to this area, that's the interesting thing. They all came over from beyond the mountains. I'm going to try and follow them back when they pack up shop.

This planet is about as strange as they come. The ice-cap covers the entire surface, and is supported by the tops of the mountain ranges. Everything lives under the ice. The light from what I guess is the sun is weak, and the ice spreads it out so it looks like half the sky is glowing. It's like living inside a table-tennis ball. There are small creatures that actually live upside down on the interior of the ice shield. They're like big helium balloons on skates. No

*intelligence to speak of. A well-aimed arrow can puncture
their skin and bring them down into your arms. Roasted
slowly over a fire, they taste of chocolate.*

I used to like chocolate.

I used to like a lot of things.

Oh, hell.

DISABLE.

2331/34/FF

PIP.

His heart pounded in time with his legs.

Chapter 4

In which the Doctor pours oil on troubled waters and Holmes goes to the dogs

'It's a rum business, and no mistake,' Inspector MacDonald sighed, running a hand through his lank blond hair.

We were sitting in the Tank: a private bar located in the basement of Scotland Yard. It was a dismal place, enlivened only by sketches of criminals torn from the Newgate Calendar and attached to the wall. Despite its unwelcoming appearance it was full to bursting. Three years ago the Irish Republican Brotherhood had bombed the nearby CID offices, demolishing a public house and injuring a number of policemen. Sordid the Tank may have been, but at least it was safe.

MacDonald, the Doctor and I sat at a small table beside a damp brick wall. I recognized one or two other occupants of the Tank from Holmes's dealings with Scotland Yard: Inspectors Lestrade and Abberline were grumbling over their pints by the bar, Walter Dew was arguing with the barman, and a sharp-faced sergeant named Cribb, whom I knew Holmes had a great deal of respect for, nursed a small whisky at a nearby table. I thought I could smell food, but nobody seemed to be eating.

'And what's "rum" about it?' the Doctor murmured, sipping at a sarsaparilla.

'I'm sure that Mr Sherlock Holmes would have a word or two on the subject,' MacDonald said, 'but I confess myself puzzled. Inspector Bradstreet called the Yard in on the suspicion of murder, but I'll be blessed if I can see how such a crime could have been engineered.'

'Bradstreet,' I snapped, 'is an imbecile!'

'There's some that would agree with you there,' Mac replied. 'He's been shuffled from pillar to post these past few years, for nobody wants to work with him. He started off at Bow Street, then transferred to B Division, and then on to M, where you met him today. Word is he's in line for the Yard.'

'But he can't possibly suspect – '

'A woman goes up in flames in a room with no fireplace, and you two are the only witnesses. And neither she nor either of you were smoking. You can see how it looks. What other explanation is there?'

'But surely you believe us?' I asked him. Mac sighed and reached for his pint of mild and bitter.

'You have to understand my position, Doctor Watson, Doctor . . .'

He looked questioningly at the Doctor, who stared back with basilisk-like impassivity.

'Er . . . yes, Doctor,' he continued. 'You're technically under arrest, both of you. By rights I should have you locked up.'

'But . . .?' the Doctor said unblinkingly.

'But Sherlock Holmes has pulled my fat out of the fire too many times for me to throw his friends in choky. Whatever happened to that woman wasn't your fault. I know that.' He gazed unhappily into his drink. 'Persuading Bradstreet might tax my skills, though. He's of the old school, like Lestrade over there: if you can't find the right man, lock the wrong one up. Keeps the arrest figures looking good.' He grimaced. 'You know what Bradstreet said to me once? "There's two types of people in the world, son: those who have been arrested and those who haven't been found out yet". That man's more of a danger to the Yard than anything anarchists or the Irish might do. If I could only think of another explanation for Mrs Prendersly's death, I might be able to convince Bradstreet of your innocence.'

'Have you ever read Dickens?' the Doctor queried.

'Dickens?' Mac was puzzled. 'Well, I picked up a couple

of bound sets of the weeklies in one of the second-hand shops along the Strand for the wife.'

'Then you may have come across his novel *Bleak House.*'

Mac's face proclaimed that he had not, but I realized what the Doctor was getting at.

'Of course!' I exclaimed, 'the death of Krook!'

The Doctor beamed at me, as if I was a backward child who had suddenly managed to grasp a complicated mathematical theorem. Mac just scratched his head.

'During the course of the novel,' I amplified for his benefit, 'the aptly named Krook is found burned to death in his room, supposedly as a celestial judgement on his sins.'

'I can't use a work of sensational fiction as evidence,' MacDonald protested.

'Mr Dickens was merely reporting a well know phenomenon,' the Doctor said calmly. 'Known generally, I believe, as spontaneous human combustion.'

'Nonsense!' My cry turned several heads around the room. After the hush was filled again by the babble of a myriad conversations, I continued. 'Spontaneous human combustion is a fallacy, an old wives' tale dusted off to explain any unusual death involving fire. It has no rational explanation, and therefore it does not exist.'

I sat back in my seat, thinking how proud Holmes would have been of me.

'I presume that you have read Carpenter's *Principles of General and Comparative Physiology*?' the Doctor asked with a slight smile.

'Yes,' I mumbled. 'Forty years old, but still a very useful book.'

'And one which admits to the existence of cases where men and women have burst into flame for no obvious reason. No doubt you have also had reason to consult Beck and Beck's *Elements of Medical Jurisprudence* in the course of your adventures with Mr Holmes?'

'Well . . . yes.'

The Doctor's voice was gentle, but remorseless. I could

not help but contrast his style of debate with that of Holmes, whose superior attitude and scathing criticisms frequently cowed me into submission. Mac watched our verbal duel, entranced.

'Those eminent gentlemen also believed in spontaneous human combustion. You may even have read an article on the subject in the *Bulletin de la Société Médico-Légal de France* last year.'

'I do know that Casper's *Handbook of the Practice of Forensic Medicine* well and truly trounced the idea.'

'Did it?' The Doctor took a sip of his sarsaparilla. 'And how did Casper explain the bizarre fate of Nicole Millet, a landlord's wife whose charred body was found on Whit Monday in 1725 in Rheims in an armchair that did not have a single burn upon it? Or that of Grace Pett, a fisherman's wife who burned to a cinder on the ninth of April 1744 in Ipswich, near a paper screen that was not even singed?'

Mac's eyes were starting from their sockets, and I was dimly aware that nearby conversations were dying away as the *habitués* of the Tank became aware of our morbid conversation.

'By 1763,' the Doctor continued, 'enough people had died that Jonas Dupont of Germany published a book on the subject entitled *De Incendiis Corporis Humani Spontaneis.* You yourself, Doctor, may have come across a report in the 1835 issue of the *Transactions of the Medical Society of Tennessee* concerning a Mr James Hamilton, who was out walking one day when a flame burst like a lighted gas-jet from his leg. Mr Hamilton was lucky enough to be able to extinguish the flame, but the Countess von Görlitz was not so fortunate. You might have read about her in the edition of *The Times* dated 18 April 1850, Inspector. She burned to a cinder on the other side of a curtain to her husband without him noticing a thing. Doctor Watson, of course, would be familiar with the more detailed reports of her death carried by *The Lancet* and *The London Medical Gazette.*'

Silence had descended across the entire room. The Doctor's voice – hushed, and yet penetrating – commanded the attention of the assembled multitude. My mouth was dry, and I drained my tankard of porter in a single gulp. I took a deep breath and wiped my moustache. The smell of roast beef somewhere in the vicinity made me acutely and incongruously aware of how long it had been since I had eaten.

'And what of Mrs Rooney, whose cremated corpse was discovered in a friend's living room on Christmas Eve 1885 – less than two years ago, gentlemen – in Seneca, Illinois, along with the body of her husband, who had slept through her death but died of asphyxiation from the smoke. There were no signs of fire in the room, save for the burnt floorboards beneath her and a slight scorching to a tablecloth, and nothing remained of her but a blackened skull, part of a vertebra, a foot and a mound of ashes.'

The Doctor's voice rolled around the final syllables as if he were pronouncing the crack of doom itself. The bar was silent, its inhabitants frozen with drinks half-way to their mouths, or cigars dropping glowing ash upon their waistcoats, spellbound by the Doctor's recitation. I felt the cold hand of terror clutch at my heart: such things should not be, not in Victoria's England, not in a rational scientific world. They belonged to an older, darker age.

'Another drink, anyone?' said the Doctor brightly. 'I appear to have finished my sarsaparilla.'

As conversations sprung up again across the room and the Doctor made for the bar, Mac's eyes met mine.

'Well, I'm convinced,' he said. 'And I've got enough evidence to silence Bradstreet. He's a superstitious man, and much afeared of the medical profession. If I can quote references at him the way your friend here did to us, there'll be no case to answer.'

The Doctor returned with a pint for each of us and another sarsaparilla for himself.

'What is the matter, Doctor?' I asked, noting his frown.

'Don't drink anything,' he whispered. 'I think somebody is trying to poison us!'

63

'Great Scott!' I cried. Inspector MacDonald lowered the glass from which he was about to sip.

'What makes you think that?' he asked carefully.

'I caught a whiff of the porter as the barman pulled the pints,' the Doctor hissed, his gaze darting around the room. 'There's strychnine in it! We may already have ingested a lethal dose from the last round.'

MacDonald laughed, and dug me in the ribs with his elbow. I could not help smiling.

'You're obviously new to city ways, Doctor,' he said. 'You'll find strychnine in most London beers. Gives it a bit of body.'

The Doctor gulped, and took a sip of his sarsaparilla.

'I trust that soft drinks are safe,' he said.

The conversation moved into other channels as we drank, and we parted as dusk fell. The Doctor and I decided to walk back to Baker Street together, the evening being so pleasant and our spirits buoyed up with drink. As we strolled, I leaning upon my stick, he swinging his umbrella, he gave me a running commentary on the buildings that we passed, illuminating minor corners of history with a sharp, incisive wit that made the city come alive in a way that I had never experienced before. He spoke with such conviction of times past that I could almost see him there, conversing with Samuel Pepys or Isaac Newton as he did with me that night. I, in turn, regaled the Doctor with tales of the cases in which Holmes and I had become involved, including some which were so sensitive or so bizarre that I could never allow them to be published. The affair of the painted pit pony, for instance, piqued the Doctor's interest, as did the strange case of Isadore Persano, the well known duellist, who was found, stark staring mad, holding a matchbox which contained a worm unknown to science. The Doctor asked about unsolved cases and I found myself describing one of Holmes's rare failures which I have occasionally thought of writing up under the title *The Affair of the Walking Ventriloquist's Dummy*. Looking back on it now, I have the feeling that the Doctor knew more about the case than I then believed. I have since discovered that nothing about the Doctor is beyond question.

We found ourselves walking around the edge of the Serpentine as Big Ben struck eight. The wind had risen, the water was choppy and the darkness hid the far side of the lake from us, so that we might have been standing on the edge of some huge ocean. I remembered how, two years beforehand, Lestrade had unsuccessfully dragged the lake for Hatty Doran's body during the case that is listed in my notes under the title *The Affair of the Noble Bachelor*, and I shivered at the memory.

'Lord St Simon deserved his fate,' the Doctor murmured.

I nodded sagely, then stopped in surprise.

'How do you know that?' I asked him.

The Doctor stopped and turned to face me. His face was shadowed by his hat, but I could swear that he was smiling at me.

'I read it in *The Strand Magazine.*'

'I do not see how,' I replied stiffly, 'for the details have never been published, to my knowledge.'

'Then perhaps I deduced it from the way you stared at the water, and from the expression upon your face.'

I was about to remonstrate with him for this impossible explanation, and then I remembered some of the deductions which Sherlock Holmes had made, based only upon the scantiest clues, and I held my tongue.

The Doctor gazed out over the Serpentine. Across the other side of the lake, someone had lit a fire. The tiny orange glow put me in mind of the moment when Mrs Prendersly had opened her mouth to reveal a hellish tongue of flame. I tried to remember how beautiful she had been, how entranced I had felt, but all I could see was flesh charred black, like an overcooked side of beef. The aroma of roasting meat rose once again to my nostrils: with revulsion I realized that it was the smell of Mrs Prendsley's cooked body which had somehow become impregnated into my clothing, like the odour of a strong cigar, and I felt my gorge rise. I pulled my hip flask out of my pocket and swallowed a burning mouthful of brandy. Gradually my stomach relaxed. Beads of sweat stood out on my forehead, and I felt hot and weak.

'I cannot accept it,' I muttered finally. 'I am a physician. There must be *some* cause for Mrs Prendersley's death.'

'You find yourself paddling in the shallows of mystery, unaware of the currents, oblivious to the nearby depths. As Shakespeare so nearly put it: there are more things in heaven and earth, Watson, than are dreamt of in your philosophy.'

'Nonsense,' I blustered unconvincingly. 'The world is rational. Everything has a cause, a reason. All that remains is to discover it.'

The Doctor said nothing, but raised his arms over his head so that his umbrella was pointing at the tumultuous clouds overhead. A fresh gust of wind stirred the ripples of the jittering lake to greater heights. He chanted something in the teeth of the wind, hurling the words into the skies. Slowly he lowered his arms towards the water. I moved back, suddenly aware that I was alone with a madman and that my revolver was in the drawer of my desk back in Baker Street.

The tip of the Doctor's umbrella touched the water, and the waves vanished in a circle around it, some twenty feet across. Where there had been a storm in miniature upon the face of the Serpentine, a spreading area of the lake lay placid and still. I stared, astounded, at the transformation.

'I don't believe it!'

The Doctor turned towards me.

'There is a reason for everything,' he said. 'But not necessarily an obvious one. I will see you tomorrow.'

And with that he walked off, into the dark. I gazed after him for a few moments, then back at the lake, where feathery ripples were just beginning to stir its surface. A gust of wind caught my hat and almost snatched it from my head.

The fire which had been lit across the far side of the lake glowed with an inviting warmth. I was tired and cold, mystified and hungry, and I wanted to be home. I flapped my arms a few times to get my circulation moving, then turned to leave.

A spindly figure scurried in front of the fire.

A sudden shudder ran through me, but it wasn't due to the cold. That shape . . . Although I had seen it but briefly, there had been something unnatural about it, something thin and febrile, and urgent. I listened intently, but apart from the rustle of leaves and the occasional cry of a goose, I heard nothing.

Eventually, feeling rather foolish, I walked off towards the nearest gate, and a hansom to take me home.

'. . . And I cannot tell you how unsettling it was to see the lake go from a state resembling the English Channel in winter to one like my shaving bowl in the morning!'

Holmes glanced across reprovingly from the other side of the table. We had just polished off a brace of woodcock with all the trimmings, accompanied by an appealing little Montrachet and followed by a spotted dick with custard. I was replete and content, and had spent most of the meal regaling Holmes with the events of the day.

Holmes had eaten well. He varied between times of immense gluttony and periods when he would pick at his food like a bird, but today, to the great pleasure of Mrs Hudson, he ate all that she placed before him with relish. He had kept up a constant string of questions concerning my tale – descriptions of Mrs Prendersly's room, her clothes, the weather, any unusual sights or sounds in the room – but I could tell that he was no nearer an expla-nation of her death than I was.

'That,' he said tersely, 'is perhaps the simplest element of this entire case.'

'Nonsense, Holmes. The man is a magician. He has powers beyond human imagining. I would not be surprised . . .' and I lowered my voice, as if the Doctor could hear me from wherever he had gone for the night, '. . . if he was responsible for that poor woman's fate. Who knows what powers he might have?'

'No more than any other mortal.'

Holmes retrieved his slipper from the fireplace. Whilst Mrs Hudson cleared the plates away and retired, he removed tobacco from it and packed it into his old black clay pipe, the unsavoury companion of his deepest meditations. I poured myself a glass of port to round the meal off.

'You have mistaken the superficial for the deep,' he explained, applying a match to the bowl and sucking deeply. 'Ah, that is better. This death is a nasty business, quite a four-pipe problem. No, the matter of the lake is easily solved. You have all the information in your hands, Watson. You are starting from a position where you do not believe it is possible, then trying to explain it. I, however, assume that it is perfectly possible, then attempt to use whatever clues I have to cast light upon the means.'

'I'm not sure I follow.'

'Let us start from the facts. The lake calmed. What can have that effect upon disturbed water?'

'Why . . . nothing, surely. Nothing but witchcraft.'

'I have told you before, Watson, there is nothing in this world but that which we make ourselves. Have you never heard of the phrase, "pouring oil on troubled waters"?'

'Why, yes. I had always taken it for a figure of speech.'

'One with a basis in truth. Oil can indeed calm waves, if of the correct consistency. It reduces the surface tension of the water, decreasing its ability to form peaks and troughs.' He sucked noisily upon the pipe. 'I would commend you to a study of the classics, Watson, especially Bede's *Ecclesiastical History* of AD 731, in which he relates how St Aidan gave a vial of oil to a priest who was about to undertake a sea voyage, saying: "Remember to throw into the sea the oil which I give you, when straight-away the winds will abate, and a calm and smiling sea will accompany you throughout your voyage". A veritable miracle, for those unaware of the trick.'

'But the Doctor . . .?'

'His umbrella was hollow, and contained a reservoir of oil. The raising of hands and the chanting were designed partly for atmosphere and partly to distract your attention whilst he used some form of release mechanism to liberate the oil. Benjamin Franklin, the American inventor and politician, used to carry out the same trick, I am reliably informed, and for the same reason: to impress credulous observers with his powers.'

'But Holmes,' I protested, 'this is all pure speculation.'

'Not so, Watson. Remember the pool of oil in our coat rack earlier, when the Doctor removed his umbrella? A leak, I think you will find.'

He smiled triumphantly, then frowned as his mind recalled other matters.

'If only the death of Mrs Prendersly were as amenable to reason.'

'Did you have any success with your own expedition?' I ventured.

'A certain amount,' he replied, moving from the table to his favourite chair, close to the fire. 'After checking that Doctor Minor was still safely ensconced within the high walls of Broadmoor, I had decided to take a look at Mack "The Knife" Yeovil, one of the men who supposedly hold the security of the Library in their hands and who, incidentally, are involved in much of the pickpocketing, extortion, prostitution and gaming between here and Whitechapel. An odd choice by the Vatican, one might say.'

I settled back in my chair whilst Holmes described, in dry and humourless terms, a picture of the dregs of society upon which Dickens could have dined out for years. Despite his jibes at my nascent literary hobby, Holmes had no ability at story-telling. Thus, for the sake of my readers, I have refrained from repeating Holmes's words as he spoke them: rather, I have taken the broad flow of events and woven them into a more pleasing narrative. This, then, is what he told me.

The smell of roasting chestnuts and excited animals hung like a miasma over the Hackney marshes. Holmes, disguised in fake whiskers, shabby moleskin trousers, a check

shirt and a leather jerkin, moved through the crowd with
a sullen expression on his face and a cloth cap pulled
down over his eyes. He had been working his way gradually inward from the fringes of the throng for some time:
moving slowly so as not to excite suspicion and keeping
his ears alert for any conversations which might prove of
interest.

It had taken no great stretch of his abilities to determine
the location of Yeovil. The entire underworld had been
buzzing for months with word of the bare-knuckle fight
to end them all. The location had only been decided at
the last moment, in order to deny the police the chance
of stopping it, but all anybody had to do on the day was
to ask in any pub or bawdy house, and they would be
told. 'Ackney's the place. Go to 'Ackney. Everybody'll
be there.'

Everybody, in this instance, would certainly mean the
man who headed one of the biggest and most dangerous
gangs in London. Hackney was traditionally on Yeovil's
patch, although the word over the past few days was that
Mr Jitter was also going to be there, and that some rough
justice would be meted out to a couple of unfortunates
who had transgressed the brutal and unwritten code of
the underworld. Holmes had a shrewd idea who those
people might be.

A train from Liverpool Street had deposited Holmes
within walking distance of the fight, and the steady stream
of people heading into the low bushes and sparse grass-
land of the marshes was sign enough that he was in the
right area. He slouched along, hands in pockets, watching,
without appearing to, for Yeovil or Jitter.

The crowd was large, almost exclusively male, and so
threateningly brutal that Holmes realized why they didn't
fear the police, now that they had settled. A team preparing the ground could be moved on, a convoy of vehicles
bearing the stalls, the sideshows and the bare-knuckle
fighters could be stopped, but a few thousand drunken
and belligerent louts were a law unto themselves. The

police, quite sensibly in Holmes's opinion, were keeping well out of it.

Holmes took a cup of warm gin for a ha'penny at a stall, contriving to slop most of it on the ground as he quaffed. The drink gave him an opportunity to look around. Every few hundred yards, groups of men were gathered around a fenced-off area of ground in which dogs or metal-spurred cocks were fighting in a flurry of action and noise. The men at the back were stretching and craning their necks: the men at the front were shouting and cheering. All over, money was changing hands.

Far in the distance, on a slight hillock, four poles had been stuck into the ground and linked by ropes. Already a crowd of several hundred had gathered around the ring, although it would be several hours yet before the fight started. The cock-fights, the dogfights and some bare-knuckle bouts were intended to whet the appetite for the major attraction which, according to custom, was to occur about an hour before sundown. Two groups of caravans parked a few hundred yards away from the ring probably held the fighters.

Holmes moved nearer one of the fenced-off areas, elbowing and swearing his way through the crowd. If the gang leaders were anywhere, it would be where large crowds were passing large amounts of money, and this crowd looked larger than most.

'Ere luv, fancy some fun for a tanner?'

A haggard woman with a painted smile, a tattered dress and no teeth tugged at his arm. He shoved her away with a curse, and slipped through the crowd until his chest was pressed against a row of wooden staves which had been plunged into the ground to form a barrier with no gaps. Brutal men with long poles, sharpened to killing points, were spaced around the perimeter of the arena. Something more than an ordinary dog-fight was planned for here, that much was obvious.

The ground was soaked with blood already, and scraps of flesh and fur littered the area. A number of bouts had obviously already been fought. The crowd near Holmes

71

suddenly parted and a man clambered into the arena holding a crate. Bewhiskered and better dressed than the rest of the crowd, although not by much, he climbed up on top of the crate and gazed around challengingly.

'All right, then,' he shouted, 'you all knows why you're 'ere. I got a little something for you which'll make everything else in this stinking field look like a flea circus! You've never seen anything like it, gents, I can promise you that. Straight from Sumatra, it is, and it killed two sailors on the way over an' all. A dark and fearsome beast the like of which has not been seen on these shores afore. We got the Natural 'Istory Museum offrin' us money for it, we got the Zoological Gardens offrin' us money for it, we got so many offers you wouldn't believe to take this evil creature off our hands, but we saved it for you this very afternoon, gentlemen. For the first time in this or any other country, see the foreign beast take on three British bulldogs! Place your bets, gents, place your bets.'

'Come on, let the dog see the rabbit then,' a rough voice yelled out from the crowd.

'You want a look?' the master of ceremonies said. 'All right then.' He jumped off his crate and moved to one side of the arena, where the staves were interrupted by a solid gate. Throwing the crate back on the ground, he used it to clamber back over the staves, and pulled it up after him.

'Ready?' he yelled to the men with the sharpened poles. They nodded. He lent over the gate, flicked the catch and quickly pulled himself back to safety.

For a long moment, nothing happened. The crowd held their breath. The men with the poles leaned over the fence, tension evident in their faces.

The gate slowly opened as something pushed against it from the other side.

A greyish-green form slunk into the arena. It was about the size of a great dane – some five or six feet from nose to tail – but thicker-set and built closer to the ground. Its head was flat and pointed, its ears lay furled along the side of its head. A ruff of coarse black fur extended

72

from its neck along its spine to where a thick tail flicked restlessly, but otherwise it appeared to be covered with rough scales. Pure red eyes, with no distinction between pupil, iris or cornea, took in everything around it – the crowd, the fence, the men with the poles – and it snarled its defiance. Two enlarged incisors at the front of its mouth gleamed with spittle.

As if the creature was not strange enough, it only had one rear leg. For a moment Holmes assumed that it had lost the limb in some other bout, but then he saw how thickly muscled the remaining one was, how it sat centrally beneath the creature's pelvis, and how nimbly the creature pivoted on its rear leg and scampered around the ring. It had obviously been born that way. Holmes had seen nothing like it.

'It's some bastard offspring of a rat!' yelled a wag in the crowd.

'A rat like you've never seen before and will never seen again,' the master of ceremonies yelled back. 'A giant rat, caught in the depths of Sumatra, the most vicious and dangerous beast you ever set your peepers on.'

As the crowd jostled for a better look, Holmes tried to place it. The resemblance to a rodent was obvious, despite the massive rear leg and the scales, but certainly not *rattus rattus* or *rattus norvegicus*. Holmes had read of *rhizomys sumatrensis*, the great Sumatran bamboo rat, but this bizarre monstrosity bore little relationship to the descriptions. It looked to Holmes more like some tripodal lizard. He watched as it made a deceptively casual scuttle for the nearest section of fence, culminating in a short leap powered by that massive rear limb. The crowd jumped back as one, all except for Holmes and one of the men with the poles, who lashed at the beast with the sharpened end. It twisted in mid-air and landed gracelessly on the blood-soaked ground. The level gaze and low hiss with which it favoured the man seemed to promise much for later. He blanched, and wiped his brow. Holmes leaned closer, watching the way the creature moved. Judging by the matting of the fur around its neck, the apparent softness of its scaled but almost human hands and the casual manner with which it treated the crowd, Holmes judged that it had seen the inside of a circus tent or a travelling exhibition more recently than it had seen Sumatra. The thought made Holmes's blood run slightly colder. What next: tiger fights in Hyde Park? Panther races across Tower Bridge?

Everybody in the crowd bar Holmes was placing bets, and the odds heavily favoured the creature. Holmes wasn't so sure. Its lack of scars and the nervousness with which it sniffed the blood which had been spilled during the earlier dog-against-dog bouts indicated that it was a newcomer to this sport. The dogs, of course, were not.

The ringmaster was watching carefully from the sidelines, and as the betting began to tail off he raised a grimy handkerchief.

'Gents, are you ready?'

A howl went up from the crowd. The creature grew agitated, as if it knew what was about to happen.

The ringmaster dropped his handkerchief.

Three squat, scarred bulldogs raced through the gate. Quick hands immediately fastened it behind them. The creature whirled at the noise of their yapping, jumping backwards in surprise, and snarling. The crowd leaned over the barrier, screaming encouragement. The first bulldog saw its prey and flung itself straight across the arena. A sudden presentiment, perhaps the first whiff of an unfamiliar scent, or a close look at the giant beast, brought it up suddenly. Too late: the beast's claws raked deep gouges across the bulldog's nose. Gushing blood, it shied away. The crowd cheered.

The other two bulldogs, more careful than their companion, circled in opposite directions around the arena. The beast switched its attention back and forth between them, retreating all the time until it was against the staves. A shower of chestnuts from the crowd above distracted its attention: the dog to its right took a chance and dived in to clamp its jaws on the beast's huge rear leg. The creature slashed back with claws extended, but the dog

74

had dived out of range. The beast tried to follow, but the third dog nipped in from behind and fastened razor-sharp teeth on its rump. The beast whirled around the arena, trying to get its teeth or its claws into the maddening distraction behind it, but the bulldog was out of reach, and hung grimly on.

The second dog launched itself through the air and sunk itself into the creature's throat. Fresh blood gushed across the arena and sprayed the faces of the crowd. Shouts, screams and obscenities filled the air. Faces contorted in a feral rage, eyes glittered in blind, mad lust.

The creature rolled over onto its back and scrabbled with its back leg, trying to dislodge the dog that had anchored itself firmly on its throat. Deep gashes appeared across the dog's stomach, but still it held on. The third dog relinquished its grip and sunk its teeth firmly into the creature's stomach. The first dog, still streaming blood from its muzzle, took the chance to run in and out, and nipping at the beast's exposed groin.

Blood gushed across the creature as its claws found an artery within the second dog's stomach. The dog's grip weakened on the beast's throat, and a shake of the beast's head flung it against the side of the arena. It fell to the ground, panting rapidly, its guts protruding from a gaping slash in its stomach.

The creature was weakening. It attempted to turn over and shield its vulnerable underbelly, but before it could climb to its feet, one dog darted round to attack its face whilst the other burrowed beneath it to continue work on the stomach.

The creature lasted another few minutes, but the fight was already over.

The bout ended with the creature and one of the dogs dead, another dog with wounds to its face, a third howling in maddened triumph, and a few men considerably richer at the expense of a large number of others.

Holmes had spent much of the time scanning the faces of the crowd, searching for Yeovil, but with no success. As the bout finished, and he could move away without attracting attention, he caught sight of a familiar pocked face. Jitter!

Holmes followed at a distance, noting how Jitter was surrounded by a knot of hard-faced punishers carrying the spiked cudgels known as 'holy water sprinklers'. They were heading for the roped-off area that Holmes had spotted earlier. A lone figure awaited them in the centre of the ring, standing beside a wooden block: a squat man with long, wispy hair and enormous sideburns. He was dressed in a long poacher's coat and a shabby broad-brimmed hat, and Holmes had seen him before. It was Mack Yeovil.

Jitter ducked under the ropes and stood on the other side of the block. The two men – the most ruthless of London's many criminal gang leaders – barely acknow-ledged each other.

Holmes drifted closer to join the growing curious crowd.

'There's somethin' that needs to be sorted out,' Yeovil snapped in a gritty voice, 'an' it needs to be sorted out in public. It's not often Mr Jitter here and I are together. More often than not, we're at each other's throats.'

There was a murmur of assent from the crowd.

'There's a job we both do together,' Jitter added. 'We guard something. It don't matter what it is, but the point is, something's gone missing from it, and it's made us look bad. We –'

'We've made it clear what the punishment is,' Yeovil interrupted. 'Our lads, the ones doin' the guardin', they didn't spot the scummy gonoph. Or p'rhaps one of them was paid to look the other way. That's what we're goin' to find out.'

He gestured and two men were pushed through the ropes into the ring. Each one was held firmly by a large punisher.

'Now you know the form,' Jitter said to the men. Despite the calmness of his voice, they were white and shaking. 'You was the ones on duty outside the place during the week when the swag was nicked. Either you was both stupid, and let the gonoph get through, or you took an alderman or two to look the other way. Now I'll make it easy for you. The man who admits taking some other bugger's shilling, I'll let him take his chances in the ring with one of Yeovil's bludgers. If you don't talk . . .'

He glanced over at Yeovil, who had pulled a huge cleaver from his coat.

'. . . Then Mack the Knife will be relieving you of your hands.'

The first cowering figure – a runtish teenager with wispy red hair – was pushed forward by one of the punishers. His right hand was forced down onto the block.

Yeovil smiled down at him.

'Did you break faith with the family, Frank?'

'No, Mr Yeovil,' Frank squealed. 'I swear, I searched everyone who came out. Nobody was carrying anything. I swear it on my dear Mother's grave!'

'Remember boy,' Yeovil said gently, 'if you admit it, I'll let you fight like a man. If you don't . . .'

Frank was crying now.

'I swear, Mr Yeovil . . .'

The cleaver flashed in the sun and buried itself in the block. Frank screamed. A fine spray of blood misted the air. His hand clutched convulsively at the wooden surface, dragging itself an inch or two away from the cleaver.

The crowd roared its approval.

'Take him away and see to him,' Jitter commanded. One of the punishers clamped a dirty handkerchief over the stump and dragged him off to, Holmes presumed, where the shady doctors who serviced the bare-knuckle fights would be waiting.

The second man, a small-time cracksman named Froome who had crossed Holmes's path before, was led to the block. His face was waxy: his eyes were almost starting from his face.

'You know the score, Alf,' said Jitter, standing at Yeovil's elbow. 'Tell us who paid you off.'

77

Froome seemed to be fascinated by the blood trickling from the blade of the cleaver.

'Tell us, Alf,' Jitter prompted.

'I been a good family man,' Froome whispered. 'You ain't 'ad cause to complain, Mr Jitter. I always been faithful to you. I ain't taken no money, an' I don't know nothin' 'bout any books bein' stolen.'

He seemed to take courage from his words. Drawing himself up, he said, 'An' that's the truth.'

The cleaver moved so fast that it had severed Froome's hand before anybody saw it move. Froome didn't even seem to feel it: he raised his arm triumphantly to the crowd, and it was only when he saw the blood jetting from the stump that his eyes rolled up in his head and he fell to the floor. He was carried off, with a grimy handkerchief acting as a makeshift tourniquet.

'That's the end of it,' Jitter shouted to the crowd. 'Let that be a lesson to anybody who thinks about crossing either of us.'

Holmes had seen enough. He was about to make his way to the fringes of the crowd when he felt a sudden stir close to his chest. He lashed back with his boot, and felt it connect with a satisfying crunch. A cry rang out behind him and a hand whipped out from his coat. He grabbed at it and turned. A small man, whose hair stuck out at all angles from his face like a fretful porcupine, was hopping up and down and cursing. He was clutching a shilling – all the money that Holmes had left.

'Give easy!' the pickpocket cried. 'You dropped it. I was only puttin' it back!'

'Ger'cha!' Holmes growled, trying to stay in character, and shoved the pickpocket away. The smaller man staggered back into a large, spade-bearded fellow, whose tattoos covered every exposed portion of his skin. He, in turn, cuffed the pickpocket into the back of a rat-faced man wearing a dilapidated top hat, who whirled and thumped the bearded lout between the eyes.

The crowd, excited by the sight of blood, was like a

tinderbox, and this was the spark it had been waiting for. Within seconds a fight had started.

Holmes, aware of the fragility of his position, attempted to extricate himself from the widening scrap. It was no use. He managed to fight his way to the fringes of the crowd, his knowledge of baritsu proving less effective than a good underarm punch to the groin, but a flailing hand caught his cheek just as he thought he was clear. He felt a tearing sensation as something ripped.

His false whiskers.

'E's wearing a sham 'tash!' somebody shouted.

'E must be a rozzer!' someone else cried.

Holmes looked around. The fight was frozen, with everybody looking at him. The rat-faced man was drawing a thin flensing knife.

'Hold him,' the man said. 'If he's a rozzer we'll find out what he's doing here, then we'll cut out his lights.'

Holmes could see several outcomes, most of them unpleasant. He briefly debated yelling out to Mr Jitter for help, but the man was unpredictable at the best of times and might not wish to acknowledge his connection with Holmes. Instead, he elbowed the nearest men aside and raced away. The crowd had thinned somewhat, and Holmes found he could easily avoid or outdistance his pursuers. His heart pounded. The stalls and the scenery blurred as he ran. The sounds of the chase diminished behind him.

'Set the dogs on him!' yelled a distant voice.

A great shout went up behind him, and, with a cold heart, Holmes could just make out the baying of the bulldogs. He increased his pace. His heart pounded in time with his legs. Hackney Downs station shimmered remotely in the distance, like a memory of childhood. Sweat trickled into his eyes, burning and blurring his vision. He shook his head, spraying the water away, but failed to see a tree root which emerged from the ground like an old, gnarled worm, and stumbled.

Behind him: a rapid pattering.

He turned and faced approaching nemesis.

The lead bulldog was less than fifty yards away, well ahead of the pursuing crowd. Its companion, the one with the scarred nose, was not far behind. He took a deep breath, and waited.

The first dog approached in a blood-dappled blur and launched itself without hesitation at his throat. He braced himself, and caught its forelegs in mid-air. Its teeth gnashed widly a few scant inches away from his face. Foam spattered across his eyes. He jerked the dog's legs apart. The dog shrieked as both shoulder joints dislocated with a terrible ripping sound. Holmes threw the carcass away as the second dog skidded to a halt before him. He started to back slowly away. Knowing that if he turned his back, the dog would fasten itself upon his calf muscles, he picked up a stone and threw it with unerring accuracy at the dog's mutilated nose. It howled, and retreated.

The crowd was only a few hundred yards away, and most of them were carrying staves ripped from the arena fence.

Holmes a deep breath, and ran.

'And that's how I come to be sitting here this evening,' Holmes said lightly. 'It was exceedingly fortunate that the train was just pulling out of the station as I ran on to the platform. I ensconced myself safely in first class and waved at the hunters as they poured onto the platform. Apart from a slight *contretemps* with a guard who challenged me for sitting in a first class compartment with a third class ticket, the journey home was most pleasant.'

He took a contented puff at his pipe.

'Still, if there's one thing that today's escapade taught me, it's that the guards on the Library door were not paid to look the other way. We must look elsewhere for an explanation for the theft, Watson.'

'But Holmes . . .'

'And I wish I knew what that creature fighting the dogs was. I have the strangest feeling that this case might hinge upon that knowledge.'

I trailed off into an amazed silence. No matter how long I lived, I would never get Holmes's measure.

Chapter 5

In which Holmes and Watson receive a summons they cannot ignore, and are vouchsafed some secrets

Following our exchange of tales, Holmes and I spent the rest of the evening quietly. Following a marvellous dinner of Coronation Chicken prepared by Mrs Hudson's fair hands, we shared a bottle of port whilst Holmes smoked his old clay pipe and I savoured one or two of the many different types of cigars which he kept as reference material should he discover cigar ash at the scene of a crime. Later, whilst he hunted through his files for references to Indian religions, I caught up on my notes of the affair which – in memory of Mrs Prendersly – I had tentatively entitled *The Case of the All-Consuming Fire*. My account of our first meeting had received some favourable attention after my friend and colleague Arthur Conan Doyle took my notes, changed our names and address to protect us from undue publicity and had them published privately under the title *A Study in Scarlet*. Indeed, Doyle and I had recently been paid the sum of twenty-five pounds to allow its reproduction in the forthcoming *Beeton's Christmas Annual*. I was of a mind to pass my notes of another of Holmes's cases to Doyle, and thought that this might prove a suitable choice.

I retired early, leaving Holmes almost invisible amongst a cloud of smoke that smelled as if he was burning leaves instead of Ships' Number One Shag. As I prepared for bed, my mind kept throwing up images of Mrs Prendersly's blazing hair and her blistering face: a zoetrope of imagination which prevented me from sleeping for many hours. Downstairs, I could hear the rustle of paper and the occasional exclamation as Holmes worked through the night.

In the absence of slumber, I spent some time considering the qualities of my fellow lodger and friend. He had the most amazing constitution of any man I had met. He could stay awake for days on end without displaying any sign of deprivation, and then sleep continuously for an entire weekend. He could also go for days without eating, then gorge himself mercilessly upon anything that came to hand. He treated his body as a tugboat captain treats his vessel: as something that should be fuelled and overhauled to keep it functional, but which deserved no special care or respect, and which could be replaced at any time. As a doctor I knew that he was mistaken, and as his friend I had told him so on numerous occasions. His abuse of tobacco and ... stronger substances ... were, I felt, a sign that his body was rebelling against the strain he imposed upon it. I warned him of the risks he ran to his physical and mental health, but he ignored me.

My last thought before sleep claimed me was that there was one thing, at least, that the Great Detective could not discover, and that was the state of his own health.

I dreamed, that night, but I do not care to recall those night terrors now, except to say that the enigmatic figure of the Doctor scurried through all of them. Mostly he was dressed in the same outlandish costume that I had already seen him wearing: once or twice, however, with the peculiar logic of dreams, he was dressed in an Inverness travelling cape and a flapped travelling cap.

I awoke to find bright sunlight streaming through my window, the sound of costermongers and flower sellers drifting in from the street outside, and the reviving smell of fresh coffee wafting up from where breakfast awaited me.

Holmes was still sitting where I had left him. His Persian slipper lay, empty but for a few strands of tobacco, by his side. Plugs and dottles from his pipe littered the floor.

Mrs Hudson was pottering around the table in strained silence, removing the cold items and replacing them with fresh ones, ready for when Holmes deigned to eat. I had seen the process before, and knew that sometimes four or five breakfasts went past before Holmes took notice.

I smiled at Mrs Hudson and bade her good morning. She scowled and limped out. Her ankle seemed to be on the mend, I observed.

'You appear to have incurred the wrath of our landlady, old chap,' I said jocularly. 'If you're not careful, we may soon be looking for new lodgings.'

'Hmm?' Holmes glanced up from the sheaf of notes which he was reading. 'I noticed no change in her demeanour.'

Remembering my thoughts from the previous night, I added human emotion to the list of things that Holmes could sometimes singularly fail to detect.

Holmes joined me at the table as I began to make serious inroads into the scrambled eggs. He ate with one hand and shuffled through the pile of newspapers with the other.

Eventually he abandoned the last broadsheet and set himself to polishing off the bacon.

'You didn't sleep last night,' I observed.

'Well done,' he congratulated me without looking up. 'I see that my example has not been completely wasted on you.'

I persevered.

'If you're not hospitalized before the end of the year, I shall eat my hat! You have completely reversed all of the benefits of our Viennese holiday. The human body was not meant to be driven the way you are driving it.'

'I sense hidden reefs beneath the seemingly placid surface of this case. I needed time to think.'

'And have you come to any conclusions?'

'Some,' he mused, reaching for the toast. 'But a fresh mind is always welcome. Perhaps you would care to summarize the salient features, Watson.'

I was familiar with Holmes's little game, whereby he

would ask my opinion on a case, only to completely demolish it with his razor-sharp wits. I always played along with him. Holmes needed his little victories and they cost me nothing, save a moment of bruised pride. To give me time to think, I pushed the saucer of jam across the table to him. He shook his head.

'Thank you, but no,' he said, with the little twitch of his cheek that passed for a polite smile. 'I am not partial to jam, or indeed to any preserve made with sugar.'

'Why is that?' I asked.

'When I was a child, I recall being told by our cook that sugar cane was purified by being put into vats where it would be mixed with bullock's blood and heated up. I have since discovered that the albumin in the blood carries the impurities to the surface, where they are skimmed off. Knowledge of the chemistry does not, however, enable me to overcome my childhood revulsion. I was a sensitive child, as you may already have appreciated.' He smiled apologetically. 'I cannot imagine what prompted Mrs Hudson to buy any jam. I have made her aware of my taste on many occasions.'

Poor Mrs Hudson, I thought, and applied some to my own slice of toast.

'A theft has occurred from a hidden library in Holborn,' I said finally, 'a library controlled by the higher echelons of the Catholic Church and containing documents felt to be subversive to the natural order.'

'One remembers Galileo, and wonders,' Holmes murmured.

'Or rather, an *alleged* theft. We have no independent evidence.'

I had the pleasure of watching Holmes's face brighten momentarily.

'A fine distinction,' he admitted, 'but a proper one.'

'We have been provided with a list of those visitors to the library who have attended since the last time the books were seen. They are our suspects, since any one of them may have committed the theft. However, all visitors are searched upon exit, by two separate and rival gangs

85

of ruffians, and we saw ourselves how thorough the search is. Your own experience at the dogfight bears out the fact that there is no love lost between Mr Jitter's gang and Mack "the Knife" Yeovil's mob. The chances of collusion are slight. Each gang seeks to catch the other out.'

'*Quis custodiet ipsos Custodes*? as Juvenal so rightly remarked.' Holmes refilled both of our cups with steaming coffee. 'His Holiness the Pope seems to have come up with an ideal solution. I detect the twisted logic of the Jesuits.'

'We have questioned two of our suspects, the Doctor and Mrs Prendersly. The one is evasive, but seems strangely honest. The other is . . .'

The coffee suddenly tasted rank. Holmes glanced across at me sympathetically.

'Bear up, old chap,' he said quietly. 'If any human agency is behind the lady's death, we will find them.'

Despite the sunshine I felt as if a dark, chill shadow was hovering over us.

'As God is my witness,' I whispered, 'the lady was struck down by a supernatural fire. I see no other answer.'

'This agency stands foursquare upon the ground,' Holmes rebuked me. 'I will have no truck with the forces of Satan. Human nature is dark enough, without a vast panoply of demons as well. All problems can be reduced to a set of mathematical relationships, and all mathematical relationships can be solved. The supernatural is not amenable to logic: therefore it does not exist.' He sipped at his coffee. 'I have been corresponding with a young man named Russell upon the subject, a philosopher at Cambridge. He believes that he is on the verge of codifying all of mathematics into a simple set of axioms. I have told him that he is taking the first step towards summing up all human endeavour as an equation. Once that is done, everything can be predicted.'

I could not help but shudder at the idea.

'What a sterile outlook,' I exclaimed.

'Not at all,' Holmes replied easily. 'Would you not like

to be able to predict exactly which horse will win the Grand National next year?'

'Not,' I said tartly, 'if everybody else in the country could do likewise.'

Holmes suppressed a smile. I realized that he had been baiting me.

'Alas, ratiocinative logic has some way to go yet. For instance, your summary, whilst admirable in many respects, fails to address the important questions. For instance, why were the documents stolen?'

I braced myself for a roasting.

'For their intrinsic value. A collector might pay highly for them.'

'Unlikely.' Holmes leaned back and stared at the ceiling. 'If we take as our premise that one of the people on our list committed the theft, then we can rule out the possibility that they wished to add the volume to their own collections.'

'Why so?'

'Because their names are not known to any of the bookshop merchants or auctioneers whom I have questioned.'

'One of them could be a secret bibliophile. The list is not exclusive, surely? Or they could be working on behalf of another person.'

'Remember the type of documents that went missing. Alternative zoology and phantasmagorical anthropology. Now we know from what the librarian, Mr Ambrose, told us that there are items in the library worth many times more to a serious collector. The unexpurgated *Malleus Maleficarum* for instance – the infamous *Witches Hammer* of the Catholic Church – or Aristophanes's lost first play *The Banqueters*. I myself saw a folio that appeared to be Shakespeare's reputedly lost play *Love's Labours Wonne*. I know men who would sell entire countries to get their hands on that one item alone. No, I think we can rule out collectors.'

'Then perhaps they were stolen for the information they contained,' I said.

'Perhaps, but why steal them? Why not copy the information down?'

'Ah.'

'Indeed!'

Holmes suddenly slapped his palms down onto the table, rattling the crockery and knocking the jam spoon out of its saucer so that it splattered the tablecloth and my shirt.

'I would venture,' he continued, oblivious to my scowl, 'that the books were removed not for the information they contained, but to prevent anybody else from reading them.'

'Really Holmes!' I was remonstrating with him over the jam, but he took it to mean I disagreed with his theory, and pursed his lips together in annoyance.

'It is perfectly plain. We know that the Doctor was recently consulting books on Indian legends. Suddenly, the documents are stolen. The perpetrator of the crime was obviously attempting to prevent the Doctor reading them.'

I wiped at my shirt with a napkin.

'It's a bit shaky, Holmes,' I said.

'Not at all. It is the only theory which fits the facts.'

I was not convinced.

'Does that mean that we can remove the Doctor from our list of suspects?' I asked.

'Yes . . .' Holmes was uncertain. 'He is obviously mixed up in it somehow, and yet . . .' His expression was troubled. 'I am loath to believe that he is the villain.'

The napkin was merely helping to spread the jam across my shirt front, and I had just decided to return to my chamber and change when the door opened and Billy, our page, walked in.

'Telegram for you, Mr 'Olmes,' he shouted.

Holmes took the proffered slip. The lad scarpered off without a backward glance. Holmes smiled.

'A bright spark, that one. He'll bear watching.'

He slipped the envelope open and read the contents intently.

'A summons, Watson!'

He handed the slip over.

'*Come at once*, I read.

'Who on Earth can it be?' I asked.

'No mystery there,' Holmes replied. 'The identity of the sender is unquestionable.'

This time Holmes was going too far.

'How can you possibly know who it is?' I yelped. 'There is no name, no address, and the communication is neither handwritten nor torn letter by letter from a newspaper, so you are unable to deduce anything from the construction. Furthermore, the message is too short to contain any hidden message or code. You are bluffing, Holmes. I've caught you out!'

I sat back triumphantly.

'Who do you know that could send such a terse message and expect it to be obeyed?' Holmes asked me, reaching for his frock coat.

'Oh.' I was crestfallen.

'Exactly,' Holmes replied. 'My brother Mycroft. Come along, Watson. Best bib and tucker.'

'But . . .!' I glanced down ruefully at my stained shirt-front.

'No time! Come on!'

I followed.

As the hansom headed towards Pall Mall, and the Diogenes Club, I recalled everything that I knew about Holmes's mysterious brother. I had first met the man upon the occasion that Holmes aided one of Mycroft's fellow lodgers – the plucky Greek interpreter Melas. Mycroft's mental powers exceeded Holmes's, but his gross obesity and his extreme laziness precluded any movement except that between bedchamber, office and dinner table. Holmes had originally told me that his brother audited the books in some Government department. He had unbuttoned enough since then to confide that Mycroft's position was more shadowy and far more influential than he had previously led me to believe. Certainly in my brief conversation with the man I had been amazed by his breadth of knowledge concerning world affairs and his profound insights into the secret pivots upon which they turned. How often had I read in the newspapers of some revolution in a distant country, or a war between two foreign states, only to remember that Mycroft had mentioned them casually in passing months before they happened?

We alighted from the hansom in front of the imposing facade of the Diogenes Club – the last refuge of the most unclubbable men in England. In a moment of refreshing candour, Holmes had once told me that he would not belong to any club that would have him as a member. The Diogenes was his exception. Not a word was to be spoken inside its walls, save in the distant, sound-proof, Visitors' Room. No social interaction of any kind was permitted. Even to glance for longer than a few seconds at a fellow member was a black-ball offence. There were men – members of the aristocracy, indeed – who maintained rooms at the Diogenes, ate in its restaurant, and had not passed out of its portals or spoken to another living soul for a decade or more. The Diogenes was so private that I had heard of men who had died whilst slumped in its massive leather chairs, and their deaths not noticed until they began to decay.

Holmes led the way inside. I was immediately struck by the vast silence, so profound that it seemed like a physical presence. The entrance hall, from which a marble staircase swept up into the club proper, smelled of beeswax polish and age. A bewigged footman led us up and along a corridor that was so deeply carpeted I could only just make out the tops of my shoes. I could hear nothing, save the swish of our clothes and a deep, regular thump that I eventually realized was my heartbeat.

We came to a doorway fully twice my height and flanked by twin statues of cherubs. They were armed with little stone bows. A strange choice for the Diogenes, I reflected, believing them to be representations of Eros, until I saw the malevolent scowls upon their faces and the eagerness with which they held their weapons.

90

The footman indicated to us that we should enter. Years of non-verbal communication had honed his skills to the point where he could mime, with superb economy of gesture, quite complicated messages. I read in his movements that we were expected, that our host was already waiting for us, and that refreshment would be provided. I also read that our presence was only tolerated on our host's personal recommendation, and that we would be expected to behave with complete adherence to the baroque rules of the Diogenes Club.

I almost thanked him, but bit my tongue just in time.

Mycroft Holmes was standing by the window when we entered. He almost completely blocked the light from it. I had remembered him as fat, fatter than anybody I had ever met, but I had not remembered the poise with which he carried himself. He moved as if the weight meant nothing to him.

'Doctor Watson,' he said in his surprisingly deep voice as he walked towards us, 'I hope that your landlady's sprained ankle has not prevented you from breakfasting well?'

'No, thank you,' I answered automatically, then paused. 'But how . . .?'

He waved a massive spade-like hand.

'A mere bagatelle. I would not bother you with the details.'

I gazed at Holmes, who smiled slightly, and shrugged.

'Holmes has told you of her injury?' I ventured.

Mycroft sighed theatrically, as if bored by the necessity to explain his thoughts.

'Oh, very well. You have a jam stain upon your shirt, but my brother has abhorred jam since childhood and will not have it in the house. The estimable Mrs Hudson would not, I am sure, have purchased it herself. *Ergo*, she is temporarily unable or unwilling to shop daily for food: a chore which, I presume, is being undertaken by a scullery maid or page-boy less familiar with Sherlock's tastes. An illness would almost certainly have resulted in her taking to her bed, but your clothes are otherwise cleaned and brushed to a high standard, suggesting that she is still taking an active part in household chores. I therefore diagnose a minor injury. The ankle was a stab in the dark, I admit, but . . .' and he shuddered slightly, like a trifle on a plate, '. . . given the seventeen precipitous steps one has to ascend in order to reach your front door, not an unreasonable one, I warrant.' He frowned over at his brother. 'Perhaps you would care to save your landlady the trouble of washing Watson's shirt by doing it yourself, since you so obviously caused the stain in the first place.'

Now it was Holmes's turn to look puzzled. The frown suddenly cleared, and he turned to me.

'The angle of the stain,' he said, as if explaining to me rather than to himself. 'Had a drop of jam fallen from your toast, it would have resulted in a tear-drop shaped blotch. In fact it is almost circular, indicating that the jam arrived horizontally.'

'I should have changed,' I said, embarrassed at the constant reference to my state of dress, 'but . . .'

'My brother rushed you out of the house,' Mycroft continued. 'When we were children he used to do the same with me: always wanting me to accompany him as he rushed around the garden, examining worms, looking at leaves and turning over stones. I said to him, "Sherlock, if I want to examine a worm, I can do it just as well from the comfort of an armchair, if you will do me the courtesy of bringing it here. Better still, I can reach out my arm and pull down a book which will tell me everything I could ever wish to know about worms".'

He looked over at his brother, and smiled. Beneath the fat which adorned his face and fell in folds to his collar, I could see the outlines of the same bone structure that showed so well in Holmes's features.

Holmes smiled back, rather fondly, I thought.

'I remember telling you, "It's the context that's important, Mycroft",' Holmes said, good-humouredly, ' "not the worm".'

Mycroft swung round on his brother like battleship preparing a broadside.

'And I said, "A worm is a worm is a worm, Sherlock, no matter where you find it." Unlike a Pope, who is quite different in Austria to the Vatican.'

A heavy pause fell across the room, broken by the arrival of the footman with a tray containing a teapot and several fine china cups.

'You cannot possibly have deduced that we have met the Pope,' I said, when the footman had left. The brothers were locked in an eye-to-eye battle of wills. Knowing the natural truculence of the Holmes family, I could see that it could go on all day, if I did not interrupt.

'Quite right,' Holmes said. 'Somebody has brought Mycroft a juicy fat worm.'

'You are meddling in affairs of state,' Mycroft said.

'You have no right to interfere,' Holmes snapped. 'I have been retained in a private capacity.'

'That is equivalent to saying that the amorous predilections of Prince Edward, Duke of Clarence and Avondale are his own concern!' Mycroft crossed to the window again, so that the light was behind him, throwing his vast shadow across the room. 'The monarchy and the state are the same. They *cannot* be separated. The same holds true for the Pope and the Vatican. Did you not wonder why the Supreme Pontiff travelled half-way across Europe in secret to consult you? Did it not occur to you that the commission, simple though it may have seemed, might have implications which could rock Europe? Help yourself to tea, by the way.'

I did so, wondering what the amorous predilections of Prince Edward, Duke of Clarence and Avondale actually were.

'Balderdash!' Holmes threw himself into an armchair. 'The Foreign Office is merely annoyed because the Pope came to me rather than to it.'

'The Foreign Office be damned!' Mycroft exploded. 'They couldn't find a cow in a field. The Queen is annoyed because his Eminence Pope Leo XIII didn't come to *her*!'

'So,' Holmes whispered, 'as I suspected.'

Mycroft shifted uneasily from one foot to the other.

'Yes,' he said, 'as you suspected.'

'The Diogenes?'

'Of course.'

'Please,' I interrupted, 'if it is not too much trouble, can somebody explain to me what you are talking about?'

Mycroft glanced at Holmes, who nodded slightly. I felt as if I had been given some sort of endorsement.

'Please do not discuss what you are about to hear outside these walls,' Mycroft began. 'I am telling you this only to ensure that my brother is aware of the truth of my position, rather than his own deductions, and because I am aware, following your commissions for the Royal Families of Scandinavia, Russia and Holland, of your honesty and integrity.'

I nodded, feeling rather proud of the faith he put in me.

'As you may know, there are certain people attached to the Foreign Office who make it their business to find out other peoples' business. One might call them a kind of secret service.'

I thought back to the Orient Express, and the Reverend Hawkins. How mysterious are the wheels of power.

'Many countries have them, Doctor Watson. Germany has agents in England even as we speak, as does Russia. We have had our own agents abroad for nigh on four hundred years, now. We operate under a rather severe handicap, however. We are a decent race.' He snorted. 'The average Englishman thinks that there is something rather sordid and dishonourable about spying, and that pretty much ties our hands as to how effective we can be.'

'There *is* something sordid about it,' I exclaimed. 'The whole idea is . . . well, just not cricket!'

'The Germans don't play cricket,' he said, scowling. 'And neither do the Russians. Unfortunately, the Foreign Office do. They run the whole thing like an Eton game. You've never seen such a group of ineffective stuffed shirts. When Thomas Beach, one of their best agents, infiltrated the Irish Republican Brotherhood and reported that the Fenians had entered into diplomatic relations with the Czar of all the Russias, and that they had actually built a submersible boat with which to attack Royal Navy vessels, what did they do? Nothing! Her Majesty was furious when she found out!'

'Her Majesty?'

'Our Sovereign is a shrewd woman, Doctor Watson, and should not be underestimated. She is not blind to the domineering ambitions of Czar Nickolas I and Kaiser Wilhelm II, and she is also perfectly well aware that the Fenians pose a greater threat to the stability of the monarchy than the Anarchists.' He hesitated briefly, wondering, perhaps, how much to say. 'Her Majesty has for some time been distrustful of what her prime ministers have been telling her. She never had much respect for poor Gladstone. "He speaks to me as if I were a public meeting," she once told me, and has publicly questioned whether he is fit to lead her country. I must say,' Mycroft added parenthetically, 'that I share her views. Not five years ago the Prime Minister proposed to the Cabinet that a Flotilla of the Royal Navy be sent to look for Atlantis!' He frowned. 'Where was I? Yes, some years ago Her Majesty decided to set up what, for want of a better word, might be called her own "intelligence organization". She, or rather, her advisors,' and Mycroft modestly cast his gaze downwards at this point, 'knew that it could not be funded from public money, lest the public protest at a secret organization in their midst. Approaches were made to the oldest and wealthiest families in the land. A cover was sought: an establishment above reproach through which this tiny band of patriots could operate.'

'And the Diogenes . . .?' I was aghast.

'. . . Is that establishment. Like an iceberg, Doctor Watson, nine-tenths of what goes on here is beneath the surface.'

'I had already deduced most of your story,' Holmes said from the far side of the room. He had poured himself a cup of tea and was sprawled in his armchair. 'Indeed, I have been following your successes with some interest. It would seem that, wherever trouble exists in the world, a member of the Diogenes Club is not far away. I notice, in fact, that the ill-fated last voyage of the Fenians' submarine vessel coincided with the honeymoon in New Jersey of one Charles Beauregard, whom I have seen dining here on numerous occasions.'

'Very perceptive, Sherlock,' Mycroft said, clapping his hands together gently. 'Very perceptive. Now, I have been frank with you. Perhaps you could return the compliment.'

Holmes stared at his brother for a long moment.

'Perhaps we can trade information,' he said finally. 'Certain pieces of the puzzle still elude me.'

He steepled his hands together, lay back in his chair until his gaze was directed at the ceiling and sketched the bare bones of the matter for his brother. When he had finished and Mycroft had asked a few incisive questions, Holmes reached into his jacket and extracted the list of Library patrons which Mr Jehosephat Ambrose had provided us with.

Mycroft's eyes scanned the list, stopping at one particular name. He glanced up and locked gazes with Holmes. They shared a long moment of unspoken communion.

'An instructive list,' Mycroft said finally, returning it to Holmes. Even I could spot the ironic understatement in his voice – a tone directed, I was sure, at his brother. 'You have questioned both the Doctor and Mrs Prendersly, but only Mrs Prendersly is dead. If we take as our assumption that she was indeed murdered, it would follow that she possessed information that the Doctor did not, and was killed in case she might pass the information on. It would also follow that Professor Challenger is not our man.'

'How so?' Holmes challenged.

'Because he set sail for South America last week on one of his scientific expeditions.'

'He could be working as part of a gang,' I said.

'Unlikely,' Holmes snapped. 'Remember William of Occam's suggestion that one should not multiply logical entities without reason. No, for the moment we will assume that our man is working alone.'

'Is your Doctor a tall chap with a shock of white hair and a penchant for velvet smoking jackets?' Mycroft asked.

'No,' I said, mystified. 'Why?'

'There's a chap who I see down in the reading room sometimes, calls himself the Doctor. Thought it might be one and the same. This one's a bit of a wag: brings newspapers into the Club dated some ten or twenty years hence and reads them as if he'd never seen them before. Got some of the members quite worried, I can tell you.'

'Apart from the coincidence in names,' Holmes said, leaning forward and fixing his brother with a hard stare, 'is there any reason why he should be the same Doctor?'

'Well spotted, Sherlock. I do have a reason. You see, a good half of the people on this list are members of the Diogenes.'

Holmes stood bolt upright, and I must admit that I was taken aback. The entry requirements for the Diogenes were notoriously stringent. To find that many of our suspects were regularly gathered together under one roof . . .

'Who?' Holmes asked succinctly.

'If we ignore the Doctor, then Challenger, Baron Maupertuis and . . .'

Mycroft trailed off. Holmes nodded. I felt completely left out. There was a name on the list that was being kept from me.

Mycroft Holmes pulled a discreet velvet cord, and within seconds a footman had entered the room. Mycroft murmured a few words, and the man left.

'I have asked Baron Maupertuis to join us, if he is on the premises,' Mycroft informed us.

'What sort of a man is he?' Holmes asked.

'A strange sort,' Mycroft replied. 'Rich – exceptionally so – and a bit of a recluse. He is of Dutch extraction, and owns the Netherlands-Sumatra Company, but has recently become a naturalized British subject. Seems to be trying to be more British than the British: friends with the Prince of Wales, goes to Ascot, you know the form. We suspect that he is mixed up in some shady business deals, which is why we encouraged him to join the Diogenes.'

'Because you wanted his help?'

'Don't be clever, Sherlock. We wanted to keep an eye on him.'

As we waited, Mycroft poured me a glass of heavy, sweet sherry, and made small talk about the weather. He was not very good at it and I was glad when the door reopened.

The man who walked into the room was tall, excessively so, and thin to the point of emaciation. His face was bloodless and completely without expression – so immobile, in fact, that it could have been carved in bone. His hair was long, ash-blond and brushed straight back: the irises of his eyes were so pale as to be almost invisible, so that his pupils were black pinpricks floating on a white void. His morning attire was impeccable. He did not offer to shake hands.

'Mycroft,' he said finally. His voice was like the wind in dry reeds. 'I trust that this is important. I have another appointment.'

'I wished you to meet my brother, Sherlock,' Mycroft said. I could tell that even he, the imperturbable Holmes, was put out.

Maupertuis's gaze settled on Holmes and he nodded slightly. Although his expression did not change by one iota, something new had been added to the atmosphere of that room, an indefinable but ominous cloud.

'Charmed,' Holmes said, sniffing slightly. 'I was saying to my brother only a moment ago that we both belong to the same library.'

Maupertuis said nothing.

'A library in Holborn,' Holmes continued.

No reaction.

'I don't remember ever seeing you there. Do you go often?'

Maupertuis reached a skeletal hand into his waistcoat pocket and retrieved an ornate gold hunter, which he consulted. I noticed that the rest of his body did not appear to move at all. He swivelled slightly so that he was looking at Mycroft.

'Time presses,' he whispered. 'You understand.'

He turned to go, and as he did so, his gaze swept across me like the beam of a lighthouse. I felt as if insects were crawling across my skin. The feeling lasted but a moment, and then he was gone.

'He did not blink,' Holmes said finally. 'Most instructive.'

'A rum character,' Mycroft said. There was a fine beading of perspiration across his forehead. he took out a handkerchief and mopped it abstractedly across his face. 'I've never got his measure.'

'I wonder whether his appointment was real or feigned,' I said. 'It occurred to me that he might have wished to avoid further questioning, and invented a spurious excuse to leave.'

Holmes crossed to the window.

'We may be able to tell something by the way he . . . ah! Yes, there he is now, climbing into a hansom.'

Holmes suddenly leaned forward, like a pointer dog on the trail of a stag. 'Hello, what's this!'

Mycroft and I moved to join Holmes. Mycroft, being nearer, got to his brother's side first, effectively blocking my view.

'Most instructive,' Mycroft murmured.

'You noticed?' Holmes said.

'Of course.'

'What's happening?' I bleated.

Mycroft moved aside and I squeezed past him to gaze along Pall Mall at a swaying two-wheeler with a baronial crest upon its side.

'I see nothing,' I said.

'You see nothing now,' Holmes corrected. 'The hansom was listing sideways before Maupertuis entered. His weight evened the suspension out.'

'I don't . . . Ah! I see! You suspect that the hansom was already occupied?'

'I suspect nothing,' Holmes replied. 'I *know*. The science

of deduction allows no room for suspicions. A fact is either true or it is not true. Did you not notice how Maupertuis was in a hurry to leave us for another engagement? I would suggest to you that he was due for an assignation with another person. The coach is obviously his, judging by the crest, and contains the person with whom he is meeting.'

It would be instructive to know the identity of the other man,' Mycroft said ruminantly. 'Save that he is elderly and does not often visit London, I can tell nothing about him.'

'He is of above average height,' Holmes added.

'Or thinner than the norm,' Mycroft riposted. Both brothers smiled. I was at a loss. I wanted to ask them how they could tell all this from the tilt of a hansom cab, but the answer would only make me feel a fool for not being able to tell myself.

Just then the hansom described a wide half-circle and began to trot towards the Diogenes again. As it passed, I craned my neck in an attempt to see its occupants. Holmes and his brother had moved back into the room, and so I was the only one to see the silhouette of a hooded and robed figure sitting next to the Baron – the same figure that I had seen in the Library of St John the Beheaded.

Chapter 6

In which Holmes and Watson make a subterranean voyage and a footman is fired

'I need to see that man,' Holmes snapped after I had imparted the news to him. 'It may be that there is nothing suspicious in this meeting – after all, we already know that the Baron is a member of the Library. Never the less, a hooded man is a suspicious figure of almost gothic proportions. Where will Maupertuis be heading now?'

'Sherlock, I'm not even my brother's keeper, let alone that of a foreign nobleman. Come, we will ask the doorman.'

Moving quickly for a man of his build, Mycroft led the way out of the Visitor's Room, along hushed corridors and down the wide marble staircase to the foyer of the Diogenes Club. Whilst we waited by the main desk, he beckoned the doorman to the steps just outside the door and flung questions at him. As he gestured to us to join him outside the club doors, I saw him slip the man a shilling.

'Jessup here says that the passenger was in shadow, but he heard the Baron tell the driver to head for an address in Euston.'

'Then we must get there before him.' Holmes looked around for a cab, but there were none to be seen.

'He has a good few minutes start,' Mycroft said. 'By the time you get there, they will have entered the house, and you may never see the other passenger. Unless . . .'

'Unless what?'

Instead of answering, Mycroft led us both back inside

the confines of the Diogenes and through the reading room – a large, oak-lined study in whose deep leather armchairs sat a cross-section of the most important, the most unconventional and the most unpleasant men in the Empire. Skirting around the back of an armchair, I found myself looking at a familiar face.

The Doctor.

He was standing in front of the armchair. Its occupant was reading a copy of the *Times*. From my position behind him I could see that he was attempting to finish some kind of word puzzle – a grid composed of black and white squares into which he was inserting words. He had one set of spaces left to fill, and from the look of him he had been stuck for some time.

The Doctor was busy writing something on a piece of paper. Seeing me, he put a finger to his lips. I looked down at the man in the chair. His hair was white and he was wearing a black velvet smoking jacket. Stumped by the clue, he rubbed the back of his neck in annoyance.

The Doctor coughed slightly. Immediately, the paper was lowered and the man in the chair glowered at him.

The Doctor held up his piece of paper.

14 Across, it read, *Sesquipedalian.*

'You bounder!' the man expostulated. The Doctor scurried off, grinning, and the white-haired man leaped to his feet as a number of irate footmen converged on him. I ran after Holmes and Mycroft, ashamed of the Doctor's juvenile antics.

Mycroft took us down a side corridor. A few yards along it was a door marked *Billiards Room*. Mycroft took a key from his waistcoat pocket and unlocked it, then led the way inside.

Excepting a billiards room, I was taken aback to find a gas-lit and carpeted stairway. I stumbled down the first few stairs into Holmes's back. In front of me, over Holmes's head, I could see Mycroft's huge bulk filling up the space from stairs to ceiling and from wall to wall. As we walked I wondered what would happen if he got stuck.

How could we get him out? Thank God he was in front, otherwise how would *we* get out?'

We walked on, and on. The stairs led down, seemingly to hell itself. A sudden *whoosh* in the distance made me jump. Seconds later a warm breeze caressed my face.

'Where are we going?' I whispered to Holmes.

'Hanged if I know,' he replied over his shoulder, 'but I doubt that it's the wine cellar.'

Light blossomed around the edges of Mycroft's body and within seconds we were standing in a spacious, brick-lined cellar from whose ceiling an incongruous chandelier dangled. Looking back up the stairs, I could see a glimmer of light. The distance was not as great as I had feared. Relieved, I looked around.

Comfortable sofas lined the walls, and tables held copies of the day's newspapers, but my eyes were caught and held by the semicircular cast-iron object which protruded from the far wall. It was about four feet across and festooned with a number of smaller pipes, one of which seemed to have a knurled wheel attached. I moved closer. It appeared to be some form of hood and, kneeling and gazing into it, I could see that it was the final few feet of a tunnel. The rest of the tunnel, which was lined with cast iron, vanished into darkness after a few feet. A large hatch, hinged at the top, hung over the opening and two rails, about three feet apart, emerged from it and crossed the cellar almost to where we stood. Sitting on the rails was what I can only describe as an large artillery shell on wheels.

'Barker?' Mycroft roared. We were obviously in another part of the Diogenes Club in which speech was permitted.

'Ere, Guvnor!'

A small man emerged from the tunnel. His skin was pale, his eyes dark, and he was dressed, incongruously, in immaculate morning dress.

'Be wantin' a trip, will ya?'

Without waiting for an answer, he threw some kind of catch and opened the entire top of the wheeled shell. The interior was padded with velvet and contained two small armchairs.

'All aboard that's goin' aboard,' he said.

I looked questioningly at Holmes. He, in turn, looked at his brother.

'Get in,' Mycroft said. Holmes shrugged, and did so. I, with some trepidation, followed.

The armchairs were a tight fit. I gazed up out of the shell at the chandeliered ceiling.

'A pneumatic railway built for the Post Office and first used in 1863,' Mycroft explained, beaming down at us. 'They used it to move post from Euston to the General Post Office at St Martin's le Grand. They abandoned it in 1880. The Diogenes bought it – through one of our members, of course – and extended the line to here. Excess air pressure – provided by the London Hydraulic Power Company from their pumping station in Pimlico – pushes the shells along, and a partial vacuum in front of them aids the process.'

'For what purpose?' I gasped.

'To get people in and out of the building unobserved,' Holmes said. I could tell from his tone that he, too, felt a modicum of discomfort.

'Quite right,' Mycroft said. 'Certain meetings held on these premises have quite distinguished guest lists. It would not do to have them observed. And . . .' his voice hardened, '. . . it would not do to have any mention of this private railway in the public domain. It shall remain our little secret.'

He made a signal to Barker.

'First stop Euston, a short walk away from Drummond Crescent, where Baron Maupertuis is making for. Pleasant journey, gentlemen. You will forgive me for not joining you.'

The lid came down.

'If anybody had told me this morning,' I said with some venom, 'that I would be shot like a bullet beneath London before lunch, I would have called them a liar.'

'I confess that the experience is a novel and unexpected

one.' Holmes voice was flattened by the padding. 'Still, look on it as a part of life's rich tapestry.

'Thank you,' I retorted. 'I'll remember that.'

We seemed to roll forward by a few feet, and a heavy thud behind us suggested that the hatch had been closed.

'I seem to remember reading about something like this in a Jules Verne book,' I said lightly, trying to keep my spirits up.

'Verne got it all wrong,' Holmes said in a level voice. 'At the pressures generated in his manned rocket shell, the occupants would have been squashed into raspberry preserve with a fraction of a second.'

There was a definite pressure building up in my ears. I swallowed. The pressure eased, only to mount a few seconds later.

'Very reassuring,' I gasped. 'Any last words?'

'The world has not seen the last of Sherlock Holmes,' my friend said. I wasn't sure if it was a threat or a promise.

There was a loud *thud* behind us and the vehicle rocked on its wheels. The armchair felt as if it was being pushed hard against my back. Something roared loudly in the background and the vehicle shook as if some unseen creature were caressing it with rough hands. The temperature rose suddenly, bringing a fine dew of perspiration to my brow. My fingers clutched at the arms of the chair and my head was forced back against the padding, making me think, for some obscure reason, of a dentist's surgery. I clenched my neck muscles and tried to force my head forward. It was hard. I felt as if Mycroft Holmes were sitting on my chest. I strained harder.

Suddenly the weight vanished from my chest. I catapulted forward, banging my nose against the back of Holmes's chair. Stars exploded in the pitch darkness. The beast outside was roaring louder now, and I had to brace myself against the sides of the vessel to stop myself sliding off the velvet upholstery. Then we were slowing down, and the tone of the roar changed. Within seconds we were stationary and the hinged lid was being pulled open from outside.

'Ere ya go, mate.'

A tattooed arm reached in and hauled me like a kitten into a room that was the twin of the one we had left. Holmes waved away the man with the tattoos, and clambered out under his own steam. I looked at him and laughed.

'If you find the experience so amusing,' he snapped, 'perhaps you would like to make the return journey.'

I suppressed my laughter. Part of it was sheer hysteria, but a large portion was due to the velvet weave pattern embossed across Holmes's forehead. I hadn't been alone in hitting my head.

We staggered out into Drummond Crescent and found ourselves outside a small, anonymous house. We looked at each other, and burst out laughing.

'Quicker than a cab,' I gasped, 'and so much cheaper!'

'Gad, I've a small place a few hundred yards away where I keep make-up and disguises,' he said between huge choking guffaws. 'And to think, I never knew . . .'

We were still laughing when a black hansom cab trotted past us. Holmes sprinted after it and I, because of the wound I had sustained in Afghanistan, followed as best I could. The hansom rounded the corner and, shortly afterwards, so did Holmes. By the time I reached the corner the hansom was stationary and the door to a small terraced house was swinging shut half-way down the street. Holmes had taken off his top hat and flung it to the pavement.

'Damn and blast!' he shouted as I approached. 'Damn and blast! I could not make out his face. Too late, by a few seconds.'

He walked along to where the carriage stood and looked up at the closed door. I joined him, mindful of the hulking figure of the driver atop the carriage.

'I know that address,' Holmes said. His lips moved as he tried to recollect the memory, then a slow smile spread across his face.

'We may be in luck after all, Watson. Follow me.'

106

With that he bounded up the stairs to the front door of the house.

'But Holmes ... Good Lord, you can't just barge in there, man!'

'Why not?' he shouted down as he rang the bell. The door swung open just as I joined him, revealing a rather seedy-looking footman whose hair was slicked down and who grinned at us in a most familiar way. I had been about to apologize for Holmes's behaviour but, after a short exchange of words, he walked in as if he owned the place. I followed, confused.

The walls of the hall were papered in a red flock design that showed patches of wear. The carpet had once been opulent, but now looked threadbare and out of fashion. There was no sign of Maupertuis and his companion, if, indeed, this was the house they had entered. A stairway led upstairs. Through a connecting door I could see a large drawing room whose walls were thankfully half-hidden by drapes. I say 'thankfully' as there were children lounging on sofas, and the murals which had been painted on the walls were of fauns and satyrs in positions of amorous entanglements with partially clad nymphs of a shockingly young age. I am no prude – my experience of women covers many nations and three separate continents – but I was appalled by the almost medical explicitness with which those paintings were rendered.

And then I looked at the children.

Most were girls, although three or four angelic boys fluttered long lashes at me. They were lolling around in postures of provocative abandon, dressed in short frocks. Very short frocks and nothing else.

I began to feel sick.

'Does anything take your fancy?' said a voice behind me. I turned. Behind me stood a woman of uncertain years wearing a dress that looked as if it had been made out of the same threadbare fabric as the flock wallpaper in the hall. She was short and wide, and her mouth was a rouged slash across her face.

'We've got some loverly little ones here, gentlemen, and

clean too, if you take my meaning. Whatever your tastes, we can satisfy them. Blondes or redheads, bold or shy. If you want them fresh, well, that comes a little extra, gents, but fresh you can have.'

She gazed up at us with bulging, frog-like eyes. I wanted to lash out at her with my stick, but remnants of gentility and Holmes's presence by my side made me stay my hand.

'Thank you,' he said. He had roughened his voice and, looking at him from the corner of my eye, I could see that he was holding himself differently, disguising his height and suggesting some congenital deformity of the spine. 'Perhaps we could take some time in choosing.'

She winked at him.

'Certainly, sir. I can see that you're a connersewer, a proper connersewer. Take your time. Talk to 'em, if you like. Give us a call when you're ready, and I'll have a room put at your disposal.'

She retreated back to whatever rock she had crawled out from under. I thought I heard her say, 'Take two or three, if you want, it's all the same to them, and you looks like you can afford it,' but the buzzing in my ears made it difficult to tell.

'Bear up, man,' Holmes's voice whispered beside me. 'Smile, and when I say the word, make for the stairs.'

I glanced again into the room. One of the boys winked at me and licked his lips. I shuddered.

On Holmes's command we moved back into the hall. As we rounded the bannister Holmes reached out and opened the door slightly, then slammed it shut.

'With luck they'll think our courage deserted us,' he said grimly. 'That harpy could tell from your face that you were discomfited.'

'*Discomfited*!' I hissed. 'Holmes, do you have any idea . . .?'

'More than you, old friend,' he said as we reached the first landing. 'The underside of London is my natural habitat. I have been able to keep most of it from you. I'm only sorry you had to be here now.'

'But Holmes, they were *children*!'

He scanned the carpet and sniffed the air like an experienced hunter in search of big game, then started up the next flight of stairs.

'The other side of the coin to our experiences in Holborn,' he whispered. 'The overcrowding in the slums and rookeries is so intense, the poverty so appalling, that many families feel they have no option but to sell their children into what may seem to them to be better circumstances.'

'And there are men willing to ... to pay money for ... And with boys as well ...!'

I could not continue. Holmes glanced over at me, his eyes shadowed.

'I have never been one to censure what two consenting adults wish to do in private, Watson, the provisions of Section 11 of the Criminal Law Amendment Bill notwithstanding. But to involve children is the lowest form of moral perversion imaginable.'

We had reached the second landing by now. The dubious trappings of respectability had faded: the walls were distempered rather than papered, the floor uncarpeted. Holmes repeated his *shikari* act, then led the way to a closed door which he opened a crack. Behind it a smaller staircase led further upward. From upstairs I thought I could hear chanting: voices raised in a deep, slow song whose words appeared to be in some foreign language. Closing the door again, Holmes whispered, 'I can hear Maupertuis at the top of the stairs. He appears to be standing guard over a room, inside which I presume is his hooded companion. We must determine what he is doing in there.'

'But Holmes, surely it's obvious.'

He gazed at me pityingly.

'This address was familiar to me not because I am an expert in brothels but because Madame Sosostris, the infamous clairvoyant, holds her devilish seances here.'

'Wasn't she mixed up in black mass ceremonies a few years back? I remember reading it in the newspapers. Shocking.'

'Indeed, and this is where she ended up, attempting to

contact the other side by using devils and demons, rather than the Red Indian spirit guides so beloved of other clairvoyants. I would give a great deal to know what this hooded man wants with her.' A thought struck him. 'Perhaps we can gain access from *this* floor.'

Holmes and I checked the nearest door. Hearing nothing, I cautiously turned the handle and opened the door a crack. The room was dark. I pushed the door a few more inches and poked my head cautiously around the edge. Apart from a stained and rumpled bed and a small plaster crucifix on the wall above it, there was nothing. The curtains had been drawn, and the room was in twilight.

Holmes went straight to the window and drew back the curtains. Beyond the fly-specked glass I could see a patch of overgrown garden bordered by chest-high walls. As I retrieved my stethoscope from my hat, Holmes threw up the window, secure in the knowledge that he could not be observed, and began to climb out onto the ledge.

'Be careful!' I mouthed. He nodded, and swung himself sideways, feeling with his fingers and toes for the gaps between the bricks.

I was just about to turn back to the room when something familiar caught my eye in the garden, half hidden by the shadow cast by one of the walls. It was a pile of tall, thin twigs with a leather pouch, like a half-deflated football, balanced on top. I tried to remember where I had seen something similar, but my mind would not co-operate.

'Watson,' Holmes hissed from his position above me, 'stop wool-gathering and see what you can hear through the ceiling!'

Chastened, I gazed upwards. All I could see were the soles of his feet. I scurried back and placed my stethoscope against the ceiling.

There were two voices upstairs. One seemed to belong to an older man, and was oddly familiar. The second was that of an old woman. Together they seemed to be chant-

110

ing a series of polysyllabic words in a regular and detached manner, like children reciting nursery rhymes.

'*I-ay, I-ay,*' the sound seemed to go, '*naghaa, naghai-ghai! Shoggog fathaghn! I-ay, I-ay tsa toggua tholo-ya! Tholo-ya fathaghn!*'

I looked over towards the window, suppressing a shudder. There was no sign of Holmes. I felt a moment of panic, but decided in the end that if he had fallen he would have made some noise, if only to warn me.

The two voices were chanting out of phase now. They seemed still to be using the same words, but the elder man's voice was two syllables ahead of the woman's. The effect was oddly hypnotic. The curious stresses within the words made the chant resonate with a strong beat as the voices alternately reinforced and competed with each other. I had heard much the same effect in Afghanistan and India, listening to the music of the native tribesmen of the hills, music based not upon the melodic structure so dear to Holmes's heart, but upon a rhythmic foundation not heard in the West.

The chant stopped abruptly in the middle of a phrase. For a moment I thought that Holmes had been discovered, until a third voice spoke. It was high-pitched and pure, without character or personality. It oozed sweetness. I had never heard anything like it in my life.

'*My children,*' it said, '*you have done well. I am pleased.*'

The man spoke again, but in English.

'When shall we bask again in your presence?' he asked fawningly.

'*Soon, very soon,*' the outlandish voice answered. Despite its peculiarities, I could make out its meaning.

'The armies are gathered,' the man said. Presumably he was well used to the owner of the strange accent.

'*You must see to it yourself. The brethren will be committed to moving me soon.*'

'I would crave a request, oh luminous one.'

'*Name it. You are my favoured son.*'

'There is interference here. I would ask that a few of the brethren are spared to protect this side of the gateway.'

111

'*Interference? You displease me. The guards are mobilizing. Soon they may realize our plans. I am loathe to spare any of the brethren.*'

'A detective and a stranger called the Doctor are investigating our affairs. They are nothing, but I would not take chances with your safety at stake.'

There seemed to be a slight quickening of interest in the voice.

'*Nothing can threaten my safety, but this Doctor may pose problems. You may have four of the brethren. They will be waiting this side of the gateway . . .*'

There was a sudden scrabble outside the window, and the sound of rubble hitting stone far below. In the moment before I tore my stethoscope away from the ceiling a silence fell across the meeting, broken by the woman's voice asking, 'What was that?'

'Some jackanapes is outside the window!' the elder man snapped. 'The connection is broken! Maupertuis! Damn you, man, attend me!'

As the door to the room above was thrown open by, I presumed, Baron Maupertuis, I rushed across and peered out of the window. There was no sign of Holmes down below.

'Watson!'

An urgent hiss attracted my attention upwards. Holmes was moving rapidly down towards me. Beyond him I could see that the lintel beneath the window must have crumbled under his fingers, sending fragments of masonry crashing to the ground.

'Damn it,' Holmes exclaimed as I pulled him in. 'All that and I hardly got a glimpse. Maupertuis was outside guarding the door, that much is for sure. There were only the two of them in the room, and the robed man had his back to me.'

'Only two of them? But I heard three voices!'

'I know,' Holmes barked as he flung open the door.

We emerged onto the landing at the same time that Baron Maupertuis arrived from the stairway. He was holding something in his hand. No flicker of expression crossed his face as he saw us. Madame Sosostris – a sour-faced woman in faded finery – cowered behind him. There was no sign of the hooded man.

'Surd!' yelled the Baron.

Holmes took two steps towards Maupertuis and tried to snatch whatever it was that he was holding. They struggled silently for a few moments whilst the woman gazed at me with horrified eyes: horrified not by what was going on, but by something else that she had seen. I was trying to decide whether to join in the struggle or make for the stairs when a grotesque figure rushed up from the floor below. He was at least seven feet tall, and wide to match. His physique was that of a prize-fighter, but it was his face that held me in thrall. Crowned by a rough thatch of black hair, it was scarred and swollen, and pulled into a grotesque expression by what seemed to be all of the many muscles of his lips and cheeks pulling in different directions. I recognized his garb: he was the driver of Maupertuis's carriage.

Holmes broke off the struggle and ran to join me.

Maupertuis indicated us with a flick of his head.

'Surd,' he whispered to the man behind him, 'kill them.'

We leaped back into the room and I slammed the door. There was a cheap bolt on the inside: I threw it, but it wouldn't stop Surd for long. Holmes tried to open the door again, crying, 'I must see the other man!', but I pulled him towards the window.

'The drainpipe!' I gasped. He picked up my meaning straight away, and clambered over the window-sill. I gave him a few seconds to get clear, then followed.

I still have nightmares about that climb. More than once I felt the bolts that attached the drainpipe to the wall start to give. Rust scoured my hands, and a bloody haze seemed to hover before my eyes as I called upon all my reserves of strength. I paused to look up at one point, and saw Maupertuis and the cowled figure of his companion leaning out of the window watching us. Of the menacing Surd there was no sign. I presumed that he was racing down the stairs to catch us. In my panic my foot slipped, and I was left hanging by a supporting bracket whilst my muscles screamed for release. My flailing feet found a brick which projected slightly from the wall and I resumed my climb, drenched in sweat. I could not tell how far I had come, or how much was left. My universe was a stretch of crumbling brick and a cast-iron pipe.

'Jump!' Holmes's voice shouted from below. Trusting him, I let go.

It felt as if I was hanging unsupported in mid-air for an eternity, but the drop could have been no more than a few feet. Holmes steadied me, then pulled me away across the garden towards the wall.

'Oy!' a voice yelled from the direction of the house. I ignored it, and pounded after Holmes. A hand caught my jacket, and I was pulled up short. Turning, I found myself in the grip of the greasy-haired footman.

'What's your game, then?' he panted. I planted a short jab to his solar plexus and a cross-cut to his jaw. He'd been in a scrap before, though, and shrugged the blows off without letting go.

Over his shoulder I saw Surd leave the house and lumber towards us. Holmes had reached the wall by now, and was urging me on. I redoubled my efforts.

Surd paused, stood upright, and gazed strangely at me. A warm breeze stirred my hair. It must have been a reflection of the sun, but it looked to me as if his eyes were *glowing*.

I tried to jerk myself out of the footman's grasp, and succeeded too well. Staggering backwards, I caught my foot in a clump of weeds. I sat down, hard.

It was that which saved my life.

As the footman grinned down at me I felt, rather than heard, a sudden *whumph*, and watched in disbelief as his head was engulfed in flames. He screamed and flailed his arms around. I scrabbled backwards through the garden on my hands and heels. He was jerking like a marionette in the hands of a drunkard. The flames were spreading down his shoulders and arms. As I watched, a fiery seam opened up across his chest. I was screaming

114

too, as Holmes hauled me up over the wall and pulled me along the road, out of sight of the burning man, but not out of range of his agonized shrieks.

Chapter 7

In which Watson and the Doctor attend a family reunion where much is explained and an unusual guest is introduced

Holmes dragged me around the corner and onto the street. My side was raw with the pain of running, and the old Jezail bullet wound in my leg throbbed with a hot, insistent beat. I kept gulping for air, but it seemed that no matter how fast I panted, it was not enough. My stomach was in revolt, and I paused for long enough to bring up a thin, acrid bile before Holmes pulled me on.

Eventually he slowed and allowed me to collapse against a lamp-post. He glanced back urgently. I tried to follow his gaze. Although my eyes were watering, I could see that the street behind us was empty. Everything seemed normal. The birds were singing, the sun shone upon scrubbed steps and a cat padded along a wall.

And yet, not five minutes walk from where we stood, a man was burning like a Roman candle.

'They do not seem to be pursuing us,' he said finally. Apart from a slight flush, he was unaffected by our escape. 'No doubt they are worried about attracting attention.'

'Holmes, who *are* they?'

He frowned.

'These are deep waters, Watson,' he said finally. 'I confess myself adrift. What we have seen today is not amenable to deductive logic, and yet . . .'

'And yet it happened.'

My breathing was coming under control now. My stamina had never fully recovered from my wounding near

Maiwand and a subsequent bout of typhoid in Peshawar. It never usually let me down when I made demands: it just extracted its price later. I would probably be laid up for a couple of days after this.

'I need to think,' he said distractedly.

'Perhaps Mycroft . . .' I ventured.

'No. No, not Mycroft . . .' Holmes glanced briefly at me, debating whether to let me in on something. I was well aware that there was some player in this mystery whose identity was being kept from me. 'But perhaps . . .'

The clatter of a four-wheeler made us both jump. It was coming from the opposite direction to Drummond Crescent, and I relaxed as Holmes hailed it with a short blast upon his whistle. It slowed to a halt as I pulled myself to my feet.

'Baker Street,' Holmes barked to the muffled cabbie, 'and double the fare if you make good time!'

He opened the door and aided me into the shadowed interior. I sank gratefully into the upholstery.

'Thank Heaven for small mercies,' Holmes muttered with heartfelt relief as the growler clattered off.

'Let's not get personal,' said a voice from the shadows. 'Small but perfectly formed, I think you'll find.'

A figure leaned forward into the light from the windows. I groped for my revolver, then remembered leaving it back at Baker Street. The four-wheeler turned a corner, and a shaft of sunlight suddenly illuminated our fellow-traveller's features.

'Doctor,' Holmes snapped, 'is that you?'

'Let's pretend it's not,' said the Doctor, 'and see what happens.'

'I presume that this is no accident.'

'Given the random nature of quantum interactions,' the Doctor mused as the cab turned again, and I saw the great hall of Euston Station through the window, 'can the confluence of any two events be truly described as anything but accidental?'

'I refuse to bandy words with you, Doctor. Give me a straight answer.'

117

'I prefer bandy legs to bandy words,' the Doctor murmured. 'An answer to what, Mr Holmes?'

'To my question.'

'You didn't ask any question.'

'I quite patently did.'

'Oh no you didn't!' the Doctor chanted, grinning.

'Oh yes I . . .' Holmes pulled himself together with an effort. 'I distinctly asked you what you were doing here.'

The Doctor gazed owlishly over the curved handle of his umbrella.

'No,' he said, 'you merely presumed that my presence here was no accident.'

'The question was implicit!' Holmes almost spat the words out.

'What question was implicit?'

'What are you doing in this cab?'

The cab swerved slightly as a growler overtook us at some speed. Our cabbie cursed the driver in earnest and graphic terms.

'I'm following someone. Or perhaps I should say some*thing*.'

'Pray explain yourself, Doctor.'

'Oh, I'm not sure I could do *that*.'

He smiled.

'However, perhaps Doctor Watson here has told you that he has been followed ever since we left Mrs Prendersly's house.'

Holmes shot a disappointed look at me.

'I have not been followed!' I protested. 'Holmes, you have taught me enough about detective work that I would be able to tell if any man were dogging my footsteps.'

Holmes smiled slightly.

'I myself have followed you during a number of our cases,' he said, 'in situations where I have anticipated some attack being made upon your person.'

'But I have seen nothing,' I exclaimed.

'That is what you may expect to see when I am following you,' he replied smugly.

'What makes you think that it is a man?' the Doctor interrupted.

'Because should any lady within a three mile radius show the slightest interest in Watson,' Holmes said, smirking, 'then he would know about it.'

The Doctor drew back the curtain of the trotting cab and indicated an alleyway ahead with his umbrella.

'Do you see?'

I peered towards the alley. It was mostly in shadow. I could make out no human form within it, just a pile of sticks set to form a rough stand, reminiscent in form of the iron 'cat' set in front of the fire at Baker Street upon which Holmes and I were wont to toast muffins on winter evenings. I had seen its like elsewhere, recently, but where?'

It vanished.

'Great Scott!' I exclaimed.

The Doctor pointed ahead to where a tree stood by a corner. A bundle of twigs was leaning up against it.

'A fast mover,' the Doctor said. 'Faster than the human eye can follow, at any rate. That probably indicates a race who are preyed upon by hunters of some sort.'

I tried to focus upon the . . . the animal, if the Doctor was to be believed . . . but it moved again.

'I've seen similar behaviour in Raston Robots,' the Doctor murmured, 'but never before in a living creature. The energy it requires is phenomenal.'

He leaned out of the window.

'Around the corner!' he yelled.

'Right, guv,' came the resigned voice of the cabbie.

The growler veered sharply to the left, and Holmes peered out of the window.

'I see nothing,' he said.

The Doctor pointed to a pile of refuse, beside which I again saw the twigs.

'But what *is* it?' I cried.

'I don't know. I pursued it here from the Diogenes Club. I think it had followed you there, and lost you.'

'You cannot possibly be serious.'

He gazed at me with eyes that seemed to contain the weight of the world within them.

'Can't I?'

I leaned back in my seat and tried to make sense of what I was being told. Try as I might, I could not fit this particular piece into the rational world-view which I held. It came from a different puzzle entirely.

The cab trotted on whilst I wrestled with my thoughts. The Doctor kept on yelling instructions out of the window, and Holmes tried and failed to see what we were following. Eventually we began to slow down, and I roused myself from my thoughts.

'Where are we?' I asked.

'Holborn,' Holmes and the Doctor said as one. I joined in as the growler halted: 'And the Library of St John the Beheaded.'

Of course. Where else?

Holmes stepped out into the street. I joined him. We were in more or less the same location in which Holmes and I had been dropped the day before. I took the Doctor's umbrella as he scrambled out of the carriage and, on a whim, examined it closely for signs of oil or a channel through which oil might emerge. The entire ferrule had been cast as a solid lump of brass: despite Holmes's claims, whatever the Doctor had used to calm the waters of the Serpentine, it was not this. I handed it back, and he smiled.

The Doctor paid the cabbie, who snorted, flicked his whip at his horses and drove off with some speed. He must have thought we were mad. I must admit I was beginning to suspect the same thing myself.

The sun was already heading for its rest and the deep chasms of the alleyways in front of us were shadowed and seething with an infestation of humanity. The stench was appalling.

'Well,' the Doctor said, 'there's no sign of the creature, but it seems clear where it went.'

'And you intend following?' Holmes snapped, stared down at the little man.

'Well,' the Doctor said softly, never quite looking up at

Holmes, 'we could pussyfoot around, check all approaches, scout the area, reconnoitre the target and all of those good things, and never get any closer to the heart of the mystery, or we could walk right in and ask some pointed questions. In the end, one way or another, we'll end up in there.'

'I'm going with you,' I said.

'Good man.' The Doctor picked his way carefully along the valley that led through the St Giles Rookery to the hidden Library of St John the Beheaded. I followed, of course. Holmes, after a moment's hesitation, overtook both the Doctor and I and led the way.

It took us twenty minutes to press our way through the throng of unwashed and unkempt humanity to the doorway that marked the only entrance and exit to the Library. As before, some form of immunity had been conferred upon us. Nobody would meet our eye: despite the crush of people, nobody touched us or spoke to us. Even the dogs seemed to ignore us.

At the door to the Library, I looked around. Two separate groups of lounging men were eyeing us. Jitter and Yeovil were still keeping watch upon the Library, and upon each other.

We entered into the darkness. Instantly we were engulfed in peace and warmth. instead of the stench of the Rookery, the musty, dusty smell of old books filled our nostrils. A black-robed man signed us in and led us along corridors lined with tottering piles of books, up stairways, down ramps and spiral staircases, through linked sets of rooms whose walls were invisible behind loaded shelves and finally up a ladder to a landing which bowed noticeably beneath the weight of the literature stacked upon it. He tapped discreetly upon a door, and withdrew.

'Come,' said a familiar voice. Holmes opened the door, and we entered.

The room was mercifully free of books. Panelled walls were interrupted only by a fireplace in which logs crackled comfortingly, and a table containing a selection of bottles and a gasogene. A desk stood at one end, in front of a massive tapestry which depicted some marbled palace. A high-backed, high-winged leather armchair had been placed between them, and turned so that its back was facing us.

Mycroft Holmes stood by the fireside. His hands were clasped behind him, and the flickering light cast his bloated shadow over us all.

'Holmes, Watson,' he nodded, 'and, I presume, the Doctor.'

'What is the meaning of this, Mycroft?' Holmes snapped, advancing across the carpet towards his brother. 'What are you doing here?'

'I followed a hunch.' Mycroft gestured towards the bottles. 'Please help yourselves to drinks, by the way. The Château Lafite is a century old, and looks fit to become one of the world's great vintages if we don't drink it all first.'

'Yes,' the Doctor murmured. 'We followed something too.'

Holmes remained glaring at his brother. The Doctor seemed engrossed in the tapestry behind the desk, and so I busied myself with a stiff whisky.

'Don't play the fool, Mycroft.' Holmes's face was contorted with rage. 'Save that for your political lords and masters. I demand an explanation!'

'What an enchanting tapestry,' the Doctor said, unheard by all except me.

As the accusations and recriminations flowed, I refreshed my drink with a spurt of aerated water from the gasogene and turned to look at the tapestry. If the Doctor thought fit to draw our attention to it, I presumed it must be important. Unlike Holmes, the Doctor seemed to prompt from behind rather than lead from the front.

From my position by the drinks table I was seeing the tapestry at an angle. The architecture of the place represented there was Indian, the style somewhat ponderous, and I could not see what kept the Doctor so raptly attentive. I confess that I lost interest. My gaze wandered across the panelled wall, the carpet, the desk, the chair and a handkerchief which had been carelessly left upon its arm. I sipped at the whisky: it had been a long day, and I had rarely needed a drink as much as I needed that one.

My gaze kept coming back to the handkerchief. I found myself idly wondering whose it was and why it had not been tidied away. I must have stared at it for a full minute or so before I realized that it wasn't a handkerchief at all. It was a gloved hand, perched motionless upon the arm of the chair. The owner was hidden from me by the high wings and, bereft of context, the hand was just an abstract white shape upon the maroon leather.

'Your spleen is misplaced, Sherlock,' Mycroft boomed. 'I know little more than you do. I merely tried to contact the last name upon the list of visitors to this Library, and found that he was still here in London. He has agreed to see us.'

There was something about his ironic tone of voice that made me suspect he found something amusing about the situation. Whilst he spoke, I surreptitiously shifted my position so that I could see the occupant of the chair.

'And where is he now, pray?' Holmes's voice was icy.

Out of the corner of my eye I could see that the Doctor was moving too, paralleling my course but on the other side of the chair. I glanced up at him. He nodded slightly towards the hand. His expression was calm. His habitually fatuous smile had vanished.

As I moved, a face came into view around the wing of the chair: such a familiar face that I had to glance back into the body of the room to check that Holmes was still there, eyeball to eyeball with Mycroft. I looked again at the occupant of the chair. The hawk-like profile, the supercilious expression, the deep lines around the closed eyes . . . it was as if the very essence of Sherlock Holmes sat before me, a distillation of my friend down to the basics that made up his character.

The Doctor appeared around the other side of the chair. He too looked back into the room, then across at me.

For a moment I entertained the thought that the face

was just a model, a wax bust perhaps, but then the eyes opened and shifted first to examine me and then the Doctor with an impassive gaze. A slight smile played around the corners of the mouth as, behind us, Mycroft Holmes called out, 'Ah, gentlemen, I see that you have discovered our host. May I present our elder brother, Sherringford Holmes!'

I was stunned, but perhaps I should not have been. It had taken Holmes long enough to reveal the existence of one brother. For him to avow another would have been asking too much.

Sherringford Holmes swung the chair around to face the room. In the light, I could see that he was twenty or so years older than Sherlock, and therefore thirteen years older than Mycroft. He had the build and demeanour of the one offset by the surprisingly mild brown eyes of the other. His hair was grey and close-cropped. Taller and thinner than either of his brothers, he dominated the room even whilst seated. His white gloves, unnecessary with his dark and rather severe suit and the travelling rug which hid his legs, added a touch of menace.

'Still an impetuous youth, eh, Sherlock?' he said in a dry, sardonic voice. 'And you, Mycroft, as smug and as well-fed as ever, I see.'

Holmes was incredulous: Mycroft amused. The Doctor glanced across at me, and murmured, 'I thought two of them was bad enough.'

'I am ... surprised ... to see you outside the North Riding,' Holmes said eventually. He seemed cowed. Turning to me apologetically, he remarked, 'There are some details of my family life to which I have not made you privy, Watson. My family derive from old Yorkshire stock. Sherringford chooses to live on as squire in the old family farmstead, whereas both Mycroft and I prefer the attractions of London.'

'Sherlock has always tried to disown his family,' Sherringford said to me. His eyes twinkled warmly, but his face appeared carved from an old, weathered, tree-trunk. 'It bothers the logical side of his nature to think that he might have irrational family loyalties above and beyond the clarion call of justice. Mycroft, of course ...' and he gazed at his corpulent brother, '... is rather ashamed of us in the exalted circles in which he now moves. That probably explains why they kept from you the fact that my name was upon the list of Library users provided by Mr Ambrose.'

Both Sherlock and Mycroft shifted slightly where they stood.

'You've a sharper brain than both of us put together, Sherringford, if only you would turn it outward upon the world rather than reserving it for crop rotation and sheep breeding,' Mycroft said grudgingly, 'but you still have not explained why you are here. What connection do you have with this Library?'

Sherringford sighed.

'Is this necessary, dear boy?' he asked.

'Very necessary. You may hold a vital clue as the identity of the thief and murderer, assuming them to be one and the same.'

'Very well. As you know, it has long been my ambition to write the history of our family. Indeed, I have had some success in tracing our roots back to Norman times. More recently, I discovered that one of our distant relatives married the Commander in Chief of the Naval Forces of His Holiness the Pope during the last century ...'

'Holmes mentioned it to me,' I blurted. 'When we were on the Pope's train a few days ago.'

Sherringford appeared surprised.

'I had always assumed that you never read the letters I sent you, Sherlock,' he said. 'Perhaps I have done you an injustice. No matter. Mention of His Holiness brings me to this Library, where I have been researching the time that our father spent in the service of the East India Company. His own journal is fragmentary, and three volumes are missing from the family archives. Eventually I tracked them down to here. I do not pretend to understand how they came to be in this Library, and Mr Ambrose will not enlighten me. I took rooms in London

125

and started to examine them. Mr Ambrose kindly put this room at my disposal.'

'But I thought that this Library contained only those documents which the Catholic Church claim could destabilize the world,' I said.

'Perhaps so.' Sherringford glanced up at me. Suffice it to say that our father's journals were amongst those stolen soon after I arrived, along with other documents relating to the Indian subcontinent, with special reference to myths and legends.'

'I have been investigating the theft of our *father's* diaries?' Holmes snapped.

'Amongst other documents, indeed. I suspect that it was my own interest in them that prompted the theft, and the interest of the Doctor here in some of the other documents.'

He glanced at the Doctor, who looked bashfully at the floor, clasped his hands before him and swung one leg to and fro.

'Mr Ambrose made me aware of his intention to notify the hierarchy of the Catholic Church of the thefts. I tried to dissuade him – the documents were not, after all, *that* important, but he would not be swayed. I must admit that I had not anticipated that the Pope himself would seek you out, Sherlock, and engage you to investigate the theft. This Library must be more important to them than I had thought.'

'Or, perhaps, the stolen books are,' the Doctor murmured. Sherringford cast him a sharp glance.

'Be that as it may,' he continued, 'you have quickly ascertained, more through luck than judgement, that the culprit is Baron Maupertuis. His motive is unclear, but no doubt it can be established by the constabulary in short order. Even better, you have regained two of the books. Well done, Sherlock.'

Mycroft, the Doctor and I all turned to stare at Holmes. He looked inclined to dissemble for a moment, then delved into a pocket and retrieved two small volumes, about the size of the palm of my hand. Sherringford waved an imperious hand, and Holmes passed them to him with obvious reluctance.

'I grabbed them from Maupertuis during the scuffle on top of the stairs,' he said. 'I had intended to produce them at an opportune moment, after I had examined them. I had no idea . . .'

'Yes,' Sherringford confirmed with an expression of relief upon his face, 'I recognize Father's handwriting. Thank you, dear boy.'

'How did you . . .' Mycroft began, but realizing that he would get no answer from Sherringford, he trailed into silence, shook his huge head, and continued, 'I wouldn't bank on prosecuting Maupertuis, or even regaining the rest of the books. My information is that the Baron is heading for India this very evening. The tickets have been booked for some time. I have men out looking for him, but since his run-in with Sherlock this afternoon, he seems to have gone to ground. I would not be surprised if he managed to slip through the web I have spun.'

'And what about the cowled man who was with him?' Holmes barked. Mycroft shook his head sorrowfully, jowls a-quiver.

'No sign of him.'

'A great shame,' Sherringford sighed. 'But at least I have father's journals back. I can complete the history of the Holmeses now.'

'I have accepted a commission,' Holmes said stiffly. 'I shall execute it, even if it means travelling to India to apprehend the villain.'

'Sherlock, be reasonable. The arm of the British Law is long, but not impossibly so. You have no powers . . .'

'Perhaps you are not aware of the fact, but two people have died in mysterious circumstances. I shall hold Maupertuis to account for that.'

'I concur,' Mycroft said, clapping Holmes on the shoulders. Holmes winced.

'The key to Maupertuis's actions,' he continued, 'would appear to be the information that Father's journals contained. Perhaps you could enlighten us, Sherringford.'

Sherringford shook his head.

'It is beyond your understanding. Let us leave it at that.'

'It is important.'

'I must agree with Sherlock,' Mycroft interjected. 'Reluctant as I am to do so. Knowledge of *why* Maupertuis requires those documents could lead us to him.'

Sherringford looked from one to the other.

'No,' he said. 'Leave it be.'

The Doctor stepped forward.

'Perhaps I can help,' he said. 'Your father claimed that there were places where the veil between this world and another could be broken, and that a determined man could cross over.'

We stared at him as if he was mad.

'The veil . . .' Sherlock said.

'This world and another?' Mycroft murmured.

'Ah . . .' Sherringford sighed. 'The Doctor . . . I should have realized. The journals . . .'

'I was young,' the Doctor said quietly, looking at the floor.

'You were old, according to our father.'

'Old, young, it's all a matter of perception. My granddaughter and I were touring India by elephant. We met your father, Siger Holmes, in the Officers' Mess at the British Army cantonment in Jabalhabad. He had been out in India for many years, working for the East India Company, despoiling the land and enslaving the natives. I was much more tolerant of injustice in those days. Your father had spent many hours in the company of the fakirs and wise men of the area. They told him of a place, up in the hills, where a man could step into another world, if he knew the right words. I was fascinated, but my granddaughter wished to travel on and I, foolishly, let her have her head. A lot of good it's done her now.' He shook his head. 'No matter. Where was I? Oh yes. I noticed that your father kept a journal, and I've been meaning to take a look at it for some years. There was a priest out in Cawnpore at the time: I suggested to him that your father was on the trail of something godless, and that the journals should be taken into safe keeping when your father died. I was a member of the Library, even then. I knew that the next time I was in the temporal vicinity, I could pop along and satisfy my curiosity. As I did. And here I am. Any questions?'

'Yes,' I said. 'Everything.'

'Who are you?' Mycroft asked. 'Your signature in the visitor's book at the entrance matches in every respect that of a member of the Diogenes, and let you look completely different. You talk calmly of things such as other worlds. You claim to have met our father in India, which would have been some forty-five years ago, and yet you stand before us aged no more than fifty. I repeat: who *are* you?'

'Have you ever read Poe?' the Doctor asked.

'I have no time for literature,' Mycroft replied.

'*I* have,' said Holmes.

I remembered listing Holmes's knowledge of literature as 'nil' shortly after we met. Either I had been wrong, or he had done a lot of catching up since then.

'In which case,' the Doctor continued, 'you may have come across his story *A Tale of the Ragged Mountains*. Of, if you prefer someone other than Poe, perhaps *The Clock That Went Backwards* and *An Uncommon Sort of Spectre* by Edward Page Mitchell.'

Holmes blinked: the only sign he gave of what I now know to have been a considerable shock.

'You claim to be some form of traveller . . . a traveller in *time*?'

'Yes,' the Doctor said simply. 'I do.'

'And further, do I understand that you claim other worlds, other planets such as Mars and Venus, can be reached with a *step*, and not a laborious and dangerous journey such as that described by Mr Verne in his book *From the Earth to the Moon*?'

Knowledge of astronomy – nil I had written six years ago. That list was looking increasingly suspect.

'If I fold a map of London such that Baker Street lies parallel to Wellington Street, could you not step straight from your lodgings into the Lyceum Theatre?' the Doctor

129

asked ingenuously. I was about to comment on the difference between a map and reality, but the Doctor continued, 'Siger claimed to have witnessed Indian fakirs pass through what he described as a "doorway", through which he could see a landscape that was unfamiliar to him. The landscape of another planet.'

'Balderdash,' Mycroft expostulated.

'Baron Maupertuis does not think so,' the Doctor said.

'What do you mean?'

The Doctor seemed to grow within his strange costume. A flicker of sparks from the fire caught his eyes and made them glow with a fierce, blue light.

'Baron Maupertuis is raising an army to invade that world in the name of colonial imperialism. He intends claiming it by force. It's a barbaric act, and it must be stopped. *I* shall stop it. Humanity's crimes will be appalling enough when it eventually develops space travel, but to have Victorian armies spreading unchecked through dimensional gateways is almost too much to bear. And if the planet in question is inhabited . . . even with your antiquated weapons, the slaughter of innocent indigents could be immense.'

There was a silence after the Doctor spoke in which the import of his words seemed to echo gently, like a struck bell.

'How did Maupertuis hear about it?' I asked, then cursed myself for getting sucked into the Doctor's deranged story.

'I don't know,' he mused. 'Somebody must have tipped him off. Perhaps this Madame Sosostris. She appears to know more about piercing the veil than I would have liked.'

'Or perhaps the cowled figure,' Holmes growled. 'I *knew* I should have stayed behind to unmask him!'

'I'm sorry,' Mycroft said, echoing my own thoughts, 'but this is all too preposterous for words. I'm not surprised that you've got sucked into it, Sherlock, you always were an excitable child, but you, Sherringford, you disappoint me. I always looked up to you as the hard-working member of the family, devoid of fancy. Now I find you accepting this lunatic's unsubstantiated word for a story more riddled with holes than a Gruyère. Talking of which, I do believe that I can hear a substantial dinner and a bottle of port calling to me, so if you'll excuse me . . .'

Mycroft began to manoeuvre his massive bulk towards the door, like a battleship attempting to come alongside a narrow dock.

'Unsubstantiated?' the Doctor said quietly, but with such force that Mycroft halted in his tracks. 'I think not. Perhaps you could introduce us to your other guest, Mr Holmes.'

Sherringford said nothing. The Doctor crossed the room and, grasping an edge of the tapestry, pulled it sharply to one side. The tapestry moved like a curtain, revealing an alcove in which stood . . .

. . . in which stood . . .

. . . I cannot bring myself to write the words, even now, without a great mental effort and a stiff tumbler of brandy. It has been said that if you shake a man's world hard enough, it is the man that crumbles, not the world. When the creature in the alcove walked forward, its five spindly legs jointed in odd directions and supporting a wrinkled and sagging body, the whole thing looking like something that a man with a handful of pipe-cleaners and a walnut might have modelled in an odd moment, I felt my mind teeter on the verge of collapse. A red mist rose before my eyes and the floor rocked beneath my feet. I could not believe what I was seeing, and yet I knew with a terrible certainty that it was no illusion or puppet. I knew, because I had seen it before. It had been hidden in the shadows outside Mrs Prendersly's house, it had moved across a fire on the other side of the Serpentine, it had been standing in the garden of the brothel in Drummond Crescent and we had followed it to the Library.

It had been following me.

'Gentlemen,' it said in a soft, sibilant voice as it halted in the centre of the room, 'we of Ry'leh need your help.'

Interlude

AF235/5/3/14
V-ON, BRD-ABLE, WPU = 546.7
VERBAL INPUT, COMPRESS AND SAVE
MILITARY LOG FILE EPSILON
CODE GREEN FIVE
ENABLE

I'm crouched on a catwalk about a hundred and fifty metres above the ground. Well, I say catwalk. Actually it's just three strips of wood running from side to side of one building to another, and they don't have cats here, just chocolate-flavoured animals with skates, and three-legged rats.

I tracked the things back to where they came from. Bit of a trek – couple of hundred klicks, I guess. It's a town, heavily fortified. The things live here and worship in this big temple thing. There's other creatures out on the plain – vicious things, killers. They seem to act like guards. Don't quite understand the set-up.

I'm hugging the wall beneath a slit-like window, trying to make out a conversation inside the temple-thing. I'm dictating this live, just in case something happens to me, like I fall, or I'm found out. I can hear voices inside the room. I'm holding the log-implant up to the window now.

'My children, you have done well. I am pleased.'

That's one's actually in the room. Odd-sounding voice, like it's not real at all. Like that old Pink Floyd song: there's someone in my head, but it's not me.

'When shall we bask again in your presence?'

Bloke's voice. Sounds like it's a long way away.

'Soon, very soon.'

'The armies are gathered.'

'You must see to them yourself. The brethren will be committed to moving me soon.'

'I would crave a request, oh luminous one.'

Crawler.

'Name it. You are my favoured son.'

God, they're all at it. It's like a convention of teachers' pets.

'There is interference here. I would ask that a few of the brethren are spared to protect this side of the gateway.'

'Interference? You displease me. The guards are mobilizing. Soon they may realize our plans. I am loath to spare any of the brethren.'

'A detective and a stranger called the Doctor are investigating our affairs. They are nothing, but I would not take chances with your safety at stake.'

Yay, Professor! Nice to know that it's all coming together.

'Nothing can threaten my safety, but this Doctor may pose problems. You may have four of the brethren. They will be waiting this side of the gateway ...'

There's a sort of scuffle, then the background noise in the room changes in some strange way I can't quite put my finger on. I think contact has been broken.

Just as I'm about to scramble down, the thing in the room murmurs something to itself.

'If only the gateway wasn't so dangerous,' *it says, like it's talking to itself. Self-pity just ladled on with a trowel.* 'If they sing one note wrong then I shall never escape this hellish place.'

Then it trails off into silence, and heavy breathing. Time to leave. I think I'll make my way back to the plain. To where the Doctor said things would be happening. Beats being bored, dunnit?'

DISABLE.

3531/748/AD

PIP.

. . . I caught a glimpse of the Doctor's diminutive
form at the prow of the ship.

Chapter 8

In which a journey is continued and a conversation is recalled

Bright morning sunshine hit the Mediterranean and shattered into a thousand silvery fragments. I raised a hand to shield my eyes and squinted into the glare. Across the glittering sea I could just make out the line of sand that marked the Egyptian coast. It seemed to float upon the water like a dirty brown scum.

We had engaged passage upon the Peninsula and Oriental Steam Navigation Company's ship *S.S. Matilda Briggs*. Two weeks out of Tilbury, bound for Bombay, we had just come within sight of Port Said – gateway to the Suez Canal. The town was just a jumble of sand-coloured buildings with the occasional dyed awning or flag fluttering in the breeze. Those passengers who had not made the trip before would no doubt flock to shore. The rest of us would be in the bar.

The stretch of water between the ship and the town was already littered with a flotsam of small boats, rafts and dinghies, all heading our way. I knew what to expect. Within the hour we would be invaded by all manner of Arab salesmen hawking insanitary food, unfashionable tropical clothing and insalubrious 'French photographs', along with an entourage of conjurors and beggars, gawkers and hangers-on. The crew would stand by to repel boarders, of course, but it would be of no avail. These peaceful but insistent pirates could not be stopped.

I turned, luxuriating in the slight movement of air across my skin. I was clad only in my nightshirt, as were all of the gentlemen on this side of the deck. Most of us had rolled up our bedding by now, and soon we would dress to allow the lascars to swab the decks. Any ladies brave enough to sleep above deck would, I presumed, be doing so on the other side of the ship.

We all had cabins, of course. Those of us who had made the trip before were travelling POSH – port out, starboard home – to escape direct sunlight. The weather had been comfortable for the first week, but as we passed Italy and Greece the calm, temperate climate of Europe had given way to the oppressive sultriness of the tropics and the captain had given permission for anybody who so wished to sleep on deck. Old hands like me knew the value of staking an immediate claim, and had bagged deckchairs in the lee of the superstructure of funnels and masts. The johnny-come-latelies would have to make do with the bare deck nearer the rails.

I dressed leisurely and wandered forward. The lascars were folding away the canvas partitions and beginning to hose down the decks. As I passed the lifeboats I caught a glimpse of the Doctor's diminutive form at the prow of the ship, standing in the same position that I had left him in the previous night.

'Did you sleep well?' I ventured, walking over to join him. Warm salt water sprayed my face as the *Matilda Briggs* cleaved the waves.

'I don't sleep,' he rejoined without taking his gaze from the glittering sea.

I took his measure. His eyes were bright, and his countenance ruddy, although his dark scowl suggested some inner turmoil. His hair was slicked back by the spume.

'I can provide you with a sleeping draught.'

'You misunderstand,' he said. 'I mean I *don't* sleep. Ever.'

'The human constitution is not designed to operate without rest.'

'Indeed,' he said dismissively, 'a crippling flaw which I would have advised against if the designer had consulted me first.'

138

I let that one pass, and gazed out across the water. I could make out small figures on the quayside now, swarming like ants. The heat was like an oppressive weight. A sudden gust of wind swept spray into my face, and I wiped my eyes with the back of my hand.

'What have you been doing all night, if not sleeping?' I said eventually, more to break the silence than for any other reason.

'Thinking.'

'Deep thoughts, then, to have taken so long.'

He turned his head and gazed at me. His eyes were violet in colour, shot through with tiny threads of orange. I had never seen their like before. I could see no expression that I recognized in them, nothing human at all.

'The deepest,' he said quietly. 'This journey worries me. We're too exposed. If Baron Maupertuis or his mysterious hooded colleague wish to stop us, we're sitting here like horda in a pit.'

'Like *what*?'

He smiled suddenly, and his face was transformed from sulky glower to almost imbecilic happiness.

'I mean, like china ducks in a shooting gallery.' He sighed. 'I won't feel safe until we get to Bombay.'

I gazed out across the water, but in my mind it was a different sea and I was just a boy.

'I remember, many years ago,' I murmured, more to myself than to the Doctor, 'travelling to Australia with my father and brother in a decrepit barque with a leaky hull and a cracked main spar. We rounded the Cape of Good Hope in the middle of a storm. I hope to God never to sail seas that rough again. I was as sick as a dog for weeks on end. I thought I was condemned to live on the ship forever, the journey took so long.'

A dash of sea-spray in my face pulled me back to reality.

'Nowadays, thanks to modern know-how,' I continued, 'a six-month journey from England to India can be accomplished in four weeks.'

A slight sneer seemed to caress the Doctor's lips.

'Modern know-how? You humans are all the same. Would it surprise you to learn that the first canal linking the Mediterranean to the Red Sea was dug over two thousand years ago? Not much more than a furrow in the sand, but they only had small ships in those days, not –' and he looked around him ' – miracles of technology such as this. That canal lasted for eight hundred years before falling into disuse. Do you think this one will last anywhere near as long?'

He cocked his head on one side and looked up at me with a bright, sparrow-like gaze. I opened my mouth to stammer an answer, but he continued speaking.

'Pharaoh Necho started to re-dig the canal a century later. The Canal of the Pharaohs, they called it. A hundred thousand men died in the digging. Perhaps they should have called it the Canal of the Dead. Necho was the son of old Psammitichus, you know? Lovely man: liked his drink, but then don't we all? Anyway, Darius took it over when Necho snuffed it, and my old friend Ptolemy took it over when Darius shuffled off this mortal coil. Or was taken upon the boat of the Night to join his ancestors, as I'm sure he would have liked to think of it. Ptolemy even built a lock in the canal: you probably thought that the English invented locks, didn't you?'

I shook my head, but the Doctor wasn't looking. He seemed to have got himself into a rut, and intended to keep talking until the subject was exhausted.

'Well, after about five hundred years the canal was impassable, and it wasn't until the Romans took over the country that anything more got done. They liked straight roads, did the Romans. They must have loved the idea of a canal. Emperor Trajan restored it, but a hundred years later it had silted up again. When the Moslems conquered Egypt the Caliph Omar ordered the governor, a little rat-faced man by the name of Amr-ibn-al-Aas as I recall, to ream it out again. They called it the Canal of the Prince of the Faithful, and it lasted until the eighth century. That was a thousand years ago. Your version of the Suez Canal has been open for – what? twenty years? – and you think you've given Mother Nature a bloody nose. What was it Shelley wrote? "Look upon my works, ye mighty, and despair!" Nothing endures, Doctor Watson, nothing endures.'

He stopped abruptly. I felt chastened.

'Your historical knowledge is exceptional,' I said eventually.

'I pick things up, here and there.'

'There's usually a trip arranged across land to see Cairo and the pyramids. You can pick up the ship again at Suez. Will you be signing up for it?'

He chuckled boyishly.

'I've had some nasty experiences around the pyramids,' he said.

The flotilla of home-made craft had almost reached us by now, or we had almost reached them. The sailors in the lead were already holding aloft their wares and shouting out how fine a bargain they were for two handsome gentlemen such as us. The beggars who had hitched lifts with them, or who piloted their own boats, were crying out for alms.

'*Baksheesh*!' they implored, their voices rising and falling like the wails of seagulls. '*Effendi, baksheesh!*'

'Breakfast?' I asked the Doctor.

He grimaced.

'With and without,' he murmured, 'have and have not.' Then, pulling himself together, 'Yes, I'll take breakfast with you.'

I was just about to lead the way when a lone voice seemed to rise above the chorus below. An English voice. A voice I recognized.

'Watson! *Watson*! Save some breakfast for me!'

I glanced over the side again. There, in the lead boat, was Holmes, dressed in a striped, one-piece bathing costume.

'Good Lord,' I muttered inanely.

'I saw him at sunrise,' the Doctor said. 'He said he was going to swim to shore for some exercise. He did ask me if I wanted to join him, but I declined.'

141

'Do you swim?' I asked.

He gazed up at me levelly.

'If pushed,' he replied. He turned and walked off abruptly towards where breakfast awaited. I made to follow, but as I did so I noticed that the wood of the rail where his hands had rested was perfectly dry, and the spray from the waves had dampened the deck all around except for two footprints where he had been standing.

Before we could even get to the hatch and descend to the saloon for breakfast, the vanguard of the local flotilla had glancingly docked with the *S.S. Matilda Briggs*. The crew attempted to fend it off with long poles, but a handful of entrepreneurs scurried up dangling cables and the anchor chain to the deck. There they proceeded to button-hole the passengers and display the cheap gewgaws and gimcracks that they had brought with them.

'Mr Mackenzie! Mr Mackenzie!'

An insistent merchant in a ragged robe plucked hold of my sleeve. For some reason they always referred to gentlemen as 'Mr Mackenzie' and ladies as 'Lillie Langtry.' I pushed past him and was three steps down the stairs when I realized that the Doctor had paused to watch. The Arab scrabbled around inside his robe for a moment, and brought out a day-old chick. I had seen hulley-gulley men before: their conjuring tricks with livestock were superficially fascinating, but no better than a second-rate music hall magician could have managed and certainly not deserving of reward. I watched impatiently as, before the Doctor's eager eye, he passed a hand in front of the chick and made it disappear. The Doctor smiled in innocent delight. The smell of bacon drifted up from the galley below. I sighed.

For the next few minutes, the hulley-gulley man plucked little cheeping bundles from his fist, his mouth, thin air, the Doctor's ears and the sleeves of passing passengers. He juggled with the creatures, carelessly dropping one over the side of the boat but carrying on like a trooper. He made them do tricks: running up his arm and back, weaving in and out of his fingers, climbing atop one

142

another to form a rough pyramid. The Doctor was entranced. Eventually the conjuror finished, threw them roughly into his pocket and held out an eager hand to the Doctor, saying, 'You like, Mr Mackenzie, you like?'

The Doctor nodded, beaming happily, and took off his hat. Reaching inside, he pulled out a large white rabbit and handed it to the astounded conjurer. As the man stared at it in bemusement, the Doctor walked over to join me with a quizzical smile upon his face.

We quitted the deck and made for the dining room. Holmes appeared just as I was chasing the remnants of my fried egg around the plate with some toast.

'I see that you haven't been wasting the morning,' he said cheerfully, pulling up a chair.

'Swimming obviously agrees with you,' I riposted. 'You should do more of it. Perhaps a dawn dip in the Serpentine every morning. As your physician, I strongly recommend it.'

'I have commented before upon your pawky sense of humour, Watson. I shall have to do something about it. Some bromide in your tea, perhaps.'

He attracted the attention of a waiter and ordered a large breakfast.

'I awoke early,' he continued, helping himself to a cup of coffee, 'and decided to take a constitutional swim. I encountered the local fleet on the way out and took the opportunity to test my spoken Egyptian.'

The Doctor smiled slightly as he gazed at the table. He did not seem to take Holmes terribly seriously.

'Baggage day, today,' I observed as Holmes's breakfast was delivered and he fell upon it like a wolf upon the fold.

'Babbage day?' The Doctor frowned. 'I wasn't counting on that.'

'*Baggage* day. The crew will bring the trunks containing our tropical wear up from the hold and replace them with the ones currently in our cabins. White drill suits replace black serge. Black cummerbunds oust waistcoats. Topees take over from trilbies.'

'Very poetic.' The Doctor looked down at his light-weight tropical suit. 'No change here, I'm afraid.'

I thought for a moment. Had the Doctor brought any luggage at all on board? Had I ever seen him in anything apart from the clothes he stood up in? My memory was hazy: I was sure that I was missing something obvious, but for the life of me, I could not remember what.

'Well,' Holmes said from around a mouthful of food, 'let us hope that this momentous day marks an end to the boredom of the past two weeks and the beginning of the *ennui* of the next two.'

Boredom? I had not been bored, although I had been aware of Holmes pacing the deck and the Doctor sitting cross-legged in a deck-chair for days on end, watching the waves. No, I had spent a large part of the journey chronicling the adventures which had taken place in London. The pages which you have already read were the result: written in longhand with a scratchy fountain pen in a ledger book brought with me for that purpose. The exercise had served to sharpen in my mind the questions that still remained: who was the hooded figure with whom Baron Maupertuis had met, and how did Maupertuis smuggle the books out of the Library of St John the Beheaded? As I had come to the end of the narrative, however – the section which detailed our discussions with Sherringford Holmes and his unusual guest in the Library – I found myself reluctant to write. I kept looking for excuses to leave my cabin. I would walk along the promenade, exchanging small-talk with the ladies and taking part in the daily lottery based upon the previous day's run. I would visit the bar and listen to the ribald talk of the men. I would sit out on deck with Holmes and the Doctor, trying to follow their abstruse discussions. I even attended the fancy-dress ball – the social high spot of the voyage – although I would not normally be seen dead at such an event. I did not wish to write of that conversation.

Now, some years later, I have gained a little perspective. Perhaps so many stranger things have happened to me since that I can recall the scene in the Library with less disquiet than before. Or perhaps I have forgotten much of what made me shy away from it. Whatever the reason, I now find it easier to cast my mind back to the week before we left London, to that oak-lined room, deep in the heart of the Library of St John the Beheaded, and the moment when the alien creature stepped out from behind the curtain.

'Gentlemen,' it said in a hissy voice, 'we of Ry'leh need your help.'

Mycroft Holmes, as I recall, spilled his wine on the carpet. Holmes leaned forward eagerly, his eyes scanning over every inch of the creature's flesh. Sherringford Holmes sat back smugly in his armchair and the Doctor, apart from raising his eyebrows, did nothing.

And I? The floor seemed to shift beneath my feet, swaying as if in an earthquake. I could hear a faint buzzing in my ears, and a small, still voice in the back of my mind kept repeating a snatch of poetry by the French writer Victor Hugo:

> *Every globe revolving round a star,*
> *Is home to a humanity near yet far.*

until I could hear nothing else. The only way I could snap back to reality was by considering the creature as a biological entity and using my medical knowledge to determine something of its life. You may gather from this that on one level, at least, I was convinced that it was real.

'My name is K'tcar'ch,' it hissed. I noted that the voice coincided with the pulsation of a small membrane beneath its sack-like body. This I labelled as the creature's mouth, although I could see no method of ingesting food.

'As the esteemed Doctor has explained, our planets are distant from one another in space, so distant that light itself would take many centuries to travel from us to you, and yet in the folds of what we call the space-time continuum, we are only a step away.' K'tcar'ch took a step forward. I watched with fascination how its spindly legs bent. Each of the five 'joints' was in fact composed of two hinges, one above the other, each acting in a different plane so that the limbs could move in any direction.

'We are a peaceful race. We have no weapons, no armies, no desire to fight. All we have are philosophers. All we wish to conquer is the realm of thought.'

'Which planet did you say you came from?' the Doctor queried.

'Ry'leh,' K'tchar'ch said. 'It is a world of no great cosmic significance. We keep ourselves to ourselves. We do not encourage visitors.'

'The name is familiar,' the Doctor said, scowling. 'If either of my brains were working, I'd remember.'

The three Holmes brothers stared at him.

'Brains?' Mycroft said finally.

'One for everyday use and one for best.' The Doctor smiled sweetly at the alien. 'Please continue.'

'Our rulers, the Great Cogitators, have known for many of your millenniums that travel between worlds was possible by using certain sounds which resonate at the basal frequency of the cosmos. These sounds can pull together areas of space which are separate, causing gateways which intrepid travellers can pass through. In that way we have met great scholars from many other races. Sherringford Holmes is one of them.'

I noted in passing that K'tcar'ch's skin was a mottled grey colour, apart from a few hard red patches which were streaked with black veins. I speculated that they might be indications of old age, injury or illness.

'How long has this been going on, Sherringford?' There was a tone of disapproval in Holmes's voice.

'Some years now,' Sherringford replied.

'And why did you not wish to tell us of this earlier?' Sherringford shrugged.

'Would you have believed me?' he asked.

Mycroft snorted.

'I remember once or twice writing to you, asking if I could visit . . .'

146

'. . . Whenever your guilty conscience got the better of you, dear boy,' Sherringford murmured.

'. . . And receiving a telegram saying that you had company. I never realized,' and he took a sip of his wine, 'how far your company had travelled to be with you.'

There was a short silence. A log cracked in the fire, making us all jump. All except K'tcar'ch. I became fascinated by what might be blood vessels beneath its skin, arranged not like the branches of a tree, as with humanity, but like a cobweb.

'We became aware, not so long ago,' it continued, 'that others had discovered how to open gateways between our worlds. Reports reached the Great Cogitators that small bands of humans were appearing in the wastelands of our planet. They appeared to be drawing maps. It did not take us long to realize what their intentions were.'

'Invasion,' Mycroft said. 'The first resort of fools.'

'I have been aware for some time,' Holmes revealed, 'that the criminal underclasses seemed to be severely underpopulated. Several thousand thugs and bruisers appeared to be lying low. I now suspect that they have been shipped secretly to India as part of Maupertuis's army.'

He smiled grimly.

'I wonder what Professor Moriarty makes of it all,' he added.

K'tcar'ch flexed its five limbs slightly, as a man might shift position to ease a cramp. I had been trying to work out how its musculature was arranged, but its baggy, canvas-like skin was thick enough to hide the movements of the muscles – if muscles they were.

'We asked friend Sherringford for aid. We asked him to find out who was planning to destroy the peace of Ry'leh.'

'I knew that Father had seen evidence of the joining of worlds,' Sherringford continued. 'It was by reading his journals that I had started experimenting, and it was those experiments that attracted the attention of the Ry'lehans. So I started with the Library, only to find that Father's journals had been stolen. And that's where you came in, Sherlock.'

I wondered, but did not dare ask, why K'tcar'ch had been following me.

'So where does this get us?' said Mycroft with characteristic directness, leaning back against the panelling. It creaked beneath its weight. 'If we accept the evidence of Mr ... er ... Mr K'tcar'ch, was it ...?'

The alien clicked in what seemed to be approval.

'... And add it to what we already know, then Baron Maupertuis is attempting to raise an army and invade the peaceful world of Ry'leh. Now, I must point out that Her Majesty's Government has no treaty or alliance with Ry'leh to my certain knowledge, and therefore, whilst we would treat any request for assistance with great sympathy, we can take no action that might result in an inconvenient diplomatic situation.'

'You have summed the situation up correctly,' Sherringford agreed.

The Doctor strode across to confront Mycroft. He was almost half the man's size and half his width, but in some strange way he seemed to tower over the diplomat.

'And so while you debate, a world is invaded? Is this British justice? Has the Mother of Parliaments been replaced by a talking shop for indecisive milksops?'

Mycroft glanced across to where Sherlock Holmes stood.

'All I can do is to advise on the official Government position,' he boomed. 'We have no control over independent agents, of course. Just as we cannot dictate the actions of Baron Maupertuis on an alien planet, neither can we legislate against the actions of a band of doughty adventurers who might wish to prevent his actions.' He waved a flipper-like hand. 'If, by any chance, you need assistance, I believe a big-game hunting expedition funded by the Diogenes is making its way across India even as we speak.'

A slow smile spread across the Doctor's face.

'So,' he said, 'once again it comes down to this: a handful

of us against the forces of darkness.' He turned to Mycroft. 'Can you arrange for our passports to India?'

'Of course, but why?'

'Because Baron Maupertuis is headed there.'

'Forgive me,' I interrupted, 'but I am puzzled.' Everybody turned to look at me as if they had forgotten that I was there, even K'tcar'ch, although I had seen no evidence of eyes. 'If these gateways can be opened from anywhere, as Sherringford Holmes seemed to indicate, then why is Baron Maupertuis heading for India?'

'A good question,' Holmes said, turning to his brother, 'and one which had been puzzling me.'

'The location is important,' K'tcar'ch replied, 'because of the relative positions of the two planets in the space-time continuum. It can only be done between India and a portion of Ry'leh that we call the Plain of Leng.'

Holmes frowned slightly, but nodded.

'A fair answer,' he said.

'We will need the books, of course,' said the Doctor, skipping across the room and retrieving them from the desk. Sherringford made to grab at them with his gloved hands, but the Doctor shoved them into a pocket of his coat and moved away.

'Surely they would be safer here . . .' Sherringford began, but Mycroft interrupted him.

'No,' he said heavily. 'If they contain information about where or how this amazing feat is to be engineered, then our brave and unofficial troops will be needing them.'

'We of Ry'leh thank you, gentlemen,' said K'tcar'ch. 'You will live in our thoughts forever.'

'I hope to live a great deal more substantially than that,' the Doctor muttered.

From there the discussion moved on. Sherringford tried once again to dissuade us from the journey, whilst K'tcar'ch remained strangely silent. Mycroft revealed that the Government had been aware that a larger than usual number of people had left the country bound for India, but in their infinite wisdom had decided not to pursue the matter. The Doctor and I debated how Maupertuis had

149

got to hear about the books, but without success. After that I remember little of our packing and making arrangements. Now, as I sat with the Doctor and Holmes in the dining room of the *Matilda Briggs*, the time in between the revelations in the Library and that moment seemed like a dream, glimpsed but dimly through a glass.

'We should start planning our itinerary for when we reach Bombay,' Holmes said, breaking into my reverie. 'Maupertuis is on the *S.S. Soudan*, and will have three days' head start on us. Watson, you're something of an expert on matters Indian. How do you suppose we can find the Baron?'

'Well, we'll need to make contact with a local man, preferably one with some influence, to make arrangements over travel and suggest likely places to check – hotels and suchlike. Then it's a question of whether Maupertuis is covering his trail or not. If he's not expecting to be followed we should be able to determine his location fairly quickly.' I shook my head. 'If only we had been able to send a message ahead to prepare the way for us.'

'We did,' said the Doctor.

'What do you mean?'

'Didn't I tell you? How remiss of me. I have already been in contact with a friend of mine, who is waiting for us in Bombay. With any luck, she will be able to tell us everything we want to know.'

'And how did you know that you would need someone in Bombay?' Holmes snapped. 'Or was it sheer coincidence?'

The Doctor gazed up at him with an ageless expression on his face, and it was Holmes who looked away first.

'Oh,' said the Doctor finally, 'I have a girl in every port.'

That was the first we heard of Professor Bernice Summerfield, a woman who was to become very dear to my heart in a very short space of time. As she is to play such an important part in the continuation of this narrative, it is only fair that I should let her introduce herself in her own words, from the diary to which she has so very kindly allowed me access.

. . . a shadow passed across the face of the moon,
like a bird with a broken wing. It was carrying
something limp.

Chapter 9

In which a new voice takes up the story, and the Doctor is picked up in a hotel

Extract from the diary of Bernice Summerfield
Bombay smells.

Yes, I know I've written the same words every morning for the past two months, but they come from the heart. Bombay smells. It smells like no other place I've ever visited. I mean, I've lived everywhere from the slums of Avernus, where dead bodies are left to rot where they drop, to a squat above a thoat-gelding shop in the mires of Zellen VIII, but I've never come across such an all-pervading, gut-wrenching stench of decay and unwashed flesh. That's what coming home means, if Earth is really home any more. Unwashed aliens just smell exotic, and more often than not rotting alien food tastes better than it does fresh. What I'm trying to say is that even a nasty alien stink has something extraordinary about it, but sheer human squalor just turns the stomach.

Especially when I'm in a city whose people think that the function of a river is to act as a latrine upstream and a launderette downstream. I'd complain, but I'm too polite. I have to be polite. In 1887, on Earth, everybody is polite. Well, everybody that matters.

But that's the general gripe over with. On to the specific.

The P&O representative told me yesterday that the *Matilda Briggs* was due in after lunch. Today, after all the usual guff – sleeping in, being woken up by the *mamlet* who wanted to clean my room, dressing, having lunch – I wandered through town towards the dock. The route was

lined with shops, hotels and offices designed to be impressive, in a gothic sort of way. I had to push my way through
crowds of workers, soldiers, beggars, lepers, amputees,
bullocks and pariah dogs before I could pass across the
vast open square to where the ocean rolled greasily
against the pylons of the dock. A battalion of British
Army soldiers was waiting to embark on one of the ships.
Their pennants fluttered limply in the breeze, their
brightly coloured uniforms were already soaked in sweat,
and one in three was yellow and wasted by malaria.
Behind them the Deccan mountains pierced the pure blue
membrane of the sky. I could almost believe that the sharp
silhouette of their peaks against the sky was actually the
coastline poking out into the waters of the Arabian Sea,
and I was standing on the mountain tops, looking downwards, far away from where the Doctor would arrive.

Eventually I wandered across to the Ballard Pier, surrounded by eager shipping agents and harassed represen-
tatives from P&O, Bibby's and British India. I was
clutching the Doctor's telegram in my hand. Every few
minutes I unfolded it and checked again that I hadn't got
the name of the ship wrong. Odd thoughts kept chasing
their tails around my mind. What if there'd been a problem and the Doctor hadn't boarded in the end? What if
I'd misinterpreted his instructions and I was supposed to
be somewhere else? What if he was angry at me for
wasting my time when I could have presented him with a
solution to his problems, all wrapped up with a little pink
bow? What if . . . ?

I knew the real problem, of course. I was scared of
seeing him again. No reason: just scared.

A beggar approached, imploring me for alms. His head
was covered in running sores. His thick hair rippled gently
in the breeze. I looked closer, and recoiled as some of it
took flight, buzzing briefly around his head before settling
again to feed. Flies – the ever-present curse of India. I
waved him away, feeling a sudden knife-stab of guilt.
There were tens of thousands of people in Bombay. I

couldn't help all of them. That was the true evil. Not Daleks, not Hoothi. Poverty and powerlessness.

From the dock I gazed out across the Arabian Sea, out to where the heat haze and the waves merged to form an ambiguous boundary, neither sea nor sky, half in this universe and half somewhere else. I was hypnotized by it. My mind blurred like the landscape. The *Matilda Briggs* had grown into a cloud the size of a man's hand before I woke up. Within an hour it was a metal leviathan, belching steam as it wallowed up to the dock.

And there he was, on deck, waving his umbrella to attract my attention. He was exactly as I had remembered. I felt my breath catch in my throat. He was small and he was trouble, but I'd missed him.

Ropes were flung back and forth, and there was a lot of jostling and bustling, most of it unproductive. Eventually a gangplank was in place.

After he disembarked he scurried up as if to give me a great big hug, but skidded to a halt inches from me and raised his hat instead.

'Doctor Livingstone, I presume?' he said.

'Doctor Doctor, I presume?' I replied.

He gazed at me for a while, checking me out from head to toe and from side to side. Around us, disembarking families wandered like ducklings.

'There's something different about you. He frowned, and looked me over again. 'Don't tell me. Let me guess.'

'Doctor, I . . .'

'It's the hair, isn't it? You've had your hair done.'

'No, I . . .'

'I know! You've lost weight.'

I sighed.

'No Doctor, I'm disguised as a man.'

He checked again.

'Are you? How very Shakespearian. Well, I'm sure you've got a good reason.'

'I have,' I said. 'Have you got any idea how they treat women in this era? You asked me to pretend to be one of the girls who comes out looking for a husband. It was

155

so *demeaning*. Do you know what the men call those girls? 'The fishing fleet'. The ones who can't find husbands are called 'returned empties'. It's disgusting. I was going mad!'

He scowled.

'You were supposed to remain inconspicuous.'

'I knocked a man out in the hotel bar one night. After that, I decided I was more inconspicuous disguised as a man than as a woman.'

The Doctor winced.

'I'm sure I don't want to know,' he said, 'but I know you're going to tell me anyway.'

'I'd just popped in for a drink when a cigar-chomping moron tried to feel me up. I politely told him to go away, but he persisted. So I told him not so politely. I think he's out of the hospital now.'

The ship's horn suddenly blasted out a sound like a drashig's mating call. The Doctor winced.

'I did tell you that women are decorative, rather than productive, in this society,' he said, scrunching his hat up in his hands. 'They do not drink alone in bars, and they most emphatically do not get involved in unseemly brawls.'

'They don't do anything! I checked out of the hotel that night, and checked into another one the next day dressed like this.'

'Where did you get the clothes?'

'From my erstwhile admirer's room. I figured he wouldn't be needing them for a while, not with his ribs in that state. So I liberated them.'

The Doctor grinned slightly, and so did I. His eyes twinkled. I couldn't match that, so I waggled my ears instead. And that's how Sherlock Holmes and Doctor Watson found us, grinning like loons and performing tricks with bits of our anatomy.

I knew there was something familiar about them when they approached, gazing around at the spectacle that was Bombay, sweat glossing their faces and a bevy of Indian porters hauling their trunks after them. Watson could have been anyone – he was handsome, in a reserved sort of

156

way, but he wouldn't stand out in a crowd – but Holmes's aquiline profile and incisive, penetrating gaze hit some deep vein of memory in me.

They were both wearing lightweight tropical suits and those topees that make people look like mushrooms. The Doctor (who once took me to a planet where mushrooms look like people, but that's another story) was dressed in his usual linen suit and white hat, and somehow looked less out of place here than usual. I could tell from the way that Holmes and Watson were standing that they were wearing those bizarre spinal pads that were supposed to protect your spine from the sun and facilitate the circulation of air, but ended up making you feel even more uncomfortable and just as hot.

'Professor Bernice Summerfield, Mr Sherlock Holmes and Doctor John Watson,' the Doctor announced.

Holmes nodded coolly at me. Watson was flustered. I wondered why for a second, then remembered that I was dressed as a man. He didn't know whether to shake my hand or kiss it.

'Professor Summerfield,' he said finally, clasping his hands behind his back. 'I'm enchanted.'

By his expression he had me figured for a lesbian. Normally it wouldn't bother me – bisexuality is the norm in my era – but I knew from my researches that the eighteen eighties weren't quite as enlightened. Ask Oscar Wilde.

'I'm working undercover,' I confided, 'and call me Bennie.' He smiled, relieved.

'Where do we go from here?' he asked.

'I've booked rooms for you in my hotel,' I replied. 'I suggest that you wash and brush up, then we'll meet for dinner.'

He nodded.

'I've been looking forward to tasting Indian food again for the entire voyage,' he confided as I gestured to the nearest group of *tikka-gharis* – four wheeled horse-drawn carriages similar to hansom cabs. After a brief argument, one of them headed towards us. Watson made to take my arm, but caught himself just in time.

'You've been here before?' I asked.

'Indeed. I passed through here on my way to Afghanistan. I fought in the Second Afghan Campaign, you know?'

'How brave.' I was being mildly sarcastic, but he didn't seem to notice.

'I was wounded in the shoulder with a jezail bullet. Still gives me gyp. Nasty things.'

'Jezail?'

'It's a sort of long-barrelled musket, fired from a rest.'

The carriage pulled up beside us and the driver busied himself fighting with Holmes and Watson's bearers for possession of the bags. Like all lower-caste Indians, they wore turbans and *dhotis* – long lengths of cloth wound around their midriffs – and little else. It had taken me a month to stop regarding them as unfortunate accident victims. Still it could be worse. The Ook of the Crallis Sector wear clothes made out of small mammals, still alive but stitched together.

Eventually, after I was satisfied that our luggage was all present and correct, I gave the driver the name of my hotel and made him repeat it. Then we set off. Watson, after fussing about trying to order the men around and failing, had bagged the seat beside me.

'You speak Hindi?' he asked, miffed, as I settled into the seat and we moved off.

'Hindustani, Punjabi, Urdu, Bengali, Tamil, Telegu, Sontaran,' I said. 'I speak them all. It's a gift.'

'Oh.'

He turned to gaze out at the sun-baked streets. I refrained from telling him that I hadn't had to learn a word: somehow my association with the Doctor had enabled me to understand any language I came across. If only he could bottle it and sell it.

I met the three of them in the hotel bar after they had unpacked. I had a couple of minutes alone amid the bamboo furniture and brass fittings before they turned up. A large sheet of woven bamboo strips swung back and forth from a hinge on the ceiling, twitched by a rope which passed through a hole in the wall to where some hapless *punkah-wallah* sat outside. There was a piano in one corner, its legs sitting in saucers of water to stop white ants from climbing up and eating their way through the instrument. A couple of florid ex-Army types with huge walrus moustaches were sitting over by it, balancing their G&Ts on the lid, to the obvious displeasure of the splendidly turbaned and uniformed *khitmagar* behind the bar. They nodded at me in a companionable way. If only they knew, I thought.

The Doctor arrived first. I suspect that he didn't even go inside his room. I'd never seen him sleep, or carry a spare set of clothes, or brush his teeth, or do any of those things that we all take for granted. I also suspect that when the rest of humanity go to bed the Doctor is either out wandering the streets or standing in a corner of his room until sunrise.

'So, what do you think of India, then?' he asked, settling himself cross-legged into a cane chair.

'I've been all over the universe with you, Doctor, and Earth in the nineteenth century is the most alien place I've ever seen.'

He smiled.

'I've always had a soft spot for it,' he confided. 'There's such a sense of infinite possibility. You feel that almost anything could evolve from this morass of science and superstition. It showcases humanity at its best, and at its worst. What about India? What have you found out?'

'I thought from the histories that it was all fairly simple. The Mughal dynasty ruled the continent for some three centuries until 1756, when their last emperor was dethroned by the British. After that, the British East India Company was allowed to run the country on behalf of the British Government for the lucrative jute, indigo and spice trade. Just like IMC and Lucifer, I guess. There was a native revolt in 1857. You know why?'

He nodded, but I continued anyway.

159

'It was so stupid: the sepoy troops believed that a new type of cartridge case was coated with either beef fat or pork fat. Of course, the Hindus couldn't touch pork and the Muslims couldn't touch beef. So they revolted – literally. After the mutiny the British Army was sent in to oversee the place, the British East India Company was abolished and the Indian Civil Service was set up. Lots of young British lads were sent out to keep the place running for the next century, and then India achieved dominion status in 1947.'

He nodded.

'You seem to have grasped the basics.'

'But that's too simplistic!' I protested. 'This place is a jigsaw. At the moment there are fourteen British-run provinces like Baluchistan, Sind, Madras, Bombay and Bengal, each with its own distinct character and geography, divided into a total of two hundred and fifty-six districts. Alongside that, there are five hundred and sixty-two *native* states like Rajputana, Mysore and Hyderabad, lorded over by an assortment of Nizams, Walis, Jams, Rajahs, Maharajahs, Ackonds, Ranas, Raos and Mehtars. Across both the British-run and the native areas, there are over two *thousand* three hundred castes, sects, and creeds, each with its own distinctive customs and religious injunctions. This isn't a country, it's a universe in its own right!'

He grinned.

'I've always thought of India as a microcosm,' he said.

'Of what?'

'If I ever find out, I'll be a wiser man than I am now.'

I grimaced.

'Yes, very deep,' said a voice behind me. I looked up to find Holmes and Watson standing over me.

'Please,' the Doctor waved to two free seats, 'join us.'

I bought the drinks. The Doctor's careful with his money. Well, to be fair, I remember a time in a bar on Barrabas Gamma when I shamed him into paying for his round. He rummaged around in his pockets, cursing all the time, and threw a handful of change onto the counter.

Unfortunately it was Cimliss money, and most of it jumped off and ran into the shadows before we could recapture it. I hear they were still finding loose change reproducing in dark corners for weeks.

Where was I? Oh yes, Holmes and Watson. They sat down, and we drank for a few minutes, swapping pleasantries. Eventually Holmes turned to me.

'As you probably know,' he said, 'we have pursued a certain gentleman here from Tilbury.'

'Baron Maupertuis,' I prompted.

'Indeed.' He cast a sour glance at me. I decided to interrupt him as much as possible.

'You are aware of the circumstances?' he continued.

'The Library, the thefts, the aliens, blah, blah, blah . . .'
He controlled himself with some difficulty.

'Has Baron Maupertuis passed through Bombay, to your knowledge?'

I took a small notebook out of my pocket and began to read from it.

'I was proceeding in an easterly direction ᵤg Rivett-Karnac Road when –'

'Benny . . .' the Doctor murmured. Holmes's snort punctuated the Doctor's warning.

'Oh very well.' I put the notebook away. 'Volume five of the Doctor's telegraph message told me that the guy with the title was on board the *S.S. Soudan*, which docked two days ago. I had the Baron paged, and spotted him when he disembarked. He was accompanied by a great hulking deaf mute named Surd. They headed here, which is one of the reasons why I did too. They stayed for one night, ate nothing and met nobody. They rose early the next morning, took a rickshaw to the station and bought tickets for Calcutta. They caught the next train out of Bombay. That's all I know.'

'An admirable summary,' Holmes said, leaning back in his chair and closing his eyes. 'Calcutta is not their destination, of course.'

'Why not?' Watson asked.

'It is a coastal city at the other end of the line from

161

Bombay. Had Baron Maupertuis wished to travel to Calcutta, he could have travelled there directly by ship, a quicker and more comfortable journey. No, the tickets are a blind. I have no doubt that they caught the train – ' he glanced sharply over at me, and I nodded. ' – but I would suggest that they disembarked somewhere along the line.'

I handed him a list of stations.

'Difficult to tell from this what their destination might have been,' he continued. 'The train passes through the major British provinces on both sides of the continent, and also the belt of native states in between. What about luggage?'

'Two trunks. Heavy by the looks of them. Surd carried them as though they were nothing.'

'Contents?'

'I . . . I don't know.'

Holmes half-opened his eyes and gazed at me.

'All right,' I admitted, 'nothing but clothing and medical supplies. I sneaked a look.'

He frowned.

'No books?'

'No books.'

'No maps?'

'No maps.'

'No weapons?'

'No weapons.'

'Hmmm.'

Watson and the Doctor exchanged puzzled glances.

'I would have expected more equipment for a planned invasion,' Holmes explained. 'Their lack does not rule out our theory, of course – the material may have been sent on ahead – but evidence would have been reassuring.'

'What about the twenty large boxes addressed to the station-master at Jabalhabad that were loaded in the guard's van?'

I was the focus of all eyes.

'What makes you think that they were associated with Baron Maupertuis?' Holmes snapped.

162

'The address labels were in his handwriting. I checked them against the hotel register.'

He smiled.

'An excellent piece of work. I could not have wished for a better agent in place.'

The Doctor raised his eyebrows at me. I smiled back. We went to dinner happy.

We discussed all sorts of things while eating. Over lobster curry with various spicy vegetable dishes Holmes and the Doctor had a running argument – good-natured on the Doctor's side but I'm not sure about Holmes – about the Basque language and its relationship to the ancient Cornish tongue while John Watson asked me what I thought about women playing sphairixtike for the first time. When I admitted my ignorance of the game he told me that it had recently been renamed lawn tennis. I was still none the wiser. Over a pudding made from boiled rice and coconut flavoured with rose essence we all discussed the recent testing of a machine-gun by Hiram Maxim. Watson ventured to suggest that it would put an end to war. I pointed out that the same was said of the bow and arrow. The Doctor muttered something about Z-bombs. We finished off with coffee and liqueurs, and debated our next move. The general concensus was that we should follow the Baron and his tame gorilla to Hyderabad in the morning.

When Holmes and Watson lit up foul-smelling cheroots, I decided to retire for the night. The Doctor and I walked through the decaying splendour of the hotel to the door of his room.

'You seem to be fitting in to the era very well,' he said.

'No thanks to you. Your Time-Lord gift of the gab is fine for alien languages but lousy on slang. I've got a feeling I'm a few decades out.'

'I'm sure nobody will notice.'

'And what's all this boat travel rubbish? Why not travel straight here in the TARDIS?'

He smiled.

'It was a ship, not a boat. And I prefer the scenic route.'

By that time we had reached his room. I didn't want to say goodnight, so I told him what I had been thinking earlier, about him probably not sleeping, or even using his room. He smiled bashfully.

'I'll be doing some reading tonight,' he said, patting his pocket. 'I've brought Siger Holmes's journals with me. Siger was definitely on to something. I've been trying to make out the underlying meaning of the chants he reproduces. I'm close, but there's still something I'm missing.'

'Do you intend getting any sleep at all?'

'I tell people that I don't sleep,' he admitted, 'but that's just for effect. I do sleep. Once every hundred years I have a kip for a decade or so.'

He yawned suddenly.

'Excuse me,' he said, 'I'm suddenly very tired.'

He vanished into his room like a rabbit down a burrow.

I stood for a moment, staring at the door in bewilderment, then turned and headed off to my room.

I was four steps down the corridor when a sudden series of crashes and thuds made me whirl and run back to the Doctor's room. I put my ear to the door. It sounded as if there was a fight going on, and it sounded as though it was a big one.

'Doctor?' I yelled. No answer.

Glass crashed inside. I kicked the door down.

The window was broken and the furniture was smashed to matchwood apart from a wardrobe which had unaccountably escaped intact. The carpet was ripped into tatters. The Doctor was standing in the centre of the room with his umbrella held in front of him like a sabre. Before him, crouched but still brushing the ceiling, was a creature from a nightmare. It was a venomous crimson colour, armoured like a crustacean, and it walked on the taloned points of its billowing leathery wings. A coiled tail with a wicked spiked club of flesh on the end brushed the floor beneath its glossy body. Its head was low-slung and vicious. It had no eyes, no mouth, just a set of thorny growths which jutted forward and seemed to swing from the Doctor to me and back, weighing up the threat.

It shuffled round to face me, the claws on the ends of its wings churning the carpet.

'Get out, Benny,' the Doctor hissed, 'it's me the rakshassa wants.'

'Rakshassa?'

'Yes, rakshassa. Plural, rakshassi. A type of Hindu demon.'

'Well, whatever it is, it'll have to get through me to get to you.'

I shuffled forward. It shuffled back. Emboldened, I shuffled forward a bit more.

It leaped for my throat, using its tail as a spring.

I dived for the floor, and felt the acrid wind of its passage as the rakshassa passed over my head and hit the doorframe. Plaster showered me. I rolled to one side. The rakshassa whirled and smashed the floor where I had been lying with its spiked tail. I scrambled to my feet. The thorny protrusions that were its face were all pointed at me and trembling. I backed slowly towards the cool breeze from the window, planning to dive out. It anticipated me, and manoeuvred me sideways, towards a corner.

I quickly scanned the room. The Doctor had vanished, sensible man. There was nothing large enough to use as a weapon save the wardrobe, and try as I might, I couldn't think of a realistic attack strategy with it. The rakshassa raised itself up on the tips of its wings and lashed its tail, preparing to strike.

I took a deep breath.

The wardrobe door slammed open and the Doctor leaped out, yelling at the top of his voice and whirling his umbrella around his head. He fetched the rakshassa an almighty crack across one of the spikes of its snout. It snapped off in a spray of pink, watery fluid. The rakshassa screamed – an undulating, unearthly noise like a nail in the eardrum – and shuffled backwards to the window.

'Thanks,' I breathed.

'I got you into this,' he admitted with a rare display of honesty, 'so I feel duty-bound to get you out.'

The rakshassa sprang across the room toward us. I tried to push the Doctor out of the way, but he took hold of my arm and shoved me into the wardrobe. The last thing I saw before the door clicked shut was the Doctor lunging towards one of the creature's wings with his umbrella, trying to puncture the membrane, then I was engulfed by darkness.

It took me less than a minute to smash the door down from the inside, and for most of that time I could hear nothing apart from my own laboured breathing. When I finally emerged, wreathed in splinters, the room was empty. I staggered to the window. The cool breeze and the scent of flowers were like something from a fairy-tale. All outside was darkness, apart from the occasional flicker of a fire. The stars glowed like the sun on waves.

And a shadow passed across the face of the moon, like a bird with a broken wing. It was carrying something limp.

The outside of the building reminded me of an
enormous wedding cake . . .

Chapter 10

In which a train once again figures in the narrative and our heroes encounter a few familiar faces

A continuation of the reminiscences of John H. Watson, M.D.

Water trickled like perspiration down the ice block in the centre of the carriage. I watched the drops as they hesitantly felt their way across the shining surface to join the water sloshing in the tray beneath. They had eroded the base of the block to such an extent that the ice was balanced unsteadily upon a thin stem. I had been waiting for it to topple for three hours now, hypnotized by its slow disintegration, my head hanging heavily and rocking back and forth with the motion of the carriage.

Professor Summerfield shifted slightly on the leather sofa opposite and murmured something in her sleep. Her eyes flicked restlessly behind closed lids. Her face was flushed and glossy. Holmes, sitting in a cane chair in the corner, was also dozing. What else was there to do in this relentless heat?

Something moved past the window. I peered intently, if somewhat blearily, through the gauze and the glass at one of the many banyans that dotted the plains. Its branches swelled straight out into a root system without feeling in need of a trunk. The sight cheered me momentarily: anything that interrupted the landscape and provided a moment of interest was worth cherishing. I gazed around for some other distraction but, apart from the scarlet blaze of a mohar tree in the distance, nothing else broke the monotony of the dusty brown landscape. The distant horizon was so straight that it could have been drawn by a draughtsman, and the sky so impossibly blue that it had to have been painted.

We were travelling on the Imperial Indian Mail train through the *mofussil* – the up-country area of India – and had been doing so for most of three days now. We had a first-class, four-berth compartment with bathroom attached. The train had left Bombay just after sunrise, heading north-east towards the town of Gadawara through the states of Nagpur and Bhopal. From Gadawara we had continued onwards towards Benares, where the train would turn south-east for the final leg to Calcutta. We would not be on it. Our goal was the small state of Jabalhabad, a few hundred miles west of Benares and a good day or so from our current position in the hinterland of purgatory.

The ice suddenly fell over with a loud *splash*! Professor Summerfield jerked awake and glared at me. Holmes merely raised an eyebrow.

I have refrained from describing Professor Summerfield, trusting rather to her own words to paint a self-portrait. Suffice it to say that I found her fascinating. Her refreshing bluntness, her vivacity and her cynicism were all at odds with the refined (dare I say prim?) ladies that I was used to dealing with back in London. To give an example: when Holmes and I burst into the Doctor's hotel room back in Bombay to find the Doctor missing and the room wrecked, I had expected to find her in a state of womanly distress. In fact she was systematically reducing the remains of the wardrobe to splinters whilst cursing fit to strike a midshipman deaf. I did not recognize many of the epithets she employed, but their meaning was clear. During the subsequent discussion, in which it was decided that the Doctor had probably been kidnapped by some creature allied to Baron Maupertuis and that our best course of action was to follow the Baron and hope to find the Doctor, it was Professor Summerfield who took the lead. Holmes and I merely stood and marvelled at her single-minded determination and her profanity.

Lest I give the impression that Professor Summerfield – or Bernice, as she encouraged me to call her – was in some way unwomanly, let me add that she was also exceedingly attractive, despite her male attire. If she was, as the Doctor had led us to believe, a denizen of the future, then all I can do is echo Shakespeare's cry: 'O brave new world, that has such people in't.'

'We would appear to be slowing,' Holmes said.

'I don't believe so,' I replied. Glancing out of the window, however, I could see the track far ahead curving towards a clutter of buildings on the horizon. 'Good Lord, we do appear to be heading for a station. How did you know?'

'You may have noticed that a proportion of the steam from the furnace has been making its way into the carriage. You had not? No matter. For the past few minutes I have detected a reduction in the amount of steam, leading me to believe that we are slowing down enough that the cloud has risen out of the way before our carriage passes through it. A trifling deduction.' He sniffed slightly. 'I am considering writing a monograph on the tell-tale odour of various types of coal. Our fuel derives, I believe, from the seams at Rewa.'

Bernice snorted. I could tell that she wasn't taking Holmes seriously.

'Who wants to move up to the restaurant car?' she asked. 'I could do with some food and a decent drink.'

'And a new block of ice,' I added.

Holmes checked his watch.

'According to our schedule, the next station after this one should be some three hours away. That should give us enough time for a leisurely lunch.'

I freshened myself up in the bathroom and emerged just as we were pulling into the outskirts of whatever cantonment or village this was. The train jerked as the engineer applied the brakes. The place looked deserted. Huts and hovels were empty, and the only signs of life were the pi-dogs pacing us as we approached the station. Far in the distance, half-hidden by the dust and the heat-haze, I thought I could make out the regular lines of a British Army fort with a flag hanging limply from its pole.

We jerked again, and dropped to a crawl. The station crept closer and I could suddenly see where everybody was. The platform was alive with a churning crowd. Hordes of people poured out from the shaded area beneath the platform itself, careless of the approaching train. I shivered, reminded of a stream of cockroaches. A terrific gabble of voices in a Babel of languages assailed our ears.

'Tahsa char, garumi garum!'

'Pahn biri! Pahn biri!'

Hindi pani, Musselman pani!'

'Beecham Sahib ki gooli!'

I turned to Professor ... to Bernice.

'Did I hear the word *Beecham*?'

'Indeed you did,' she replied. 'He's offering us some of Mr Beecham's little pills. Does that mean anything to you?'

'Indigestion tablets!' I laughed.

'Well, you learn something every day,' she murmured. 'But is it ever useful?'

The train shuddered to a halt. Beyond our window a wall of faces watched us with no hint of decorum. We stepped out onto the station. It felt good to be able to stretch my legs. Holmes locked the door and the crowd cleared a way for us as we made our way along the platform towards the dining car. Beggars implored us for alms, sweetmeat sellers beseeched us to buy their wares and those Indians who were travelling onward from here in the third or fourth-class carriages bustled around with broken umbrellas looking self-important. Those unable or unwilling to pay for tickets on the train were climbing onto the roof, joining those who had been there since Bombay. Ahead of us a small cadre of British soldiers had disembarked and were trying to form up into some sort of order before marching off.

172

Bernice dickered with an ice seller, then borrowed a key to the carriage from Holmes so that she could leave it to cool the compartment down. We found the dining car and secured a table in its cool, dark interior.

'This may seem like a stupid question,' Bernice said when she joined us, 'but how come we can find huge great blocks of ice at these one-horse towns in the middle of God's own oven?'

'The Carres Ice Machine,' Holmes pronounced. He loved to show off. 'Most stations will have one. The device contains a cylinder of ammonia which is heated and then plunged into water. The liquid, confined in such a small space, absorbs heat from the metal and then the water in order to evaporate, causing the water to turn to ice. A most interesting device. I was involved in a case recently where a Mr Matthew Jolly was murdered with a Carres Ice Machine.'

'I don't recall that case, Holmes,' I said stiffly.

'I believe I did draw some of its features to your attention.'

The train quivered, and began to heave its vast bulk out of the station. For the first half of our journey, station-masters had politely sought Holmes's permission for the train to leave their stations – something to do with him being the most senior traveller. Somebody more important must have joined the train at Gadawara, as we were no longer bothered by such requests.

A great wail went up outside. I looked out of the window, only to find it blocked by a swarm of naked children who clung to the frame and gazed at us with imploring spaniel eyes. The stewards rushed up and down the aisle rapping their little knuckles with spoons until they dropped away, screeching.

'Don't leave me in suspense!' Bernice said eagerly. 'What happened to Mr Jolly?'

'His wife, Josephine, had purchased one of the devices some months beforehand. On the night in question, she waited until he fell asleep downstairs, as was his habit

173

after drinking heavily, then manoeuvred the device so that his head was resting in the water. She then activated it.'

'You don't mean . . .?' She was aghast.

'His brain froze whilst he slept. She waited until the water had thawed again and then moved the machine back to the pantry. He was found dead by the maid in the morning without a mark upon him.'

Bernice shivered. 'What a way to go. Why did she do it?'

'Every evening for ten years he had taken his false teeth out after dinner and hurled them at her. One day she finally snapped. I cannot find it in my heart to blame her. Knowing how much I get on Watson's nerves, I occasionally wonder if my last sight on this Earth will be of him standing at the foot of my bed with a syringe of cyanide in his hand.'

I coughed to hide my smile.

'And how did you detect the crime?' I asked, trying to deflect the conversation into a different course.

'Mr Jolly had a glass eye. The rapid cooling, followed by the significant rise in temperature as the rising sun shone upon it, had caused it to crack.'

'You're making it up,' said Bernice.

At that moment a figure loomed into sight behind Holmes's back. I half rose from my seat. The figure clapped its hands on my shoulders and shook me.

'Watson! Good God man, what on Earth are you doing here? Do you *live* on trains?'

That florid face: that huge walrus moustache. A conversation about violins.

'Warburton?'

'The very same.'

In amazement I cast my mind back to the Orient Express, where our adventure had started a few short weeks ago. Colonel Warburton had been one of the passengers. He and his wife had been on their way to . . .

'Jabalhabad, wasn't it?' Holmes said casually. 'I remember you saying that you were the Resident there.'

'Mr Holmes, good to see you again. Yes indeed, we've

174

been back for a few weeks now. I left the *memsahib* sorting out the mess the servants had made of the bungalow and headed to Gadawara on business. I must say, I hadn't expected to find you here. On a case are you? The little lady *will* be pleased. I thought you were on your way back to dear old Blighty after that odd business with the other train. You never did tell us what that was about. Some secret assignation, was it?'

I could see from Holmes's slightly glassy expression that he wasn't entirely sure which question to duck.

'We find ourselves heading for Jabalhabad as well,' he said finally. 'Quite a coincidence that we should come across each other again.'

'Mind if I join you?'

Warburton eased his large frame into the seat opposite Bernice.

'I don't believe I've had the pleasure,' he continued, extending a hand.

'Colonel Warburton,' I blustered, 'this is ... er, Miss ... er *Mis*ter ...'

'Benny Summerfield,' said Bernice, shaking Warburton's hand. He winced slightly at her firm grip.

'Pleased to meet you. Are you part of the mystery too?' Bernice smiled.

'Aren't we all?' she said.

The stewards came along then, and took our orders for lunch. We dined well and drank even better. Holmes and Bernice ordered copious quantities of weak whisky and soda: Warburton and I, old hands at the tropics, stuck with gin and tonic. Many was the toast to the Queen-Empress that afternoon. Warburton was eager to find out what we were doing heading for Jabalhabad, but Bernice was singularly skilled at turning the subject back to the Colonel's life in India. He told us about the Nizam of Jabalhabad, who ruled the small province to which Warburton had been posted as the representative of Her Majesty. God alone knows how it happened, but by the time lunch was over, Bernice had inveigled Warburton into inviting us to stay at his bungalow and attend an official dinner – a *burrah khana*, or big feast, as Warburton called it – to be thrown by the Nizam in a few days time. Even Holmes was taken aback at the speed with which Bernice worked. I felt my admiration for her growing by leaps and bounds.

Extract from the diary of Bernice Summerfield
It's been a couple of days since I've made an entry. The Doctor's kidnapping threw me into a furious rage, most of which I took out on poor Watson. We decided that the best thing to do was to follow the plan and set off for Jabalhabad, there to try and trace the recipient of Maupertuis's boxes.

We staggered off the train at Jabalhabad two days ago. I haven't had time to make an entry since then. The area is hilly and green, and a lot cooler than the plains. Have you ever heard of a heat rash? It's like lots of little pimples, all over your body, so close together that you can't slip a pin in between them. Itches like crazy. Thank God Watson's a medic.

We've been spending our time trying to find those boxes. A couple of locals say they saw them being unloaded at the station, but after that the trail goes cold. Jabalhabad is a large place, and they could be anywhere.

Colonel Warburton has been a brick (is that what they say in Victorian times? Slang is so ephemeral: here today, old hat tomorrow). His bungalow is a large, rambling, mud-brick building. It's thatched on top, has walls made of reeds covered in cow-dung and whitewash, rattan screens over the windows and muslin ceilings. I've always been good on materials. I'm sure there are things living up there: I can hear them moving round, and the muslin shifts from time to time as if something has rested its weight on it.

We were introduced to Warburton's secretary: a thin, rather diffident man who held out his hand for shaking like a man might proffer a rather dubious anchovy. His name was Smithee. I decided straight away that I didn't like him: an impression reinforced at dinner yesterday when a kitehawk managed to swoop down and make off with the roast as it was being carried along the veranda from the kitchen to the dining room. The rest of us cursed and raved, but Smithee walked calmly out and took pot-shots at the bird with a revolver. It wouldn't have done any good – the food would have been inedible, whatever happened – but it seemed to make him feel better.

I was getting ready for this beanfeast tonight up at the Great Panjandrum's palace, when I realized I was missing something. I'd 'liberated' a full set of evening wear from my disappointed suitor back in Bombay, and studied enough men one night to know where the cummerbund went, but somehow I must have dropped one of the cuff-links. I couldn't eat dinner with one sleeve dangling in the soup, so I decided to borrow one from Colonel Warburton. I wandered around the bungalow – which was TARDIS-like in its deceptively spacious interior – but couldn't find him. I popped out on to the veranda, just in case he was out there, and found his wife Gloria instead. Her hair was piled high on her head, and she was wearing a floor-length gown and white gloves up to her elbows. That didn't faze me: the archaeology of fashion was a minor interest of mine. What *did* surprise me slightly was the Indian bearer on his knees beside her with his hands under her gown.

'Could I trouble you for a cuff . . .' I said, and trailed off into silence. Don't get me wrong – I'm no prude, it's just that all the research I've ever done on nineteenth-century Earth suggests that the British were sexually repressed to an incredible degree. The rumour that they put little skirts on piano legs is probably just a joke, but I did read once about a Victorian woman who had little suits made for her goldfish, and another one in France who set aside money in her will for clothes for snowmen. Faced with this scene, I had one of those moments I've started getting recently where, for a second, I don't know where or when I am.

She must have seen my confusion and mistaken it for embarrassment.

'Insecticide,' she confided. 'Keeps the mosquitoes out.'

The bearer withdrew his hands, stood up and bowed to her. He was holding a large, syringe-like object. I could see faint wisps of a white, powdery substance creeping from beneath her hem.

'How do you avoid the snakes?' I asked snappily. 'Use a mongoose?'

She smiled and changed the subject.

'My husband and Mr Holmes are taking a turn around the grounds. Was there something that I could help you with?'

I smiled back.

'No, thank you,' I said, turning to go.

There was an explosion somewhere nearby. The sound was curiously dull and flat. I could smell an acrid, burnt odour. Cordite? Mrs Warburton and I looked at each other.

I ran to where the sound had come from. It was the bathroom. There was nothing but an ominous silence in there now. I kicked the door in.

Watson was sitting squeezed into the little hip bath. He was naked and held a gun. He didn't seem to register my presence. Instead, he was staring fixedly across the room. I followed his gaze.

At first I thought two snakes were coiling furiously on the floor, over by the large wooden object that was euphemistically known as the 'thunderbox'. Then I saw the blood, and realized that he had shot a cobra in half.

'Good shooting,' I said, noticing the rip in the muslin above his head through which the snake had dropped.

Watson, realizing that I was there, grabbed for a towel to hide his modesty.

'I'll see about getting that mongoose,' Mrs Warburton's voice sang out from the veranda.

A continuation of the reminiscences of John H. Watson, M.D.

We had taken a carriage up from the bungalow; Warburton, his wife, his secretary, Holmes, Bernice and myself.

178

The outside of the building reminded me of an enormous wedding cake: all tiers and pillars and white surfaces edged with rose. Two other men had arrived at the same time as us. Warburton introduced us: one was a red-headed missionary named O'Connor and the other, Lord John Roxton, was hunting big game up in the hills. A man in long golden robes and a white turban met us beneath a huge scalloped archway.

'I am Ghulam Haidar,' he said, bowing deeply to us. 'The Nizam bids you welcome.

Turning, he led us into a vast cloistered area whose lofty ceiling was held up by row upon row of the most impressively carved marble pillars. It was as if we had entered a forest of marble. I half expected to see a deer peering around one of them, or a squirrel running up it.

We were escorted through cool corridors to a large room hung with embroidered material. A low table in the centre of the room was piled high with food of all descriptions. A man in his early twenties was sat on a large golden cushion. His robes were silken and flowed around him like a glossy waterfall when he moved. Jewels glinted in the fold of his turban, and a single emerald the size of an egg sat at its front.

'Mr Holmes, I'm so pleased to meet you at last,' he said with a broad smile.

Holmes, if he was surprised at the Nizam's urbanity, did not show it. Bowing deeply, he said, 'I am honoured to meet your Highness. May I compliment you upon your excellent grasp of our clumsy tongue.'

Tir Ram laughed joyfully.

'I was at Eton and Cambridge, Mr Holmes. I even speak Hindi with an accent now.'

He shook our hands firmly, to the obvious displeasure of Ghulam Haidar.

Shortly we sat cross-legged for the meal. I shall not dwell overmuch upon it. Silent servants waited on us. The food was unusual but not unappealing, and the drink flowed freely. Most Indian rulers are either Hindu or Muslim, but the Nizam seemed to have few religious injunctions concerning what he could or could not eat. I sampled yellow, red, green and purple rices, along with various spiced meats which were served swimming in butter and garnished with sultanas and almonds. Coffee was served between every course. Lord Roxton proved an interesting conversationalist, and gave me some tips on hunting tigers that I hope I will never need to use. He was a strange man: small and wiry, with a thin moustache and a small goatee beard.

'An experienced man can tell from the blood marks where the animal is hit, young fellow my lad,' he said, leaning forward and poking me in the chest for emphasis. 'If it's been hit in the lungs the blood will be dark red and frothy, if in the liver or near the heart it will be dark red, sort of port-wine colour, if you get my drift. If you're unlucky enough to bag it in the stomach the blood comes out pale and watery, and anywhere else it will be a light red. Fancy a day's shootin' tomorrow?'

Bernice seemed to be locked into conversation with Warburton's secretary, Smithee. She occasionally cast glances in my direction which started off as entreaties to rescue her and ended up as threats of physical violence if I did not. Holmes, Warburton and Tir Ram carried on a spirited discussion concerning the British public school tradition, and Mr O'Connor sat in silence for most of the meal. From what I knew of the byzantine complexities of British Empire etiquette, he was considerably further down the social scale than Warburton and, by extension, us. He obviously felt it.

Oddly enough, on the couple of occasions I glanced over to find O'Connor gazing at me with a faintly sardonic expression. There was something about his eyes that I recognized: they blinked too much. I noted Holmes staring at him as well, but he had no more success in identifying the man than I did. Surely hair of that fiery hue would not be easy to forget?

I found myself at one stage talking to Tir Ram. He was a handsome youth, self-assured and pleasant with a sly sense of humour.

'Quite a change from Cambridge,' I ventured.

'Indeed,' he replied. 'I was all set for a career in the City when my father and elder brother both succumbed to cholera.'

Nodding in acceptance of my hasty but sincere condolences, he continued: 'I was forced to return to my home to rule what must seem to you like a minor province with nothing in particular to recommend it. A degree in the classics hardly prepared me for the life I now lead.'

'I'm sure there are many people who would envy you this life,' I said, indicating our surroundings.

'One can tire so easily of ostentation. My favourite place in the whole palace is a cave below us. The local *thuggee* sects used to worship Kali in it. They claim that rakshassi have appeared to them there.'

'Rakshassi?' Bernice asked. I had not realized that she was listening to the conversation. I thought I saw a warning glance pass between Warburton and the Nizam, but I could have been mistaken.

'Hindu demons,' Tir Ram said with a sad smile. 'A part of our heritage. I must not scoff. Ghulam Haidar will be angry with me.'

Colonel Warburton interrupted to tell us all a rambling and rather bawdy story about his early experiences in the army. The meal ground to a halt, and servants brought round betel nuts on silver trays. Holmes, O'Connor and Roxton popped them in their mouths and chewed wholeheartedly. Bernice and I refused. I know that they are meant to aid digestion, but I am also aware of their narcotic properties. I had an orderly in Afghanistan who became addicted to them.

I felt the need to visit a cloakroom. Divining my need, Ghulam Haidar assigned a white-gowned servant as my guide.

As I left the impressively marbled room, I looked around for the servant. The corridor stretched in both directions: empty. I cursed. I had not bothered memorizing the route from the banquet, assuming as I did that I would be led back.

181

I waited for a few minutes, then began to walk in what I thought was the right direction. Even if it was wrong, I would probably come across a servant of some description who could point me in the right direction. The only thing to be careful of was wandering into the Nizam's harem, if Nizams *had* harems. If they did, the ladies would undoubtedly be attractive.

It was in this frame of mind that I turned a corner and walked straight into a massive figure. Before I could react, a hand was clamped across my mouth and I was thrown against the wall. A red haze filled my vision. I tried to shake my head to clear the ringing in my ears, but the hand was forcing my head up the wall. I tried to take a breath, but could not. My feet left the floor. My chest felt as if a rope were being tightened around it. I tried to bite the hand, in fact I *did* bite it, but the pressure on my jaw increased remorselessly.

And then my eyes came level with the face of my assailant, and all thoughts of my own pain vanished.

It was Baron Maupertuis's manservant: Surd. Seen close-up, his face was a jigsaw-puzzle of stitches and glossy scar tissue. His hair, however, was full bodied and fine, hanging in a neatly coiffured fringe across his eyes. His glowing eyes.

I lashed out with my feet and caught him in the groin. He grunted, and shifted his grip. I tried to wriggle free, but his fingers were pressing into the soft flesh beneath my jawbone. The pain was incredible. I started to slip in and out of consciousness: every few seconds I would awake from a nightmare of agony only to find that it was real. The skin of my neck was pulled so taut that I expected to feel it pop at any moment and find his fingers clutching at my windpipe.

The next time I awoke it was to find myself sprawled against the cool stone wall. The agony was receding like a wave across a beach, always promising to return.

Surd was a shadow blocking out the light. From behind him, a soft caress of a voice said:

'Your friend Holmes is slightly less stupid than I had

assumed. You should be in Calcutta by now, searching for me in vain. I had not anticipated that you would penetrate my alliance with the Nizam so soon.'

I tried to speak, but the tide rolled over me again and withdrew, leaving me shivering.

A white-gloved hand raised my chin.

'You are pathetic,' Maupertuis said. I managed to raise my eyes to gaze into his thin, impassive face. His eyes seemed to sear into me: somehow the experience of his gaze was worse than all the pain.

'We can find out everything we want from your friends. How much they know. What sort of threat they pose. Why they persist in following me, when all I want is to restore the glory of the Empire and extend it to other worlds. You, however, are irrelevant.'

I could hear the rustle of a gown as somebody else joined us. For a moment I had hopes of a rescue, until Ghulam Haidar said, 'The Nizam wishes you to join him. The others have been subdued.'

'Very well,' Maupertuis whispered.

The gloved hand released my chin. I tried to keep my head up, but failed. I could feel consciousness ebbing away with the tide.

'Surd,' he said, turning away, 'kill him.'

Chapter 11

In which Holmes stands alongside an unlikely companion and a villain falls for Bernice and Watson

Maupertuis's footsteps echoed like the knell of some huge bell as he walked away. Surd bent to take my head in his huge hands. I tried to look away, but I was fascinated by the twin sparks glowing deep in his eyes. I swear that I could *feel* the heat emanating from them. I made my peace with God. Surd, seeing my acceptance of my fate in my expression, smiled twistedly.

I wrenched my head downwards as the fire in Surd's eyes reached out for me. Heat seared the top of my head and I heard a massive *crack!* as the wall exploded. Chips of marble stung the back of my neck. Surd fell backwards, clutching at his face. Blood seeped between his fingers. I scuttled crab-fashion away from him and climbed precariously to my feet. The last things I saw before I staggered away were a scorched pit in the wall where my head had been resting, and Surd wiping the blood from his eyes and looking round for me.

I ran. I ran until my lungs were heaving and my legs would not carry me any more. I ran until I no longer knew where I was. I ran until I could no longer avoid the question that pounded in my brain to the exclusion of all else. What could I do now?

My funk lasted for a few minutes, and left me shaking and soaked with perspiration. What pulled me back from the brink was the thought of my friends in danger. I could not allow anything to happen to them. I am not a brave man by any stretch of the imagination – I have seen too much pain and suffering in the lives of others to face it with equanimity myself – but there is a code that transcends all else, and its name is honour. I had to help.

I slipped quietly through the whited sepulchre of the Nizam's palace, looking for some stretch of corridor or ornamental feature that I recognized. The coolness, the silence and the marble all reminded me of the Diogenes Club back in London. I found the comparison strangely calming. The sweat dried on my brow and a warm glow of courage spread through my limbs. Perhaps I *could* achieve something after all.

A sound! I hesitated, then flung myself flat against the wall as a small group of people emerged from an adjoining corridor ahead. I was as invisible as a fly on a bedsheet, but fortunately they turned and walked in the other direction.

Three burly servants dressed in *dhotis* and turbans were carrying the unconscious bodies of Holmes, Roxton and the red-headed O'Connor over their shoulders. Four others were attempting to carry Bernice, who was swearing and struggling in their grip. My mind raced to piece together the evidence. If Bernice and I were conscious and the rest were not . . . The betel nut! It must have been drugged, and the absence of Warburton, his wife and secretary, and the Nizam would suggest that they were implicated in the scheme. I cursed bitterly. How could Warburton, a fellow officer, have allowed himself to fall amongst thieves in this way?

I followed the group for a few minutes. Watching Bernice's face, I noticed when she caught sight of me over the shoulder of one of her captors. To her credit, she made no sign. In fact she twisted more furiously in their grip, slowing them down so that the other three bearers trudged on ahead with their unfeeling loads. We were passing a junction at the time, and she caught my eye for a fraction of a second and flicked her head. What did she want? I frowned in an exaggerated manner. She rolled her eyes, then flicked her gaze quickly towards one branch of the corridor and back to me. Did she want me to go by a different path, overtake the bearers and somehow rescue her? Flattered as I was by her confidence in my skills, I could not see it working. And surely she was no more familiar with the layout of the palace than I was. I shook my head.

'Hide round the corner, you damn fool!' she yelled in the middle of her stream of profanity, then carried on blaspheming without drawing breath.

I nipped back to the corner and turned to the right, halting a few yards down. Hopefully the bearers were unfamiliar with English. Or perhaps Bernice assumed that they were as stupid as I was.

Extract from the diary of Bernice Summerfield
After Watson finally got the hint and hid round the corner, I managed to twist my body around and push against one wall with both legs. The guys carrying me were thrown off-balance, and staggered towards the other wall. It was easy for me to deliberately catch my head against the marble. A spike of sick pain shot through me. I went limp. It was all I could do to keep myself conscious.

The guys stopped and had a little conference. One of them tried yelling after the ones up ahead, but they were too far away and didn't respond. The guys patted my face a couple of times but I didn't react. When one of them raised my eyelids I had rolled my eyes so far up that I could almost see the roots of my hair. They talked a bit more, then four of them turned and headed back along the corridor while the fifth sighed deeply and picked me up again. I almost laughed in relief: it had worked! Gazing through my eyelashes at the departing Indians, I suddenly realized why. There was a very convincing streak of fresh blood marring the stonework of the corridor, and I suddenly became aware of something warm trickling down my neck. There is such a thing as being *too* convincing.

When the four who had left vanished around a corner – not the one that Watson had gone around, thank God – I went into action.

A continuation of the reminiscences of John H. Watson, M.D.

I watched with a palpable sense of relief as the four bearers turned the corner and walked away from me. Emerging into the main corridor, I saw Bernice standing over the body of the fourth man. There was blood everywhere. As I got closer I realized that it was hers, not his.

'Let me have a look at that,' I said in tones more suitable for my Kensington surgery than Mughal India.

'No time,' she hissed. She was obviously in pain.

'It won't do any of us any good if you pass out through lack of blood.'

I gave her a quick once-over. The blood was issuing from a shallow scrape on her scalp, and was coagulating as I watched.

'You'll have a headache for some time, but apart from that you'll be all right.'

'A headache. Thanks for warning me: I'll be sure to watch out for it.'

'What now?'

She looked around.

'Well, there's not much option, is there? We have to follow to find out where they're taking Holmes. If we're really lucky, the Doctor might be there as well.'

The path taken by the three Indians was quite clear. The damp marks of their bare feet on the marble flagstones had not yet evaporated, and we made good time. We turned a corner to find them some yards ahead of us, at a point where the corridor opened out into a large open space. Sunlight glared on stone, and the heat and stink of the outside world suddenly assailed us. In the centre of the space, a large circular pit seemed to absorb the light. I could make out the first few steps of a stairway which spiralled around its edge before the shadows lapped over it like black water.

The Indians carrying Holmes, Roxton and O'Connor did not hesitate, but plodded down the stairway into the pit.

With barely a hesitation, Bernice and I followed.

Stale air drifted up from the dark heart of the pit. The steps were almost invisible beneath our feet. Three times I wandered too close to the edge and would have fallen had Bernice not grabbed my sleeve. Gazing upwards I could see birds wheeling across the deep blue circle of the sky. I started to count steps, and got up to several hundred before I gave up. The comforting light above us receded to the size of a guinea, then a farthing and then a sixpence. My feet fell into a pattern – step, step, step – and my mind wandered free. I suppose that I had fallen into some kind of hypnotic state, a dream land where logic is conspicuous by its absence. I seemed to be standing in a familiar city of tall buildings. There were people thronging the pavements and buckboard carriages manoeuvring through the refuse-laden streets. I was trying to warn passers-by of the danger they were in – although I did not know what that danger was myself – but they were ignoring me. I screamed to them to take cover, to beware, but it was as if I was invisible to them. And then a huge crack opened up across the street, and buckboards fell into it, their occupants' faces contorted in terror. Buildings around me wavered and crumbled. Chunks of masonry fell and buried themselves in the dusty ground. I stared at the devastation, knowing that I could have prevented it but uncertain how.

A hand tugged at my sleeve and woke me from my day-dream. I was in darkness. The stairway continued on as before. Bernice's face was lit by a flickering orange light.

'Are you all right?'

'I'm not sure . . . I think I blacked out for a while,' I replied.

'Can't say I blame you.' She grimaced. 'I think we've arrived somewhere.'

She indicated downwards. A few steps past where we had stopped, the pit seemed to open out into a vast conical cave with us at its apex. I crept down a few steps. The stairway hugged the sides of the cone, descending in a spiral to a rocky floor some half-mile across its base.

The three Indian bearers carrying Holmes, Roxton and O'Connor were trudging down the sides of the cave like ants on the inside of a flower pot. Pools of brackish water littered the plain like malignant sores. In between them, a host of men were sitting, lined up in rows with kit bags at their feet and rifles across their shoulders. There were larger weapons in evidence as well: Gatling guns, elephant rifles and the like. Some of the soldiery were British, some were Indian, but they were all wearing uniforms of bright blue and silver, but looked uncomfortable and self-conscious in them: more like dressed-up apes than soldiers. This, I presumed, was Maupertuis's army.

Around the edges of this ragtag invasion force, groups of Indian men of the type known as fakirs were sitting in groups around fires, staring vacantly into space. They were singing.

'*I-ay, I-ay*,' their voices echoed through the shadows, '*naghaa, naghai-ghai! Shoggog fathaghn! I-ay, I-ay tsa toggua thola-ya! Thola-ya fathaghn! I-ay Azathoth!*'

The chant soared through the vacant space, filling it and echoing back upon itself in a complex web of sound. Sometimes the song reverberated in a single pure note loud enough to make the stairs beneath my feet tremble: moments later I could distinguish individual voices raised in sweet harmony. I had heard this before. I racked my mind trying to remember where, and then it came to me. Mrs Prendersly had repeated those words to the Doctor and I in her house in Deptford just before she had burned to death, having heard them from the lips of her husband. It was also what Maupertuis' mysterious hooded companion had been singing in the brothel in Euston.

I caught sight of a movement in the centre of the cave. There amidst the singing wise men, Maupertuis, Tir Ram, Colonel Warburton, Gloria Warburton and Smithee were making their way towards a raised dais which contained three ornate chairs. The gigantic Surd was following his master. I nudged Bernice.

'I'm way ahead of you,' she said. 'Look over there.'

She gestured to the bottom of the stairway, where the

three Indians with their captors had just reached the ground. A fourth man had been waiting for them. He was holding the Doctor by the scruff of the neck.

'Now is the time for all good men to come to the aid of the party,' I murmured.

'What?'

'We have to rescue them!'

Bernice sighed.

'I'm open to suggestions,' she whispered.

By this time the Doctor, Holmes, Lord Roxton and Mr O'Connor had been dumped at the foot of the dais upon which Maupertuis, Warburton and Tir Ram sat. Mrs Warburton and Smithee stood behind the chairs. The Doctor, still clutching what was by now a rather battered umbrella, gazed up balefully at them. The other three prisoners seemed to be recovering from the effects of whatever narcotic drug the betel nut had been adulterated with. Holmes was pulling himself painfully to his feet, whilst the other two were holding their heads and groaning. Maupertuis leaned forward to stare at them.

'You have each tried to interfere in my plans,' he said. 'You have crept on your bellies into this country and followed me here to the country of my friend Tir Ram, ready to stop me in my grand venture.' His voice was as quiet as wind in dry grass, and yet I could hear him clearly above the background chanting.

Mr O'Connor removed a small notebook from his jacket and began making notes: of what I could not guess.

'I do not understand,' Maupertuis continued. 'My only aim is to extend British influence to the stars, bringing more dominions under the control of the Queen.'

He gestured to the regiments lined up in the shadows.

'My army, drawn from the ranks of the poor and the powerless in the slums of England's great cities, trained and commanded by my brave general . . .'

Warburton preened himself.

'. . . will march through the portal created by the wisdom of my ally, whose land is best placed to be the launching point for this glorious enterprise . . .'

Tir Ram smiled slightly.

'. . . and place this virgin territory, its goods and its chattels, its spices, oils and minerals, its people and their treasures, under British dominion. Yet you try to stop me. Why?'

The Doctor stepped forward.

'You will be spreading death and destruction across the cosmos,' he cried. 'The British Empire is based upon oppression and slavery. You offer not the hand of friendship but the jackboot of tyranny! I shall prevent your plans!'

'Ah,' said Maupertuis, 'a liberal. There are always those whose hearts bleed for the underdogs. You fail to understand: there will *always* be underdogs. You cannot prevent it.'

He turned to Holmes.

'And you, Mr Holmes. What interest has a private detective in my affairs?'

Holmes grasped the lapels of his linen suit and stepped forward to stand beside the Doctor. His expression was calm, supercilious even.

'A number of books were stolen from a library in Holborn. A lady named Kate Prendersly was murdered in Deptford. A footman was also murdered in Euston. It is my intention to bring you to justice for those crimes.'

Maupertuis leaned back in his throne. A faint sneer etched itself across that bone-white face.

'How petty. I offer a bountiful land of opportunities: new spices, new sources of power, whole continents to colonize, and what do you greet my beneficence with? A handful of minor grievances. There are no laws in this new land, Mr Holmes. You cannot touch me there. I will be king. I will be God.'

His gaze moved on to Lord Roxton.

'And you, big game hunter and peer of the realm. What pitiful excuses do you offer?'

Roxton joined Holmes and the Doctor, standing proud before the dais.

'You talk of openin' up this alien world for the greater

191

good of Britain. As a representative of the Queen, I repudiate your claims. The Empire is based upon fairness and incorruptibility. We will not have men of your ilk sourin' our reputation.'

'You claim to speak for Britain?' Maupertuis scoffed in a voice that grated like rats' feet over broken glass.

'I speak for the Diogenes Club,' Roxton said triumphantly, 'and they speak for Britain.'

Of course! I turned to Bernice and whispered, 'Holmes's brother Mycroft said that he had people in the area.'

'Nice to know they're doing as well as we are,' she snapped.

Far below, Maupertuis turned his attention upon the fourth man, the meek O'Connor.

'And you, what pathetic reason do you offer for attempting to obstruct my plans?'

O'Connor put away his notebook and climbed to his feet, avoiding Maupertuis's searing gaze.

'Your regiments, as you call them,' he said hesitantly, 'are drawn from the criminal classes of England. You've taken away my thugs, my bullies, my bodyguards and my enforcers.' His voice was growing stronger and more familiar. 'You've created your own army by depleting mine, offering them more money and greater glory. Oaths were taken when they entered my employ. I intend to see that those oaths are honoured.'

'And who are you?'

O'Connor straightened up from his cowering position and met Maupertuis's gaze. He seemed thinner, gaunt even, and his head seemed to have developed a slight tremor. With a sudden movement he pulled the bright red wig from his head and cast it to the floor, revealing a large expanse of domed forehead. He stared malevolently up at Maupertuis with puckered, blinking eyes.

'I am Professor James Moriarty,' he exclaimed. 'The greatest criminal genius that the world has ever known!'

Holmes's eyes widened in sudden shock. I felt unsteady on my feet, and Bernice clutched at my shoulder, afraid that I might fall into their midst.

A ripple of unease washed across those of Maupertuis's troops who hailed from Britain as they recognized their erstwhile employer, the criminal genius who sat at the centre of a web of crime that stretched across the civilized world, the man whose lieutenants – men such as Mr Jitter and Mack 'The Knife' Yeovil – were mere babes in arms when compared to him. He gazed over them with a promise of retribution in his eyes. They quailed, but they did not break.

He turned to stare at Holmes.

'Dear me,' he said quietly. 'I had hardly expected to be standing by your side, Mr Holmes.'

'Nor I yours,' Holmes replied grimly.

'A common outlaw,' Maupertuis scoffed. 'To add to a spineless apologist for the weak, a small-minded detective and a secret agent for a government too blinkered to understand what I am offering.'

Behind him, the chanting of the fakirs had continued unabated. Now it rose to a crescendo. The air itself seemed to throb in anticipation.

'Not a patch on the Isley Brothers,' Bernice murmured.

'Behold,' Maupertuis screamed above the pandemonium. 'Behold the gateway to glory!'

Bright light flooded the cavern. It issued from a *rip* that had appeared in the air to one side of the cavern, a rip that pulled itself apart into a rent, and then a hole.

And through the hole, another world.

Its sky was a pearly white colour, and was held up by purple mountains. It was like a tapestry suspended in mid-air, except that I could smell its dry, lemony odour and feel the cool touch of its air.

Warburton was issuing orders through a megaphone. The army, stunned by the sight of their objective but too stupid to let it bother them, prepared to march.

Maupertuis reached into his jacket.

'I have no use for you,' he said to the small but defiant group of men before him. Removing a small whistle from a waistcoat pocket, he raised it to his lips and blew. I heard no noise, but felt a sudden stab of pain in the centre of my forehead. Bernice winced.

Fetid air ruffled my hair. I glanced about, but saw nothing. My stomach churned. Something was coming, something *evil*, but I could not tell from which direction it approached. I turned to consult Bernice, but she was gazing upwards in horror. I followed her gaze, and felt my bowels turn to ice.

The tiny circle of daylight at the top of the shaft was obscured by a shadow that was growing larger with every passing second. Wings flapped. I could not move. It was almost on top of me.

I felt a leathery wing brush past me, saw a sudden flash of pebbled scarlet hide, and then it was past me, and I was looking down upon a creature from delirium as it plummeted towards the ground. I recognized it from Bernice's description. It was one of the creatures that had abducted the Doctor.

Another one dropped past me, almost knocking me from the stairs with the wind of its passage. Opening its wings to their widest extent, it circled around the dais. The spikes that comprised its face quivered in anticipation of the kill.

A third creature dropped from the shaft, and a fourth. They flocked for a moment like blood-soaked vultures around a carcass. I pulled my revolver from my pocket, but Bernice grabbed my hand before I could fire.

'You'll give away our position! Let's see whether or not they need us first.'

The first creature swooped for the Doctor.

He ducked as its mace-like tail swept through the air where his head had been. The wind from its mighty wings beat Holmes and Roxton back as it gained height again; then, folding those wings against its body, it plummeted towards the Doctor's prone body. He rolled to one side. The tail smashed into the ground beside his face, its spikes drawing deep scratches down his cheek.

'What *are* they?' I hissed.

'The Doctor called them rakshassi. I guess they're

native to the planet through the gateway. They look barely intelligent to me. Maupertuis probably brought some back with him and trained them up as glorified penis-substitutes.'

'Glorified *what*?' I exclaimed.

'Go have a chat with Freud,' she replied cryptically.

The vanguard of Maupertuis's army were filing apprehensively into the gateway now. They gazed around, not sure whether to be more frightened of the alien world ahead or the alien creatures behind. Grizzled sergeant-types kept them moving.

The three other rakshassi had engaged Holmes, Roxton and Moriarty, harrying them from the air, lashing them with their tails and clutching at them with the talons on the ends of their wings. They hissed in anticipation of the kill. It was all the men could do to keep out of their clutches. There was no chance of fighting back.

Smiling cruelly, Maupertuis leaned back in his throne to enjoy the fun. Besides him, Tir Ram was looking a little sick.

One of the creatures had cornered Holmes by one of the pools of water. He had nowhere to back away to as the thing hovered above him, preparing to dash his brains out with its tail. Moriarty lurked behind it, unable or unwilling to intervene.

I didn't even know I was going to fire until I felt the gun buck in my hand. My shot hit where one of its wings met the body, exploding the joint in a shower of bone and blood. The creature screamed shrilly and plunged to the ground. Moriarty was on in a flash, snapping the bony ribs of the wings and tearing at the membranes between them. The creature thrashed about, but Moriarty fought like a daemon. Taking a bunch of the sharp spikes of its face in each hand, he pulled sharply in opposite directions. Watery fluid sprayed up from the rent. The creature convulsed and was still.

'Oh well,' said Bernice, pulling a tiny double-barrelled Derringer from her sleeve and searching for a target.

Maupertuis was up and out of his chair, gazing around

195

and trying to find the source of the shot. His gaze flickered wildly around the cavern. He didn't think to look upwards.

The Doctor managed to poke the ferrule of his umbrella into the thorny face of his rakshassa opponent. The creature hissed at him and sprang into the air, spraying pink blood from the wound. The Doctor bounced to his feet and held the umbrella before him like a sword as the beast dived at him, neatly impaling it. Its death cry rang out across the cavern, almost drowning out the constant chanting of the fakirs and causing the rent between Earth and Ry'leh to wobble alarmingly. The onward marching regiments hesitated for a few moments, waiting for their destination to come back into focus.

Roxton was throwing rocks at the rakshassa that had been harrying him. It flew higher and higher, striving to escape the persecution. As it came within range of her weapon, Bernice fired. A small rent appeared in its wing. Its blind head snapped around, targeting her for death, but the rent suddenly opened out into a tear and its wing folded up. It fell into a spiral, screaming all the while, and hit the ground in a crumpled heap.

The shot had attracted Maupertuis's attention. His face convulsed with rage. Gesturing to Surd, he shouted, 'Kill them! Kill them!'

Surd lumbered towards the rocky stairway and began the long climb up to the apex of the conical cavern, and us.

The fourth rakshassa was stalking Moriarty across the cavern floor. Holmes and Roxton were shadowing it, but it lashed its tail violently to discourage them from getting too close. It was gaining on the Professor as his stamina gave out. I would have been quite happy to see him perish, but I knew that for the moment we were all in it together, and so I shot at the back of its head. The wound would have been fatal in a human, but it just jerked slightly, then turned its head to fix me with a blind and baleful gaze.

Holmes took his chance. Springing on the back of the beast, he took hold of the shafts of its wings and jerked backwards, as one would pull the wishbone of a turkey. A distinct *snap* reached my ears. The spines of its face

196

seemed to bulge, and it slowly fell forward into one of the pools that dotted the cavern floor. Holmes clambered off its back and kicked it a few times, but it remained still.

We had killed all four of the rakshassi.

I waved a triumphant hand at Holmes. He grinned and waved back. Nearby I could see Moriarty bending over one of the fallen creatures, examining the carcass. The rank and file of Maupertuis's army marched past them, still heading for the dimensional gateway. Maupertuis himself was standing on the dais gazing malevolently up at Bernice and I. Suddenly he switched his gaze to the section of stairway leading up to us, and smiled in triumph.

Without thinking, I flung myself backwards, hitting Bernice. We fell in a tangle of limbs onto sharp rock.

'What the . . .'

Fire exploded across the cavern wall where we had been standing. Hot air washed across us, blistering our skin. I threw an arm across my eyes to protect them. Bernice cried out in pain behind me.

When I lowered my arm, Surd was standing in front of us. The jigsaw of scars that made up his face were distorted into a leer. Pinpricks of insane flame danced in his eyes.

I scrambled back slightly to shield Bernice as best I could. Her breath was warm against my neck.

'It's been fun,' she whispered.

'We must do this again,' I murmured in reply. She laughed, bright and clear.

Hell reached out for us.

And then there was nothing but blessed coolness. Where Surd had been standing there was just an expanse of seared rock. A faint *crack!* drifted up from the cavern below.

Bernice twisted her body to gaze over the edge. I edged closer and looked out into the void.

Turning like a sycamore seed, Surd's body fell away from us. For a long while he seemed to move very slowly, hardly getting any smaller, and then with a sickening rush his body shrunk to the size of a doll and crashed into one of the pools of stagnant water. Water sprayed everywhere, dousing several fires.

A few yards away, Lord Roxton lowered the rifle from his shoulder. One of Maupertuis's soldiers was sprawled unconscious at his feet.

'One good turn, an' all that rot!' he yelled.

'Well,' Bernice said, 'if you ever hear me say that the aristocracy was a useless vestigal appendix on the body of society, you have my permission to spank me soundly on the bottom.'

I turned my head, and found myself gazing into her eyes from a distance of less than six inches.

'Can I have that in writing?' I asked.

'Ask me again when this is all over.'

There was a long moment of silence between us. Somewhere in the background a lone voice was raised in song. By the time I realized that it was one of Maupertuis's fakirs, still chanting his incomprehensible chant, the voice had stopped and the cavern was suddenly a lot darker.

The dimensional portal had closed.

As we gazed around, the extent of our meagre victory became apparent. We had won the battle, but the war was far from over. There were more dead bodies than live ones down on the cavern floor. Maupertuis had gone. His troops had gone. His fakirs had gone. Warburton, his wife, his secretary and Tir Ram had gone.

And so had the Doctor.

Chapter 12

In which Surd undergoes a hair-raising experience and a jolly travelling song is sung

Bernice and I descended the steps into the cavern, feeling remarkably like actors who watch the curtain rise only to discover that the audience has already left. Holmes and Lord Roxton were examining the ground where the gateway to Ry'leh had been. Professor Moriarty was some distance away, bent over the corpse of one of the rakshassi.

'Good work, Watson,' Holmes said as we approached. The fires cast a flickering orange light upon his features, rendering them even more gaunt than usual. 'I knew I could count on you.'

'That was damn good shootin', both of you,' Lord Roxton agreed. 'Remind me never to invite you up to my estate. The grouse'd never recover!'

I knew that he was jesting, but the compliment brought a blush to my cheek. Bernice also was pleased.

We gazed around in silence for a moment at the remnants of Maupertuis's army. Wherever we looked we could see abandoned mess kits, churned ground and blankets. There was nobody left, though. Nobody at all.

'So we've lost the Doctor again,' I murmured. 'This is getting beyond a joke.'

'He's always getting lost,' Bernice replied. 'It's what he's best at. Like a bad penny, he'll turn up again.'

'The little fellah?' Roxton asked. 'Seemed like a plucky sort of chap. Didn't see him go through that ... that *thing* ... though, whatever it was.'

'It was a gateway,' I confided.

'To another world,' said Bernice, smiling at Lord Roxton and daring him to disbelieve us.

'Another world, eh? I dare say the huntin' there would be an experience an' a half.'

'I take it from what you said earlier that you are one of Mycroft's agents,' I said to him. 'What brought you here?'

He rubbed a hand across his beard.

'I work for the Diogenes on and off. Nothin' formal, but I occasionally pick up the odd snippet of information here an' there. Feel it's me duty to let someone know. Mycroft knew I was comin' to India on a tiger shoot an' asked me to have a sniff around, see what I could come up with. Cabled me last week, told me you were comin' out as well, an' asked me to keep an eye on you.'

'What made you come to Jabalhabad?' Bernice asked. 'We only came across a clue that led us here by accident.'

'I've been tryin' to track the members of Maupertuis's ragtag army,' Roxton admitted. 'They've been comin' ashore all around the place – Calcutta, Bombay, Lahore – an' some even slipped across from Afghanistan. I picked up a hint of some Englishmen headin' for here when I was in Sind, so I popped across to have a look-see.'

He frowned.

'Knew Tir Ram from fox-huntin' back in Blighty,' he added. 'Members of the Quantock, both of us. Surprised to find him mixed up in all this.'

'I suspected from the start that we had walked into a trap,' Holmes snapped.

'Is that why you accepted the drugged betel nut?' Bernice asked.

He gazed superciliously at her.

'I palmed the nut and feigned unconsciousness. I felt it was the best way to force their hand.'

'You were takin' a bit of a risk,' Roxton said admiringly. 'Hate to admit it, but I was taken in completely. Me head feels like a ruddy rugger ball after the International.'

Bernice leaned towards me.

'Do *you* believe him?' she whispered.

'Of course.'

'It occurs to me that your Mr Holmes is a bit of a show-off. Doesn't like to admit that he can be wrong.'

'He so rarely is.'

She smiled.

'How do you know?'

Leaving me with that thought, she walked off towards where Surd had fallen. For a moment it occurred to me to protect her from the sight, but I quickly realized that she would not thank me. She gave the impression of having seen a lot worse. I turned my attention back to Holmes and Roxton.

'It was Colonel Warburton's reappearance that alerted me,' Holmes was saying. 'I believe that our initial meeting with him on the Orient Express was accidental – he was, no doubt, in the process of winding down the overland transfer route for Maupertuis's troops – but our second meeting here was pre-planned. Either Maupertuis suspected that we would be following him or the mysterious hooded man back in England alerted him via some preternatural means. Either way, he sent Warburton to lull us into a false sense of security and reel us in, like a trout on the line.'

'This is all a bit above me head,' Roxton admitted. 'Where do we go from here?'

Holmes looked around.

'I would suggest a comprehensive sweep of the cavern for clues. I shall divide it up into areas, and assign each of you to an area. The process of searching is a painstaking one: I have often thought of writing a monograph on the subject. I shall give you all precise instructions on how to search, and what to search for. Until then, touch nothing and try not to move around too much.'

The thought of all of us scuttling like cockroaches across the floor of the cavern as Holmes tutored us in his hallowed techniques struck me as funny. I chuckled to myself. Holmes glanced over darkly.

'That young lady is having an unfortunate effect upon

your dignity, Watson,' he snapped. 'Perhaps you should remember your age, and act accordingly.'

I stifled an incipient fit of giggles. Holmes could be so terribly pompous if he thought he was being made fun of.

'Young lady?' Roxton asked, confused. 'What young lady?'

'It's a long story,' I replied.

A slight prickling at the back of my neck made me turn. Professor Moriarty was standing a few feet away. His deep-set eyes examined me as he might examine a simple but rather tedious problem in mathematics. Of course, most mathematical problems were simple and rather tedious to Professor Moriarty. He was, so Holmes had led me to believe, one of the foremost authorities in the world on asteroid dynamics, having derived a result for the three-body problem using the binomial theorem and gone on to generalize it to situations involving four, five and six bodies. The whole thing sounded rather distasteful to me, but Holmes assured me that it had been a *bête noir* of mathematicians and astronomers ever since the time of Newton. Apparently only three other people were capable of understanding the subtleties of Moriarty's work: two of them disagreed so violently over the implications that they had come to blows during an international conference and the third one had suffered a bout of brain fever following three sleepless nights checking the details.

I had once asked Holmes why, when he had international fame and presumably fortune in his grasp, Moriarty spent so much time indulging in criminal pursuits. Holmes had puffed away on his pipe for a few moments.

'For the same reason that I resort to cocaine,' he said finally. 'To alleviate boredom. And besides, I doubt that he wastes more than half an hour a week pulling the various threads of his web of villainy. No, Moriarty is a dilettante malefactor, albeit a highly dangerous and successful one.'

Now, as I met his gaze, I tried to fathom something of the depth of purpose, the iron will, the phenomenal intellect that Professor Moriarty must possess. I failed. He could have been a minor bank manager or a crusty old prelate. He was unimpressive.

His head oscillated slightly from side to side. Holmes had described the phenomenon before, and even imitated it for me, but I still found myself slightly hypnotized by the motion. I found myself grasping for a stray butterfly of memory. I had read descriptions of symptoms such as his before, in an article by the French neurologist Gilles de la Tourette. The tics and twitches of the head, allied with the phenomenal quickness of thought and the relaxation of 'moral' guidance, were typical symptoms. Could it be that Professor Moriarty suffered from a minor form of Tourette's Syndrome?

'I do not intend to spend my time scrabbling around the floor for you, Mr Holmes,' Moriarty said quietly. 'I have done what I set out to do, and traced my missing men. They are beyond my reach now. Naught else remains. I shall return to England.'

'Really?' Holmes snapped back. 'You surprise me. Are there no *dacoit* or *thuggee* gangs with whom you can debate unusual techniques of murder? Can you not spare a few weeks to travel to China and discuss plans for world domination with the Si Fan's Council of Seven?'

'Such sarcasm,' Moriarty whispered. 'You should take care. It may be the death of you.'

'Should I take that to be a threat?'

'I do not issue threats, Mr Holmes. Merely predictions.'

'Then I shall reply in kind. I shall see you in the dock ere long, Professor. You have my word on it.'

Moriarty smiled: a thin, wintry flexing of the lips.

'Of what worth is the word of a drug addict?'

Holmes flinched. Moriarty turned to leave.

'Professor?'

He glanced over at me.

'Doctor Watson?'

I waved a hand to indicate the cavern and, in a wider sense, all that had occurred there.

'You seem remarkably unaffected by all of this. Does it not surprise you in any way?'

He thought for a moment.

'I have no expectations, therefore nothing that occurs in the world is a surprise. But, if it makes you feel better, the mathematics of folding higher dimensions are relatively simply. I am currently writing a paper on the subject. Perhaps I could send you a copy?'

'I cannot promise to understand it,' I rejoined.

'Nobody will understand it, apart from myself.' He did not appear to be boasting.

'You don't want to be understood?' I was intrigued. Perhaps this provided the key to his character.

He gazed at me for a few long moments, his head moving like a cat eyeing up a bird, or a cobra preparing to strike.

'I merely wish to be noticed,' he said finally, and smiled slightly. He knew what I was digging for.

'That's hardly an excuse for your crimes,' Holmes interjected.

'It is not meant to be an excuse,' Moriarty said, still gazing at me. 'It is meant to be an explanation.'

He took a step toward me and held out an object in a thin hand. It was a page torn from a notebook, covered in a thin, spidery handwriting.

'You may find this advance preview of my paper useful,' he said.

And with that he left.

'If you've finished playing dominance games,' Bernice shouted from where she crouched, near to the scattered remnants of one of the fires, 'then you might be interested in this.'

I crumpled the piece of paper up and shoved it into a pocket. Holmes and I walked over to join Bernice whilst Roxton set to work cleaning the rifle with which he had shot the rakshassa. Moriarty's footsteps echoed for some little while as he climbed up the stairs towards the Nizam's palace.

Bernice was bending over the body of Surd, which looked larger in death than it had in life. I bent and quickly checked the cadaver over. Most of his bones were shattered or twisted, and his face had impacted upon a sharp fragment of rock. Fortunately, his glossy thatch of hair had fallen forward to cover the ruin.

I couldn't say that I was sorry about his fate.

Holmes bent, took a firm grip on the back of Surd's head, and pulled. The results were startling. Surd's hair came away in his hand, revealing a naked scalp, criss-crossed with thick, worm-like scars.

'Interesting,' he commented dryly, and examined the hairpiece inside and out.

'A fine piece of work,' he murmured. 'Made by Meunier of Grenoble, if I don't miss my guess. What do you think, Watson?'

I opened my mouth to answer but as usual he wasn't listening. Instead, he sniffed at the wig, then spent some moments parting the hairs and subjecting the surface in which they had been woven to a close examination, as if he were searching for lice.

'Hmmm. Most instructive.'

Placing the wig into a pocket, he turned his attention upon the corpse itself, running his fine, sensitive fingers over the fissured skin of Surd's head.

'There's something about these scars that intrigues me,' he muttered, retrieving his magnifying glass and scrutinizing Surd's scalp from close range. His forefinger traced a path amongst the cicatrices: along for a few inches, then down towards the nape of the neck, across for a few more inches and finally up, arriving at the point he had left.

'They're too regular,' he finished.

Bernice gasped.

'But that's . . .'

'Impossible?'

'I was going to say "ingenious".'

I could contain myself no longer.

'What are you suggesting?' I asked.

Instead of replying, Holmes removed a penknife from his pocket. Choosing a small blade, he placed its edge against one of the scars, as if he was going to make an incision.

205

'Surely surgery is my province?' I joked. Holmes did not smile.

The blade slipped too easily out of sight, as if a cut had already been made. Holmes twisted the knife, and I watched in astonishment as a section of Surd's skull, some four inches by three, lifted away in Holmes's hand.

'*Voilà*,' my friend exclaimed. 'The perfect smuggler's hiding place.'

I gazed at the small, dark space thus revealed. It had been lined with velvet, now slightly stained by the cranial fluids, and stitched to the skin of the scalp. I presumed that the stitching had also sealed the gap in the *dura* and *pia mater* membranes. I estimated that about half of Surd's brain must have been removed to create the space.

'Fascinating,' Holmes murmured.

'Sick,' said Bernice. 'Are you seriously suggesting that the books were smuggled out of the Library inside the head of this ape?'

'The space is obviously not large enough to hold more than a few pages, tightly folded. Perhaps the books were smuggled out a piece at a time. There is some collateral evidence to suggest this.'

'What evidence?' I asked.

'Do you not remember your interview with Mrs Prendersly? Did you not repeat to me her assertion that she had seen the shadow of a man eating books? I put it to you, Watson, that what she actually saw was Surd here inserting a small volume into this space.'

'And that was why she was . . . killed in such a terrible way?'

'Quite possibly, although she did repeat to you the chant that her husband had overheard and which, it transpires, is the key to unlocking the dimensional gateway. I can imagine that Maupertuis would wish to silence anybody who knew that information. The question remains, however: how did Maupertuis determine that she knew anything?'

I tried to think, but I found that I could not look away from the gaping space in Surd's head.

'I cannot accept that Maupertuis would do this to his servant.'

'I admit that it is a length to which even the recently departed Professor would not stoop. Still, as a method of conveying stolen materials past guards it has its advantages.'

He frowned.

'But why stop there?' he asked himself. He reached beneath the body and gently eased it onto its back. Surd's face resisted the attempt for a few moments, finally coming free with a glutinous sucking noise. The features were no longer recognizable, being how subsumed into a mass of raw meat. I felt my stomach lurch. Holmes, unconcerned, began to unbutton the shirt.

'Aha!'

Surd's chest, like his scalp, was a mass of scars.

'The man is a walking suitcase!' Holmes observed, pulling at a flap to reveal another, larger leather-lined space in the position where I would have expected a lung to be. Either it had been shunted aside or removed entirely.

'I wonder how many poor souls underwent Maupertuis's surgery before one survived,' I mused.

Holmes turned a rueful gaze upon me.

'You do right to remind us that this is an abomination committed against our fellow man,' he sighed. 'I find it hard to believe that anybody could survive such massive trauma, let alone evade infection afterwards.'

'I have seen worse,' I replied. 'During field surgery in Afghanistan, I worked on men whose heads had been half-obliterated by cannon-fire, and I was still able to hold a conversation with them. Much of the brain is under-utilized, and many of our organs are duplicates which we can do without – kidneys, for instance, and lungs and . . .' I hesitated, conscious of Bernice's rapt attention, '. . . er, other things. In fact, it is amazing how little of our bodies and our brains we actually use.'

Holmes just looked at me.

'Well, some of us,' I amended.

'What I find myself wondering about,' Bernice mused, 'is those powers of his.'

'You mean the spontaneous combustion?' I asked. 'What connection could there be?'

'It's been shown that damage to one part of the brain results in other parts – possibly dormant parts – taking on the extra workload. Like if fire destroys your bedroom you might start sleeping in the attic.'

'Where has that been reported?' I asked.

'Well, maybe it hasn't yet. Anyway, it's also been shown that mental powers like telepathy and telekinesis and the like are related to unused areas of the human brain – the attic and basement areas, if you like. So . . .'

I carried on the thought to its logical conclusion.

'. . . So if some part of Surd's brain was surgically removed, it might follow that other parts could come into operation!'

Whole vistas of medical and mental science began to open up before me. I was entranced.

'Telepathy, of course,' Holmes said, frowning. 'From the Greek for feeling at a distance. Telekinesis, therefore, would mean movement at a distance. Most intriguing.'

Bernice's expression suddenly changed.

'What it is?' I asked.

'The Doctor always warned me about interfering in history. "Don't reveal more than they already know," he said. "Such gifts don't come cheap". And I think I've just done it. He won't be pleased.'

'I'm not,' said the Doctor from behind us. We whirled around. Bernice flushed a bright red.

'Good Lord,' exclaimed Roxton, who was standing beside the Doctor and peering at Surd's corpse. 'What a poacher that feller'd make!'

'You seem to have a remarkable facility for turning up when least expected, Doctor,' Holmes said.

'You don't seem pleased to see me,' the Doctor replied. His linen suit was stained with a pinkish fluid and his hair was covered in some sticky substance. He was a mess.

'What happened?' I inquired.

'Ask Bernice.'

Bernice frowned. 'I don't . . .' she began, and then started to laugh. 'Oh no! You can't be serious!'

'I'm *always* serious, even when I'm being trivial,' the Doctor snapped.

I just looked from one to the other. Eventually the Doctor saw fit to put me out of my misery.

'I was underneath the last rakshassa that you shot down. It knocked me out. When I woke up, everything was dark and sticky. I thought I'd gone to Time Lord hell. It was only when I heard your voices that I realized I was lying beneath its wing.'

'What's Time Lord hell like?' Bernice asked.

'Earth,' the Doctor replied.

There was no answer to that.

Holmes dragooned us all into a search of the cavern, but we found nothing of any import save odd scraps of clothing and a few personal possessions left behind by the departing army. I tried to imagine where they were now and what they were engaged in, but my mind would not stretch that far. How would the men stand up to Ry'leh? How well had they been trained? Would K'tcar'ch's people be waiting for them or would their entry be unopposed?

I could hear part of a conversation between the Doctor and Bernice concerning his period of captivity. Apparently his flight across India had taken almost as long as our train journey. He had only arrived a day or so ahead of us, and had been held captive in the Nizam's palace. The books, of course, had been taken from him.

'There's nothing here,' Bernice said finally. She sounded dejected. 'The action's moved on and left us all dressed up with nowhere to go.'

'The lad's right,' shouted Roxton from his little area of ground. I looked around for a moment before realizing that he meant Bernice. 'We're on a wild goose chase.'

'I have no choice but to follow them,' the Doctor said decisively. 'Thank you for your help so far.'

'We will accompany you,' Holmes said. 'Watson, can you remember the words of the chant?'

'You have to be joking.'

Holmes just stared at me.

'You're not joking,' I said finally.

'You've heard it three times now, Watson.'

'But I've got a tin ear.'

'I'm not exactly one of the De Reskes Brothers myself, but it's the only chance we have.'

I walked across until we were standing virtually nose to nose.

'Holmes,' I said quietly, 'has it occurred to you that we could just turn around and go home? We've done our bit. We can't be expected to do any more. Alien planets are outside our bailiwick.'

'I accepted a commission. I shall see it through. And besides, can you really see the Doctor succeeding?'

I glanced over to where the diminutive man was shaking rakshassa blood out of his umbrella, and sighed.

'Well, I had to try.'

Holmes smiled.

'The better Roman Emperors had servants who would whisper in their ear, "You too are mortal". I value your level-headedness, Watson. Don't ever think that I don't.'

I didn't, of course, and I never have since.

'Lord Roxton!' Holmes called. Roxton came over.

'You'll be needing an old *shikari* like me,' he said. 'I've shot everywhere on Earth. Might as well have a crack at baggin' game up in the heavens.'

'I'm afraid not.'

Roxton sighed, and nodded.

'I thought as much. You'll be needin' someone to report back to your brother, and you can't trust Moriarty.'

'I'm glad you understand.'

Roxton held out a hand and Holmes shook it.

'You're a credit to your country, Mr Holmes, and there's not many I'd say that about.'

As he shook my hand, I wished him a safe journey.

'Gad, I hope not!' he cried, and laughed.

Bernice took his hand and pumped it vigorously.

'I hope you'll seek me out and tell me the outcome of this adventure when you get back to Blighty,' he said.

'Oh, Doctor Watson is the teller of tales,' she said diplomatically. 'I'm sure he'll be only too pleased to turn a minor skirmish into a major adventure.'

The Doctor saluted Roxton with his umbrella.

'Fare thee well,' he said.

Roxton looked one last time at us, saluted, and walked towards the stairway which coiled up the side of the cavern. I felt as though some vital force had been drained from our enterprise.

'Well,' said the Doctor finally. 'Let's get on with it.'

'How do we start?' I asked.

'We must all do our best to remember the words which were used in the ceremony,' Holmes snapped. 'I have trained my memory to the point where it rivals the Daguerreotype for accuracy. You, Professor Summerfield and the Doctor may be able to aid me in problems of intonation.'

I rummaged around in my pockets.

'I'd better write down what I remember, then.'

Pulling out a piece of paper and a fountain pen, I was about to start writing when I realized that it was the piece of paper Moriarty had given me. I tried to decipher his scrawl. The words were meaningless gibberish. Gibberish like . . .

'Holmes! Moriarty has written down the words of the chant!'

'Indeed. What a fortuitous piece of luck,' Holmes said dryly, walking over and taking the paper from my hand. 'Indeed, these are the words as I remember them, with phonetic notes as well.'

'I remember him writing *something* just before the attack,' Bernice said, 'but why would he want to give it to us? Could it be a trap?'

'I think not,' said Holmes after a moment's thought. 'I am an irritant to the good Professor, and he has already tried to kill me on a number of occasions. How convenient

211

for him if we died on this alien planet, and thus allowed him to continue extorting, blackmailing and terrorizing his way through England and ultimately the world?'

'So you trust him?'

'In this instance, his aims and ours coincide. Now, to business.'

Like members of a choir, we gathered around Holmes and the piece of paper.

'On the count of three. One ... two ... three!'

'*I-ay, I-ay,*' we managed before Bernice and I collapsed in fits of giggles. Holmes and the Doctor stared at us with lips pursed.

'When you have quite recovered ...' Holmes said.

'That's quite enough of *that* ...' the Doctor barked.

Without daring to look at one another, Bernice and I clustered around them and tried again.

'*I-ay, I-ay Naghaa, naghai-ghai! Shoggog fathaghn! I-ay, I-ay!*'

The phrasing was wrong and we stumbled over the unnatural words, but there was something there. We tried again, and again. Under Holmes's tutelage we must have spent a good hour rehearsing that damned chant. Even now I can hear it echo in the labyrinthine passages of my mind: a dark, malevolent sound that has a life of its own and induces feelings of dread in me whenever it pops into my mind.

'*I-ay, I-ay. Naghaa, naghai-ghai! Shoggog fathaghn! I-ay, I-ay tsa toggua tholo-ya! Tholo-ya fathaghn!*'

After a while, we were confident enough that we could introduce a phasing in the chant, with Holmes coming in a beat after Bernice and myself, and the Doctor's fine baritone soaring high above on the descant. The nature of the chant altered in subtle ways: sometimes Holmes's voice was a powerful engine behind us, pushing us on, and sometimes it seemed to be dragging us backwards. Our voices seemed to be echoing in a deeper and larger space than the cavern.

And then, after what seemed like an eternity but must have been only half an hour, I thought I could detect other voices singing along with us: soft, sibilant voices pronouncing words in a subtly different way. A hallucination? Perhaps, but we took our cue from them and tried to shape our palates to form the same sounds as they did. It was not easy. I suspect now, so many years later, that if they were real then they were not human in form. We must have produced a close enough approximation, however, for it was shortly after that when Bernice plucked at my sleeve and indicated that our shadows were being cast in front of us from a bright source of light behind. Still singing, I turned to look.

Through the gates of delirium I saw an alien world blazing in all its glory. A wide plain spread before us, curling up in the distance to form tall mountains of knobbly purple rock. The sky was white and glowing, and seemed to cut the mountains off as if it were solid. A citrus-scented breeze ruffled my hair.

Still chanting, we walked into another world.

Interlude

GGJ235/57/3/82-PK3
  V-ON, BRD-ABLE, WPU = 1.244
  VERBAL INPUT, COMPRESS AND SAVE
  MILITARY LOG FILE EPSILON
  CODE GREEN FIVE
  ENABLE
They know I'm watching them now. I made too much noise
getting down from that window the other day, and attracted
a bit of unwelcome attention. It ended up in a chase through
the alleys. Since they can fly and I can't, I reckon it was a
bit one-sided, so I brought one of them down with a sort-
of home-made bolas and another two with smart missiles.

  I keep having to move my base camp. They're very good
at searches: that's what flying does for you, it gives you a
different perspective on where people might hide. For
a while I hid out in nooks and crannies that couldn't be
seen from the air, but they caught on and started using
packs of those three-legged rat things with the red eyes. I
had to look for somewhere else. Base camp's only a ruck-
sack anyway, so moving isn't too much hassle.

  Time to get back to the plain, I guess. Hope the Professor
makes it through okay. If not, I guess it's chocolate-flavour
animal for tea forever.

  DISABLE.
  2757/3/FF43
  PIP.

Chapter 13

In which our intrepid heroes arrive in the New World and Watson takes up scouting

Extract from the diary of Bernice Summerfield

I suspect that midnight has passed by, back in India, so I'll distinguish this entry with a new date. I've been awake for almost forty-eight hours and I feel ready to drop. In fact, I keep falling asleep in the middle of writing this diary entry. Four times I've tried to start it now, but each time I get a few words in and suddenly my pen will start sliding down the page. When I snap back to wakefulness a few moments later, I don't know where I am and I've only got a sketchy idea of who. So: if you've just woken up, Bernice Summerfield, and you're reading this for some clue as to what's happened, the Doctor's made some coffee and I think I can cover the past few hours before the big black bag goes over my head again.

First question: where am I? Well, it's an alien planet. Not just any alien planet, either. This one's stranger than most. Stranger than Moloch, the hollow moon of Lucifer that's linked by a bridge to its sister Belial. Stranger than Eusapia and Zeta Minor, half in this universe and half in another. Stranger than Tersurus, with its clone banks and its singing stones. Stranger even than Magla, whose crust is a shell covering a vast, dreaming, creature. No, Ry'leh is the strangest planet I've ever seen. I'm not a geologist, but I suspect that it's an old world. At some point in its past the local star must have gone nova, blasting much of its matter away into space to leave a colder, smaller core. Soon after that Ry'leh's atmosphere must have frozen, leaving it looking like a great cue-ball hanging in space. The frozen jacket doesn't fit tightly though: the heat from the planet's core has melted the interior layers of ice back into an atmosphere, leaving valleys, fissures, channels and plains with an oppressively solid sky hanging above them, supported upon the pillars of the mountains. And that's where you are, girl: sandwiched between rock and a hard place.

The wind whistles through the canyons like a demon. It plucks at your clothes and whips your hair into your eyes. It snatches things from your hands and whirls them gleefully away from you. It hates you.

The plants hate you too. Only the strongest and most stubborn life-forms survived the sun going nova. Their razor-sharp bruise-coloured vanes catch at your clothing as you clamber past them, and make rents for the wind to get in and sap the warmth from your bones. Some of them hiss and thrust their roots between your feet as you pass. High above, up where the sky is hard and cold, small black specks wheel. Rakshassi? I wouldn't be at all surprised.

You get the picture? Ry'leh is not a nice place to be.

As we emerged from the gateway the wind snatched the words from our mouths, and it collapsed behind us. When we turned, India had vanished. We were just a step away from Earth in one direction, a million light-years in another.

We were standing at the foot of a mountain range. The dusky purple ground rose gently for a few miles, then jabbed sharply upwards into a set of harsh peaks, all of them truncated by the ice sky. The sun was a lighter spot through the ice, too weak to cast any shadows. Turning, I could see that we were surrounded by the mountains. Valleys led away in three directions. It was as if we had been dumped in the middle of a giant's maze.

Gravity seemed to be about Earth normal. I find it difficult to tell – I've been on so many worlds that I forget what my body was designed for sometimes – but neither Watson nor Holmes were falling down or falling up. The

216

Doctor walked around as if he owned the place. Which he might well have done, of course.

Holmes gazed around in some shock. I think that the reality of an alien planet was turning out to be completely different to the theory. He bent down and investigated the ground, then plucked a small weed-like flower from a crack. It bit him, and he dropped it with a cry. Watson tended to the wound. It wasn't serious, but I think he might have been worried about poison. There's a theory I once heard suggesting that there is no logical basis for alien poisons to work on humans, and vice versa, because the two ecologies would have evolved different chemical bases for life. Personally, I don't believe it. Summerfield's First Law of Planetary Evolution states that anything not specifically designed to hurt you will still manage to find a way. Or, to put it another way, the buggerance factor of the universe tends towards a maximum.

Watson was turning gradually around, a bit like a weather vane influenced by the wind. Eventually he came to a halt facing down one of the valleys towards a misty horizon half-glimpsed through the distant mountains.

'That way,' he said. 'Maupertuis's troops went that way.'

'How can you tell?' the Doctor asked.

'Not sure. It's a matter of instinct, more than anything. I spent some time talking to an old Afghan tracker during the war, you see. He was a prisoner of ours, but he'd been injured and I had to treat him. Picked up some tips on hunting.' He smiled boyishly. 'I rather fancy his skills at treating wounds improved as well.'

'Fascinating though this is,' I interjected, 'where do we go from here?'

'We try and get in front of Maupertuis's troops,' Watson said, 'and alert the appropriate native authorities to the fact that they are being invaded. We then request their help in taking Maupertuis into custody.'

'Of course,' I said. 'Simple, isn't it?'

Watson shrugged.

'Well, as a broad plan I think it has its strong points.

217

Obviously there are some details which remain to be ironed out . . .'

'Such as: how do we persuade a peaceful, philosophical race like K'tcar'ch's to join together to fight Maupertuis's marauders?'

'We shall have to play it by ear,' he said stiffly.

'But back in the Nizam's cavern you said that you had a *tin* ear.'

He gave me a exaggeratedly withering glance that had an underlying vein of humour in it. Ever since I surprised him naked in the bath, he seemed to believe that he and I were sharing something special. I hated to disillusion him.

We set out in the direction that Watson had identified, on the basis that it was no worse than any other choice. Watson marched on ahead, and the Doctor and I followed behind. Holmes brought up the rear. He was uncharacteristically silent. Whenever I turned to make sure he was still there, I found him striding along with his hands in his pockets and a distinct glower on his face.

'What's the matter with him?' I asked the Doctor, indicating Holmes with my thumb.

'He's been thrown completely out of his element,' the Doctor explained as we walked. 'Mr Holmes's deductions rely upon a comprehensive knowledge of the way things work, or so Arthur Conan Doyle wrote. He knows London back to front, for instance. He can identify the typefaces used by all of the daily newspapers, he knows the secret signs employed by vagrants and down-and-outs to identify households prone to charity, he can identify the profession of any man based upon the small changes made to their hands, or their clothes, or the way they stand. In the provinces his knowledge is probably less comprehensive. I doubt, for instance, that he knows much about the regional variations in shoeing horses, but he probably *does* know where to research the subject, should the need arise. In Switzerland, to pick a country at random, he could well be at a disadvantage, as his base of knowledge would be largely useless and his opportunities to research would be limited, but here on Ry'leh he has nothing at all upon which to work. None of the signs that he looks for are valid. On the other hand, your friend Doctor Watson, being a man who works on the instinctive rather than the intellectual level, comes to terms with new sets of rules remarkably quickly. A very adaptable man, and one much after my own hearts.'

'He's not my friend,' I murmured, not liking the way the Doctor had rolled the word around his mouth, getting every last nuance out of it.

'Don't you like him?' the Doctor said innocently.

'I like him, but . . .'

'I thought you two were getting on rather well.'

'We were. We are. But I'm not going to have an affair with him.'

'Well, that makes a change,' he murmured. 'I'm worried enough about Ace's amorous predilections without every male you meet falling for you left, right and centre.'

He glanced at me with a twinkle in his eye. I smiled back, but beneath his serious surface and his humorous interior I could see something else, a deeper, more fundamental worry.

'What's the matter?' I asked.

He shook his head.

'A word, that's all.'

'A word?'

'Something I heard back in Tir Ram's cavern. Something in that chant.'

I shook my head.

'I couldn't make any of it out,' I said. 'It didn't sound like a real language at all. I'd have understood it otherwise, surely?'

The Doctor pursed his lips for a moment. I took the opportunity to look around. Nothing had changed. The plain was still plain, the mountains still touched the sky. Watson still walked too fast. Holmes was still sulking.

'It wasn't a language as such,' he mused finally, 'more a polyglot collection of words which I've heard before on half a hundred worlds across the universe, although with translations as varied as "window", "reddish-green" and "happily unicycling in an easterly direction". The actual chant was meaningless, but one of those words made me think.'

'Don't leave me in suspense. Which one?'

' "Azathoth",' he said gloomily.

Now it was my turn to frown.

'I know that word. I've seen it somewhere. An article, or a journal, something. Maybe on Braxiatel . . .'

'Azathoth is a god of anarchy and chaos: one of a pantheon whose worship sprung up on various planets across the universe at more or less the same time. The Silurians, for instance, venerated them before mankind was even a gleam in evolution's eye, as did the gargantuan entities that ruled Earth a hundred thousand years before them. Hundreds more races sacrificed in their names. There was even a cult amongst the Shobogans at one time.'

'Shobogans?'

'New Age Time-Lord drop-outs, but that's not important right now. Azathoth is a representation – an avatar, if you like – of one of the Great Old Ones.'

'And they are . . .?'

The Doctor sighed explosively. Watson looked round at the sudden noise, tripped over his feet and almost fell.

'I was hoping not to have to go into this.'

'Start at the very beginning.'

'A very good place to start. Very well: the universe is cyclical, which means that it periodically goes through cycles of expansion and contraction, punctuated by a series of big bangs.'

'I think we can skip the history of the universe, if it's all the same to you.'

'No, no,' he complained, flapping his hand at me, 'the Great Old Ones predate even that. In the dying days of the universe *before* this current one, which is forever separated from us by a point where time and space do not exist, a group of beings discovered how to preserve themselves past that point where their universe ceased.

They shuttled themselves sideways, into a parallel universe which, for various reasons that I will not even attempt to explain now, ceased a split-second *after* our one. With me so far?'

'No.'

'Good. Just before *that* universe ceased, they jumped back to *our* one, which had just started expanding afresh after a moment of nothingness. The trouble is, the universe before ours was set up differently. Fundamental physical laws such as the speed of light and the charge on the electron were different, which means that the Great Old Ones have powers undreamed of by anybody in this universe. Powers that make them look like gods, to naive races. And they're a pretty nasty bunch, too.'

'Great. I *thought* I'd heard the name before. I went to a seminar on Felophitacitel Major, a few years back. There was a Draconian who had this theory about various cults springing up across the universe, all worshipping the same gods. We all laughed at him.'

'He was on the right track. The Great Old Ones *are* those gods. There's Cthulhu, who we met in Haiti, if you recall, and the Gods of Ragnarok, who Ace will tell you about if you ask her nicely, and Nyarlathotep, who I sincerely hope never to encounter. And Dagon, who was worshipped by the Sea Devils, and the entity known as Hastur the Unspeakable who also goes around calling himself Fenric and who Ace will *not* tell you about no matter how nicely you ask. And Yog-Sothoth, who I met in Tibet and again in London, and Lloigor, who settled quite happily on Vortis . . . oh, there's a lot of them. All alien to this universe and its laws, both moral and physical.'

'It's amazing, the stuff you can remember sometimes.'

'I wish I could remember more,' he scowled. 'I failed practical theology, back in the Academy.'

'Did you pass *anything*?'

'I was highly commended for my landscape gardening.'

'Very useful.'

'You should have been with me when I fought the

221

Vervoids.' He suddenly looked confused. 'You weren't, were you? No, of course you weren't. I have a bit of trouble with that period in my life: bits of it appear to be in the wrong order. Never mind, many a mickle makes a muckle, as somebody once said to someone else.'

'What does that mean?' I asked, confused by the rapid changes in conversational tack, just as I suspect he intended me to be.

'I don't know. I just like the sound of it. I wish I knew who said it – was it Robert Burns? My previous incarnation would have known: he was very good at obscure quotations.'

'And you don't know anything else useful about this Azathoth character? Or what his connection is to all of this?'

'I've got a book that might help, back in the TARDIS. *Every Gallifreyan Child's Pop-Up Book of Nasty Creatures From Other Dimensions*. You'll like it.'

'Don't you think I'm a bit old for a pop-up book?'

'Not compared to a Gallifreyan child. And besides, the pop-ups *are* four-dimensional. But I *really* think that we should discuss it later.'

'Why?'

'Because we've just found Maupertuis's army.'

At that moment I walked into Watson's back. He had stopped, and had been gesturing to us to do the same.

We had been walking for some time and had penetrated some distance along the floor of the valley. The mountains rose to either side of us. Although it was beginning to get dark, I could make out the beginnings of a plain, far ahead. At its edge, a splash of colour and movement stood out.

'They're setting up camp,' Watson murmured. 'Smart move on Colonel Warburton's part: keep them moving after they go through the gateway so they don't have a chance to worry about where they are, then pitch tents when they're good and tired.'

'I suspect that there is a small native town across the plain,' Holmes said, surprising us all.

222

'How can you tell?' the Doctor asked. I got the impression that he wasn't so much questioning Holmes as giving him a chance to explain his thought processes to us.

'The sky appears to be reflective,' Holmes replied, more hesitantly than usual. 'Perhaps, like Dante's inner circle of hell, we have ice above us. If you look closely, you will see a reflected glow from something over the horizon. The nearest Earthly equivalent would be the lights of a town or city.' He coughed. 'I am merely speculating, of course. It could be an incandescent chicken the size of the North Riding for all I know.'

'Maupertuis is probably intending to attack it on the morrow,' Watson said. 'We must bypass the camp and warn the natives.'

'I think they already know,' said the Doctor, pointing up the slope of the left-hand mountain, just above Maupertuis's camp. For a moment I couldn't make anything out through the gloom, then, squinting, I began to make out what looked like bundles of sticks set upright on the slope behind some rocks. Bundles of sticks in armoured suits.

'K'tchar'ch's people,' Watson breathed, and shivered suddenly. He was right, of course. Once he had said it, I could see that they were living beings, but then he and the Doctor had seen them before, whereas I had made do with a second-hand description. 'I wonder what they're doing up there,' he continued. 'Observing, perhaps.'

Silently the Doctor indicated other areas of the mountain slope, and areas of the right-hand mountain as well.

'There are several thousand of the creatures,' Holmes snapped. 'This is an ambush in force.'

'But Maupertuis's army has only been on Ry'leh for a few hours,' I protested. 'How come the Ry'lehans had time to set up an ambush?'

'Perhaps more to the point,' the Doctor added, 'why are a race who claim to be peaceful philosophers armed and armoured?'

'As we suspected,' said Holmes, 'we have been misled.'

I think the phrase is, 'some discussion ensued'. It went

around in circles, but the upshot was that everything K'tchar'ch had told Holmes, Watson and the Doctor was now in doubt, and we didn't know who was the friend and who was the foe. On the face of it, the points were still racked up against Maupertuis, but he had never actually lied to us. Just tried to kill us.

Eventually, as I feared he would, Watson said, 'There's only one thing to do. I'll have to sneak closer and find out what's going on.'

'It's too dangerous,' Holmes urged. 'I should go.'

'You cannot.' Watson placed a hand upon Holmes's upper arm. 'Your ratiocination got us here. Leave the rest up to me. This is what I do best.' He took a deep breath, and looked directly at me. 'I'll be back soon,' he said, and vanished into the deepening shadows.

He wasn't, of course. It's been almost half an hour, and there's no sign of him. Holmes is sat by the fire that the Doctor lit with his eternal matches and some of the local vegetation. The fire squirms every so often, but Holmes is too wrapped up in his own thoughts to care. I hate to see him like this. He seems to have given up.

The Doctor found some sachets of instant coffee in his pocket, along with an unopened bottle of mineral water. We were three thousand years before the use-by date of either of them. The resulting brew tasted so bad that I added a slug of brandy from my hip-flask. It still tasted awful, but at least I could drink it.

The fire is burning low now, and the Doctor and Holmes are both staring into its depths for answers. As for me, the coffee is wearing off, and I'm gradually falling asleep.

A continuation of the reminiscences of John H. Watson, M.D.

I made the mistake of using a bush for shelter as I approached the cluster of canvas tents. It made a lunge for me and I quickly backed off, hoping that its disappointed hiss wouldn't echo through the night air. Fortunately the wind was blowing toward me from the camp, carrying with it the smell of cheap tobacco and roasting meat but hiding any noises that I might make. It had been hours since last I ate, and I had vomited most of that up in the corridors of the Nizam's palace, so the smell of food forced sharp little pangs through my stomach. I quelled them and moved closer.

The camp was set out sloppily: the guards were congregating around a camp-fire rather than patrolling the perimeter and the arrangement of the tents would make it easy for any attackers to duck and dive, and hard for any defenders to marshall their forces. I was surprised at Warburton, but perhaps he could be forgiven. After all, he was organizing the invasion of a planet. He had enough on his plate already. No doubt he had delegated to some old sweat who was more concerned with comfort than carrying out a commission.

Oddly enough, I could see no sign of the fakirs whose chanting had opened the gateway to this world. Perhaps they had set their camp elsewhere.

I glanced up to where the dark shape of the mountains loomed against the icy sky. Somewhere up there, the Ry'lehans were gathering. What did they want? Perhaps if I could discover whether Maupertuis was aware of their presence I would know the answer to that question.

As I crept closer, I saw that the guards were roasting an animal on a spit and telling vulgar jokes. The creature's flesh was greasy and green, and it had three legs. A pair of sightless red eyes gleamed as the juices from the roasting flesh ran over them. I recognized the thing from Holmes's description as being akin to the creature at the dog fight in the Hackney marshes.

I waited, hoping for a particularly crass joke to be told, and whilst the sentries were convulsed with laughter I slipped past them and into the camp. I had to locate Baron Maupertuis, Colonel Warburton and Tir Ram, and to eavesdrop on their conversation. I knew it was a risky course of action, but I felt that it was worth it. The thought of impressing Bernice Summerfield with my courage and feats of derring-do had nothing to do with it.

I slipped like a wraith between concentric circles of

rough tents. The guy-ropes were as unmanageable as a cat's cradle, and I had to pick my way carefully through them, listening all the while for sounds of activity from within. Snoring and muted conversations were all I heard. Nobody was about. I began to take more risks: rather than slipping beneath the ropes I would stand up and step across them.

A cough made me dive for the ground. I held my breath, positive that I must have been seen. After a minute or so during which no alarm was raised and no shots fired, I took the risk of looking up. For a moment I saw nothing, then a match flared in the darkness, illuminating the face of one of Maupertuis's private soldiers. After lighting his cigarette he threw the match towards me. I closed my eyes, and felt it lodge in my hair. For a few agonizing moments I could feel the increasing warmth from my scalp and smell the singeing hair, but dared not move. The feeling of relief that swept over me when he walked away was something that I will remember to my dying day. I swept my hands back and forth across my head until I found the match – dead and cold. Imagination is a powerful enemy. After a few deep breaths I crawled off again.

After ten minutes, I stopped to take stock of my situation. The brave venture was beginning to seem more and more like a misguided attempt at false valour. The camp was larger than I had thought: I could wander around for hours without locating anything of importance.

I turned back.

I had moved five yards when the ground behind me exploded in blue fire. The concussion almost stunned me into insensibility. Tents were engulfed in flame: their occupants spilling out, cursing and screaming. Another explosion, some thirty yards to one side, flung bodies into the air. They fell again to the ground in broken, charred heaps: some of them whimpering, some lying ominously still. Amid the bodies I thought I could make out the crinoline dress worn by Warburton's wife.

I looked wildly around, trying to locate the source of

the attack. Tents burned, soldiers ran around like ants whose nest had been disturbed, but of the attackers I could see nothing.

And then I looked upwards, towards the invisible mountain. A small turquoise flower bloomed upon the slope and faded again to black. Moments later, another explosion knocked me off my feet.

Picking myself up, I began to run back towards the point where I had entered the camp. Nobody bothered with me. They had enough to worry about. Two questions at least had been answered: the Ry'lehans on the slopes of the mountain were not allied to Maupertuis; and they weren't peaceful philosophers either.

A soldier rose up from the collapsed wreckage of his tent. He yelled something at me, but I elbowed him aside and ran on.

Another blast flung me into a collapsing tent. I became tangled in guy-ropes and thrashed about for some moments before I could extricate myself. Standing, I noticed a figure to one side, silhouetted by an azure conflagration. I made to move off, but it raised a hand. A hand holding a gun.

'I should have had you killed back in England,' Baron Maupertuis screamed above the pandemonium. 'You will pay in coins of agony for the trouble you have caused me!'

I tensed, ready to dive, but a cold caress of metal at the nape of my neck made me pause.

'The Baron would prefer to keep you alive for the moment, old boy,' Colonel Warburton's voice drawled in my ear, 'but I think you'd look just as good dead.'

'Haven't you got other things to worry about?' I asked as another of the Ry'lehans' infernal devices exploded nearby.

Maupertuis looked wildly around, his ash-blond hair falling in lank strands around his gaunt face.

'What have you *done*? My army! You have destroyed my army!'

227

'Look elsewhere for your attackers, Baron. Much as I would wish to take credit, I cannot.'

'Then who ...?'

'Your intended victims.'

He sneered.

'The natives of this God-forsaken planet are lily-livered philosophers. They rejected arms millenniums ago.'

'Your hooded friend obviously misinformed you,' I continued, anxious to divert the Baron's attention for as long as possible from whatever plans they had for me. A hit, a very palpable hit. Something moved behind his eyes: a flicker of annoyance, and perhaps even distrust.

'You know nothing.'

I decided to make a stab in the dark.

'I know that you have been played for a fool by whoever it is that you work for.'

A series of explosions punctuated my words.

'Baron,' Warburton interrupted from behind me, 'perhaps we should ...'

'Insects!' the Baron screamed at his troops as they milled around us. 'You were supposed to be an all-consuming fire, spreading out to conquer this planet in the name of the Empire! Now you run like *insects*!' His cold gaze turned to Warburton.

'You assured me that their training had turned them into an efficient fighting machine. You guaranteed that they were ready for anything!'

The pressure of Warburton's pistol vanished from my neck. Surreptitiously I edged sideways.

'You gave me a month!' Warburton snapped. 'It takes years to build up an army, and you gave me a month!'

'It was not my decision,' Maupertuis said coldly. 'I agreed with your strategy. I was overruled.'

'Whoever our mysterious benefactor is, he knows as much about building a fighting force as I do about ballet dancing.'

Maupertuis looked around. The camp was almost deserted now. The landscape of burning tents was bereft of movement.

228

'As I have no army,' he said calmly, 'and no need of a ballet tutor, it would seem that I no longer require your services.'

He shot Colonel Warburton between the eyes. I watched with mixed feelings as Warburton stumbled backwards, staring at Maupertuis with a puzzled expression on his face. Blood streamed from the wound.

'Gloria?' he said in a quiet, almost conversational tone, then fell to his knees. 'Gloria . . .?'

He pitched forward onto his face. His fingers clutched at the cold, hard ground for a moment, and then a great shudder ran through his body.

'God forgive your sins,' I murmured to his departing spirit.

'There is no sin,' Maupertuis said, swinging his pistol so that I was staring down the rifled barrel. 'There is only disobedience in the face of a higher authority.'

'And who elected you to be a higher authority?' I said scathingly. 'You bring the whole human race into disrepute.'

As an epitaph, I wish I had been given time to polish it a bit, but it would do. As Maupertius's finger tightened on the trigger, and I watched the tiny gleam at the end of the barrel that I knew was the tip of the bullet that would shortly be tearing through my brain, I tried to recall Holmes's face as an example to give me courage. I could not. All I could remember was an afternoon thirty years ago, when the bright Australian sun shone down upon a creek, and my father and brother and I sat and fished together. It was the happiest day of my life, but I had not realized it until now.

The world seemed to explode around me. My eyes were filled with a red mist. So this was death.

The mist settled on my face. It was sticky and tasted of salt and hot metal. I licked it from my lips. I had spent enough of my youth tying off spurting arteries that I recognized it as blood. Mine? Reflexively I wiped a hand across my eyes.

Maupertuis was still standing in front of me, gun raised,

but there was a large hole in the middle of his chest. The rim was charred and I could see the edges of his rib-cage projecting into the void where his heart should have been.

His face was noble in death. Noble and unreal, like a marble statue. He fell like a statue too: without bending.

A young woman stood behind him. She was holding a device the size of a Maxim gun, but a lot sleeker.

'Hi,' she said. 'My name's Ace. And you're grateful.'

The sharp-edged rocks tore at my fingertips . . .

Chapter 14

In which Ace and Watson pit themselves against nature, and come out on top

She was wearing a smooth armoured bodice like the carapace of some glossy black beetle. Her shirt and leggings seemed to be composed of some fine-mesh metal weave. She was wearing spectacles, but of such a deep hue that I could not make out her eyes. I could not help but wonder how she could see out of them in the dark. She was so shorn of the identifying badges of her gender that the only clues were her long hair, her voice and the curve of her bodice.

Her weapon was trained firmly upon my midriff.

'My name is Watson,' I said, and swallowed. All I could see in her spectacles was my own distorted reflection. I hoped that the panic evident in my expression was caused by the distortion rather than the circumstances. 'Doctor John Watson, at your service. I presume that you are another of the Doctor's companions, Miss . . . ah?'

'Ace, like I said. And what makes you think I'm with the Doc?'

'A wild guess. He seems to have a fondness for leaving young ladies in situations fraught with danger.'

She looked around.

'Young ladies? Oh, I get it. You must mean Bernice.'

She stared strangely at me.

'Are you for real?' she asked.

'Indubitably. Shall we go?'

She lowered the gun and, with a couple of quick twists,

disassembled it into components which she hung off her belt.

'Show me the way.'

I pointed, and without another word she moved off. I took a last glance back at Baron Maupertuis's ruined body. I could not find it in my heart to regret what Ace – I supposed that I should call her by that appellation – had done to him, but something in me had responded to his fervent, if misguided, patriotism.

But what now? Would his invasion fall apart with his army scattered and its general dead, or would the mysterious hooded man that Holmes and I had seen in Euston weld it back together again? Only time would tell.

We moved across the ravaged landscape, trying as far as we could to avoid the bodies. The explosions seemed to have ceased, but I could see a large number of survivors forming up into lines closer to the slopes of the mountain. It looked to me as if they were preparing to take the fight to the Ry'lehans.

Ace quickly impressed me with her skills. She moved quickly but carefully, maintaining a constant watch upon our surroundings. She threw questions back over her shoulder and, under their prompting, I told her the story of how we came to be there.

'He shouldn't meddle,' she said at one point. 'He doesn't know the half of what's going on here.'

'What do you mean?' I asked, but she gestured impatiently for me to continue.

I finished talking as we passed the last row of tents, and persuaded her to wait for a few moments whilst I found the beast which had been roasting as I entered the camp. The spit had been knocked over during the attack, but the carcass was still in one piece, and I managed to pull two of the legs off. They did not look appetizing, but I was ravenous. I rejoined Ace, who refused the food I offered with a secret little smile. As we walked off I asked her how she came to be there. Whilst I ate the tender, spicy flesh, she explained in a few terse sentences that the Doctor had left her on Ry'leh in the same way that he had left Bernice in India, and for the same reasons. She was meant to scout out the area, prepare the way for the Doctor and report on anything interesting that happened. Having seen my confrontation with Maupertuis, she had decided to act.

'Does he always do this sort of thing?' I asked.

'What sort of thing?'

'Move you and Bernice round like pieces in a game of chess?'

'You don't know the half of it. Trouble is, I've seen him play chess, and he's crap.'

By now I had finished both legs and discarded the bones. My stomach was beginning to rebel against its unfamiliar contents, but I ruthlessly suppressed the incipient insurrection. I would not give Ace the satisfaction of seeing me ill.

The camp was a few miles behind us now, and we were approaching the area where I remembered leaving my friends. Looking round, I could see no sign of Bernice, Holmes or the Doctor. I caught hold of Ace's arm to stop her whilst I got my bearings. At the touch of my hand she whirled and knocked me to the ground. My head slammed against rock: I blacked out for a moment, and awoke to find her fingers pressed into my windpipe.

'A word of warning,' she hissed. 'Don't touch me. Too many people have done that already, starting with a scumbag named Glitz. I don't like it, and these days, what I don't like, I stop. Violently.'

'Glawp!' I said. It was all I could manage to get out of my compressed larynx.

'I'm glad that's understood.'

She stood up and looked around.

'So where's the party, then?'

I rolled over to enable my arms to take the strain of lifting my body, bruised and battered by recent events, to its feet. A dark stain on the ground caught my attention. I touched it tentatively, and my fingers came away sticky.

It was blood.

I ran a hand across the back of my head to determine

whether I had hit the ground harder than I had thought, but my scalp was clear of any wounds.

'Ace,' I said.

'I know.'

I rose, to find her holding the torn remains of the Doctor's paisley-pattern scarf.

'Why is nothing ever easy where he's concerned?'

To that I had no answer.

Casting around, we found little else to indicate that they had ever been there. The most significant discovery was a patch of charred ground where a fire had obviously been lit. The ashes were still warm.

As a pearly, directionless sheen spread across the sky, heralding the approach of a new day, I sat down upon the hard, cold ground. A patch of moss squirmed beneath me, so I shuffled sideways. It tried to follow, so I stood up again and watched it cast itself unsuccessfully upon my boots.

Sounds of gunfire suddenly drifted across the plain. Maupertuis's shattered army had regrouped enough to go on the offensive. I wondered who was leading them now.

Hearing a sound, I glanced round to where Ace was talking softly into a small box. I wondered if it was some marvellous form of communication, but I soon realized that she was leaving no space for a reply. A dictation machine, perhaps, akin to the phonograph but much smaller.

I glanced around at the harsh landscape now emerging from the shadow of night. The murmur of Ace's voice ceased.

'Who do you think took them?' I asked.

'How do I know?' She sounded bad-tempered. 'It could have been this Baron's men, or it could have been the spindly sack-things with five legs, or it could have been those winged creatures with the spiky tails. We won't know till we find them.'

'I doubt that it's the rakshassi,' I said patronizingly. 'They're only animals.'

'Rakshassi?'

'The winged creatures. The red ones.'

'Who told you they're only animals?'

I frowned.

'Well . . . it seemed obvious.'

'Nothing obvious about it, mate. They're as intelligent as you or me. Well, you at any rate.'

I didn't know what to say for a moment.

'But . . .' I stammered finally, 'they've never shown any sign of intellect . . .'

She looked pityingly at me.

'Well they're not going to do crosswords on the train, are they, dick-brain? Remember that seance you told me about? The one in Euston with this hooded geezer?'

I nodded.

'Well, I was listening to the other end of it. There's a large township a couple of hundred clicks away . . .'

'Clicks?'

'Kilometres. A bit over a hundred miles. Anyway, I was scouting around a big temple-type building, and heard something big inside opening hailing frequencies. The town itself was occupied by the rakshassi.'

'Occupied? You mean, they were *living* there?'

'Yeah. Worshipping at the temple, too.'

'Worshipping what?'

'I don't know, but it wasn't Sonic the Hedgehog.'

She took pleasure in watching the stunned expression blossom on my face. Foolishly, perhaps, I had made certain assumptions about the nature of the new reality in which I had found myself. Now, one by one, those assumptions were being overturned. If only Holmes were there to make things clear for me.

'They could have taken him anywhere,' I whispered to myself, disheartened.

'Not quite,' Ace said. 'The plants here kip during the night, and they get a bit ratty if something disturbs them. If we're lucky, we can tell which way the kidnappers went by checking how quickly the plants react to us.'

'How do we do that?' I asked stupidly.

237

'Stick your finger out and see how long it takes them to bite it.'

Ace watched on, a sardonic smile upon her face, as I hesitantly knelt and tempted the mosses with my outstretched digit. It quickly became apparent that those lying towards the distant mountains responded significantly faster than those in any other direction. So quick were they that they almost ripped my nail out with their thorny little mouths.

'Well,' she said, 'that settles it.'

'Do you think they're poisonous?'

'I wouldn't have thought so. They're probably more at risk biting you than you are being bitten.'

'Somehow that fails to reassure me.'

'It wasn't meant to.'

We set out shortly after that.

The walk to the lower slopes of the nearest mountain took us some hours. Every few minutes I would check the plants in the vicinity to ensure that we were heading in the right direction, but our course was as straight as a die. It was hard to tell when we actually began to climb the mountain slopes: it was only after I complained to Ace that I was tiring, and she agreed that the going suddenly seemed to have become hard, that we realized we had been walking uphill for some little time. We rested for a few moments, and I took the opportunity to appreciate the view in the manner of a tourist, rather than a tired doctor.

The slope fell away from us, blending gradually into the purple plain below. I could see Maupertuis's quondam encampment and, through the haze of distance, men in blue and silver uniforms in close combat with five-legged Ry'lehans. Further than that, the ground rose up to form more mountain ranges whose tops were lost to the ice. Ry'leh seemed to be a planet composed of peakless mountains. From where we stood I could see along three major valleys. It was like standing in Cheddar Gorge back on Earth, and looking between the stalactites and stalagmites,

238

but on a far vaster scale. What was God thinking of when he created this place?

We seemed to have risen above what, on Earth, I would have termed the tree-line. The vegetation had died away, but we had been moving in a straight line for so long that we saw little point in altering our course.

We were closer to the sky now, and I could see features upon it: patches of shadow, deep gouges and little black specks that seemed to move.

'Animals,' said Ace when I pointed them out to her. 'Good to eat, too. I shoot them down with a bow and arrow when I get the chance. They taste of chocolate.'

'But how can . . .?'

'They're like big balloons full of some gas that's lighter than air. They float up against the ice.'

'I see. So how do they move around?'

She looked at me as if I was slow-witted.

'Skates,' she said succinctly.

We moved on. The going was getting rougher now: we were having to use our hands, more often than not, to pull ourselves along. Sometimes, when I looked up, the sky was a milky white wall towards which we were crawling. At one point I grasped at a rock which came away in my hand and rolled down the slope with an increasing clatter of smaller stones following it until it was out of sight. The echoes of its passage lived on for some time.

It was getting colder. Much colder. I turned the collar of my coat up and bound strips of handkerchief round my hands, but it was of little use. Ace did not seem to be bothered by the cold.

'You should try doing route marches on Ragnarok,' she snapped when I offered her my jacket. 'The only inhabitants are a tribe of brass monkeys who all look like they've lost something.'

I did not understand her meaning, so I smiled and climbed on.

By this time I was forced to seek out crevices with my hands and feet to anchor myself before taking a step. The sharply edged rocks tore at my fingertips, and the blood

239

seeping from the wounds made my handholds difficult. I wished that I had brought gloves. The weight of my body constantly threatened to tear me from the rock and send me hurtling down the slope. I dared not look down. My world was a few square feet of rock, my one aim to find enough purchase to enable me to pull myself onwards to another world: another few feet of rock. Every so often, but not often enough, Ace called a halt. In those periods I gazed ahead, toward the oppressive ice barrier. Wave-like formations of thin clouds seemed to chase each other across its surface and crash against the mountainside where it penetrated the ice. The inflated bladder-like animals skated across the sky in flocks of ten or twenty, looking rather like fat pheasants, or perhaps puffed-up goldfish. The thought of chocolate began to obsess me.

We passed a stream of some viscous turquoise substance that wound its way through the rocks. My throat was dry, and so I made as if to drink some. Ace warned me off.

'It's not water,' she said. 'More like a liquid atmosphere. Oxygen and nitrogen, mainly, although it should be gaseous at this temperature. Probably some kind of allotropic form that we don't get on Earth. A-level chemistry's all right for a few bangs, but not much use on alien planets.'

Over the course of a few minutes, I found it increasingly difficult to breath. My lungs seemed to be on fire, and I felt as if spikes were being driven into my temples. Finding handholds was almost impossible: I seemed to be able to concentrate on a smaller area of ground than before and my hands were having to scrabble in the grey areas on the edges of my vision until they found something which would take my weight. Twice I found nothing, and had to retrace my path and find a new one. I cursed myself for eating that alien creature. Its flesh was obviously poisonous, and I had obviously ingested an incapacitating, if not fatal, dose. It was only when I noticed that Ace was also having problems that I remembered the symptoms of oxygen deprivation, and suggested that we go back and dip handkerchiefs in the stream. If we tied them around our necks, I reasoned, the heat of our bodies should cause the liquid to evaporate back into a breathable vapour. Although sceptical, Ace complied with my suggestion. I am glad to say that it worked, and we were able to climb onwards refreshed. We made sure that we climbed alongside the stream, and when the effort of drawing a breath became a chore again, we would re-moisten our handkerchiefs. Ace took me more seriously after that.

We were constantly attempting to find the easiest path up the side of the mountain, choosing those sections which appeared to have more cracks which we could use as hand- and footholds, detouring around large outcrops of stone and sections of friable rock, always trying to look ahead and predict which channels, chimneys or ledges would lead to fresh paths and which would lead to dead ends. Sometimes we got it right, and could gain ten or fifteen feet in a few minutes: sometimes we got it wrong and would have to retrace our steps and find another path. Frequently we would have to spend as much time travelling sideways, edging along precarious ledges, as we did climbing upwards.

A cramp hit me as we traversed one such section: a fairly broad lip of rock beneath a jutting boulder made of some striated element more impervious to the weathering effect of the wind. I fell to my knees, clutching at my calf. The pain was agonizing, as if a ligament had snapped or a muscle had torn. I was familiar with the sensation – I used to play rugby for Blackheath – but it as no more welcome for that. Fortunately Ace was also familiar with cramp, and forced me to lie flat whilst she massaged my calf until the muscle relaxed.

'Are you sure that we're headed in the right direction?' I asked as her fingers probed my leg.

'No. I haven't seen anywhere for them to have diverted, though, so it looks like we're headed for the top.'

The wind picked up as we climbed higher. It attacked us first from one direction and then from another, circling around to find our weakest spots, sometimes insinuating its cold, hard fingers into our clothes and sapping the strength from our limbs, sometimes buffeting us hard and making us lose our precious fingerholds. There was no mercy here: the elements were pitting their strength against two pygmies who had dared profane this sacred place. Perversely these natural attacks gave me some small measure of comfort, for compared to them the evil of men such as Maupertuis and his mysterious master were as nothing. If we could defeat the mountain, I felt that we could defeat anything.

That epiphany proved to be the turning point of the climb. Perhaps the cold had finally got to me and numbed my marrow but I felt warmer and more confident after that. Even when the rock vanished, to be replaced with a sheer wall of black ice, I did not quail. Ace and I took turns with her miraculous weapon, which she had set to produce a thin knife of sunlight, cutting steps into the ice. I took my cue from her: each step that she cut was precisely the right size, no deeper than it should be, and spaced apart from its neighbours by a comfortable distance. My own initial attempts were farcical but I soon learned how to wield the device, and I found that I could match her delicacy of touch.

At one stage, when Ace was above me, cutting away, and I was clinging to the steps that I had recently cut but which had refrozen within seconds, I looked past her. The mountain could only have been a few hundred yards in diameter at that point, and I was shocked to discover that the sky was only a few body-lengths away. At that range the ice was pitted, rough and grey. Gaps existed between the ice and the mountain: black voids, like wounds in reality. The river of liquid atmosphere, just a trickle at this elevation, emerged from one of them. The view was half-hidden by tendrils of mist which curled around us. Looking down, first a few inches, then a few feet, and then further, I found that I could no longer make out the ground. We were suspended between heaven and hell, cocooned in the mist.

'Jesus, I didn't realize we were so close.'

Ace's voice surprised me out of my reverie. I climbed past her and took the light-gun.

'A few more minutes should see us to the top,' I grunted, and set to work cutting a set of steps and then a rough platform for us to stand on, side by side.

Reverently, I reached up and touched the sky. It was as hard as the mountain had been, and as cold. I craned my neck and looked out, upside down, along its surface. My mind played funny tricks with perspective, for a moment I couldn't tell which direction was up and which was down, what was surface and what was sky. Some primitive part of my brain kept screaming that I was going to fall, but only for a moment.

And then a distorted face thrust itself out of a patch of mist at me, and I *did* scream.

Ace laughed.

'It's only one of the skaters,' she said.

Catching my breath, I looked closer. The face, which looked so much like a gross caricature of a well-fed, gout-ridden Dickensian gentleman, or a rector straight out of Trollope, gazed with an expression of bovine stupidity straight from a spherical, semi-transparent body some ten feet in diameter. Three stubby limbs rose from the top of the body, each terminating in what looked for all the world like a skate, made of some bony substance. A pouch of skin drooped below the creature. I wondered for a moment what its function was, but I was enlightened when the creature grew bored with me and unfurled the pouch to form a sail with which it caught the breeze and skated away across the surface of the ice.

'Your face,' Ace said, and laughed again.

'They taste of chocolate, you say?'

'Yeah. They have these big macho dominance fights, sometimes, and they use those skate-things as weapons. The loser gets his balloon punctured and falls all the way down to the surface. I got hungry one night, and one just dropped out of the sky, virtually into my lap. "That's 'andy, 'Arry," I said, and bunged it on the fire. After that I made myself a bow and arrow. No time to eat now, though. We've got a job to do.'

'Where do we go now?'

She looked around.

'Where else is there? Onward and upward.'

'Upward *where*?'

She indicated the gap where the ice did not quite meet the rock.

'Up there. To the *real* surface. To the outside.'

'Are you *mad*? There's no reason to think that they've been taken up there! The chances are that we missed the signs of a camp or a cave further down the mountain, and we've been climbing blindly ever since!'

Ace nodded to a larger fissure some thirty or so feet away.

'Look at that. The edges aren't natural. They've been clawed away. That's where they were taken.'

'But..' I was searching round for excuses now. I did not want to climb any further. Every muscle in my body ached with the accumulated toxins of fatigue. '. . . But the air is too thin. How will we manage to breathe? How did *they* manage? You must be mistaken.'

'That's a bit of a poser,' Ace admitted, frowning. 'You're right of course. If the atmosphere's this thin here, it'll be non-existent if we climb much further. They probably had suits of some kind. We'll have to improvize.'

I didn't like the sound of that.

'Improvize?'

'What's the matter, never seen *Blue Peter*?'

'No.'

'Lucky man. Now think: how do we ensure a supply of air for ourselves?'

'We've managed with the handkerchiefs so far,' I offered.

'True, but the path might move away from the mountain side, like in a tunnel through the ice or something. We can't rely on still being able to use the stream to refresh them.'

'So we need a larger supply,' I mused.

'Good thinking, Sherlock.'

I frowned at her and she blushed, embarrassed.

'What about the animals?' I asked, as an idea suddenly struck me.

'The animals? You mean, cut a couple of them open, get rid of the gas inside and replace it with air?' She grinned. 'Ace!'

Luring the creatures over was, paradoxically, the easiest part. They were not wary of humans in the way that animals on Earth might have been. We had a few teething troubles in the butchery department: Ace used her light-gun on the first one, and it exploded with a surprised expression upon its face, singeing my eyebrows. The gas inside appeared to be inflammable, as well as lighter than air. The next one was almost as bad. I held it whilst Ace made a slight incision in its tough but flexible skin with my pocket knife. It burst in my arms, splattering me with a gelid blue substance. If I hadn't been so cold and so tired, the farcical elements of our actions would have set me laughing. As it was, both of us were getting increasingly angry. By the time we had captured a third creature, we had evolved a strategy. I pinched a section of its skin, and Ace cut off the protruding section. I could then gradually let the gas out using my fingers as a crude valve. It died struggling, and in confusion. The gas made me slightly light-headed, but I welcomed the feeling as it cushioned my tiredness somewhat. It also made me feel slightly better about what we were doing. I did not enjoy killing them, especially in such an undignified manner, but we were desperate.

Once we had two deflated skins, we set about cutting away the limbs and protruding members and refilling the remaining bladders. We carefully held the rents beneath the surface of the stream until some liquid got in. Whilst I held them closed again, Ace filled two oddly shaped canteens with liquid as well, and hooked one onto my belt.

'Additional supplies,' she said, then climbed inside one of the skins. I did likewise with the other. We knotted the rents from the inside. As we had hoped, the warmth from our bodies vaporized the liquid and inflated the skin.

Urgency had lent skill to our endeavours: the scheme had worked, and we were left standing within two tough, translucent, taut spheres that used to be living creatures but now functioned as crude reservoirs of breathable air.

Ace waved at me. I waved back, and followed her as she carefully climbed up towards the dark opening. The skin of the life-preserving integument deformed beneath our fingers and feet, enabling us to climb, but was tough enough to resist tearing against the rock.

We entered the dark channel. A tunnel led upwards through the ice at a shallow enough angle that we could walk along it in comfort. Ace turned and bestowed a triumphant smile upon me. I pretended not to see it.

We walked for what seemed like hours. There were no side tunnels, no choices of path. Although the walls were rough ice, I gained the impression that they had been carved, rather than formed naturally. They glowed with what I first took to be an inner effulgence, but later realized was the light from the planet's sun, refracted through the ice. It got brighter as we walked, and more directional. Upon Ry'leh's interior surface I had not been able to tell where the sun was, merely that it was up. Now I could have pointed to it with some accuracy. I stumbled numerous times, but each time I managed to pick myself up and carry on. My friends were depending on me. All I wanted to do was sleep, but I kept on putting one foot before the other, slogging away like a trooper. The air within the balloon became stuffier and stuffier, and the skin grew tauter and tauter as the pressure outside reduced, but the trapped warmth of my body combated the cold which stung my fingers whenever I inadvertently touched the skin. I was on the verge of passing out when I remembered the canteen that Ace had provided me with. With clumsy fingers I untied the knot and tried to bleed some of the stale air away. The reduced pressure outside snatched at the rent, but I managed to hang on. I retied the skin when the balloon was half empty and carefully poured some liquid from Ace's canteen. Within seconds the balloon had reflated, and I felt refreshed.

246

I glanced over to where Ace had stopped. She was engaged in the same activity. From the haggard look upon her face, she had almost left it too late.

We started walking again along the monotonous tunnel. I had completely lost track of time, and was dreaming about roast turkey and plum pudding, when Ace stopped. I bumped into her, and rebounded. She pointed ahead.

There was an irregular black opening some ten feet away. Cautiously, we crept closer and peered out.

We had emerged at the base of a sheer cliff. The landscape that surrounded us was like illustrations I have seen of the surface of the moon. Tremendous spires of rock – the tops of the mountains – soared into the jet-black, star-speckled sky. Broken escarpments and jumbled, irregular cliffs vied with large expanses of flat ice. A bloated red sphere, spotted with black, hung above our heads, casting a maleficent light across the terrain.

I have reconstructed the view at my leisure, to set the scene for the adventures that were to come. At the time, it was not the alienness of the landscape that captured and held our attention but rather the group of wooden caravans that sat not twenty feet away from us. Their seams were sealed with some black, sticky substance and they sat upon huge metal runners that cut deeply into the ice. The central caravan was cathedral-sized and ornate, with symbols carved deeply into its sides and ten or eleven doors spaced around its circumference. The others were smaller, clustered like ducklings around their mother. Great grooves in the ice led away towards the horizon. They had been brought here.

Surrounding them: hundreds of rakshassi. They too were encased in inflated skins, forcing them to fold their wings up against their backs. Some of them were busying themselves with ropes, a handful of others were connecting the larger caravan to one of the smaller ones with a tube which seemed to have been sewn together out of the same flexible skins that Ace and I wore, and inflating it.

As we watched, a door in the largest caravan opened and a figure emerged wearing a hooded robe. Climbing down from the caravan to the ground, the figure walked calmly through the tube towards the smaller caravan. Two rakshassi followed it. It was hardly a shock to me, but a shiver still ran up my spine as I recognized Maupertuis's mysterious superior, the person at the seance in Euston.

Ace touched her balloon against mine.

'Well,' her voice said faintly, 'it looks like a party. Shall we gatecrash?'

Chapter 15

In which Holmes discovers that all things are relative and Watson sees the face of God

Extract from the diary of Bernice Summerfield

Well, despite having two of the best brains this side of the planet Arcadia on the team, we've been captured. Comprehensively and unquestionably captured. Imprisoned. Shut up in a wooden caravan. The tinkle that I heard just after the door slammed was probably them throwing away the key.

I could write a traveller's guide to places not to be locked up in. This one gets three stars: it's clean, at least, and you can stand up without hitting your head but, as you can probably tell from the handwriting, it's dark. I'm writing by the light of the Doctor's everlasting matches, but they flicker too much to let me write in a straight line. In the shadows I can hear Holmes pacing up and down and muttering to himself. I can't say I blame him: he's had a hell of shock. All I can see of the Doctor is his eyes gleaming in the darkness. He doesn't move or make any noise for ages, then he murmurs something, like, 'Of course, the Anglo-Saxon name for a council of kings was a micklemote,' and subsides into silence again.

But I'm getting ahead of myself (so easy to do when you're a time traveller). Where did I leave us at the end of the last entry? Oh yes, camping out on the plain, waiting for Watson to return. Well, I fell into a fitful sleep, punctuated by bright blue flowers that bloomed noisily across my mind's eye. It was only when the Doctor shook me awake that I found that there was some sort of attack going on in Maupertuis's camp. The Ry'lehans on the mountainside were firing at the humans down below. There was general confusion, and I can't say that I blame them. My heart flip-flopped a couple of times when I thought about Watson being caught up in it. I mean, he's such an innocent abroad, I'd hate it if anything happened to him.

'As von Clausewitz so nearly said,' Holmes muttered dryly, 'war is the continuation of philosophy by other means.'

A movement overhead caught my eye. I glanced up. A bat-winged silhouette was dropping rapidly towards me. Bloody hell, I thought, it's a rakshassa! I shouted at Holmes and the Doctor, and tried to dive out of the way. The creature's claws hit the ground where I had been sitting, striking sparks from the rock. I rolled sideways, but it was too fast for me. With an ungainly hop it straddled my body, blocking any escape with the shrouds of its wings. I recoiled in disgust as it lowered its spiky face toward mine. In the valleys between the spikes I could see small red orifices fluttering open and shut.

'So . . .' it hissed, its breath rancid and steaming, 'we have the unbelievers who killed our brothers. We forgive you. We forgive you.'

The shock of hearing it speak, and realizing that it was intelligent, made my head whirl. I glanced to one side, looking for Holmes and the Doctor, hoping that one of them at least had managed to put up some resistance, but the creature's crimson wing blocked my view.

'Don't worry . . .' Its voice was warm in my ear. 'We have the other two heathens.'

'Let me *go*!' I shouted.

'Or what?' it asked, amused. Small droplets of its spittle rained down upon my face. I tried not to gag.

'Or I'll . . . Look, what do you want with us, anyway?'

It cocked its head slightly.

'You will see the light,' it said.

'Oh, great. And this will happen when?'

'Worry not, human. The ceremony of innocence will soon begin.'

Before I could move, it reared up on its wing tips and wrapped its tail tightly around my rib-cage. Springing into the air, it spread its wings wide and flapped, gaining height rapidly. I tried to take a breath but the damned thing was holding me too tight. The world stared to fuzz out, like static on an open comm-link. Air buffeted my face as the rakshassa's wings clutched at the air and pulled us aloft, but I couldn't seem to get any of it where it would do the most good. I tried to prise the segmented coils of its tail apart, but they were unmovable. I hit out at its cold, hard body but it didn't even seem to notice.

And then a gust of wind caught us and it shifted its grip on me slightly. Enough to breathe. I sucked in great gulps of precious air, too concerned with staying alive to bother about the sudden and catastrophic turnabout in our fortunes. After a few minutes of that, after my heart settled down and stopped threatening to jump through my chest, I took a look around.

And wished I hadn't.

The camp was a small blot on the landscape. Below us, and slightly to one side, another rakshassa soared upwards with the Doctor held tighty beneath it. He waved reassuringly at me. Irrationally, I felt like punching him on the nose. Morose for no reason and cheerful in a crisis. I don't know how his other companions managed to stand him for so long. Or maybe they didn't. Maybe they're all in therapy now.

'The battle is still going on,' Holmes cried faintly from somewhere above me. 'Maupertuis's men appear to have successfully counter-attacked.'

As we rose higher, I could see that although most of the tents were on fire, Maupertuis's men in their bright shiny uniforms were putting up quite a fight out on the plain. They had a number of Gatling guns set up, and were raking the Ry'lehan lines. Although the Ry'lehans had superior firepower they appeared to be surprised at

251

the resistance they were getting. A number of little five-legged shapes were lying dead upon the ground.

Something odd was happening on the far side of the camp. I could see winged shapes – rakshassi – diving down and picking up the occasional figure. They were very selective, swooping low over the heads of the soldiery and choosing only the occasional victim. Gradually I realized what they were doing.

'It's the Indian fakirs!' I yelled. 'The rakshassi are only picking up the Indian fakirs! The rest of Maupertuis's men are being left to fight the Ry'lehans.'

'I cannot see Watson,' Holmes shouted. The Doctor remained silent, but I could see the scowl on his face.

We flew higher, and higher still. The fires of Maupertuis's camp dwindled until they were just a bright glow on the ground. As I saw more of the landscape of Ry'leh, I began to appreciate its raw, uncompromising beauty. Valleys snaked away in every direction and the ice sky reflected the mountains so that it looked as if we were rising from the surface of one world, past twisted pillars, towards the surface of another. After a while I became disoriented, but as we got closer and closer to the ice I could see that it had its own topography and its own ecology. Looking around, I saw that we had been joined by a number of other rakshassi, each clutching a bewildered fakir in its tail. Some of the fakirs were chanting prayers, others appeared to have passed out. I thought I could see Tir Ram, the Nizam of Jabalhabad, dangling from the tail of a rakshassa in the distance, but it was difficult to be sure.

Eventually, the rakshassi settled onto the upper slopes of a mountain like a flock of birds congregating on a church steeple. I tried to take a breath, but the air was so thin that I found myself gasping. My eyes streamed but I could see a large crack in the ice where the mountain pierced it. A translucent tunnel poked out of it like some bloated worm. It looked like it had been made from circular patches of material or skin sewn together. It bulged, as if filled with air, and there was a zip-like arrangement at one end. It looked to me remarkably like a crude but workable pressurized corridor. The rakshassi were picking up their prisoners, one by one, flying them up to the mouth of the tunnel and throwing them in, then pulling up the zip after them. Dimly, through the skin of the tunnel, I could see another rakshassa inside the corridor operating another zip. Okay, it was a crude but workable pressurized corridor with an airlock. I had to admire their ingenuity, if not their good looks and personal hygiene.

Eventually it was my turn, and not a moment too soon. I was on the verge of passing out. After a short flight I was thrown into the tunnel, and after the zip was fastened behind me the rakshassa inside opened *his* zip and pulled me through into the main body of the corridor. A sudden rush of oxygen made me dizzy. Where was it coming from?

I reached out to touch the walls. They were smooth and leathery, and marred every few feet by a rough stitched seam. Beyond them, the smooth walls of an icy tunnel led upwards at a gentle angle.

My fingers ran over what felt like a distorted nose and a puffy cheek. I didn't want to know.

The rakshassa at the tunnel mouth grabbed my shoulder and pulled me past its hard body to join the end of a line of turbaned and breech-clothed fakirs. We all trudged along through the dark and the cold. The fakirs were singing some kind of gentle song, but I didn't know the words. I tried calling out for the Doctor or Holmes, or even Tir Ram, but there was no response. For the first time I felt truly alone.

We emerged after what seemed like hours onto the surface of Ry'leh. The sight of the stars shining down on us cheered me up for a moment. Through the translucent skin of the tunnel I could see that the peaks of the mountains erupted through the ice all around, giving the planet the air of a frightened hedgehog.

A group of large wooden caravans on skates were huddled together out on the ice. Gouges in the ice showed that this was the end of their journey, not the start. Mostly they were small, but one enormous one loomed over the rest, so big and so heavy that the ice seemed to bow slightly beneath it.

The pressurized tunnel, which I now realize was sewn together out of animal skins, led to another airlock, which was connected to a large wooden caravan on skates. This place was getting wilder and wilder. A rakshassa at the end of the tunnel was throwing prisoners willy-nilly into its dark interior. A queue had already formed. Every so often there would be a hold-up while the airlock was resealed and the caravan was towed away by teams of rakshassi pulling ropes, to be replaced with another one. The rakshassi outside the tunnel were all squeezed into impromptu spacesuits. They had to fold their wings up to fit in. I hoped it hurt.

I shuffled forward, a few steps at a time, trying to come up with some witty comment but failing miserably. Miserably, yes, that was the word. When I got to the end, the rakshassa took a closer look at me, then pulled me roughly inside.

'You are special,' it assured me.

'Tell me something I don't know,' I snapped, but it was already busy throwing more fakirs into the caravan.

I slumped against the wall of the corridor for a while, glad of the chance to rest. One by one, the fakirs filed past me.

'Mr Summerfield!'

I jerked out of my reverie to find the youthful figure of Tir Ram standing in the line. His fine robes were ruined, but the Indians around him still knelt in his presence. My brain floundered for a moment, then I remembered that I had attended his feast disguised as a man. I was still wearing the same formal attire, but it was just as ripped and stained as his was by now. Considering the rips, I was surprised that he still referred to me as 'Mr'. He was either being polite or he'd led a sheltered life.

'Happy?' I asked.

'I do beg your pardon?'

'Are you happy? Have your plans worked out the way you thought?'

254

Sarcasm was wasted on him.

'I think that I was misled by the good Baron,' he said without any trace of irony. 'He promised me a new empire. He said that Jabalhabad would be a new port, a landbound harbour through which the trade of two worlds would flow.'

He smiled, rather shamefacedly.

'I'm afraid I believed him,' he continued. 'I didn't want Jabalhabad to remain a backwater province too small even for you British to bother about. Was I wrong?'

There was desperation in his voice.

'Ask them,' I said, gesturing towards his subjects. He opened his mouth to reply, but the rakshassa picked him up and threw him into the airlock.

I saw the Doctor's hat bobbing in the distance, and called out to him. He was talking earnestly to one of the fakirs, but waved his hat in the air in reply. A few minutes later we were reunited as the rakshassa pulled him out to stand beside me. We hugged in greeting. Holmes joined us shortly afterwards, but I didn't hug him.

The next caravan to come along was for us and us alone.

'We're honoured,' I murmured as I climbed through a simple but effective wooden airlock arrangement into the dark interior.

'There are times,' the Doctor said, joining me, 'when it pays to be one of the crowd.'

'You suspect that we have been singled out for something special?' Holmes asked.

I could just make out the Doctor's sombre expression.

'It seems to be the story of my life.'

Holmes laughed briefly.

'And mine as well. We make a fine pair, Doctor.'

The heavy *thud* of the door cut off my retort. Darkness descended upon us.

And that's where we are now. The caravan moved off shortly after that, but stopped a few minutes later. It looked like we were parking until all of the prisoners had been transferred from the tunnel. The Doctor lit a couple of his wonder-matches and stuck them into his hatband, so we could just about see what we were doing.

Which wasn't much.

Holmes paced up and down, and the Doctor made gnomic little utterances from time to time. To keep myself amused I did my usual trick of going back over my diary entries for the past few days and sticking yellow labels over the pages, then writing an alternative, more dramatic version of events in which I played a much larger part. After a while, even that palled.

When we heard the outer airlock door *chunk* open, then shut, I was so glad to have my boredom relieved that I didn't even feel scared. It was only when the inner door opened and a figure in a hooded white robe and white gloves stepped into the room, flanked by a massive rakshassa, that I felt a shiver run through me like a seam of silver through rock.

The figure stood silently for a moment. I could feel its gaze pass across me, although I couldn't see any features within the hood. The light from the Doctor's matches gleamed on the hard, chitinous skin of the rakshassa.

Holmes gazed at the figure. He looked anguished.

'Why?' he whispered. 'Why did you do it?'

Raising his gloved hands the newcomer threw back his hood. The sharp face and close-cropped grey hair were familiar. Very familiar.

Holmes's lips tightened slightly. His body-language told me that he was not surprised.

'Professor Summerfield,' he said quietly, 'may I introduce my brother, Sherringford.'

'Two meetings in a month,' said Sherringford Holmes with a smile. 'Wouldn't Mother have been pleased to see how well we're getting along?'

A continuation of the reminiscences of John H. Watson, M.D.
'Well?' Ace said, 'what's it to be?'

I looked across from our coign of vantage to the cluster of caravans.

'How much air have we got left?' I asked.

'Haven't got a clue.'

'What are the chances that Holmes, Bernice and the Doctor are held captive down there?'

'Don't know.'

'How do you see us proceeding, assuming that we can get to those caravans undetected?'

'You've got me there, squire.'

'It strikes me,' I said, with some asperity, 'that, as plans go, it leaves a lot to be desired.'

'Listen, spunk-brain, if you've got a better one . . .'

'Any alternative plans I might have rather depend on different things having occurred over the past few hours,' I said placatingly. 'Given the current situation . . .'

'I'll let you into a secret,' Ace said. 'I've been in more sneaky situations than you've had hot dinners, and the best plan is usually not to have one. Any plan you can think up, the enemy can anticipate, and the more complicated it is, the further away they can see it coming. Take it on the fly, and it confuses them.'

'Do you always think in terms of enemies?'

A dark shadow passed behind her eyes.

'Who else is there?' she murmured. Without waiting for an answer, she moved off down the slope. Reluctantly, I followed.

We moved carefully over the icy terrain, the more so because of our globular suits. I kept worrying that they would tear on sharp shards of ice, but they were remarkably resilient. The rakshassi were fussing around with ropes at the front of the caravans, obviously preparing to move, and so we crept around to the back where it was safer. We managed to sneak through the line of caravans to the huge central one without being detected. Close up it was even larger than I had thought. Sheltering beneath it, in the lee of one of is vast metal runners, standing beside one of the parallel gouges in the ice that marked its journey, we debated out next move.

'Whatever is in there is heavy,' I pointed out, indicating

257

the way the floor bowed towards us. 'It might just be a storehouse.'

'I'm going inside anyway,' Ace insisted.

'Why? It's obviously important to them, whatever it is.'

'That's exactly why.'

'I'm not going to risk it!'

'I didn't ask you to.'

True to her word, Ace moved away from me towards the edge of the caravan, where the lip of one of the doors jutted out. Cursing, I followed. She checked that the coast was clear, and then emerged into the open. The spherical suit made it difficult for her to swing up to the door, and in the end she reluctantly let me help her up. Somehow I managed to scramble up beside her without bursting my own bubble. The incised sides of the caravan loomed above us. It must have been some ten or twelve yards high.

Ace examined the edges of the door.

'It's an airlock,' she announced.

'A what?'

'It keeps the air in. Look at the seals. There must be another one, just inside. Fair enough, unless they've got a pump or something they'll lose whatever air is trapped between the doors, but I guess that doesn't worry them. They can probably replenish it. Shall we go?'

'Are you sure about this?'

'Does the Pope wear a funny hat?'

'Not the last time I saw him,' I replied. She grinned at me, shedding a lot of years as she did so. I smiled back.

She pushed at the door. It opened easily, giving us access to a chamber about the size of a large wardrobe. I closed it behind us, and noticed that it pressed against a door-seal which was made of some material like gutta-percha. There was a door ahead. Judging by the hinges, it opened away from us. It too had a rubbery seal. Ace pushed against it, but it resisted her.

'Air pressure,' she grunted. 'Give us a hand.'

I added my weight to hers. For a moment nothing happened, then a crack appeared between the door and the seal. A sudden hiss made me jump. My bubble misted up and began to wrinkle.

'Pressure's equalizing,' Ace said. Her envelope was also sagging. She pushed the door fully open.

I did not know what to expect when I entered that foul, awful place. My mind could have conjured up a myriad possibilities, but never, never in a million years, could it have hit upon what I actually saw.

The interior of the caravan was one huge space. Flying buttresses braced the sides against the floor and the high ceiling. Windows of coloured glass, high up in the caravan's sides, admitted the weak crimson light of the sun to cast illumination upon a creature that should have remained in darkness forever.

Extract from the diary of Bernice Summerfield
As Sherringford Holmes stood over us, flanked by his gargoyle-like rakshassa bodyguards, I felt a terrible sinking feeling in my stomach. Or 'breadbasket', as Watson would have called it in his po-faced Victorian way.

The Doctor chuckled slightly, surprising me.

'You knew!' I accused him.

'I had my suspicions,' he admitted. 'So did Holmes, although he didn't want to acknowledge it. Sherringford was so against us pursuing the Baron to India that I began to smell a rat.'

'Hang on,' I said, 'it can't be Sherringford. I mean, it *is* Sherringford, but it *can't* be. Didn't Holmes and Watson see this mysterious hooded man in Euston just before you all met Sherringford in Holborn?'

'Yes,' the Doctor said earnestly, 'but we were almost forced off the road by a carriage which raced past us. Sherringford must have been inside it, doing a quick-change act on his way back to the Library to meet Mycroft. And then there's those curious gloves...'

'The gloves? What about the gloves?'

'Well, that's the curious thing...'

'The Doctor leaned back with a self-satisfied smile on

259

his face, and looked up to where Sherlock Holmes was staring at the gaunt, grey-haired form of his brother.

'I had hoped that my reasoning was faulty . . .' Holmes said finally, and trailed off into silence. He looked pretty stunned. I guess I would to, if my brother turned up as the villain of the piece. Especially since I haven't got a brother.

'I had hoped that you were in blissful ignorance, dear boy,' Sherringford said. 'Once Mr Ambrose in the Library told me of his intention to recommend you to the Pope, I sent Colonel Warburton out to Vienna to follow you, and then detailed K'tcar'ch to monitor your investigations in London, but they both reported that your suspicions were directed at Maupertuis. Out of interest, what gave me away?'

'A number of minor clues, most important of which was Father's journal.'

'What of it?'

Explaining his reasoning seemed to be helping Holmes calm down. He wasn't quite as pale as he had been, and his eyes weren't quite as glazed.

'I asked myself why only one of our party should be kidnapped from the hotel in Bombay. Why not take all of us? The only answer I could come up with was that the kidnapper wanted not the Doctor but the book that he carried, the book with the chant in it. Not only did you evince a strong desire to keep the book back in England, but you were also one of the few people to know that we were heading for Bombay.'

'How careless of me,' Sherringford sighed. 'I needed the book in order to open the gateway, of course. When I knew that it was coming to India with the Doctor, I sent a message ahead to Maupertuis and followed on the next ship.'

'You must know by now that your scheme has been scotched.' Holmes's voice rang with a kind of righteous indignation, brother or no brother. 'The army which Baron Maupertuis raised for you has been scattered. You may have retrieved your fakirs from the fray, but you cannot proceed with your invasion of Ry'leh. You may as well give yourself up and return to England, where I can . . .' The words seemed to catch in his throat. '. . . I can promise you a fair trial.'

'Oh Sherlock,' said Sherringford, 'you can never abandon a theory once you've got your teeth into it, can you? At least Mycroft, lazy though he may be, is flexible in that regard.'

He smiled in brotherly affection.

'We aren't invading Ry'leh,' he said. 'We're invading Earth.'

Chapter 16

In which God wants to have a word, and an evil from the dawn of time is debunked

'Invading the *Earth*?' Holmes snapped. 'I've never heard anything so preposterous. Why in Heaven's name would you betray everything that you hold dear in the name of some alien race?'

Sherringford leaned forward earnestly.

'Have you heard the word of God?'

There was a moment of silence as we tried to work that one out. The Doctor was the first person to come up with an adequate response.

'Were you thinking of any god in particular, or would a general chit-chat with any deity suffice?' he piped up eventually. 'You see, I've come across enough gods in my time to stock several pantheons and still have a few left over for a *Gotterdammerung* or two. There's even a planet I could point you to where they worshipped *me* for a few generations, but then, I suppose that's understandable. I hope you don't want references, because I'm not on good terms with very many of them. Apart from myself, of course, and even then we had our differences.'

He frowned, as if rerunning the spiel in his mind to check that it all made sense. I knew that the whole thing was a trick to give him time to think, and to make Sherringford underestimate his intelligence, but I couldn't help thinking that he was overdoing it a bit.

Sherringford had heard the Doctor out in good humour.

'You are a heathen, Doctor, but that will change.'

'I doubt it,' the Doctor said. 'I've bandied words with

bigger megalomaniacs than you without any noticeable change in my opinions.'

The rakshassa took a step forward. Its claws gouged holes in the wood and its spiked tail swung ominously. I'd felt the strength in that tail, and I didn't particularly want to come up against it again.

'You will regret those words, heretic . . .' it whispered.

'Worry not, Brother K'tcar'ch,' Sherringford said soothingly. 'God will protect me.'

'K'tcar'ch?' the Doctor exclaimed. I could see he was surprised, and suddenly remembered the name. K'tcar'ch was the alien that they had all met in the Library in Holborn, but I thought the Doctor had told me that it looked like a large walnut with five legs, like the Ry'lehans fighting on the slopes of the mountain.

'We have already met, Doctor,' K'tcar'ch hissed, 'but now I know the Peace of God, and have abandoned my body of flesh for this spiritual form!'

'Brother K'tcar'ch has been converted to the One True Faith,' Sherringford said with some pleasure. 'Another of Her miracles. Once you have heard the Word, you too will know Peace.'

'*Peace*?' spat the Doctor, 'I've seen more, bigger and nastier wars than you've pulled wings off flies, and most of them were the result of the members of one faith thinking they were better than the members of another. I abjured religion a long time ago. You may have come across some creature that *claims* to be a god, but I will eat my hat if it is the real thing.'

'You will meet Azathoth shortly,' Sherringford assured him with a benign smile, 'then you will understand.'

Now there's a familiar name, I thought, as the rakshassa made a complex sign across its armoured and studded chest, and the Doctor's face fell.

'Azathoth?' he said.

Sherringford beamed.

'Not *the* Azathoth?'

'Indeed.'

'Not the amorphous blight of nethermost confusion that

263

blasphemes and bubbles at the centre of all infinity, co-existent with all time and conterminous with all space?'

Sherringford's face broke into a joyous smile.

'Doctor, I had no idea that you had studied the Faith!'

The Doctor cocked his head and gazed up at Sher-ringford.

'Oh, I've come across some of your sales literature in dentists' waiting rooms and the like,' he said with a straight face. 'I may even have attended a jumble sale or two. What confused me is what an omnipotent, omniscient god like Azathoth is doing here on Ry'leh.'

'This is hardly the time for a theology lesson,' Holmes muttered.

'On the contrary,' his brother corrected him, 'your tran-substantiation will be easier if you are prepared and if you understand what hearing the Word truly means.'

Holmes sneered and turned away. Sherringford turned to the Doctor and me and smiled.

'After giving birth to the cosmos, Azathoth drifted, dis-corporate, through the void,' he said in the tone of voice reserved for priests and religious lunatics the universe over. 'Across the Universe, Her followers prayed that She would be born into a physical body. After hundreds of billions of years, their prayers were answered, and Aza-thoth became incarnate amongst them. As a mark of Her special favour She spread the Word amongst them, so that they might be more pleasing in her sight.'

'You see,' the Doctor said, turning to me, 'how the truth becomes distorted and woven into the legend? Azathoth must have floated around in the vortex for billennia before managing to find a gap and manifest itself corporeally on somebody's home planet. It was always the weakest of the Great Old Ones, according to legend.'

'They went out into the universe in their star-spanning craft to spread the gospel of Azathoth,' Sherringford went on, 'but the unbelievers took arms against them. There was a *jihad*, a holy war. Azathoth, in Her infinite mercy, would not lay waste to the forces of darkness, and was vanquished. They wanted to kill Her – as if a God could

264

be killed! – but they were too weak and divided, and banished Her to this cold, hard world with the most faithful of her followers.'

'For which,' the Doctor murmured, 'read "Azathoth tried to spread her religion around a bit via a sophisticated sort of mind control, and got stomped on".'

'It's a bit hard on the inhabitants of Ry'leh,' I said. 'Having a god dumped in their laps.'

'Inhabitants?' the Doctor asked.

'His lot,' I said, pointing to K'tcar'ch. 'The ones with five legs.'

'The Shlangii?' He shook his head. 'No, they don't live here. The Shlangii are the most feared mercenaries in the known universe. I presume that a couple of garrisons of them were stationed on Ry'leh to stop Azathoth escaping. They are notoriously unreceptive to new ideas, which makes them ideal choices to guard a creature with a natty line in mass hypnosis. Unfortunately, it looks as if Azathoth has managed to convert a substantial number of them. I *knew* that it reminded me of something back in Holborn, but I couldn't remember what.'

Sherringford had been following our conversation.

'Alas,' he said, 'the remainder have taken steps to prevent themselves hearing the message. Some form of surgery, I believe. Poor, misguided creatures. If only they knew the glories that they have blinded themselves to.'

'So they're not peaceful philosophers?' I asked, just to make sure. He just laughed.

'That's why they were attacking Maupertuis's men,' the Doctor said. 'They must have thought that Maupertuis had come to rescue Azathoth.'

'Which, of course, he had,' said Sherringford. 'Although he did not know it. But we tarry too long. It is time that you heard the Word yourselves.'

Holmes was staring at his brother's hands.

'I have been wondering ever since we met in the Library why my brother has been wearing gloves,' he said suddenly. 'An affectation, I thought, or perhaps a disfiguring skin disease. I noticed then that his nails had not been cut

265

for some time – the material of the gloves was stretched to a point in an unmistakable way – but it has just struck me that his nails are considerably longer now than they were in the Library. Longer than they could feasibly have grown in that time.'

'The Mark of Azathoth,' the Doctor said quietly.

Sherringford raised his right hand.

'Our stigmata,' he said, flexing his fingers. Something seemed to ripple beneath the glove, which suddenly split along the seam. Scarlet flesh swelled out, revealing fingers that were clawed, pebbled and veined with black. Scraps of white material fluttered to the wooden floor of the caravan.

'Such a relief,' he sighed. 'I have been trying to hold this back for weeks.'

His shoulders began to swell.

'Dealing with pagans and unbelievers, I have been forced to retain this debased guise, hiding any changes beneath by clothes, but now I can allow my transubstantiation full rein.'

We were all backing away from Sherringford now. Holmes was horror-struck. He held out his hands towards his brother in a way that was either an entreaty, an offer of help or a warding off. The Doctor was looking on with a detached scientific interest. I just wanted to get out.

Sherringford's shoulders erupted through his robes into moist, filmy wings. I could see the pulsing of veins as blood pumped into them, filling them out as I watched. Droplets of some fluid sprayed across my face. The wings stretched until they touched the ground. As soon as his wings could take his weight his legs began to wither away into an armoured tail.

'You will be so happy when you have heard the Word,' he hissed.

A continuation of the reminiscences of John H. Watson, M.D.

The creature was vast and swollen, like the carcass of a beached whale that had become bloated with putrefaction.

A discharge of some mucus-like substance hung in thick, cobweb-like strands from its rugose skin to the floor. It was a vivid purple in colour, with irregular black spots marring its surface. I saw no limbs, no eyes, no organs of sense at all, just one huge toothless maw that slobbered incessantly at us. The wooden planks of the floor were bent under its weight, and pitted as if it sweated some acidic substance.

'Oh my God!' I whispered. There was a stench within the caravan: a stench of something old, and decayed, and evil.

'*My child . . .*'

I whirled, looking for the speaker, but we were alone. 'Where . . . ?' I said.

Ace inclined her head towards the . . . the *thing* in front of us.

'There,' she said.

'*You poor lost souls, you have made your way to salvation.*' The voice continued. It was mellifluous and curiously hypnotic. I could not believe that it came from this swollen leech.

'Who are you?' I cried. '*Where* are you?'

'*I have been known by many names,*' the voice continued, '*but you may call me Azathoth.*' I could not determine whether it was a physical thing or whether I was hearing it within the confines of my own skull. '*I am everywhere. I am here for you. I am your saviour.*'

'Talks like the R.E. master at school,' Ace muttered.

'*Approach me, and feel the warmth of my love for you.*'

'No fear.'

There was something in that voice that touched a chord deep within me. It approved of me. It forgave me.

'*Come closer . . .*'

I took a step forward. Ace caught at my arm and tried to drag me back, but I pushed her away.

'What do you think you're doing?' she yelled.

'*Come close to me, and receive my redemption.*'

I gazed lovingly up at its rough hide.

'I want . . .' I began, then trailed off in confusion.

267

'*You want to be loved,*' it said. I nodded dumbly, and took another step.

Ace's arm snaked around my windpipe and pressed hard. Choking, I fell back into her arms.

'Don't listen to it,' she yelled in my ear, but it was still whispering in my mind, and I struggled in her arms. Somehow, as I fought to get free and she fought to drag me back, we staggered sideways just enough to bring a figure into view around the side of the creature's bulk. A figure that was kneeling before it, dressed in ragged embroidered robes of peacock blue.

'Tir Ram!' I cried, forgetting for a moment that insistent voice in my mind. He did not react. He seemed to be in a world of his own, worshipping Azathoth.

'Who . . .?' Ace asked.

I shook my head to try and clear it. My thoughts were muddy and confused.

'He's . . . he was allied with Baron Maupertuis . . .' I said, stumbling over the words. 'I told you about him . . . it was his fakirs who created the gateway through which we arrived here.'

'*The gateway that brought you into my light,*' said Azathoth calmly. '*Tir Ram has joined me, as you will join me. Follow his example, and submit yourself to my love.*'

I managed to elbow Ace in the pit of the stomach. She fell back, coughing, and I ran forward to take hold of Tir Ram's shoulder. His head was bowed and his dark hair fell across his features. I am still not sure whether I wanted to drag him away or join him. A part of me had succumbed to Azathoth's message, but a part of me still rebelled against its seductive lure.

'Tir Ram!' I cried.

He turned to look at me.

His face was a forest of tiny crimson thorns.

Extract from the diary of Bernice Summerfield
The pressurized tunnel had been rearranged to connect us to the vast central caravan. Waves of cold radiated at us from the bulging walls. As the three of us crossed the

open ground, escorted by the two rakshassi, and started up the steps of the cathedral-like caravan, I could see, through the mist of condensation, rakshassi in pressurized globes attaching ropes to anchor-points all around the caravans. I was confused. If they were intending to pull the caravans across the ice, why attach ropes all the way around?

Sherringford was having a bit of trouble walking on his shiny new wings. It's not the sort of thing that you can practise beforehand.

'I take it,' the Doctor said to him as we walked, 'that all of this business has been in order to rescue your putative god and get it to Earth.'

The door in front of us began to creak slowly open, like something out of an old horror film.

'Indeed,' Sherringford said in a hiss-laden voice. 'Azathoth suspected that natural gateways had long existed between Earth and Ry'leh – the occasional Indian mystic had managed to open a window through which they had seen the occasional rakshassi. Tir Ram's *thuggee* forebears believed Ry'leh to be the realm of Siva, the Destroyer, and built a temple to worship in.'

'Not far wrong, were they?' I murmured.

'However,' Sherringford continued, 'neither Azathoth nor Her faithful followers could open the gateway between the worlds from Ry'leh.'

'Why not?' The Doctor seemed genuinely eager to know. 'I would have thought that escape would have been Azathoth's priority. After all, what sort of god would put up with the shame of eternal detention on a cold ball of rock?'

Sherringford's spiked face swung around until his facial spikes were quivering a few inches from the Doctor's snub nose.

'As you have already found, the only way to open a gateway is by use of certain musical tones which vibrate at some underlying universal frequency – that harmony of the spheres. One of the drawbacks of this form is that we cannot sing.'

'And Azathoth couldn't conjure up a voice box?' The Doctor kept his face straight as he baited Sherringford. 'Not much of a deity, if you ask me. What do you think, Bernice?'

'Perhaps Azathoth could have equipped her flock with harmonicas.'

'Or kazoos,' he agreed. 'I'm a dab hand with the old comb and paper.'

Sherringford turned away.

'Azathoth had been weakened in Her long battle against the forces of darkness,' he explained.

It was too much like 'God moves in mysterious ways' for me, and he didn't exactly sound convinced himself.

'It was fortunate for Azathoth,' he went on, 'that I had discovered our father's diaries in the Library of St John the Beheaded. He reproduced the chants he had heard. I was intrigued, and began to experiment with opening a gateway. Travelling to India, I stayed with Tir Ram and managed, with the help of his wise men, to find my way to Ry'leh. After Azathoth had opened my eyes to the Truth, I willingly returned to Earth to make preparations to open a larger, more permanent connection so that we could spread the Word far and wide.'

'And that's where Maupertuis came on board?' the Doctor asked.

'Indeed. Poor Maupertuis. He was so looking forward to his invasion. We needed him to create a diversion, of course. Once I had determined how to move Azathoth from the city of Kadath in the Cold Wastes to the Plain of Leng where the transfer had to take place, I needed to keep the nearest garrison of Shlangii busy while the gateway was opened and Azathoth escaped to Earth. I knew Maupertuis through the Diogenes, and I knew how bright the flame of glory burned within his breast.'

We were walking up the steps to the big doors now. The caravan loomed overhead, dwarfing everything nearby. It looked like a fitting place for a God. No, actually it looked like a very big dog kennel, but I'm a sucker for religious architecture. I've dug up so much of it in my time.

270

'Why did you not convert more innocents to your cult?' Holmes asked. 'Why the subterfuge? Why not spread the Word to Maupertuis, or Warburton, or Tir Ram?'

The door opened to K'tcar'ch's push, and Sherringford stepped forward. Well, lurched. He wasn't getting the hang of those wings.

'The Mark of Azathoth is not easily hidden, as you can see from Brother K'tcar'ch' he said. 'Azathoth's faithful worshippers would have attracted too much attention to themselves. In order to raise an army to rescue Azathoth from this purgatory, Maupertuis and Warburton had to travel. In Her infinite wisdom, Azathoth decided not to take the risk. I, of course, had little contact with anybody, and could hide whatever physical changes occurred beneath my robes. And besides, the Word is not something that can be explained quickly. Its subtleties and intricacies take time to explain. We did not have time to spare.'

'Vast amounts of physiological and psychological data to transfer,' the Doctor murmured to me as we followed Sherringford into the darkness. 'Even given data compression techniques and broad-band telepathy, it still takes an appreciable time.'

'And why did you steal the books?' Holmes asked as the airlock door closed behind us and embedded itself in some kind of rubber seal.

'Because the Doctor had asked to see them, dear boy. It was apparent that somebody had stumbled on our plans and we had to cover our tracks. I had to act, and act quickly. Once you began to show an interest in the books, Maupertuis's brutal manservant was the perfect choice to steal them.'

'Yes,' the Doctor said, 'that manservant. Did Azathoth have anything to do with the surgery?'

'Oh no,' Sherringford said, rather shocked at the idea. 'That was all Maupertuis's doing. He seemed to enjoy that sort of thing.' He shook his head at the folly of the world. 'Brother K'tcar'ch followed you, of course, to see how far your investigations had progressed, but alas you followed it back to the Library and we were forced to invent a tale to satisfy you. It seemed best to tell you the same story that we had told Maupertuis, with some small modifications.'

The Doctor obviously wanted to ask more, but the inner door opened, revealing a dark, echoing space, crisscrossed by beams of light from windows high above. In the middle of the space sat what I can only describe as a big fat slug. A big, fat slug with a mouth that drooled thick strands of black saliva. The stench alone made my eyes water.

'If that's God,' I said, 'then somebody should shoot Michelangelo.'

I glanced sideways at the Doctor, but he had an odd expression on his face. It looked like disappointment.

Sherringford was on his knees again, with his forehead touching the floor. Deciding that discretion was better part of valour, I joined him. The Doctor, scowling, followed my example, but I saw him sticking his tongue out as he bent his head.

Something cold and slimy infiltrated itself into my mind. I shook my head violently to try and dislodge it, but I could feel cupboards and drawers being opened and ransacked, and old memories being held up to the light. I tried to turn my attention inwards and fight this thing that was skulking around inside my personality, my *me*ness, but it was like trying to catch a rat in the beam of a torch.

It was disgusting. It was rape.

And then it was over. The touch withdrew, leaving a nasty taste in my mind.

'Azathoth!' Sherringford cried, 'all praise!'

The rakshassa repeated the words in its hissing voice.

For a long moment nothing happened, and then Azathoth spoke in a voice as sweet as honey.

'*Sherringford, my child . . .* ' it began, '*I am concentrating my energies upon the spiritual plane to ensure our success. You have done well. Disturb me not.*'

Sherringford seemed surprised at this abrupt dismissal.

'I have brought you two more worshippers, oh great Azathoth.'

Azathoth seemed to pause, as if it was listening to something.

'*Leave them here. I shall deal with them in my own time. You must oversee the preparations for my descent to the surface.*'

Sherringford frowned.

'Alone? Unguarded by your faithful?'

Another pause.

'*Do you doubt my power?*'

Backtracking quickly, he cried, 'No, oh Great One! My concern for you overrides my good sense.'

'*I have . . . converted two intruders to the cause,*' Azathoth said. '*I shall send them to you. They will serve as my guards.*'

I glanced at the Doctor. He looked back with a foreboding frown. I knew what he was thinking, and it was bad news.

He glanced across at Sherringford.

'This One True Faith lark,' he said. 'It sounds as if you have something more literal in mind than a quick dip in the holy water.'

'*Once you have heard my Word, Doctor,*' Azathoth's voice murmured seductively in my mind, '*then your doubts will evaporate like dew in the sunlight, and you will receive my Mark as a sign of my special favour.*'

'Hypnosis? Mind control? I was hoping for something a little more impressive than that.'

He turned to me.

'I've spent a thousand years fighting the Great Old Ones and their servants, and this pathetic specimen isn't one of them. It's nothing but a confidence trickster with the power to make people love it: a cosmic cuckoo masquerading as a trans-dimensional power and trading on the reputation of a being far greater than it could ever be. How pathetic.'

'Clutch at whatever straws of explanation you like, Doctor,' Sherringford whispered, 'but you will think differently when you have heard the Word.'

'That,' the Doctor said, 'is what I am afraid of.'

He turned to look at me.

'Imetay otay ogay,' he said, 'When I say the "R" word . . .'

'Message understood.'

'Make sure Holmes comes too.'

I quickly glanced over to where the Great Detective stood. His face showed no expression now, and he seemed to have got stuck in a particular pose.

'He's in shock,' I said. 'Not surprising. I'll try and pull him after us.'

'Run,' the Doctor cried.

I turned, and froze.

Ace was standing behind me. She looked fine, apart from an unnatural hump across her shoulders. Beside her, Watson was holding his hand out to touch my face. The hand was a hard glossy crimson thing veined with black, with fingers that ended in vicious claws.

'Ah, the newcomers to the congregation,' Sherringford hissed. 'I'll leave you in their capable hands.'

Chapter 17

In which our heroes are finally reunited but their celebrations are suspended for a while

A continuation of the reminiscences of John H. Watson, M.D.

There was a long pause after Sherringford Holmes and K'tcar'ch walked out of the caravan and into the airlock. There was an expression of complete and utter resignation on Holmes's face, as if he was trapped in a dream and could not wake up. Bernice's face registered a mixture of horror and betrayal, whilst I could read nothing from the Doctor.

After we heard the outer door to the caravan open and then close again, Ace gazed at the Doctor's rumpled linen suit and battered hat.

'It's Kolchak the bleeding Night Stalker, isn't it?' she said.

A slow smile spread across the Doctor's face.

'I've never known you to be convinced by anybody else,' he said, 'so why should a god find it any easier?'

'I used to fancy this guy, when I was a kid,' she replied, twisting so that she could pull the bundled-up floater skins from beneath her jacket, the ones that had given the impression of nascent wings. 'But he was one of the happy-clappy God Squad types. Used to take me to church discos on a Saturday night. No booze, no fun, and it all finished at half past ten. I've had more fun watching *Question Time*. Didn't stop him trying it on when he walked me home, though. Anyway, got chatting to the vicar one night, and come closedown I'd thrown so many spanners into his faith that he had to go off to a monastery in the Hebrides for five years to recover. He lives in a squat in Woolwich now, or at least he did the last time I asked. So, don't talk to me about religion.'

Bernice's eyes were darting between Ace and myself now as she tried to work out whether or not we had converted to the cult of Azathoth. I reached out a hand to comfort her, but she recoiled. Cursing my clumsiness, I pulled the rakshassa hand off my own and threw it away. She watched it fall.

'Now I've seen everything,' she said to herself.

'It was Tir Ram's hand,' I said. 'He was in the process of changing into one of those creatures. He tried to explain to us about the cult of Azathoth, but Ace ... well, she dispatched him, I'm afraid.'

'She *what*?'

'She killed him.'

Bernice smiled.

'Well, no surprises there.'

'I had to,' Ace interposed, casting a glance over towards the bloated bulk of Azathoth. 'That thing was trying to pass the Word on to us. I had to distract its attention somehow.'

'Thanks for saving us,' Bernice said. 'It's good to see you again.'

Stepping forward impulsively, she hugged Ace. Surprised, the girl hugged back.

The Doctor looked down at the scarlet object on the floor.

'And what about Mr Ram's hand, then?'

Ace was unrepentant.

'Well he wasn't going to use it any more, was he?'

'Sometimes,' the Doctor mused, 'just sometimes, I hanker for the good old days, when all my companions ever did was scream and ask me stupid questions.'

'So what's going on, then?' Ace asked.

'Yes, that was a favourite one. Well, Bernice, perhaps you would care to summarize the present situation.'

'Fine.' She nodded towards Azathoth. 'Well, that's one

alien creature pretending to be an ancient god from another dimension. It can control your mind, and when it does you worship it and turn into something that looks like it might be more at home in the larder of a seafood restaurant. It's imprisoned here, with the five-legged things as guards, and it wants out. Unbeknownst to the people who put it here, there's a short cut between Earth and Ry'leh that can be opened by singing, but none of the lobster things can sing. Sherlock Holmes's father heard the local wise men in India singing the song and wrote it down in his notebook, where brother Sherringford found it. Sherringford managed to open a gateway between the worlds and arrived here, only to find himself having a face-to-face talk with God. Once his mind had been given a good pummelling, he and God hit upon a plan to escape. He would travel back to England, raise an army and bring them back to India where the Indians would open another gateway. The army was necessary to create a diversion. The guards would try to repel all boarders, and in the confusion, God and all hands would head for Earth. Does that cover all the salient points?'

Ace looked stunned.

'I've never heard such an implausible idea in my life!' she said. 'Apart from the imprisonment bit. The big maggot lived in a city some way away, worshipped by the winged things. The five-legged things were in little garrisons around the city.'

'That was the problem,' the Doctor added. 'Getting Azathoth out of the city and past the garrisons to the plain of . . . what did K'tcar'ch call it? The Plain of Leng. That was the only place where so few people could open such a large gateway.' He gazed over to Azathoth. 'I presume that you have managed to turn the tables upon our host, Ace.'

'*You blaspheme my temple,*' Azathoth said in a voice that was all sweetness and light. '*You cannot stop me. I shall escape this world. I shall!*'

'Shut it,' said Ace. She put her fingers to her lips and emitted a piercing whistle. A small black object, about the size of my hand, whistled round Azathoth's bulk and knifed through the air towards her. Bernice and the Doctor ducked, but the object terminated its trajectory a few scant inches in front of Ace's face.

'Smart missile,' she said. 'I used to read about these things in Iain M. Banks's books, then I found that Space-Fleet issues them like the Civil Service issues biros. That's the nice thing about the future: it's full of little things you've already read about.'

She murmured something to her little infernal device and it whipped away, back to its sentry position in front of Azathoth's face, where we could hardly see it.

'I've never threatened a god before,' she continued. 'I could get used to it.'

'It was you who dictated what Azathoth was saying just now,' Holmes said suddenly.

'Yeah,' Ace replied. 'Once we topped Tir Ram, Azathoth knew we were serious, so I made a deal. If it didn't try to convert us, I wouldn't blow its face off.'

'Sounds fair,' said Bernice.

'When you lot came in, and Watson here recognized Sherlock's brother, we were a bit stumped. Then Watson reckoned that we could get rid of him and his minders by getting Azathoth to tell him to leave. When he played up a bit it threw us, but I worked out that if he thought you were being guarded by a couple of new converts, he'd be happy. Good thing the rakshassi are crustaceans,' she added, 'otherwise Watson would have had trouble dressing up as a true believer. As it was, he could slip the hand on like a glove. After we'd scooped it out, of course.'

Azathoth shifted its massive bulk slightly.

'It's being very quiet,' I said. 'Does that not strike you as odd?'

'Probably had a shock,' Ace said. 'I mean, nobody's ever talked to it like that before.'

She seemed inordinately pleased with herself. I was not so sanguine about our position.

The Doctor appeared to be listening to something.

'Can anybody hear a whispering sound?' he asked. We all shook our heads. 'Hmm. Perhaps I'm hearing things.'

Judging by his scowl, he was not convinced.

'Anyway, they're preparing to descend to the plain,' he continued. 'To the area where we came through to Ry'leh, the weakest point of contact.'

'How can they get Azathoth down there?' Bernice asked. 'The rakshassi can fly, but their god's powers seem to be strictly limited in that department.'

'A fair question,' the Doctor said, 'but they've shown a remarkable ability to get around problems so far. They've evaded the Shlangii mercenaries by building these pressurized caravans and taking Azathoth across the icy surface, they've built rough and ready space suits for themselves . . . No, I don't think that we can rely on them falling at the last hurdle. And remember, they had to get Azathoth *up* here somehow.'

'They will obviously use Tir Ram's fakirs to open a gateway back to Earth,' Holmes added. 'Once in India, the cult would spread like wildfire. Within a few months, the entire world would be united in Azathoth worship, I have always nurtured a hankering for a united world, but not this way.' He shook his head. 'I am presuming that the fakirs have been converted?'

'We were locked in that caravan for long enough,' the Doctor said.

I cleared my throat.

'Tir Ram assured us that all of his people had been blessed by Azathoth.'

I noticed a smile appear on the Doctor's face. I was just about to ask him what he had in mind when there was a tremendous *bang!* and the entire caravan rocked suddenly, throwing us off our feet. Ripples ran through Azathoth's moist bulk. I thought I could feel a sigh of satisfaction emanating from it.

'Bloody hell!' Ace scrambled back to her feet and looked around wildly. 'We're under attack.'

'I think not,' the Doctor replied calmly. 'Climb up to

one of those windows, if you will, and see what's going on.'

Like a monkey, Ace scrambled up the rough wooden walls of the caravan to where the coloured glass windows were set. Some remnant of my usual gallantry – severely dented by these capable women of the future – rose to the surface. I climbed up behind her.

'This is no place for women,' I said as I came alongside her.

'Sod off,' she said succinctly.

I kept quiet, and gazed through the thick red glass of the window at the panorama thus revealed.

The sun cast a low red light across the jumbled terrain, and the twisted spires of the mountain tops reached for the star-speckled sky as before, but near where our caravan sat the icy surface of Ry'leh was marred by a jagged hole a few hundred yards across. I could hardly see it for rolling banks of mist. The grotesque silhouettes of rakshassi clustered around the opening.

'Looks like they've blown a hole in the ice,' Ace said. 'Dunno if they've got through to the interior yet. Depends on the explosive.'

'Could they be using the gas from the floaters?' I asked.

'Good thinking,' she said. 'Probably take them a few goes, then. That stuff's not a patch on nitro-nine even.'

As she spoke, another enormous explosion made the caravan judder. My fingers slipped and for a moment I had to scrabble for a hold. Metal squealed beneath us as the massive skates ground against the ice. A column of vapour shot upwards out of the hole like a waterfall in reverse, plunging into the obsidian sky until it was lost to sight.

'I lie,' she added. 'Looks like they've done it in two. Those floaters must live on beans, or something.'

'The vapour . . . That's Ry'leh's atmosphere?'

'Uh-huh. Not much of it at this altitude, of course. If there was, the pressure would've caused the entire ice sheet to fracture.'

'There's a reassuring thought,' I said dryly. She smiled.

'You've got hidden depths to you, mate.'

I would have replied, but then I felt the entire caravan lurch towards the fissure. I cried out. Craning my neck, I tried to see down the wooden side and was rewarded by the sight of ten or so rakshassi pulling on ropes. They appeared to be dragging the caravan towards the column of mist.

'I would not wish to worry you . . .' I started, but Ace interrupted.

'Heads down, folks,' she said. 'We're riding for a fall.'

Holmes stepped forward.

'Quick, Watson, how many pressurized suits did you bring?'

'Just the two.'

'Not enough time to get us all out, then. Miss Summerfield, Miss . . . er, Miss Ace, I suggest that you make your escape and leave us to survive as best we can.'

'Not a chance,' said Bernice.

'Seconded,' Ace said from her position beside me. 'Besides, the Professor's got a card up his sleeve.'

She looked pointedly at the Doctor, but he did not react.

'Haven't you, Professor?'

'Why do you have to rely on me to get you out of everything?' he said, scowling. 'Use your native intelligence.'

'The rakshassi aren't going to risk the life of their god,' Bernice said. 'Whatever's happening, they intend to happen.'

I switched my attention back to the window. We were a hundred or so yards away from the hole now. I could see the melted ice that made up its sides. It was easily large enough to accommodate the caravan.

'I believe that we have only another few moments,' I said. 'I would suggest that you brace yourselves.'

The caravan slid another few yards, and I found myself staring down the funnel-like hole. Thankfully, mist wreathed its depths. I think that my last vestiges of calm might have fled if I could have seen Ry'leh, far below.

Another lurch. The rakshassi were yanking hard on the ropes. Like a malevolent eye, the hole grabbed my attention and held it. The column of vapour was rising straight past the window, blocking any sign of the surrounding landscape.

'Uh, Watson?' Bernice said hesitantly. 'Do you think you should come down now?'

The precariousness of my position should we be shoved over the edge suddenly struck me. I glanced over to warn Ace of the danger, only to find that she was already climbing down. I took one last look out of the window before following her, but what I saw caused me to stay, glued to the glass.

The rakshassi were rising up past the window, their wings spread wide, borne aloft by the rising current of air. They had removed their globes – no doubt because the atmospheric column could now sustain them. Each of them was holding the end of a rope in its tail, and, as they rose and the ropes pulled taut, I felt the caravan lurch, then rise unmistakably into the air! The rakshassi were supporting us!

'What's going on?' Bernice asked.

'We're flying!'

'Be serious.'

'I am serious. The rakshassi are holding us up.'

The caravan swung sickeningly, and the hole disappeared beneath us. I felt the unmistakable sensation of descent. Within moments I could make out the melted ice of the hole passing a few hundred feet away through the upflowing vapour.

'Exceedingly ingenious,' Holmes said.

'I've always been in favour of low-tech solutions,' the Doctor murmured.

'They don't come much more low-tech than this,' Bernice sighed. She was looking a little queasy. Glancing up at me, she said, 'How can you stand it, up there? Don't you feel the remotest bit ill?'

'No,' I said. 'In fact, I'm quite enjoying myself.' The feeling reminded me irresistibly of a balloon ride that I

282

had undertaken as a child in the grounds of Batty's Grand National Hippodrome in Kensington.

I turned my attention to the sight outside the window, where we were just passing the inner lip of the hole that had been blasted through the frozen sky. Clouds had gathered around the rent, and the caravan was buffeted by gusts of wind. Gazing upward, I could feel the strain evident in the almost heroic poses of the rakshassi. Whatever else I thought of them, I had to admire their dedication to their god. Thoughts of Azathoth quickly turned me to a consideration of what was ahead of us. As the ground grew ever closer, I began to make out vegetation and the remains of Maupertuis's encampment. Bodies lay about, human and Shlangii, allies in death. Nothing moved apart from the odd three-legged scavenger. My spirits fell. How could we prevent this profane invasion of everything we held dear?

High above us, a number of square dots had appeared amid a web of rope. The other caravans, the ones carrying the fakirs. Everything was going according to Sherringford's plan. The local Shlangii garrison had been distracted and defeated by Maupertuis's army, and by the time more could be shipped from other garrisons, it would be too late. The gateway would have opened and closed.

I looked down. We were dangling a hundred or so feet above the ground.

'Perhaps we should think about our escape,' I said tentatively.

'Ace,' the Doctor commanded, 'how many of those suicidal robots do you have?'

'If you mean the smart missiles, why not say so?' she snapped.

'Because it's exploiting a thinking creature, and I don't approve.'

'Professor, they're programmed to do what they do.'

'That's no excuse, Ace. The American CIA used to strap bombs to dolphins' backs and train them to swim up to Russian submarines. Training, programming, what's

283

the difference? Don't answer that, just tell me how many you have left.'

'None, apart from the one that's keeping Azathoth occupied.'

'None?'

Ace looked away.

'No,' she said.

'Why not? You used to have hundreds.'

'Some I've used, the rest deserted back on Peladon. They said they were going to set up a union with the mining machinery.'

The Doctor smiled, thought for a moment, then walked over to the moist grey bulk of Azathoth.

'Can you hear me?' he cried.

Azathoth remained stubbornly silent. The Doctor waved a hand at Ace.

'You can answer,' she said. 'The missile won't explode. Yet. But if I hear anything that sounds like it might change my mind in a way I won't like, I'll make sure that your mind changes into a pile of mush on the walls.'

'*I hear you,*' Azathoth replied sulkily. '*Blasph . . .* '

'Yes, yes, we'll take that as read, thank you very much,' the Doctor said. 'Azathoth, I offer you a choice.'

'*There is no choice. I am God. I do what I wish.*'

'You are no god, and you know it. You're just a fake deity whose powers are limited to a rather forceful form of persuasion.'

There was a thud as the caravan settled to the ground. I could hear the hiss of ropes sliding down the outside as the rakshassi released them.

'*What is your offer?*'

'Stop this invasion. Stay here on Ry'leh.'

'*And what do you give me in return?*'

'Your life.'

Azathoth laughed: great quaking peals of laughter that caused its body to quake and the wooden floor beneath it to creak alarmingly.

'*What power do you puny creatures have over the life of mighty Azathoth?*'

'Have you forgotten the missile that guards you?'

'If you mean the most recent convert to the cult of Azathoth, no. We have been enjoying a long conversation.'

The Doctor's face fell, and he began to back away.

'Missile,' Azathoth continued, *'kill the Doctor.'*

Chapter 18

In which one disaster is sought and another one narrowly avoided

The tiny black object that had been hovering in front of Azathoth's slobbering maw suddenly darted away.

The Doctor turned to run. Circling quickly, the missile sped for the Doctor's back in a blur of ebony. The Doctor tripped over his own feet and went sprawling, leaving the missile to overshoot its target.

'Disengage!' Ace yelled. 'Do you hear me, disengage!'

Azathoth was giggling.

I dropped to the floor and whipped out my trusty revolver. The missile was heading straight for the Doctor's face, but I managed to deflect its path with a well placed bullet. For a moment I thought that I had crippled it, but it recovered its momentum quickly and headed straight for the Doctor again. He had climbed to his feet and was pressed against the wall with nowhere else to run. The missiles sped directly for his wide-eyed face. I fired again, but missed.

The Doctor threw himself to the floor. The missile hit the wall and exploded, sending a hail of wooden splinters across the caravan. Several of them hit Azathoth, who howled in pain. Through the hole I could make out the rocky surface of Ry'leh.

'Quickly,' I shouted, 'before anybody investigates.'

I stood by the hole and helped the others as they scrambled through. The Doctor was last, and caught his coat upon a projecting spar of wood.

'With friends like Ace . . .' he muttered as I disentangled him.

Within seconds I was outside with the rest of them. As we ran off, Azathoth's plaintive voice tugged at my mind.

'*Listen to me . . .*' it shouted, its voice growing fainter and fainter. '*I can offer you peace and happiness and a place in heaven . . .*'

I was not the only one to stop and look back, but we kept on going none the less.

We took refuge finally in a small clump of bushes. They snapped at us tentatively, but the size and mood of our party obviously frightened them and they returned to sleep with their buds safely tucked beneath their leaves.

'Look,' said Bernice, gazing upwards in wonder. Her face seemed to shine. At first I thought that it was her inner beauty, but then I followed her gaze. For the first time in a thousand years the sun was shining upon the surface of Ry'leh. Its rays were pouring through the hole in the sky, surrounded by concentric rings of cloud, and shone down like a stage spotlight upon the plain where the caravans were landing. Rakshassi hovered high above, looking for us, the shadows of their wings skimming across the ground like lithe black animals.

'There is a crack in everything,' the Doctor whispered. 'That's how the light gets in.'

'Pardon?' I said.

'A line of poetry from my home planet. I think it loses something in translation.'

In the distance, illuminated by the finger of light, the fakirs were emerging from the landed caravans. They immediately formed up into lines and began to chant.

'*I-ay, I-ay!*' The words echoed across the plain. '*Naghaa, naghai-ghai! Shoggog fathaghn! I-ay, I-ay tsa toggua tholo-ya! Tholo-ya fathaghn! I-ay Azathoth!*'

The words repeated, growing louder as more voices joined the chorus, throbbing like a heartbeat in the distance. I felt, as I did the last time that I heard those words, that a pressure was building up behind my eyes.

'They don't waste much time, do they?' Bernice said.

'It's their big moment,' Ace replied. 'And besides, the Shlangii will soon be here.'

'How soon?' the Doctor asked.

'The nearest garrison is a small one, so let's assume that it's been wiped out during the battle with Maupertuis's men. The next one is half-way around the planet, but they've got skimmers. Giving them an hour to work out that something has happened, and another fifteen minutes to mobilize . . . I guess half an hour until they arrive.'

'Too long. Azathoth will be through to India by then.'

'So what are our options?' Holmes asked.

'I don't know,' the Doctor said.

Bernice gazed sceptically at him.

'No cards up the sleeve?'

'None.'

'No long-range plans?'

'Not one.'

'Scout's honour?'

'May my woggle fall off if I lie.'

'That chant,' Ace said thoughtfully. 'You said it weakens the fabric of reality, whatever that is, enabling a gateway to be opened, and you also said that this fabric thing is already weakest between India and this plain.'

'Indeed.'

'Well, how easy would it be to move the gateway? What I mean is, could we change the chant and alter the aim point?'

The Doctor thought for a moment.'

'Hmm. A canny notion, and one well worth bearing in mind. What made you think of it?'

Ace smiled. 'Something I overheard while I was hanging around waiting for you to arrive,' she said.

Delving around in his pockets, the Doctor finally pulled out a piece of green chalk. 'No paper,' he complained. He looked around for something to write on, and his eyes lit up as their penetrating gaze crossed Ace's battle-armour.

'Ace, turn around.'

'You what?'

'Just do it!'

288

He began to scribble on the matt-black surface, quickly covering it with symbols and small diagrams, some of which I recognized from the inscriptions on Azathoth's caravan. Sometimes he would go back and rub a line out with his sleeve: once or twice he retrieved chalks of other colours and added notes in and around his original ones. Holmes was following the Doctor's calculations so closely that he ended up with chalk-dust on the tip of his nose. The Doctor kept up a running barrage of commentary, muttering phrases such as: 'Of course, the rho-meson flux must be taken into account . . .', 'it's important to remember that E equals MC *cubed* in the exo-space time continuum . . .' and 'for heaven's sake, keep *still* Ace!'

The chant was building up, with individual voices soaring above the main theme, and a strong beat pushing it along. My head was beginning to throb in sympathy.

Finally the Doctor leaned back and sighed.

'This would have been so much easier with the books from the Library, but Sherringford still has them. Fortunately I had a quick flick through some of them, and I also managed to chat with one or two of the fakirs when we were on our way to the surface. I *think* we can do it.'

'How?' said Ace, stretching after sitting in a cramped position for so long.

'The whole thing is frequency-specific. It's the subtle shifting of discords that weakens the structure of space-time, enabling the connection to be made with the nearest world – Earth. If we introduce a specific set of new discords, we can move the point of connection.'

'But why didn't Azathoth or Sherringford think of that?' I asked.

'Because they were thinking in purely spatial terms,' the Doctor replied. 'And the frequencies required are just too high to achieve. It never occurred to them to move the aim-point in *time*. The calculations are harder, but the frequencies can be sung, and the further forward or back in time we move the aim point, the wider our spatial error can be.'

'In *time*,' Holmes breathed. 'You mean . . .?'

'I mean I'm looking for suggestions as to the best place to dump an evil god and its worshippers. Somewhere that they can't do any major harm. A geological disaster would do perfectly. Eighteen eighty seven, plus or minus fifty years, and on the Earth's surface. That's our window of opportunity. Once we dump them, we can sing our own way back to Tir Ram's cavern, and from there we can make our way home.'

Bernice thought for a moment, then said, 'What about Siberia, nineteen-oh-eight? The TARDIS explosion?'

'No,' the Doctor snapped. 'If I start mixing dimensional rips they could end up anywhere.'

'Krakatoa!' I exclaimed. 'Four years ago. If it's an explosion you're looking for, that's the biggest one I can remember.'

'Is that east or west of Java?' the Doctor said, then thought for a moment. 'A distinct possibility,' he added, 'but a trifle dangerous if we get caught up in it. Ditto the Titanic in nineteen twelve, which I was also considering, with the added problem that we would be interfering in our own pasts. Has it occurred to you that we seem to have toured most of the major disasters of the late-nineteenth and early-twentieth centuries in the past few months?'

'California,' said Ace quietly. 'Nineteen-oh-six. The great San Francisco earthquake.'

'Perfect!' the Doctor shouted. 'We missed that one. What made you think of that?'

'Personal interest,' she replied. 'It was an old school History project.'

History?, I thought, then let it slip away.

The Doctor delved in his pockets and pulled out a large, leather-bound book.

'My five-hundred-year diary,' he said, catching my inquiring glance. 'All sorts of information that's completely pointless unless you are trying to avert an alien invasion.'

He flicked through the pages.

'Now let me see ... We'll need a location which is

known to have been completely wiped out. We can't risk them escaping. That rules out quite a bit of the town . . .'

His scowl deepened as his fingers riffled through page after page.

'Town Hall . . . no. Agnews State Insane Asylum . . . no. Palace Hotel . . .'

A smile broke across his face.

'Yes! Razed to the ground.'

His face fell again.

'But what's the address?'

'Market Street,' I said. To Bernice's inquiring glance, I added, 'I lived in San Francisco for nearly a year.'

'What are the galactic co-ordinates for Market Street?' the Doctor asked. 'Never mind. I'll estimate.'

Wiping across Ace's carapace with his sleeve, he began to scribble down staves and sets of crotchets and quavers.

'No time to lose,' he urged. 'Ace, get your armour off!'

Under his direction, and all clustered around Ace's armour, we began to sing. Ace was shivering in an immodest singlet, and so I gave her my jacket to wear. I thought that she might throw it back in my face, but in fact she accepted it gratefully. The song was a collection of words similar to the chant that the fakirs were singing, but the notes spanned theirs, weaving around and between their weird harmonies, forming a straightjacket for their chant and forcing it in a different direction. The Doctor was forever darting in and scribbling an additional sharp or a flat, or altering the length of a note, until we got it right.

We knew that it was working when the deep, underlying beat of the fakirs' chant began to alter into a double beat, and their descant picked up some of our notes. It was working. We were changing their song, but were we changing it enough?

The first indication we had that something was happening was when light – yellow gaslight, not the diseased red glow that illuminated Ry'leh – shone across us. We looked up, still singing, to see a vast tear in the fabric of reality through which a stretch of carpet and a marble wall could be seen. Silhouetted against it, I could see the winged figures of rakshassi and Sherringford Holmes's still-robed form. He seemed agitated. It must have been obvious to him that this was not India but, unwilling to stop now and disappoint his god, he went onward, leading Azathoth's followers in. Most of the rakshassi went first, in case of trouble, then Azathoth's personal honour guard pulled its temple through the rent, straining to move the metal runners across the rock. The fakirs followed, still chanting. I could smell smoke and, oddly, freshly made coffee.

The chant was swelling towards some final crescendo now, and I watched, wide-eyed, not wishing to miss a moment of Azathoth's downfall.

Bernice tugged at my sleeve. I tried to shrug her off. Insistently, she tugged again. I tore my gaze away from the rent and glanced at her. She was looking back, over the terrain of Ry'leh.

I followed her gaze, and drew a sudden breath as I glimpsed a number of metallic shapes trailing fire as they arrowed through the air towards us.

A deep rumble shook the ground. The Doctor turned. His eyes widened in shock as he saw the craft. He chalked a quick message on Ace's back.

Shlangii mercenaries! it read.

A blue-green line of fire lanced from the leading craft and melted rock not ten feet to our right. The Doctor shook his head and, before I could stop him, ran towards the rent in the air.

We followed him. We had no choice.

The fakirs stopped singing just as we passed through behind them and felt the carpet beneath our feet. We were in a huge, high-ceilinged ballroom whose walls were cracked and whose carpet was thickly smeared with dust. Nobody else was present. A feeling of peace washed over me. I was home. I didn't care that it was, if Ace could be believed, almost twenty years since I had left. At least it was the same planet.

I turned and looked behind. The surface of Ry'leh hung like a painting on a wall of the ballroom. Tiny five-legged shapes were rushing across the ground towards us, clutching weapons, as the metal shapes flew overhead like a flock of birds.

The gateway closed behind me, close enough for me to feel the sudden *whoosh* as it collapsed.

The Doctor led us into a deep recess in the wall. From there we watched the rakshassi milling around the temple, whose runners had cut deep gouges in the carpet. I could not see Sherringford.

'I thought you said half an hour,' he said to Ace.

'Anyone can make a mistake,' she said.

'Looks like a frying pan and fire situation to me,' Bernice added, looking around. 'How do we get back to the TARDIS from here?'

'We can worry about that later,' the Doctor said. 'Are we in the right place?'

'Search me,' Ace replied. 'I did all my research from an old copy of the *Reader's Digest*.'

'It's the Palace Hotel,' I said.

Holmes looked at me sceptically.

'It *is*,' I insisted. 'I practised medicine in San Francisco for nearly a year. I took rooms here when I first arrived. You sent telegrams to me.'

'It looks like we're too late,' the Doctor muttered. 'The earthquake has already happened. The hotel is still standing. I don't understand!'

'So they can still invade?' Bernice asked.

'More fool me, yes they can. And in the middle of a national disaster, it will be even more difficult to fight them. Still, at least we're here to try.'

In the centre of the ballroom, Sherringford emerged from Azathoth's temple.

'My brothers . . .' he began.

He got no further. A deep shudder ran through the fabric of the hotel. Sherringford looked around wildly.

With a tremendous explosion, the doors to the ballroom burst open to reveal a wall of flame. Gluts of red-tongued fire leaped up the walls, scorching the plaster and cracking the marble. A wave of heat rolled towards us.

'Fire?' Holmes mouthed.

Ace grinned.

'Started after the earthquake when some stupid woman tried to cook breakfast after the gas main cracked. Caused more damage than the earthquake itself. The army tried to stop it by dynamiting the buildings, but they spread it even further. I remember the dynamite, it's why I enjoyed the project so much.'

An ominous cracking made me look upwards. What I saw made me shout: 'Run, run for it!'

We got to the door just as the ceiling gave way and huge chunks of masonry fell into the centre of the room. Rakshassi staggered around, blinded and deafened, their wings alight. A cloud of dust and smoke rolled towards us, hiding the hellish scene. Holmes led the Doctor, Ace and Bernice along the corridor. I stopped to look back. I thought that I had heard a voice, a sweet voice screaming, '*No, I cannot die, I cannot die! Help meee!*'

I took a step into the room, but the heat drove me back towards the door. A gust of superheated air drove the dust and the smoke away from me for a moment, and I saw that the temple had been smashed open by a falling concrete beam. Azathoth flailed helplessly in the wreckage, pinned by the beam. Its skin was burning.

'*Watson!*' it screamed, '*help meee!*'

I took a step into the room. I wanted to help. I had to help.

From the smoke, a figure emerged. Its white robes were in tatters and its wings were ragged and torn. Its chitinous armour had been seared by the fire. It swayed uncertainly as it looked me over.

'Forgiveness only goes so far,' Sherringford hissed in a pained voice. 'You have killed my God. No punishment can atone for that.'

He took a step towards me, his spiked tail swinging in readiness. In the midst of the spikes that constituted his face I could just make out two human eyes that gazed at me in bloodshot hatred.

Holmes walked past me. He was holding a length of iron pipe that had fallen from the ceiling.

'No,' he said simply. 'Watson is my friend.'

He lashed out with the pipe, catching Sherringford across his chestplate. Pale pink fluid splashed out of a crack in the living armour. Sherringford staggered backwards and flailed at Holmes with his tail, but Holmes stepped out of the way and snapped Sherringford's wing with a short jab. Sherringford fell sideways as the wing crumpled. He lowered his head for a long moment, then looked back up at his brother. There were tears in his eyes.

'The horror . . .' he said quietly. 'The horror!'

Holmes brought the pipe crashing down on the back of his brother's head, splitting it open and bending the pipe. A shower of sparks drifted down from the ceiling and lodged in the folds of his wings. Tiny flames began to flicker. His other wing buckled beneath his weight, sending him sprawling.

I turned to Holmes. His gaze met mine.

'I had to,' he said.

I nodded.

'I know.'

Something exploded on one of the upper floors. Flames and drips of molten metal issued through the cracks in the ballroom ceiling. We left in a hurry, running through rubble-strewn corridors until we found ourselves in the deserted foyer of the hotel. Its fine antique trappings were wrecked.

We emerged, coughing and choking, into bright sunlight and ran across the road to a barricade where the Doctor, Ace and Bernice were waiting anxiously for us. Behind them, uniformed men watched the destruction. They were pale and haggard, as if they had walked through the valley of the shadow. I glanced back at the hotel. Every window was a glimpse of hell. Nothing could survive that conflagration. Nothing.

The last thing I saw before I turned away was a tongue of flame licking up the flagpole on the hotel roof and setting fire to the Stars and Stripes.

Chapter 19

In which our heroes have breakfast in the ruins, and the Doctor makes a surprising offer

There was, as is usual in Holmes's cases, no distinct *finalé*, no crescendo and clash of cymbals to mark the end of the case. Rather, there was a long, slow diminuendo, a trailing off into silence. Even now, four years later, the case of the All-Consuming Fire still haunts us both, and yet it is that moment, as we wandered amid the ruins of San Francisco, that marks *an* end, of sorts.

We walked for a little while, the four of us. We were not heading for anywhere in particular. We just needed to get away from the scene of Azathoth's destruction.

The city was devastated. Cracks crossed streets and houses without any distinction. Many areas were in flames, or had been afire but were now charred and smoking. Whole streets had been blown up as makeshift fire-breaks, scattering bricks, twisted metal, items of crockery and personal items to the winds. One of those houses had been mine. In it I had wooed and won my wife. Now she was dead, and a part of me wished that I was too. I was tired. I was so tired.

We saw things as we walked that I cannot explain. At one point we turned a corner to find a group of Chinese men attacking a maddened bull with machetes. I wanted to intervene, but Bernice held me back. Later we had to hide from a group of soldiers who were firing indiscriminately at looters. Later we found a quiet square on the edge of the city and sat there for a while, saying nothing and trying hard not to think. As we did so, a man started to sing in the sweetest, purest voice I have ever heard. His clothes were torn and covered in dust, but he did not seem to care, and neither did his listeners. Hearing him, I felt a small bud of hope flower from the ashes within me. Life went on. Life went on.

'Enrico Caruso,' the Doctor said eventually, after the man had finished his recital and had begun to argue with a companion. 'You are lucky to have heard him sing.'

'I wish I had been in a better mood to appreciate it,' Holmes said dryly. 'Forgive me, Doctor, but if you are to be believed, we are several thousand miles and nineteen years from home. Do you have any suggestions?'

The Doctor blinked owlishly.

'As usual, the time is no problem,' he said. 'It's the space that might be difficult.'

The Doctor walked off around the corner, telling us that he would be back in a moment. Indeed, he was. A miraculous contraption appeared out of the air before us, a blue cabinet of the Doctor's own construction that can travel through the aether at his direction. He told us that after walking round the corner he had made his way across America by rail and engaged passage in New York upon a ship bound for London. Once there he had located his miraculous time-travelling cabinet, which remained exactly where he had left it at the home of Professor Litefoot, and travelled back to the moment at which he had left us.

I did not know whether to believe him or not, at least, not until we travelled back to Baker Street in that same cabinet: nineteen years removed from the life of the world in as many minutes. I cannot help thinking that such power is dangerous, and yet I cannot think of safer hands to hold it than those of the Doctor. He is a strange little man, but he engenders such trust.

Bernice and I talked for some of those nineteen minutes. We were standing in a corner of the control chamber of the Doctor's mighty craft, a room whose oak-panelled walls and brass railings give no hint as to its true function. With the Doctor's permission Holmes had opened a round panel in one of the walls, and was asking pointed but, I fear, ill-informed questions as to the source of its energy. Ace was standing near Holmes. I assumed that she was watching to make sure that he did not interfere with the workings of the mechanism.

I asked Bernice if I might see her again. Perhaps, I offered, a night at the theatre might amuse her, or a meal at the Savoy. She smiled.

'I'm a good six hundred years too young for you,' she said, handing me a package wrapped up with string. 'Have this instead.'

'A gift? Really, I . . .'

'It's not a gift, it's some of my diary entries. You might find them useful when you come to write this case up.'

I started to protest, but the Doctor wandered over.

'Perhaps you would like to stay,' he said. 'There's room enough for more travellers.'

Bernice looked askance at him.

'Well, why not?' he asked defensively. 'I've been thinking that one of our problems is that there's just the three of us, cooped up in here, getting on each other's nerves. It might do us good to broaden the team a bit. Bring some fresh blood in.'

'This isn't *Mission* bloody *Impossible*,' Ace muttered.

'A tempting offer,' Holmes replied, shutting the panel decisively. 'I greatly wish to see more of these worlds you talk about, and the shining marvels that technology will bring us in the future. And yet . . .'

He glanced over at me, a question in his eyes. I nodded. I knew what he was thinking: the same arguments had occurred to me as well.

'. . . And yet I fear that we would be out of our depths. The adventure we have just shared with you has brought us both to the edge of our sanity. The human brain cannot take too much information at once: it must be given time to sort, to index, to catalogue. We need our London around us once more, like a comfortable overcoat.'

'Perhaps . . .' I ventured.

'Yes, Watson?'

'Perhaps in a few years. When we have distanced ourselves from the events of the past few days.'

He smiled.

'A wise prescription. We would be happy to travel with you, Doctor, but not just yet. Not, at least, until I see that scoundrel Moriarty dangling at the end of a noose.'

We soon arrived in our sitting room at 221b Baker Street, frightening the life out of Mrs Hudson, who was tidying the room and had just popped out for a fresh duster. By the time she returned, Holmes and I were sitting in our usual seats and the Doctor and his companions had gone. I was still blushing after Bernice had kissed my cheek.

We discussed the entire affair over dinner with Mycroft and Lord Roxton, who had arrived safely back in London and was eager to hear of hunting opportunities in this New World. Mycroft undertook to pass a sanitized report back to His Excellence Pope Leo XIII. I did not envy him the task.

It seemed to me that the more Holmes and I recounted our adventures to Mycroft or Roxton, or discussed them with each other, the less real they became. It was as if by telling them as a story, they became a story. Perhaps it is for the best. I still wake from nightmares in which I see Azathoth twisting in the flames. In some of them, I am burning too.

Holmes threw himself into more mundane cases immediately upon our return. In quick succession he solved the bizarre problem of the paradol chamber, investigated the loss of the British barque *Sophy Anderson* and cast light upon the grotesque affair of the monkey and the plywood violin. Other adventures followed, and I was proud to stand with him during them.

I am ashamed to say that the memory of Bernice faded, and I married again. My wife and I had a happy few years together before a congenital weakness of the heart robbed me of her wit and her beauty. Had it not been for Holmes's friendship, I too would have perished, of a broken heart.

Following the success of my memoir entitled *A Study*

in Scarlet, I embarked upon another account of my adventures with Holmes: *The Sign of the Four*. To my surprise (and, if truth be told, to Holmes's chagrin) the public rather took to these little amusements, and so I began to write more of them. I composed *A Scandal in Bohemia* in shorter form as an experiment, and found that its popularity far outstripped either of the two longer works. I was a middling to fair physician, but I found that I had a talent for fiction. My medical colleague and co-author, Arthur Conan Doyle, became well known to the public. The *noms-de-plume* with which he protected the identities of Holmes and myself became equally famous, but Doyle never revealed our real names. After a while, we both found ourselves in the curious position where we would answer either to our real names or to our fictional ones. Secretly, we both preferred the latter.

On a number of occasions I had attempted to set down the circumstances of our meeting with the Doctor, and their shocking outcome. On each occasion I found myself floundering, wondering what people would make of them. It was Holmes, of course, who came up with the solution.

'Write for yourself, Watson,' he said. 'Write the book, let the doctor friend of yours pretty it up for you, and then lock it away somewhere.'

I did write the book, this book, and it helped. Seeing aspects of the narrative from the point of view of Bernice Summerfield helped me to find a wider perspective. The notes she had written on strange, yellow scraps of paper with a sticky margin, have been integrated into the text almost verbatim. I do not pretend to understand much of what she says, and some of it jars with my own recollections, but I admire the way that she says it.

When I look back and ask myself what I learned, I can say that I now know the universe to be a far stranger place than I had, in my prosaic British way, imagined. Far stranger, and far richer. I also find myself intolerant of the pronouncements of clerics of any sort. They may talk of Hell, but I have seen it.

And Holmes? He refuses to talk about his brother

Sherringford. He seems to have retreated inside himself. He is dismissive of love, friendship and family ties.

He has also taken to wearing gloves.

There is a confession that I have to make. I have suppressed a deal of material in preparing this narrative, even though it will never see print. Our interview with Doctor Minor in the Broadmoor asylum, for instance, is too appalling to consider setting down on paper, and the circumstances surrounding the mysterious deaths of Patrick Grice-Patterson and Cardinal Tosca on the island of Uffa, germane though they are, would only serve to confuse an already fragmentary account.

And now we sit here, Holmes and I, warming ourselves before the fire. I write these words in my ledger and Holmes busies himself with the newspaper. It is four years to the day since we said goodbye to the strangest man we have ever met.

I sip my brandy. Rain splatters across the window. There is a storm in the offing.

Holmes looks up and smiles at me. I smile back, and wonder whether we will ever see the Doctor and his companions again.

More rain, like gravel thrown against the glass.

And thunder, echoing far away.

Epilogue

March 1843 – Jabalhabad, India

As Bernice read the last few words, she shivered.

'Any good?' Ace asked casually.

'Not bad. Want to read it?'

'Nah. I'll wait till the film comes out.'

Bernice laughed.

'I don't know how much of this is Watson and how much is Conan Doyle, but whoever it was is all right,' she said. 'It's a bit verbose at times, but the plot moves fast. A lot of the facts have been changed, mind you. I don't remember half of these things happening. And it's odd reading about Holmes and Watson, rather than—'

'What about the characterization?' Ace interrupted.

'He's got you down perfectly, but I think he misses the essential me.'

Ace grinned.

'What about the Professor?' she asked.

Bernice glanced at the Doctor, who was resting his chin on the handle of his umbrella and gazing sombrely across the lawn towards the old man and Siger Holmes, father-to-be of Sherringford, Mycroft and Sherlock.

'A good question,' she said quietly.

The Doctor's gaze shifted from his former self to his latest companion. The corners of his mouth twitched slightly in what passed for a smile.

'A question,' Bernice said.

'Fire away,' he replied, his voice muffled by the umbrella handle.

'I wouldn't say that too loudly when Ace is around.'

This time his mouth curved into a definite grin. Ace snorted, but her eyes were laughing.

'This book . . .' Bernice continued.

'What about it?'

'Well, a lot of the material about Victorian London is bizarre. Odd. Grotesque, in fact.'

'That's the way it was.'

'But surely there wasn't really an air-driven underground railway running out of Euston?'

'There was indeed.'

'And strychnine as an additive to beer, and sugar being refined with bull's blood?'

'Without a doubt.'

'And the Fenians building a submarine to attack the Royal Navy with?'

'Indubitably.'

'The more I delve into history, the weirder it gets.'

'My sentiments exactly.'

'Something I don't get,' Ace said, frowning. The setting sun cast a rose-tinted glow across her face, and she squinted. The Doctor smiled at her.

'Go on,' he said.

'Well, the big worm-thing, Azathoth, was turning its worshippers into the lobster things – the rakshassi.'

'Indeed it was.'

'Why?'

'Ah. A good question. I suspect that Azathoth was still in the larval stage of its race when it developed its powers, and had become trapped there, a mutant imago, if you like. Perhaps, had it been normal, its adult form would have resembled the rakshassi.'

'So it made everyone love it and then made them look like mum and dad,' she said scornfully.

'It's only a theory,' the Doctor replied, affronted.

'It's well weird, that's what it is.'

The Doctor gazed across at where the girl sat painting the landscape.

'Families are,' he murmured.

Across the lawn, the old man pulled a gleaming Hunter

watch from the fob pocket of his waistcoat and consulted it. Unconsciously, the Doctor mirrored the action. Bernice gazed from one to the other, stunned more by the fact that it was the same watch than the same person.

'It's five past time to leave,' he said.

They rose. The Doctor gestured to his two companions to go first, sighed deeply, then raised his hat to the old man and walked away.

He didn't look back.

CAT'S CRADLE: WARHEAD
Andrew Cartmel

The place is Earth. The time is the near future – all too near. As environmental destruction reaches the point of no return, multinational corporations scheme to buy immortality in a poisoned world. If Earth is to survive, somebody has to stop them.

ISBN 0 426 20367 4

CAT'S CRADLE: WITCH MARK
Andrew Hunt

A small village in Wales is visited by creatures of myth. Nearby, a coach crashes on the M40, killing all its passengers. Police can find no record of their existence. The Doctor and Ace arrive, searching for a cure for the TARDIS, and uncover a gateway to another world.

ISBN 0 426 20368 2

NIGHTSHADE
Mark Gatiss

When the Doctor brings Ace to the village of Crook Marsham in 1968, he seems unwilling to recognize that something sinister is going on. But the villagers are being killed, one by one, and everyone's past is coming back to haunt them – including the Doctor's.

ISBN 0 426 20376 3

LOVE AND WAR
Paul Cornell

Heaven: a planet rich in history where the Doctor comes to meet a new friend, and betray an old one; a place where people come to die, but where the dead don't always rest in peace. On Heaven, the Doctor finally loses Ace, but finds archaeologist Bernice Summerfield, a new companion whose destiny is inextricably linked with his.

ISBN 0 426 20385 2

TRANSIT
Ben Aaronovitch

It's the ultimate mass transit system, binding the planets of the solar system together. But something is living in the network, chewing its way to the very heart of the system and leaving a trail of death and mutation behind. Once again, the Doctor is all that stands between humanity and its own mistakes.

ISBN 0 426 20384 4

THE HIGHEST SCIENCE
Gareth Roberts

The Highest Science – a technology so dangerous it destroyed its creators. Many people have searched for it, but now Sheldukher, the most wanted criminal in the galaxy, believes he has found it. The Doctor and Bernice must battle to stop him on a planet where chance and coincidence have become far too powerful.

ISBN 0 426 20377 1

THE PIT
Neil Penswick

One of the Seven Planets is a nameless giant, quarantined against all intruders. But when the TARDIS materializes, it becomes clear that the planet is far from empty – and the Doctor begins to realize that the planet hides a terrible secret from the Time Lords' past.

ISBN 0 426 20378 X

DECEIT
Peter Darvill-Evans

Ace – three years older, wiser and tougher – is back. She is part of a group of Irregular Auxiliaries on an expedition to the planet Arcadia. They think they are hunting Daleks, but the Doctor knows better. He knows that the paradise planet hides a being far more powerful than the Daleks – and much more dangerous.

ISBN 0 426 20362 3

LUCIFER RISING
Jim Mortimore & Andy Lane

Reunited, the Doctor, Ace and Bernice travel to Lucifer, the site of a scientific expedition that they know will shortly cease to exist. Discovering why involves them in sabotage, murder and the resurrection of eons-old alien powers. Are there Angels on Lucifer? And what does it all have to do with Ace?

ISBN 0 426 20338 7

WHITE DARKNESS
David McIntee

The TARDIS crew, hoping for a rest, come to Haiti in 1915. But they find that the island is far from peaceful: revolution is brewing in the city; the dead are walking from the cemeteries; and, far underground, the ancient rulers of the galaxy are stirring in their sleep.

ISBN 0 426 20395 X

SHADOWMIND
Christopher Bulis

On the colony world of Arden, something dangerous is growing stronger. Something that steals minds and memories. Something that can reach out to another planet, Tairgire, where the newest exhibit in the sculpture park is a blue box surmounted by a flashing light.

ISBN 0 426 20394 1

BIRTHRIGHT
Nigel Robinson

Stranded in Edwardian London with a dying TARDIS, Bernice investigates a series of grisly murders. In the far future, Ace leads a group of guerrillas against their insect-like, alien oppressors. Why has the Doctor left them, just when they need him most?

ISBN 0 426 20393 3

ICEBERG
David Banks

In 2006, an ecological disaster threatens the Earth; only the FLIPback team, working in an Antarctic base, can avert the catastrophe. But hidden beneath the ice, sinister forces have gathered to sabotage humanity's last hope. The Cybermen have returned and the Doctor must face them alone.

ISBN 0 426 20392 5

BLOOD HEAT
Jim Mortimore

The TARDIS is attacked by an alien force; Bernice is flung into the Vortex; and the Doctor and Ace crash-land on Earth. There they find dinosaurs roaming the derelict London streets, and Brigadier Lethbridge-Stewart leading the remnants of UNIT in a desperate fight against the Silurians who have taken over and changed his world.

ISBN 0 426 20399 2

THE DIMENSION RIDERS
Daniel Blythe

A holiday in Oxford is cut short when the Doctor is summoned to Space Station Q4, where ghostly soldiers from the future watch from the shadows among the dead. Soon, the Doctor is trapped in the past, Ace is accused of treason and Bernice is uncovering deceit among the college cloisters.

ISBN 0 426 20397 6

THEATRE OF WAR
Justin Richards

Menaxus is a barren world on the front line of an interstellar war, home to a ruined theatre which hides sinister secrets. When the TARDIS crew land on the planet, they find themselves trapped in a deadly reenactment of an ancient theatrical tragedy.